11254

THE SOLUTION

THE
SOLUTION

Edward Stewart

HEADLINE
FEATURE

First published in Great Britain in 1998 by
HEADLINE BOOK PUBLISHING

A HEADLINE FEATURE hardback

10 9 8 7 6 5 4 3 2

British Library Cataloguing in Publication Data

Stewart. Edward, 1938–
The Solution
1. Thrillers
I. Title
813.5'4[F]

ISBN 0 7472 1761 0

Typeset by Avon Dataset Ltd, Bidford-on-Avon, Warks

Printed and bound in Great Britain by
Mackays of Chatham PLC, Chatham, Kent

HEADLINE BOOK PUBLISHING
A division of Hodder Headline PLC
338 Euston Road
London NW1 3BH

THE
SOLUTION

July 5

The spilled blood spread in eddies across the varnished teak floor of the yacht's lounge. It edged past the brass fittings on the legs of the large table and almost reached the shoes of the man holding the gun.

The highly polished eight hundred dollar custom Cordovans stepped back.

The body lay on its left side, eyes staring in paralyzed, disbelieving shock. Spasms passed through the right cheek, dislodging a crimson tear. Despite these small twitches, no one in the lounge could doubt that the elegantly dressed man with the coiled brunette ponytail was dead. The bullet hole just above the left eye allowed no other conclusion.

The yacht rocked gently in the wake of a passing launch.

The young man standing by a porthole turned his head. 'US Coast Guard, Señor Bosch.' His black hair, raptor's-beak nose, and ruddy skin identified him as less Spanish than the other two men in the lounge; and less Spanish than the dead man as well. At least three-quarters Central American Indian. 'There could be trouble. I'll go check.' Leather heels clicking smartly, he headed for the steps leading up to the deck.

'No need to worry,' Miguel Bosch said. 'The Coast Guard know I'm here, they're protecting me.' The oldest man on the yacht, Bosch was a silver-haired contrast to his sleek companions. Even his silk suit seemed silver in the light of electric candles set into wall sconces. 'It's a government courtesy to a distinguished foreign financier vacationing in these peaceful Miami waters.'

The Indian gave a deferential nod and returned to his post at the porthole.

Bosch acknowledged the nod, then stepped away from the advancing pond of blood. He signaled with his gun hand.

A young assistant snapped a Gucci scarf from his breast pocket and sopped up the blood drifting toward Bosch's shoes.

Watching him, Bosch was reminded of a hungry dog. The sheen of perspiration on the young man's forehead and upper lip indicated either excitement or fear.

This one won't live long, Bosch thought. During his more than thirty-five years in the business, he had developed a sense about such things. 'When the cutter passes, weight him and let the sharks feed on a fool.'

'They are not going to like this in Lima,' the young man said. 'He was the Peruvian padrone's nephew.'

Bosch studied the young man, wondering whether he was still called Pablo or, now that he was more or less permanently rooted in Miami, Grant or Scott.

'Send a wreath to the padrone,' Bosch said. 'Black.'

Two stewards entered to lift the corpse from the floor.

'Use hooks and spare anchors,' the Indian directed.

Two deckhands began to slop up the blood into buckets. Within minutes the sparkling polyurethane floor varnish had once again proved its worth.

But Bosch was dissatisfied. 'It smells of death and shit in here.' He had trouble deciding which smell offended him more.

'Yes, sir.' The Indian opened the porthole. A smell of salt water and diesel fuel gusted in. It wasn't enough.

There was only one sure way to get that stink out of his nostrils. Bosch chose a cigar from the mahogany humidor on the table. He clipped it and lit it with a match from a book embossed with the name of his yacht: *Santa Rosa*. When the cigar was drawing properly, he tossed the match into a pail of bloody water.

The sound of an approaching launch floated through the open porthole. The Indian turned. 'Your guests, Señor Bosch.'

The yacht lifted and rocked slightly. Voices could be heard chattering in English.

Bosch handed the pistol back to Pablo or Grant or whatever the boy's name was now. 'Do something with this.'

As Bosch stepped on to the deck, the sun was setting and the Miami skyline glowed against the night sky like a tiara designed for an extrovert giantess.

Six men and two women were climbing up the side of the yacht: the men were Mike Bosch's brain trust. Since 1987, when illegal drugs had become America's largest-grossing industry, he had laundered his profits through legitimate banks and invested them in legitimate businesses. As a result, American finance was hooked on drug dollars – and uneasy about its addiction. To calm the money mandarins, he allowed their representatives to advise him twice a year. It was a courtesy on his part, nothing more. He respected hired brains no more than he did hired brawn; he considered them both to be as replaceable as toothbrushes.

On the other hand, there was nothing replaceable about either of the women.

'What would I do without you, Esme.' Bosch kissed the younger, dark-haired woman. 'Thanks for picking up the guests.' His arm went round her and he was aware of the toned tautness of the body beneath her silver dress. The mouth that she offered him was completely slack, moist, and inviting. He felt his loins stir.

He turned quickly to the older woman and relieved her of some of the folders and rolled charts and maps that she carried clutched across her chest.

'Señora.' He smiled. 'You are very courageous to be with us.'

'This is not an act of courage, Señor Bosch.' Tall and middle-aged, she wore her graying fawn-colored hair in an unflattering swept-back style. 'It is an act of necessity.'

Her rimless bifocals told Bosch that she had long ago capitulated in any war she might have fought to attract men. Her plain, loosely cut mannish suit, her unostentatious silver cross hanging on its simple chain told the story of a starved heart; yet the line of her lips, the unblinking gaze behind those glasses, the confident posture gave powerful signals of resolution and purposefulness. Bosch was intrigued.

'Gentlemen.' He greeted his male guests with handshakes. It amused him that five of them still subscribed to the Commodore Vanderbilt notion of yachting and wore blazers and white linen trousers. Only the epidemiologist from Johns Hopkins wore a business suit.

'Gentlemen. And ladies. Please.'

Bosch gestured toward the semi-circle of director's chairs that had been placed on the deck facing the Miami skyline. His guests arranged themselves.

'Great yacht, Mike.'

'How many horsepower?'

'Can you get Cable?'

Two waiters took drink orders.

Bosch's cigar had gone out. He handed it to a waiter, who brought the humidor.

'Would any of you gentlemen care for a smoke?' Bosch winked. 'Genuine State Department Havanas.'

No takers.

'Ladies?'

Silence.

Bosch selected a beautiful, plump, dark-skinned H. Uppman. His young woman leaned toward him with a lit match. The flame danced in her pupils.

He inhaled till the tobacco caught, then exhaled. 'I've asked you here, my friends, because we are in a battle for our lives. We are fighting not simply to save the cocaine business; we are fighting to save Colombia and the United States.'

The smiles faded from his guests' faces. Spines stiffened. Glances were exchanged.

'If present trends continue, we shall suffer irreparable harm not only to ourselves and our families, but to our countries and our cultures, to the international money market, and to the very economic stability of the world. Do not forget who we are.'

He saw their eyes blink and knew that they understood his meaning: Do not forget who I am.

'We are the major source of distribution for cocaine throughout the world. The Peruvians and the Bolivians and the others exist and compete with us only because we allow them to. They are simply our back-up. We allow them to use our routes and carriers because we sometimes have losses and shortages. Such concessions are a quid pro quo and they make sense in times of expanding markets. But when the market itself is under assault, we must review our policies. At the moment, we are in a state of catastrophic contraction. Immutable forces have set themselves against us.'

The man from Harvard Business School interrupted. 'Could you be a little more specific, Mr Bosch? What forces?'

'There are four,' Bosch said. 'The law, the traitors, the careless, and the inscrutable intervention of God.' He doubted Harvard Business School had heard of any but the law. 'In this case, we ourselves have been the careless ones.'

'In what respect?'

'Two respects. In the first place, we have been too generous to the Peruvians. We can no longer afford to give them a free ride. The time has come to put aside the policy of helpful co-existence.'

'I'm sorry,' the same man, the same snidely patrician tones, 'do you mean *break the truce*?'

'The only truces that deserve honoring are truces between equals. The Peruvians have a confused government; we have armies. They have poor transport; we command the oceans and the air. They have no allies; we have half the governments of Mexico, Bolivia and, if pressed,

4

enough of the United States Border Patrol and the DEA to reduce them to motherless, marketless babies. We will starve them until they conform or wither away. They will do business our way, as our subordinates, or they will cease to exist.'

'Impressive rhetoric.' A different voice this time, but still annoyingly Harvard. 'But how realistic?'

'Realism is will, and we have the will. If necessary we will suffocate them in an avalanche of cocaine wider than the Amazon and higher than the Andes. Then if they are so *indecent* as to try to dig themselves out, we shall strangle them one by one.'

The man from Chase Manhattan seemed troubled. 'This strategy seems rather short on specifics.'

'You don't need to know the specifics. I'm briefing you on the war, not asking you to run it.'

Chase Manhattan's brows contracted. 'War?'

'The first shot was fired less than,' Bosch consulted his gold Rolex, 'thirty minutes ago. One of their emissaries brought an unacceptable offer.'

An uncomfortable silence descended. Bosch smiled. They were wondering if sitting here made them accessories to murder.

'You said we've been careless in two respects.' The man from First National Cayman twirled the ice in his Stoli and soda. 'What's the second respect?'

'The worst carelessness of all. We've allowed our market to die. And I mean that literally.' Bosch snapped his fingers. A waiter set up an artist's easel, angled so that all could see. Bosch turned to the doctor from Johns Hopkins. 'Bartle, if you don't mind?'

The doctor rose and placed a graph on the easel. He explained that the red line represented AIDS deaths in tens of thousands over the past ten years in Europe and South, Central, and North America. The blue line below it represented AIDS deaths among cocaine users in the same period and region.

'As you can see, after four years of steady rise, the red line shows a leveling off. Whereas the blue line, after six years of relative stasis at thirty per cent of the total, shows an explosive increase bringing it to seventy per cent of the current death load. And still climbing.'

The doctor turned to face his audience. His expression was grim. 'The conclusion is inescapable. The epidemic is gutting our market.'

'Tell us, Louis,' Bosch asked Harvard Business School, 'in terms of sales, how far are we down?'

5

'Eight per cent from last year.'

'Seventeen per cent from the year before,' MIT added, punching keys on a calculator. 'At present trends, in three point four two years, we'll have one-tenth the market we enjoy today.'

'And today,' Bosch reminded them, 'is not our best year. It's obvious what we must do.'

Silence answered him.

He scanned his guests' faces and saw that it wasn't obvious, at least not to any of these men; not obvious at all. 'We have to take up the fight against AIDS. We have to succeed where all the others have failed. *We have to find the cure.*'

'Oy,' Harvard Business School muttered.

'There appear to be four promising avenues of research.' Johns Hopkins substituted a new graph. 'Nutrition therapy; Chinese bitter melon; aspirin; and Sperilac. The first three are highly speculative at this point.'

Bosch let the explanation go on for another three minutes and then impatience got the better of him. 'Let's be realistic,' he interrupted. 'There's no way you're going to persuade our customers to observe proper nutrition. Their money goes to coke, not to organic pasta. As for Chinese bitter melon, my daughter Rosa – may she rest in peace – drank the juice of one of those every day while she was dying; they look like cucumber with venereal warts and they taste like snake venom – there's no way our customers are going to be persuaded to go near them. As for aspirin . . .' Bosch sighed. He'd heard of equally improbable miracles, like the cow kick that cured smallpox.

'If it works, OK. Why not? And if it doesn't work, we go for option four.' He extended an arm toward the older woman. 'Señora, would you tell us about Sperilac?'

She rose and spread a large chart on the easel. The two waiters rushed to tack down the corners.

'Sperilac is a broad-range anti-viral with a demonstrated affinity for all the currently known HIV viruses and mutations. Unlike other anti-virals, it achieves its effect by boosting the body's own intra-cellular immunity. The patent is controlled by Forbes Biochemtech.' Her fingers trailed across the yard-wide sheet of paper. 'This is a table of mortalities and use that we kept during our Phase One tests. Naturally, all of this is highly unofficial, even a bit speculative at this stage, but it's too suggestive to be ignored. I believe that in Sperilac we've found what we've been hunting for.'

Her finger touched the red line.

'This line shows that while your trade dropped due to rising mortality among your clients, test subjects who continued to smoke or inject your product while taking Sperilac did *not* die, did *not* get sick, *and* the sick ones even got well.'

She indicated a black line that wavered occasionally but still climbed toward the upper right-hand corner.

'However, the number of test subjects was so small that it didn't cause a significant dent in the overall mortality rates.'

'But this is astonishing,' Johns Hopkins cried. 'Why on earth haven't you continued with your tests? If Sperilac does what you say, it would mean enormous profits for your company.'

'Great profits sometimes demand great investments and an even greater willingness to take risks.' The woman offered a grim smile as she rolled up the chart. 'At this point in history, Biochemtech, like most of American business, has neither.'

Bertolt Devereux, president of Bertolt-Bienvenue Pharmaceuticals and a long-time Bosch collaborator, shook his head. 'These are amazing claims for a drug that was turned down by the FDA.'

'In my opinion the FDA made a mistake. Sperilac passed its Phase One and Phase Two trials and if the FDA had allowed a Phase Three, it would have easily passed that as well.' She gestured toward a stack of manila folders sitting beneath her chair. 'You're free to review the complete statistical figures.'

He made no movement toward the folders. 'Do you have the authority to put Sperilac at the disposal of this cartel?'

'I'm in charge of inventory and export. I have the authority to sign the necessary releases.'

'I find that hard to believe when you're not even an executive of Forbes Biochemtech.'

'I exercise powers of a junior executive nature. At my own request I've remained middle management.'

'You turned down an executive salary?'

'One moment,' Miguel Bosch interrupted. For twenty-two years Devereux had acted as Bosch's fifth column in the world of legal drugs, but if the lady from Forbes-Biochemtech joined them, Devereux would have to share that distinction. Bosch caught a whiff of jealousy. 'Why are we cross-examining an ally who comes to us in friendship?'

As Devereux turned, the lenses of his eyeglasses flashed. 'Because I can think of only one motive for this lady's behavior – government entrapment.'

Miguel Bosch leapt to his feet. The chair behind him crashed to the deck. 'I have personally confirmed every word she says. You will apologize.'

'No. Please.' The woman raised her hand. 'These are honest doubts and they deserve honest answers. I find the present-day level of executive salaries an affront to morality. Which is why when one was offered to me I turned it down. I also find it an affront to morality that the medical establishment rejected Sperilac.'

'And why did they do that?' Devereux said.

'Because they considered Sperilac's mode of action a challenge to their own AIDS paradigm. Forget that no drug or treatment strategy engineered on that paradigm has yet worked. As a result, hundreds of thousands of men and women are dying needlessly. Which is why, as a last resort, I approached Mr Bosch.'

Devereux was clearly unconvinced. 'Then you're acting out of moral conviction?'

'I'm acting out of medical conviction and moral necessity.'

'You're a doctor?'

'I am not.'

'You're a Catholic?'

Her hand reached for the cross at her throat. 'I am.'

'But two of the major vectors of AIDS are drug addiction and homosexuality. Don't you regard these behaviors as sinful? Why would you want to help people who practice them?'

'They're dying only because they bear the weight of human weakness. God commands me to love them, not to condemn them – just as he commands you, Mr Devereux.'

Bosch saw that this stork of a woman was ready to transform herself into an eagle. At that instant he made up his mind.

'You heard the lady. She says we can stop the dying.' His foot slammed down on to the deck like a cannon shot. '*Then that's what we're going to do!*'

The hired brains were silent, faces perplexed and anxious.

Only the Indian standing by the stairway seemed indifferent to Bosch's decision, as though it touched him not at all. As he gazed out at the rising and sinking horizon of the sea, the reflected light on his dark sunglasses made his eyes invisible. His face had the serenity of a carved idol's.

'Someday, Señor Bosch,' the woman's voice was a hoarse whisper, 'someday they are going to call you the second Jesus Christ.' Her fingers tangled in the chain and cross. The chain snapped and a shard of light lashed off the cross as it fell into her hand.

Bosch allowed himself a monosyllable of a laugh. 'God willing, gracious lady, they will never know my name. Now, please, if you will give me that necklace, I shall have it repaired.'

At long last the meeting had broken up. The guests had returned to shore. The waiters had cleared the dinner dishes and the drinks and Mike Bosch and his young friend were finally alone on the deck of the *Santa Rosa*.

'What happened to Valdes?' She seemed thoughtful, remote. 'Why didn't he stay?'

Mike Bosch shrugged. 'Valdes had no interest in solving problems. He came to create new ones.'

She frowned. 'New problems?'

'The Peruvians are fools. I have no time for fools. I have obligations, a family, a business undergoing reverses, a nation I love that is crumbling. If my time is to be wasted, I'll waste it myself. I don't need others to do the job for me.'

Something in his voice must have clued her. She flinched back. 'He was a *boy*!'

'That's no excuse for being a fool.'

'Did you?'

'Did I what?'

'Kill him?'

'Don't try to run my business.' Mike Bosch got up and walked to the bar. aware that he was limping more than usual.

'When you're bad-tempered,' she said, 'it makes you limp.'

'Fools make me limp.' Thirteen years ago, a hireling DEA agent had gotten off a lucky shot – lucky for the DEA, unlucky for Mike Bosch. Mike had driven himself through ten months' unrelenting physiotherapy, learned to walk again, dance again, swim again, play polo again. Lately when he was tired, which was more and more often, the limp had returned.

He held up the Johnnie Walker bottle. 'Nightcap?'

She shook her head. 'None for me.'

He sensed sullenness. Was she really angry because he wouldn't tell her the details of an ugly, unimportant murder? He poured himself a stiff double.

'Why do you drink so much?'

'I only drink this much when I'm alone.'

'You're not alone, you're with me now.'

'I'm alone with you.'

'It's bad for your liver.'

'My liver's shot and my heart's getting there, so what difference does it make?'

'What are you trying to forget?'

'I'm not trying to forget.' He belted back half the drink. 'I'm trying to die. Ever since God took my Rosa I've been trying.'

'I think you misunderstand God.'

'You're my mother, my psychoanalyst, and now my priest too?'

'I'm only trying to be your friend.'

'Why can't you just shut up and be my lover?' He slammed down the glass and pulled her toward him. 'I've been wanting another of those kisses for the last five hours.'

Her head tipped back and her mouth opened to him. His hand went to the small of her back and into her zipper and down to the elastic of her panties.

'Wait a minute.' She drew away. 'I have to go to my cabin first.'

'Why?'

'To freshen up.'

'Fresh is for yuppies.'

'And I want to do a little coke first.'

'And so is coke. You criticize my drinking and you do that shit. You're a beautiful little hypocrite, with your ruddy-skinned angelic face, your teeth as bright as burning phosphorus, your perfectly worked-out body . . . I want you now.' He wrapped his arms round her and amused himself squeezing the breath out of her.

'Not here, Mike,' she gasped. 'People can see.'

His eye swept the harbor. There were no yachts moored nearer than two hundred yards, and they were all dark. To humor her, he switched off the deck lights, leaving only the glow that spilled through the lounge portholes.

'Now where was I?' He reached for her again.

'Hey, slow down a little.'

'Why?' Her thrashing only excited him more. His fingers probed into the panties.

'Mike, please, you're hurting me.'

But he wasn't hurting her. He wasn't even touching her. What he was touching was a thin metal wire.

10

He yanked it out and stared. Rage exploded. 'What the hell is this?' Her expression came apart like a mirror struck by a rock.

'Goddamn you!' he screamed. 'You're wearing a wire on me! On *me*! Who are you with?' He slapped her across the face. The sound echoed like a round from a 9-millimeter Glock. Somewhere across the bay a foghorn answered mournfully.

'Are the Peruvians paying you?'

'No!'

Another slap, back of the hand. 'DEA?'

'No!'

In a single movement he looped the wire and snapped it round her neck. 'Tell me the truth, Esme – you only get one chance. *Who?*'

She didn't answer. He could feel her heart pounding beneath her ribs like the timer on a car bomb. Fear burned in her eyes.

Mike Bosch whistled for the Indian. 'Key, come here! I need you!'

August 3

Cleaning up files that a transferred agent had left behind in the Miami office, Eddie Arbogast came across a month-old photo of the one man on earth he hated.

The photo was black and white, fast film, available light, night shot. It showed pleasure craft docked in one of the downtown marinas. The telephoto lens had mashed the masts into a fence of spindly pickets.

Moored on the far side of the fence, a hundred-foot two-decked cruiser flew Cayman insignia. On the canopied, brightly lit aft deck, two waiters in white jackets carried trays of drinks. A group of men lounged in director's chairs.

Eddie Arbogast recognized only one face in the group. Miguel Bosch. The oldest. Known to his acquaintances and to his hunters as Mike. He held a cigar in a jeweled, confidently gesturing hand. A young woman in a silvery cocktail dress touched a lit match to the cigar.

The chairs had been placed in a semi-circle round an artist's easel. The easel held a three-foot graph.

Eddie laid the photo on the metal desktop and scanned through his magnifying glass. He could make out the words 'mortality (in 10,000s)' and a line that shot up like a drunken rocket.

A prim-faced middle-aged woman wearing rimless eyeglasses and a cross stood at the rail, her back toward the discussion. She was staring without knowing it straight at the Agency's camera. Her face had a gloomy expression, as though she'd have given her soul to be anywhere in the world but on Mike Bosch's yacht.

And I'd have given my soul to be there, Eddie Arbogast thought. He'd never met Mike Bosch personally, but he'd met the man's work.

Twenty-five years ago, as a rookie assigned to liaison with the Colombian *guardia civil*, he'd kicked open a cellar door and gotten a nun's foot in his face. She was hanging by a meat hook. Her thumbs were crushed blue pulp and her eyes had been stabbed. Flies crawled in the bloody fluid that streaked her face.

'Mike Bosch,' one of the *guardia* said. Even in Colombia, they called him Mike. It was sexy, American. Like a movie star. '*Su firma.*' His signature.

12

What Mike Bosch and his men had done to the other three nuns was even worse. But the worst was the little girl. Eddie Arbogast looked at that child, realized what he was seeing, and vomited.

'Why did he do it?' he asked.

The officer shrugged. 'They refused to carry cocaine. It's very bad to refuse Mike.'

Eddie had never again vomited on the job. And he'd never forgotten the promise he'd made himself that day in that cellar: *I'm going to bring Mike Bosch in. He's going to pay.*

Twelve years later, in a Panama City whorehouse, Eddie had been close enough to fire a .38 round into Bosch's left leg. Bosch had gotten even last year on a pier in Bimini, when one of his gunmen fired three rounds into Eddie's left kidney. Since then, without exactly saying he was grounded, the Agency had given Eddie desk work. He'd opted for early retirement. Technically, he could keep his agent's badge and his gun another seventeen months, but with eight months of cumulative personal holiday due him, he'd be out next April.

Till then he was a file clerk. When he thought about his status, his gut ached. After thirty-four years in the field, after steering twenty-two operations, four of them in Latin America, after bagging three of America's most wanted drug capos and busting two of the nation's biggest coke rings, after eight departmental and two presidential citations, Edward G. Arbogast was sitting indoors nine to five, doing work any secretary with a level-two clearance could have handled.

And Mike Bosch was running free.

The manila folder held fourteen photos. You'd never have known that all of them had been taken from a catamaran moored two hundred yards away. Three were such tight telephoto close-ups that Eddie could practically count each strand of Mike Bosch's thickly waved gray hair. He had no trouble counting the teeth in Mike's smile. Sixteen state-of-the-art Hollywood caps.

It was a smile that turned Eddie's stomach to ice. A smile that said: mine. This illegal Havana cigar, this yacht, these men, these women, this harbor, this city, this hemisphere. Mine.

There were rumors about Mike Bosch: rumors of deals with the CIA, rumors of US senators vacationing at haciendas Mike had put in the names of relatives, rumors of tens of millions of laundered drug dollars contributed to PACs of American politicians.

Nowadays, drug money conferred a level of arrogance that no other form of wealth could approach. It offended Eddie's sense of decency.

13

Presidents and kings were answerable. Mike Bosch wasn't.

In addition to the photos, the folder held a two-hour-long tape and a transcript. Eddie swung the arm of the reading lamp lower. He polished his steel-rimmed reading glasses, put on his earphones, snapped the tape into the Walkman. He adjusted the volume up.

The men were speaking English, but the sound quality was rotten. The agent was wearing that tight cocktail dress over her wire and the silver Mylar crackled every time she breathed. After two minutes, Eddie estimated that the transcript was fifty per cent guesswork.

Every now and then the bored Ivy League-trained voices came through the crackling. 'Soaring death rate . . .'

'The epidemic is gutting our market . . .'

Eddie made a mental note: *epidemic*.

'How far are we down?' Mike was putting on his don't-bother-me-unless-it's-important voice. There was barely a trace of Spanish accent.

'Eight per cent from last year . . .'

'Seventeen per cent from the year before . . .'

'So where's it going?' Mike again, impatient.

'At present trends . . .' *Crackle, crackle.*

'Find the cure.' Mike was angry now.

Eddie jotted the word *cure* on a notepad. He added a question mark.

'There appear to be four promising avenues of research.' A patronizing voice. A voice that didn't know you don't talk to Mike Bosch that way if you expect to keep your nuts. The transcript identified the speaker as Dr Bartle Warner and a footnote mentioned the faculty of epidemiology at Johns Hopkins. 'Nutrition therapy; Chinese bitter melon; aspirin; and—'

The next word was unclear. Beyond the initial *sp*, the transcriber hadn't even guessed.

'The lady (*crackle*) says we can stop the dying.' Mike Bosch almost spat the dental consonants. 'Then that's what we're going to do!'

Eddie knew that when Mike Bosch commanded, it got done. But what exactly were they talking about?

His eyes skimmed forward in the transcript. No help there. After ten tantalizing, ambiguous pages Mike Bosch's guests said their good-nights.

'We're agreed, then?' Dr Warner asked.

'Agreed,' Mike said. 'Sleep well.'

What was agreed?

There was barely a half-page of words from here on. From the sound of it, Mike began making love to the agent. The wire crackled beneath his hands like a bonfire. Understandably, she tried to get away.

Wrong tactic. You don't say no to the man who owns the world.

'You're wearing a wire on me!' Mike Bosch's disbelieving voice trembled and broke. It was the first time on any recording that Eddie had ever heard him completely lose his cool. 'On *me!*'

There was a sound of ripping cloth. A slap, gunshot-sharp. A wounded-animal whimper, cut short by a second slap.

And then nothing but the soft horrible hiss of blank tape.

The next photo showed the agent, Esme Rodriguez, after shore patrol had scooped her out of Miami Bay. Eddie winced. Mike's men had tortured the girl with the savage inventiveness of adolescent boys on crack.

Mike watched. Certainty beat in Eddie's blood. He stood there and watched while they did this to her.

The final photo showed the body of Paco Valdes, nephew of Peru's drug king, also fished out of the bay and also suspected to be Bosch's victim. By Mike Bosch standards, this was a clean, almost merciful death: a single bullet hole over the left eye.

Eddie closed the folder and laid down his earphones. His ears ached and his head throbbed. He took off his glasses and stared out the window at a sunny world of flowing traffic and purposeful pedestrians.

He had met Esme Rodriguez two years ago. He recalled a bright-eyed, motivated young woman who was fiercely opposed to drugs because of what they'd done to her kid brother.

Some day, Eddie told himself, Mike Bosch was going to go too far: kill an innocent American citizen, or kill a US politician. Somehow Mike Bosch was going to cross the line and his protectors would be forced to desert him . . .

God grant me one wish before I die, Eddie prayed. Let me be there when it happens. Let me nail Mike Bosch.

At a plastic-topped table in the corner of the cafeteria, Eddie stirred more sugar into his coffee than it needed. 'I heard a weird rumor.'

Tom Schmidt's fork deposited a pile of chicken salad in his mouth. 'Mmm?'

'I heard Mike Bosch is getting into medical research.'

Tom's deeply suntanned face registered amazement. He wiped his lips with a bunched paper napkin. 'That's crazy.'

'You haven't heard anything about it?' Tom was just back from a two-year tour in Bogota, and Eddie figured if anyone would have heard something, it was Tom.

'Things are pretty much the same down there as up here. The cartel is going legit, parking money any place they can make a profit. Some of it's medical – HMOs, nursing homes, hospitals. But *research*?' Tom shook his head. Beachboy hair flopped. 'Give me a break.'

Tom was the twenty-eighth co-worker Eddie had asked. The whole bureau probably thought he was a nut. But Eddie was certain that Mike was branching into new territory – territory he didn't know or control.

He was certain that Mike Bosch was approaching the line.

Late that evening Eddie drove home to a small white house in Coconut Grove. The air smelled heavily of bougainvillea.

'You're in a mood.' Amy set two frosted margaritas on the patio table.

'Tell me something I don't know.' Eddie sank into a deck chair. 'Twenty-eight agents say I'm crazy.'

'Only twenty-eight?' Amy had been his wife for thirty-two years.

'On the other hand, they didn't hear the tape.' Eddie touched his tongue to the rim of the glass, savoring the shock of the salt.

Amy didn't answer.

He glanced over at the darkness of her eyes. He felt something radiating from her, something unhappy that was directed at him. But he couldn't see if she was worried or annoyed or what. In the dim light the skin around her eyes was smooth, like a girl's. Lately she'd allowed a small decorative wave of gray in her pale brown hair.

'If it was just a brainstorming session to kick loopy ideas around, why kill Valdes? Why kill Esme? Why throw the proof in our face? What the hell was at stake?'

'They kill a lot of people, Eddie.'

He could hear in her voice that she didn't want to continue this conversation. But he needed to.

'What they did to Esme they reserve for special people on special occasions. What's bugging me is, *what the hell was special?*'

'Hey.' Her voice was stern. 'Am I telling you what my summer-school kids did today? Am I whining who threw spitballs? Who beat up who? Life goes on – thank God.'

He stared up at the almost-night sky. The evening star was a pin-point of brightness at the trembling edge of a palm frond. Some-times he forgot to remember the miracles. Amy had survived a breast cancer scare last year and he'd survived three and a half decades with the DEA. Just last month they'd become grandparents.

'Sorry,' he said. 'Didn't mean to bring it home.'

The house was a hundred yards from the ocean. The waves made a carpeting, peaceful murmur that was hard to distinguish from distant traffic.

'The supermarket had a special on lobster. I bought two.' Amy's voice had changed key. Now it was sly and cajoling. 'How about it?'

August 5

At 3 a.m. the morning of August 5th, in the radio room of Sombrerte airport in the foothills of Mexico's Sierra Madre, Raul Sanchez lifted his head from his desk and listened. Had he heard it or dreamt it?

Now he heard it again: the buzzing sound of a two-engine prop plane approaching from the north. His ears estimated its distance to be five kilometers, the altitude five hundred meters.

No radio message had disturbed his sleep.

He pushed aside his unfinished dinner of refried beans and searched flight plans. Between the hours of midnight and 7 a.m. there was not a single plane scheduled to fly over Sombrerte.

He peered through his binoculars and saw low cloud cover, nothing else. The buzzing was a kilometer closer, almost overhead.

Raul realized the plane was flying without lights.

He yanked open a steel drawer and grabbed the US Air Force nightscope. Rapidly adjusting focus, he was able to make out the glowing silhouette of a 1962 Grumman Gulfstream. Nobody used that plane nowadays except drug and arms smugglers.

He pressed the *on* button of his radio mike. 'Grumman Gulfstream, *me entiende*? Grumman Gulfstream, do you hear me? *Identifiguese.* Identify yourself.'

The pilot didn't answer.

The buzzing crescendoed as the plane passed overhead, then faded.

Raul ran it through his mind. No lights. No radio. The problem was, the plane was heading south, away from the United States, and the US Drug Enforcement Administration offered a bounty only on smugglers flying north. On the other hand, there was no flight plan; other airports had reported no sightings.

Raul radioed the *guardia civil* station twelve kilometers south. The *guardia* had American anti-aircraft bazookas. 'Do you hear me, Lobos? This is Sombrerte. Do you hear me? Over.'

'This is Lobos.' Static spat. 'I hear you, Sombrerte. Over.'

'Listen, Enrique. A Grumman Gulfstream is flying south, altitude five hundred meters. They'll be over your head in five minutes. They're flying dark and they don't answer the radio. There's no flight plan and no one else has reported them. If you want to claim the bounty, I'll back you up.'

A young woman stepped round Eddie's desk and handed him a fax. 'This just came in from Mexico.'

Eddie read it twice.

Sombrerte, February 23. At approx 3 o'clock this a.m. unmarked 1962 Grumman Gulfstream was detected flying north without lights. Pilot refused to answer radio calls. *Guardia civil* shot plane down. Pilot dead, no ID. Serial number on engine block identical to plane registered to Billy Boy Imports, Arkansas. Company is on list of known/suspected drug cartel fronts.

Recovered cargo, buffered time-release aspirin.

Eddie frowned. The Mike Bosch transcript had mentioned aspirin. But that didn't explain why the cartel would risk a pilot's life flying the stuff into the US.

Eddie's Delta jet to Mexico City was half empty. He sat by the window and spent the flight reviewing the Mike Bosch transcript, listening and re-listening to the tape for some scrap of information he might have overlooked.

Aeronaves de Mexico had overbooked the connecting two-engine flight to Sombrerte. He flashed his agency ID and managed not to get bumped.

The local DEA man met him at the two-landing-strip airport. They drove in a bouncing jeep down to the crash site at Lobos.

Eddie walked slowly around the pile of charred, twisted metal.

'A bazooka shell shattered the fuel tank.' The agent pointed. 'You can see the leak in the sand.'

Eddie's eye followed the black line of oily dots and dashes that wavered a half-mile northward. 'Then the plane must have been flying south. Not north.'

The agent nodded.

Eddie couldn't figure it out. There was no more sense in the cartel's flying aspirin south than flying it north. 'The cable said you recovered some of the cargo.'

'Not a whole lot. Another shell ripped open the hatch door. I'll show you what we've been able to find.'

The agent took Eddie to the only hotel in Lobos. Upstairs he unlocked a door and snapped on the light. A shipping carton sat on the closet floor, bagged in plastic. He pulled it into the open.

It was partially burned and there were mostly ashes inside. Eddie smoothed the plastic and made out stencilled lettering on one side: 'Bayer time-release buffered aspirin'.

'This is all?'

'Except for one thing.' The agent took a small, plastic-bagged bottle from a bureau drawer.

The child-proof safety cap was still unbroken. Pills rattled when Eddie shook it. 'What is it? More aspirin?'

'Sperilac. The label was almost loose. I bagged it separately.'

'Never heard of Sperilac.'

'Me neither.' The agent handed Eddie the label: 'Sperilac 150 mg 100 caplets. Manufactured by Forbes Biochemtech, Bethesda MD, USA.'

Eddie felt cheated. He'd used two of his personal holidays coming down here. He'd spent twelve hundred dollars of his own money. For what? A bottle of commercial caplets legal in the USA.

February 28

*U*rgent, the message had said, with no explanation. Sharon Powell's heart was pounding as she stepped off the elevator on to the third floor of Georgetown University Hospital.

Dr Andy Horner, tall and curly-headed, hurried down the corridor toward her. 'Thank God you got my message.' He embraced her. 'He's been calling for you.'

She felt touched yet baffled and more than a little apprehensive. 'It seems so strange, we hardly know one another. All we did was play Scrabble once at the clinic.'

'Dementia does funny things. How strong are you?'

'How strong do I need to be?'

'I don't want you breaking down.'

'Come on, Andy, I've been doing volunteer work with AIDS patients for over two years.'

'But you've never seen one die.'

Her eyes flicked up. 'You mean Alex is . . .'

Andy nodded.

'But he was getting Sperilac.'

'He was getting Sperilac at the clinic; he's not getting it here.' A licenced MD with a degree from Harvard Med, Andy ran a small outpatient clinic that specialized in alternative AIDS treatments. He'd achieved impressive results – 'anecdotal results,' his critics said – but the medical profession considered him a maverick, and a dangerous one, and patients who required hospitalization were rarely allowed to continue on his protocols.

Sharon gritted. 'You mean he's dying because of some idiot regulation?'

'He's dying because he's a very sick man and he started Sperilac too late. And if you can't handle it, please just turn around and leave. Don't make it worse with hysteria.'

It was a stupid, insensitive thing to say, and she had a hunch Andy said it because he was close to hysteria himself. She swallowed her annoyance. 'Of course I promise.'

'All right.' He motioned her to follow him.

They passed a central station staffed by three nurses. There was a curious absence of urgency about their movements. They sat making notes in metal-bound folders, glancing occasionally at moving lines on the screens of monitors placed in easy view.

One of them, a stoutish woman wearing steel-rimmed bifocals, glanced up at their approach. 'You'll have to wear these.' She handed them two bundles of disposable sanitary hospital wear: rubber gloves, lime-green face masks, gowns and caps. 'He's at a highly infectious stage.'

Sharon remembered something she'd underlined years ago in a high-school biology text: *death releases toxins*. She'd shivered when she read the line. She shivered now.

Andy helped her into her gown. She drew on the gloves and tied the mask over her mouth and nose.

Andy dressed himself, then led her down the corridor and stopped at a half-open door. From behind drawn green curtains, she could hear incoherent cries, alternately weak and pathetic, then shrill and violent.

'Prepare yourself,' Andy said.

The smells were already preparing her – an astringent odor of disinfectant masking the sourness of vomit and feces. The combination reminded her of rotting fish and wilted flowers.

Death's bouquet, she thought.

Andy stepped forward and drew the curtains. A man who looked a hundred years old lay on the bed, wearing only an absurdly outsized padded diaper. A tube pulsing with driblets of thick black fluid ran out of the crotch of the diaper to a large jug on the floor. His skin was taut and gray, every rib etched and visible, his knees and elbows grotesquely swollen knobs on fleshless limbs.

Black feverish eyes stared at Sharon. 'Is she going to kill me?' he croaked.

Sharon had last seen Alex Field three weeks ago. He'd already been Dachau-thin and riddled with opportunistic infections, but his mind had been clear and his spirits optimistic; he'd still had control of his bodily functions, and there hadn't been a hint of dementia. Her mind recoiled at the realization that this reeking, raving skeleton was the same 32-year-old man who had laughed and joked and beaten her at Scrabble.

'Hello, Sharon. God bless you for being here.'

Sharon turned toward the voice and recognized the eyes over the mask as those of Martin Baumer, Alex's lover. He sat on a small stool by the bed, his gloved fingers interlaced with Alex's naked fingers.

'Sharon! Is that green person Sharon?' Tendons trembling in his neck, Alex struggled to lift his head an inch from the pillow. 'Is green the fashion statement for killers this season? If you are Sharon behind that mask, please, don't let them kill me.'

'His brain is ulcerated,' Andy whispered.

'He comes and goes.' The tone of Marty's voice was both defeated and defensive. 'Sometimes he isn't quite here.'

Sharon moved to the opposite side of the bed. A network of intravenous lines ran from something that resembled a beeping computerized hat rack into veins on Alex's arms. The thickest tube, almost a small hose, was attached to a needle in his jugular. She reached through the IVs and put her hand on his forehead. Even through the glove, she could feel the burning of his parchment-dry skin. 'No one is going to kill you, Alex.'

He stretched dry, crusted lips, exposing a mouth filled with yellow boils and sores. 'Oh, *shit*!' he screamed. 'The elves have come with knives. They're taking out my kidneys.' He lay gasping for a few seconds. 'Marty, Marty,' he sighed.

'Yes, baby, I'm right here.'

'I have to tell you something.'

Marty leaned forward to listen.

Alex made a strangling sound. A spout of clotted ebony vomit spewed out from his mouth directly on to the exposed portion of his friend's face. Andy and Sharon yanked Alex upright, pounding his back to clear his throat.

'Oh, Marty.' Apologetic and embarrassed, Alex heaved for breath. 'I've killed you. I blew my lunch and killed you.'

'Don't worry.' Marty used a corner of bedsheet to wipe mucus and phlegm from his eyes and cheeks. He glanced at Sharon. 'It's all right. I already have the virus.'

'Oh oh oh oh!' Alex screamed. 'They won't let me use the bathroom!'

A seepage of liquid fecal matter began to ooze from the bottom of the diaper. A flood of bright fresh blood surged after it, spreading across the bed and spilling on to the floor.

Andy whirled and called to the nurses' station, 'He's hemorrhaging!'

Running feet sped toward them. 'Don't touch him!' a voice cried. Donning protective gear, a nurse pushed Sharon and Andy aside and began to unfasten the diaper.

There was an eerily calm look in Alex's eyes, as though he was meditating or focusing on some infinitely distant point. Sharon tried to remember where she had seen that look before. And then it came to

23

her: it was the same forlorn gaze her cat had had when she and the vet had held it down on the examining table, when the animal had finally realized there was no point in further struggle.

A pang went through her.

'Get a mop in here!' the nurse shouted. 'The rest of you step outside and give me some room!'

Andy took Sharon's arm and pulled her out of the cubicle. An orderly dashed past them with bucket and mop. The curtain snapped shut behind him.

'Are you holding up?' Andy said.

Sharon tried to blink him into focus through tearing eyes. 'Is it always like this?'

'A few lucky ones die fast.' Andy wiped his eyes. 'Alex isn't one of them.'

'Why don't you put him on a morphine drip and let him slip away?'

'He *is* on a morphine drip. He's getting enough to slaughter an elephant.'

'Then why isn't it working?'

'I don't know. Something is making him resistant. Panic or the will to stay alive – or maybe a past drug habit.'

'You're his doctor, Andy. Help him.'

'I run a small not-for-profit AIDS clinic. I'm not accredited to this or any other hospital.'

'It's not right. It's not fair. He's a human being.'

'Dr Sanders has done everything he can. Any further sedation would push Alex over the brink.'

The curtain slid open and the orderly came out carrying a plastic bag with the legend BIO-TOXIC WASTE printed across it in red letters.

Newly diapered, Alex lay breathing in short gasps. Leather restraints now held his arms and legs immobile. His hands clenched and un-clenched in a furious fight against an invisible adversary. His nails had already torn into his palms, and blood trickled on to the freshly changed sheets.

'Don't let them kill me.' His voice had become a high, childlike entreaty. 'Whoever you green people are, don't kill me.'

In her gloved hand, the nurse held a large syringe with the longest needle Sharon had ever seen.

'She's going to steal my soul!' Alex cried. Brown froth gathered at his lips. 'She's going to stick that in me and take away my soul!'

The nurse wiped his chest with an alcohol pad.

'Oh God,' he screamed, 'don't let them kill me and feed me to the cat!'

With a movement that was fast and practiced, the nurse thrust the needle into his chest below the ribs and depressed the plunger. Alex stared at the ceiling in open-mouthed shock.

Sharon had to look away from his eyes.

The nurse jerked the hypodermic free and patted a bubble of blood with a cotton swab. 'Just Valium, directly into the heart,' she whispered. 'It won't kill him, but it will calm him down, at least for the time he and his friend need.' She threw the used syringe into a kidney-shaped stainless steel bowl on the bedside table.

Alex's breathing became more regular and his head rolled to one side. Tears slid down his face.

Marty reached a hand to brush them away.

'Did you see that?' Alex said. 'She took my soul.' He seemed puzzled. 'How do you suppose I'll get along without it?'

'You've still got lots of soul,' Marty said. 'More than enough for both of us. I love you, Alex.'

Alex stared at Marty as if he had just made a discovery of something far too wonderful to imagine. 'Oh, and I love you too, Marty.' He paused, trying to catch his breath. 'But you're going to have to forgive me, Angel. I think I've worn out my welcome at this party and I guess I'd better go now.' He fell silent, his eyes studying his lover.

Marty pulled off his mask. 'You go when you want to.'

'OK.' Alex gave a long sigh. 'Will you be here?'

'I'll be here to say goodbye.'

'I might not be able to say anything back.' Alex smiled. 'But I'll be waiting for you.'

'I understand.' Marty laid his head upon his friend's chest and wept.

Alex closed his eyes. 'This is good. Just stay there, please?'

The nurse motioned Andy and Sharon. 'Why don't we just let these people be? They'll call if they need us.'

In the corridor, Sharon turned to Andy. 'No one should have to die like that. I hate this disease. I hate what it does to the people who catch it and I hate what it does to the people who love them.'

Andy's expression was grim. 'I agree.'

They walked to the elevator.

'There must be something we can do,' she said.

Andy nodded. 'There's plenty we can do. The question is, how far are we willing to bend the law?'

March 6

'Tell me about aspirin.' Eddie Arbogast kept his tone shooting-the-breeze casual. 'Do you know of any epidemic it's supposed to cure?'

Eddie and Dr Ida Lovejoy were strolling along the palms on the bay side of Biscayne Boulevard. The midday sun had burned away its circumference, and a blinding white glow spread high above the mirroring ocean.

'Epidemic?' Behind her sunglasses, Lovejoy arched a pale, questioning eyebrow. 'Not unless you're talking about an epidemic of headaches.'

She was a senior researcher with the National Institutes of Health, stopping over in Miami after a two-month Latin American disease tour. Eddie doubted an epidemic could exist anywhere in the world without Lovejoy's knowing something about it.

'What about Sperilac?' Eddie reached into his wallet and drew out the label. Its creases were neatly flattened in a sheet of folded plastic.

Lovejoy stopped walking. She studied the faded lettering for a long, frowning moment. 'Where on earth did you get hold of this?'

'From the foothills of the Sierra Madre, in the wreckage of a drug cartel plane.'

A Cuban family had spread sandwiches and fruit on one of the picnic tables. Latin music flowed from their radio, a high, beseeching threnody over clicking drums.

'Tell me about Sperilac,' Eddie said.

'What's to tell?' Lovejoy walked faster, annoyed, getting away from the music. 'It looked like a possible treatment for AIDS six or seven years ago. A lot of smart money bet on it and a lot of people lost their shirts.'

'What went wrong?'

'The FDA wouldn't OK it.'

'Why not?'

'I don't recall the exact reasons, but there were problems.' She handed the label back. 'Ask the FDA.'

Eddie watched two dark-skinned children playing on the sea

26

wall. 'Has aspirin ever been touted as a cure for AIDS?'

'Surprisingly enough, in a test tube, aspirin knocks the AIDS virus dead.'

'And in a living human being?'

'The problem in a human being is, you can't build up an effective saturation in the blood without ulcerating the intestine. You kill the patient before you kill the virus.'

More and more, it seemed to Eddie that the drug cartel capo and his guests must have been discussing a cure for AIDS. The notion struck him as ridiculous, yet the telltale bits of evidence were mounting up. 'What about Chinese bitter melon?'

Lovejoy shrugged, minimizing the idea. 'It tastes foul but it kills a broad spectrum of viruses – in vitro and in vivo. There've been claims that it kills the AIDS virus, but no one's published a double-blind.'

Eddie sensed a doctor's disdain for remedies that lacked patents and trade names. 'Have you ever heard nutrition touted as a cure for AIDS?'

'Ad infinitum, by the same nuts who advocate meditation and acupuncture.'

At that moment Eddie knew he had all the pieces. And impossible as it seemed, they fitted: aspirin, bitter melon, nutrition, Sperilac – and the cartel.

'What would you say if I told you the drug cartel is looking for a cure for AIDS?'

Lovejoy turned into the breeze, pushing pale hair from the frames of her glasses. 'I'd say you're crazy.'

'So would I. But I have the craziest feeling I'm not.'

March 23

When the phone rang, both Sharon Powell's hands were full with vials from the refrigerator.

Her co-worker Wendy reached round the microscope and answered. 'Lab five. Wendy Johnson.'

Sharon arranged the vials in the holding rack on the counter.

Pale inquisitive eyes flicked up at her through bifocals. 'She's right here.' Wendy covered the mouthpiece and whispered. 'It's Mr Mysterious again.'

Sharon took the phone. 'Sharon Powell.'

'Can you talk?' Andy's voice was low, urgent.

She glanced over at Wendy, whose face quickly bent toward the microscope. 'Not really.'

'We need more Sperilac. Right away.'

'I'll try to get some after work.'

The storage vaults were exactly that – vaults. Sharon slipped her electronic pass card into the slot and a heavy motor-driven steel door opened just far enough and just long enough for her to squeeze through into the steel-walled chamber.

The stern-faced woman wearing rimless eyeglasses looked up from her desk.

'Hello, Sharon.' When Helen Weller smiled, she possessed the slightly ragged beauty of an Aztec princess nearing her middle forties. But obviously she prized efficiency above beauty. The chain of cards and keys that she wore draped round her neck had badly creased her dove-gray blouse. 'How can I help you?'

Everyone assumed that Helen was a spinster, but she answered impartially to Miss, Ms or Mrs Weller. Inevitably, after a few encounters, she would insist on being called Helen.

'Hi, Helen.' Sharon smiled. 'I need the usual. Amitol. Female problems. I love your blouse.'

Helen shook her head. 'I guess gray suits me because I'm getting close to the time when I can forget about PMS.' She pushed back in her chair. 'Shall I get them for you?'

'Save yourself steps. Just open up and I'll help myself.'

Helen tapped a code into her computer. Behind her, a wall of bars shielded a second vault door. Though the inner door was open at the moment, it possessed an untamperable time lock. Helen Weller was reputed to be the only person in the firm who could override the undefeatable system in case of emergency.

The bars swung back and Sharon walked through. She glanced behind her to be sure Helen's eyes weren't following. Moving quickly, she went to the bins where the small square plastic bottles of Sperilac were stored. Each bottle contained 100 capsules. She stuffed five into the pockets of her lab coat.

As she rearranged the remaining containers to conceal her theft, six bottles fell to the metal floor. The clatter ricocheted around the steel walls like gunfire.

Sharon bent down to pick the bottles up.

'Having trouble finding what you want?'

She started at the sound of Helen Weller's voice immediately behind her. She hadn't even heard Helen leave her desk. She realized she'd have to bluff it out.

'No, no, I just knocked these off the shelf.'

'I didn't even know that bin was open.' Helen gave Sharon a questioning glance. 'Well, I'll get your Amitol for you.' She turned and went back up the aisle.

Sharon hastily straightened the Sperilac containers in even rows. As she slid the bin door shut, her hands were trembling.

Helen was waiting at the desk. She held out a large-sized Amitol. 'This enough?'

'That's perfect. Thanks.'

'Sharon.' Helen came round the desk. 'You've been using an awful lot of Amitol lately. You know, a Swedish study has shown it upsets the electrolyte balance and depletes cellular potassium. Low potassium's been linked to migraine. That could be your problem.'

Helen was a statistician, but she knew a lot more about biochemistry than she could have picked up over the walls in Biochemtech's ladies' room stalls.

'Do you think maybe you should have a doctor look at you?'

Sharon felt herself begin to blush. *She's worried about me and here I am lying to her.* Helen was a devout Catholic, nun-trained, easily offended by bad language and bad manners. Scuttlebutt had it she'd kept a crucifix on her desk until management demanded that it be removed. Scuttlebutt also had it she held three university degrees.

'I go to a terrific woman.' Helen jotted a name and phone number on a piece of scratch paper and handed it to Sharon. 'Just tell her I sent you.'

'Actually, the reason I'm out of Amitol is I knocked my last bottle down the john.'

Helen's gaze was motionless, like fresh lake ice. 'Really.'

She knows I'm lying. Sharon felt the blush deepen.

'Anything else you need?'

'No. Thanks. I'm fine.' Sharon fought back the guilty impulse to flee. Her mind flailed for some easy topic of chitchat. 'Am I mistaken, or are our bins emptier than usual? What's the extra storage space for?'

'Our sales are up thirty per cent worldwide. We've also been authorized by the FDA to dispose of redundant drugs to make room for special shipments. And we've been moving out unauthorized pharmaceuticals that are beyond their time limits. Sperilac, for instance. My inventories indicate a lot of that seems to be going out. But I'm sure there's an explanation.'

Sharon felt a tiny quiver run down her spine. 'If anyone can find the explanation, it will be you, Helen.'

'I hope so.' Helen began to gather up her coat and purse. 'I just don't see any point in making a fuss about a discrepancy in the count of a drug nobody uses, do you?'

Is she warning me? Sharon watched as Helen shut down her computer.

'I do this every night,' Helen said. 'We don't want any hackers breaking into my files, do we? Now, if you'd just sign this log for the Amitol, we'll be all square.'

Security people at Forbes Biochemtech had the authority to check employees' purses and briefcases and shopping bags, but the guard at the side entrance smiled and let Sharon pass.

'Pleasant evening, Sharon.'

'You too, Hank.'

She crossed the parking lot with quick strides and slid into her Mazda hatchback. It was a twenty-minute drive from Forbes Biochemtech headquarters in Old Georgetown Road, in Bethesda, Maryland, to the seedy section of Washington, DC, where the Harvey Milk Clinic was located. The ramshackle Victorian frame house at 14th and U Streets was set back from the sidewalk by a littered rectangle of bald earth.

She pushed the buzzer beside the steel security door. A haggard female face peered through a window and there was a click. She stepped into the hallway and nodded toward a young man waiting on a bench. His face wasn't familiar but the emaciation and hopeless eyes were.

Andy Horner, sandy-haired and lanky, stood in the doorway of his office. 'You're an angel.'

She closed the door and set her purse on the paper-strewn desk. 'Keep asking for good deeds, and your angel's going to wind up in jail one of these days.' She cleared space for the five pilfered bottles.

'So might we all.' Andy studied the expiration dates. 'Has Biochemtech manufactured a new lot?'

'I don't know why they would, there's no market.'

'These have a later date. That gives us a two-year reprieve. Not that five bottles will last us a week.'

Sharon poked through envelopes addressed to Dr Andrew Horner. She held up a report from Schlesinger Labs. 'Is this patient on Sperilac?'

Andy nodded.

'Mind if I look? I'm not being nosy, I just like to see how we're doing.' She opened the envelope and skimmed figures. Tim Wyatt's T cells were 420, up from 390 last month; his liver function was low normal, he was negative for hepatitis A, B, and C, and he carried antibodies to A and C. 'Is that Wyatt sitting out in the hall?'

'That's Wyatt.'

'His T cells are up.'

'Of course they're up, he's been getting Sperilac for two months.'

'If Sperilac could do this for him, why couldn't it save Alex Field?'

'No two cases of AIDS are the same.' Andy sighed. 'Besides which, Alex started Sperilac when his T cells were fifty-five. It was too little, too late.'

'He would have killed for a blood profile this good. Why's Wyatt so depressed?'

'His lover died yesterday. It was worse than Alex.'

Sharon fell a chill. She slid the report back into its envelope. 'Wasn't the lover getting Sperilac?'

Andy shook his head. 'We had to triage him out. Too far advanced. Speaking of triage . . .' Andy rummaged through papers and pulled out another blood report and handed it to her. 'Here's someone I want you to look at.'

Sharon gritted. She hated it when market forces determined the life

31

and death of human beings. 'If only we had more Sperilac.'

This had been the single greatest problem confronting them since Sharon had begun work with the Harvey Milk Clinic over a year ago. She'd volunteered after a close friend had died of AIDS. She'd liked Andy immediately, admired his calm in the center of never-ending crisis and approved of his flexible, non-traditional approach; and when she'd learned he and his patients were actually willing to try Sperilac, it wasn't long before she'd started smuggling the drug to him. As a result, a hundred or more lives had been saved.

Which wasn't nearly good enough when hundreds of thousands were dying.

'You work for the manufacturer,' Andy said. 'Tell them to up production.'

'They're only manufacturing for research, and nobody's doing research.'

'We are.'

'You're not legal.'

'Ouch. Don't remind me.'

Sharon opened the report and studied the stats on Isabel Mahler, age twenty-six. Andy had highlighted the bad news in yellow: positive for TB and MAI; positive for candidiasis, positive for hepatitis A and B; advanced anemia; liver function wretched, T cells vanishing.

Sharon had no medical training, but she had lab experience and she could rank Sperilac prospects into good, middling, and poor.

'I don't know,' she said. But she knew.

'Can't say or won't?'

Andy only asked when the case was borderline and he was having trouble making up his own mind. She resented being dragooned into casting the deciding vote. 'Andy, I don't know, OK?'

'Then come meet her. She's here.'

'You bastard. You show me this and then you—'

'You'll like her.'

In a room with a sloping greenhouse wall, a dark-haired girl rested, eyes shut, on a deck chair. A knitted afghan lay across her legs and her face had a translucent, sickly beauty.

Andy made introductions. 'Sharon, Isabel. Isabel, Sharon.'

A strapping, dark-haired young man rose from a canvas lawn chair. 'My sister's asleep. I'm sorry.'

'Don't wake her.' Sharon said.

32

'And this is Joe, Isabel's brother. Joe, Sharon.'

'Hi, Sharon.' Joe Mahler had burning dark eyes. 'She wanted to stay awake and meet you. But when she gets tired, she just doesn't have the strength.' He also had a hint of a Spanish accent; it went with his appearance, but not with the German name. 'She shuts her eyes and boom, out like a light.'

'That happens.' It happened in the final stages, and Sharon hated to hold out false hope. She's seen good results from Sperilac, but Isabel looked awfully far advanced.

'My sister's been to fourteen doctors and nine hospitals. Three years of standard therapies. I think it's hurt her.'

'Possibly.' Sharon wondered if the girl could hear them. She decided not. 'Some of those standard therapies are toxic.'

Joe nodded. 'I have a feeling that's how she developed anemia.'

'Very possibly.'

'Andy says you're the resident expert on Sperilac.'

'I'm not a resident, and I'm not an expert.' She didn't mean to snap, but it was her ingrained response to being pressured. 'How did you hear about Harvey Milk Clinic? Who told you about Sperilac?'

Joe looked uncertain, as though she was testing him. As though there were right answers and wrong answers and he had to score high to save his sister.

'I have a gay friend.'

One of those, Sharon thought. The gay thing bothers him.

'You have a gay friend and . . . ?'

'I was looking through one of his magazines, I saw an article. I thought, that's it, we're going to try that.'

A stereo was playing soft pan flutes and there was a faint breeze from an air purifying machine. Potted plants hanging from the ceiling by copper chains stirred as traffic rumbled by.

'Sharon had a look at your sister's blood work,' Andy said.

'You did? What are her . . .' Joe Mahler didn't say the word: chances.

'I've seen some amazing recoveries on Sperilac.' Sharon held out a hand. 'Nice meeting you, Joe.'

'You too.'

She felt desperation in his handshake.

In the corridor, with the door shut behind them, she said, 'It's not my fault there isn't enough.'

'No comment,' Andy said.

It's terrible to want to shout when you have to whisper. 'What the hell do you expect from me? She's not a good risk. You don't need me to tell you that.'

'Three years of wrong therapy.'

'All right, she's been through hell.'

'If you could steal a little more Sperilac, we could start her on the protocol.'

She wheeled on him. 'I'll say yes this one last time. But don't ever do that to me again.'

Eyes of manipulating innocence. 'Do what?'

March 30

Thursday morning the following week Joe Mahler phoned Sharon at the lab. His voice bubbled over. 'Isabel is doing fantastically. I have to thank you.'

'That's great. You're welcome.'

'Her appetite is back, she's holding down food, she's gained *a pound and a half.*'

'Fantastic.'

'The night sweats have stopped and you know what? This last week I haven't had to get up once to change her sheets.'

'A good night's sleep can make a difference. For her and you both.'

'You don't know. Hey, could you join Andy and me for lunch? There's a proposition I want to discuss.'

The maître d' led Sharon through a busy, buzzing room to a table beside a wall of whaling prints. Andy and Joe Mahler were halfway through their drinks and from the giddy vibes she knew it wasn't their first round.

'And something for the lady to drink.' Andy motioned.

'Mineral water for me.' Sharon angled a cheek to Andy's kiss. 'I have to focus a microscope this afternoon.'

'I have to squint at a computer screen,' Joe Mahler said.

She couldn't believe the difference a week had made. Joe's pallor was gone, his face had filled out, his dark eyes danced. 'What kind of work do you do, Joe?'

'Nothing so useful as you two.'

'Joe keeps the economy going.' There was an edge of good-natured needling in the way Andy said it.

'I work for Vestcate,' Joe said.

'Vestcate?'

'We're an international investment syndicate. I'm East Coast rep.'

'And what does East Coast rep entail?'

'In my case, a fair amount of research.'

'Joe's researched you,' Andy warned.

Sharon had a sense that this conversation was not so much happening as following a prepared script. 'And what did Joe find out?'

'You were a Westinghouse scholar,' Joe said. 'Your father is Lucas Powell. Twenty years ago he devised the liver enzyme test for determining *in utero* if a foetus was at risk for vitamin B6 deficiency-linked brain and lung abnormality. It won him a Nobel Prize. Eight years later he developed Sperilac. You helped him.'

'Gross exaggeration. I transcribed his notes.'

'Forbes Biochemtech controls the patent. Sperilac went through Phase One and Phase Two FDA trials seven years ago, and then it bogged down in pharmaceutical intrigue and bureaucratic delays. It's still bogged down.'

'It's not bogged down. It's dead. It's gone to drug limbo.'

'Which is what I want to discuss. I've spent the better part of a week reading the trial reports. They impress me. And frankly, what impresses me even more is what I've seen with my own eyes – Isabel's improvement. I want to back new trials.'

Disbelief took Sharon. 'But—'

'More precisely,' Joe said, 'I'm recommending to my partners that we invest. Vestcate has five hundred and sixty-three partners worldwide, and they're going to be as enthusiastic as I am.'

Sharon wasn't so sure. 'Maybe not when they learn Forbes Biochemtech sank a hundred million into Sperilac seven years ago.'

'The problem wasn't the drug, it was Biochemtech. They couldn't access capital. The best product in the world will fail without adequate backing. Vestcate can provide that backing.'

'Joe, I wonder if you understand how the pharmaceutical world works. My father invested twenty years of his life and almost all his savings to develop Sperilac. When he needed further capital, he sold the rights to Biochemtech. He knew he had a good drug and so did they. But they discovered Sperilac has one fatal flaw – it challenges orthodox AIDS theories.'

Andy explained. 'Mainstream treatment tries to kill the AIDS virus with chemicals. Sperilac works by boosting intra-cellular immunity so the *immune system* kills the virus. The fact that Sperilac works shows that the mainstream approach is wrong.'

'Major pharmaceutical companies stood to lose billions,' Sharon said. 'So they closed ranks and pressured the FDA to turn Sperilac down. The shock and disappointment almost killed my father. He suffered two severe strokes and now he's paralyzed and has to speak through a computer.'

Joe nodded somberly. 'I understand. What they did to your father was tragic. And criminal. But when the public sees that Sperilac works – and they *will* see it, believe me – the establishment will have to yield. And your father will finally be vindicated.'

Sharon wondered if after all these years it might really be possible. 'If that ever happened, it would make Dad the happiest man on earth.' And me the happiest woman, she thought.

'What's more,' Joe said, 'Forbes Biochemtech will make back six to eight times its loss.'

'I'm sorry.' Sharon shook her head. 'But you're going to have a hard time persuading Harry Forbes of that.'

'Which is why I want you to talk to him.'

'Me?' This was going too fast. 'I don't think so.'

'But you're the perfect choice. You know the drug. You've worked with Andy, you know the disease.'

She shook her head. 'None of that's going to impress Harry Forbes.'

'The Harvey Milk Clinic records will do the impressing. Two hundred and thirty-nine persons with AIDS have taken Sperilac and two hundred and twelve have achieved viral dormancy. That's a success rate no other drug can touch, and other drugs are making *fortunes*.'

Sharon stared at Joe Mahler a long, deliberating moment. 'It's not ethical to show those records. The clinic wasn't running a trial. Andy's patients didn't sign consent forms.'

'I'll handle the medical ethics,' Andy said. 'You handle Forbes.'

April 2

Harry Forbes, CEO of Forbes Biochemtech, saw that he had an appointment penciled in for 3:15. The handwriting was his secretary's. He lifted the telephone and tapped a digit into the keypad. 'Miss Lyons, who the hell is this Sharon Powell I'm supposed to see?'

'She's Lucas Powell's daughter, sir.'

Lucas Powell. Forbes flipped through his mental Rolodex. Bio-chemtech's one and only Nobelist. Annoyance rose up in him. 'But Powell's daughter is that loud little child with pigtails.'

'Oh no, sir. She's been working down in research for four years now.'

'Any idea what she wants?'

'All she mentioned was— She's here now, sir.'

Forbes steeled himself for fifteen wasted minutes. 'Send her in – but buzz at three thirty sharp.'

The mahogany door opened and a slender, bright-faced young woman stepped in. She carried an enormous loose-leaf binder tucked under one arm. 'I appreciate your seeing me on such short notice.' She smiled uncertainly.

'No trouble.' Forbes could see the resemblance to the loud little girl, and he was surprised at the improvement a few years had effected. With a little more heft topside, she would have been exactly his type. 'How's your dad?'

'He's in good spirits, but since the second stroke . . .' She let a headshake say it. Her dark blonde hair swayed. 'You know.'

Forbes didn't know. He'd heard nothing about Powell's strokes and, knock wood, no one in his family had ever had one. His own health was perfect for a man of sixty-one. He lifted weights with a personal trainer at seven in the morning, twice a week.

Powell's daughter was looking at one of the small twilight landscapes on the wall. 'Is that a Corot?'

'Why yes.' Forbes was proud of his Corot and pleased on the rare occasions when visitors commented. 'Do you know art?'

'Not really. I minored in art history.'

'We'll have to talk about that some time. Unfortunately, I can only give you ten minutes today.'

'I understand.' She sat in a leather armchair facing his desk, her weight forward, the ungainly binder balanced on her knees. 'It's about Sperilac. As you may recall, my father developed the drug as a cure for—'

'Of course I recall.' Forbes had a painfully clear memory of that hundred and twelve million dollar black hole in Biochemtech's balance sheet. 'Sperilac went through a brilliant Phase One trial and failed after Phase Two.'

'I've got a backer who wants to put it back in production.'

The effortlessness of the effrontery amazed Forbes. As though he would ask a lab employee to pass the tin cup on the company's behalf. 'You have a backer,' he said without intonation.

'Vestcate, an investment syndicate. A representative approached me and—'

'Ms Powell, when the FDA says no, they mean no.'

'The FDA can be wrong, and in this case they are. Sperilac works.' She leaned forward from the chair and placed the binder on his desk.

He averted his eyes from her neckline. 'What's this?'

'It's the medical log of an underground treatment center. The Harvey Milk Clinic. They treat people with AIDS with promising untested drugs. They've been giving their clients Sperilac for the last year, and the results are – well, you can see for yourself. Some of these people are in virtual remission.'

Forbes opened the binder and thumbed through a depressingly thick stack of lab reports.

'With the International AIDS Conference coming up in Amsterdam next month, you couldn't have a more perfect opportunity to relaunch Sperilac.'

'Ms Powell, where has this clinic been getting its Sperilac?'

Silence rolled in, and it was as though someone had boosted the humming sound of the little refrigerator where he kept his pre-mixed martinis.

'The drug was just sitting on the shelf.' There was no apology in her green eyes. If anything, reproach. 'Doing no one any good.'

'Do you realize the position that puts this company in? Sneaking behind the government's back? Ms Powell, this company cannot function without the good will and approval of the FDA.'

Her eyes met his levelly. 'I understand that, but what about the Vestcate offer?'

'The pilferage must stop before you get this company shut down. As for the offer.' Forbes slammed the binder shut. 'Absolutely not.'

Shortly before four, Harry Forbes' secretary buzzed to tell him his wife was on line two.

'Lucinda.' He tried to sound agreeable.

'Just a reminder.' Lucinda's voice, as always, was orange-blossom honey. 'The Cosmos Club at eight. Black tie.'

'Christ.'

'Bad day?'

'Rotten. It looks like the government's going to force us to re-price Seranox.' The drug, one of Biochemtech's top earners, had a huge share of the Veterans' Administration and nursing home market, but this new Congress had gone cost-cutting crazy. 'And to top it off, one of the employees came bouncing in with an offer to put Sperilac back into production. *Sperilac*. Of all the lunacies.'

'But that would cost hundreds of millions.' Lucinda's tone was thoughtful. 'How do you suppose an employee could access that kind of backing?'

'Her father won a Nobel Prize. I'm sure she knows how to trade on it.'

'What did you tell her?'

'What do you think? I told her to go to hell.'

Cursing the end-of-the-workday headache pounding at his temples, Harry Forbes stepped into the company parking lot at 6:05 p.m. He unlocked his moss-green Mercedes SL300 and slid into the front seat.

He took the Advil bottle from the glove compartment, shook two caplets loose, and swallowed. The smell of new leather consoled him.

As he was turning the key in the ignition, high heels rat-a-tatted across the asphalt and a dark-haired young woman came running up to the window.

'Mr Forbes?' She had a Hispanic accent, dark eyes, flawless Hispanic skin, and *mucho* topside. She was very much his type.

'Yes?'

'I hope you don't think I'm forward – I'm Maria del Lago, in book-keeping?'

She seemed to expect the name to mean something to him, but of course it meant nothing. The company had over three thousand employees in the District alone.

'Yes, Miss del Lago?'

'My car's broken down.' She tossed a harried nod in the direction of employee parking. 'The AAA say they'll pick it up in two hours, but I have to get home – and don't you live in Chevy Chase?'

He wondered how she happened to know his address, and then he remembered last Sunday's *Washington Post* profile on Lucinda. 'I live in Chevy Chase, yes.'

'My place is on your way. Would it be too much trouble to ask for a lift?'

She was leaning so close that it was impossible not to smell her perfume – a rich rose attar with intriguing citrus and thyme dissonances.

Why not? Harry Forbes thought. I'm not due at that Cosmos Club wake till eight . . .

His headache had vanished. He pushed the button that unlocked the passenger door. 'Hop in.'

Twenty minutes later Maria del Lago was directing him down a quiet street of middle-income wood frame houses, most of them for sale.

'Last house on the left.'

The two young cherry trees in front were obvious transplants, and they weren't doing well. Harry Forbes' foot touched the brake and the car glided to a buttery stop.

'I can't thank you enough, Mr Forbes. You saved my life. Really.'

She reached for the door. He'd locked it from the driver's control, which overrode the passenger's. Her eyes came round to his, questioning.

'Are you in a hurry, Maria?'

Something changed in her expression. He couldn't tell if she was flattered or contemptuous.

'I don't often get a chance to meet my employees one on one.'

'My day care's expecting me.' She snapped open her purse. A mysteriously pleasing smell floated up. His nose identified anisette but there was something else too.

She took out a small comb. 'May I?' Angling the rearview, she centered her reflection and neatened her hair with crisp, quick little strokes.

'You're a very attractive young woman, Maria.'

Was that smile for her reflection or for him? She placed the comb back in the purse. He could hear her hand scrabbling like a mouse through packets and coins.

'I wouldn't mind just sitting here a moment and talking.' He leaned toward her and his right hand slipped along the calfskin upholstery till

41

two fingertips were touching her marvelously narrow waist. 'How about it?'

Her scrabbling hand pulled a slender object out of her purse. His eye caught a wink of metal. His brain registered an incongruity. What's she holding? That doesn't make sense.

Maria del Lago, turning to offer her open lips, punched the blade between Harry Forbes' ribs straight into his heart.

April 4

Eddie Arbogast sat in the patio, legs up on the diving board, skimming the Sunday edition of the *Miami Herald*. He was almost a happy man: the day was sunny, the house was paid for, the swimming pool was almost paid for. But as he turned a page, his mind red-flagged the word 'Biochemtech' in the obits.

'Harry Churchill Forbes – CEO of Forbes Biochemtech slain.'

Eddie made the connection instantly: Biochemtech, Sperilac.

The *Herald* listed Forbes' wives, his children, his professional accomplishments. Then came the interesting part.

'Mr Forbes was apparently mugged and murdered in his car.'

Eddie paused to polish the lenses of his steel-rimmed reading glasses with his napkin. He placed them on his nose and continued reading.

'Police speculate that the assailant, possibly a woman, entered his car when Mr Forbes stopped for a red light.'

Eddie found that improbable. He didn't believe any CEO would drive in any major metropolitan area of the USA with the car doors unlocked.

He went into the den. Amy had littered his desk with travel folders. Color photos of fjords and pagodas, ski slopes and chateaux socked him in the eye.

'Amy,' he shouted, 'what did you do with my manila folders?' His last day at the office, he had Xeroxed every document and clipping related to Miguel Bosch that he could find in the files. 'I left them right here on top of the desk.'

It was an old battle: she was always re-organizing him.

'In the chest,' she called.

He lifted the begonias and family photographs from the rosewood chest and placed them on the floor. He swung open the iron-hinged lid and saw that Amy had placed his folders at the very bottom, under their wedding photographs. Wishful thinking on Amy's part. He had to smile.

He spread the manila folders on the sofa and chair and floor and finally found what he wanted: the report on Mike Bosch's car-mugger murders of two Supreme Court justices in Colombia in '72.

The MO in the Forbes killing was a carbon copy.

Every instinct in Eddie's body shouted that Mike Bosch had finally done it: he'd killed a US citizen with no involvement in illicit drugs. Mike Bosch had finally given him the hook he needed to reel him in.

Eddie began throwing underwear into a suitcase.

'Could I be nosy?' Amy stood in the doorway. Her artist's smock was daubed with oil paint. 'Where are you going?'

'Chevy Chase, Maryland.'

'Now?'

'Next plane to DC.'

'We have a bridge party tonight.'

'You don't seriously expect me to play bridge when Miguel Bosch is on the move again.'

'You're obsessed.'

'Tell me something I didn't know.'

'You're retired.'

'Don't remind me.' He kissed her. 'I'll phone.'

Captain Tod Farmer of the Chevy Chase Police stepped round his desk to examine Eddie's DEA credentials. He handed them back, frowning. 'Miami division? A little far from your home turf, aren't you?'

'That's right,' Eddie said agreeably.

'Did your people phone us or fax, Mr Arbogast?'

'Sorry. There wasn't time.'

'If you'd given us prior notification, we could have prepared and that would save *you* time. How can we can help you?'

'I need to see the file on the Harry Forbes killing.'

Sharon Powell sat in the rear of Saint Agnes' Episcopal Church and let the sonorous male voice with its Boston Brahman vowels stream over her.

'Harry and I were rivals in the pharmaceutical business, rivals on the golf course, rivals for the hand of Lucinda Barrett, and throughout it all best of friends.'

Sharon's eye wandered, counting heads in packed pews. Sunlight streamed through stained glass saints and martyrs. A man with pepper-and-salt hair was seated just across the aisle. He seemed to be staring at her.

She directed her attention to the lily-banked altar. Beeswax candles cast wavering halos on drifting clouds of incense.

'Harry,' the voice concluded, 'how can I ever thank you for forty unforgettable years? God bless you.'

There were sniffles, purses clicking open and hankies pulled out. Harry Forbes' rival stepped down from the pulpit and a golden-haired minister took his place.

'Let us pray.'

Head bowed, Sharon peeked at the man across the aisle. He was still staring at her. She'd never seen him before in her life.

The family formed a reception line on the church steps. In her pearls and black Chanel and matching pillbox hat, Harry Forbes' widow looked younger and wealthier than the three stepdaughters beside her.

Sharon introduced herself. 'I'm in the research lab.'

'You knew Harry?' Lucinda Forbes seemed surprised.

'I spoke with your husband the day he . . .'

Lucinda Forbes' hand clasped hers with a strength that was almost brutal. 'We're having Harry's relatives and friends to the house – please join us.'

In Harry Forbes' fieldstone mansion the rooms were photographer-ready, English antiques gleaming. Caterer's men circulated with trays of canapes and drinks. Guests in designer cocktail dresses and two thousand dollar suits spoke in low tones of shock: 'What a horrible thing – mugged in his own car.'

A discreet pianist played Chopin nocturnes.

'Chopin was Harry's favorite,' Lucinda Forbes said. 'Mine too.'

'It's consoling music,' Sharon said.

At that moment, the man with pepper-and-salt hair took Lucinda Forbes' hand. 'I'm so sorry, Lucinda. So sorry.'

'Thank you.'

Sharon watched him return to the crowd. 'Who's that man?'

'I don't recall. He's not one of the relatives.'

It seemed to Sharon that he wasn't dressed like any of Harry Forbes' friends. His suit looked lived-in, off-the-rack.

'Let's go somewhere we can talk.' Lucinda Forbes led the way to a paneled study with shelves of leatherbound first editions of Dickens and Thackeray and a complete run of *National Geographic*. A hulking young male servant with exotic eyes and graceful hands was emptying an ashtray.

'What are you drinking?' Lucinda Forbes said.

Sharon had work to do that afternoon. 'Maybe some mineral water.'

Lucinda Forbes asked the servant to bring them two Perriers, ice and lime. He closed the door behind him.

'The board has asked me to take over Harry's job.' Lucinda dipped two fingers into a desk drawer and lifted out a piece of scribbled scratch paper. 'I found some notes in his office. Apparently a place called the Harvey Milk Clinic has been running unauthorized trials of one of our drugs. Sperilac.' She dropped into a red leather armchair, her crossed leg swinging like a cat's tail. 'There was a mention in Harry's datebook that he met with you the day he died.'

Sharon sat in the facing chair. She weighed her options and decided there was no point lying or even trying to shade the truth. 'For the last year, I've been taking Sperilac from the storeroom and giving it to a doctor at the clinic.'

'What doctor?'

'His name is Andy Horner. He's been giving the drug to AIDS cases.'

Lucinda Forbes' voice betrayed no more emotion than her face. 'And?'

'And it works. And an investment syndicate by the name of Vestcate heard about it. They wanted to back new trials. I took the offer to Mr Forbes and he turned it down.'

There was a knock at the door. The servant brought two Perriers on a silver tray.

'Thank you, Key,' Lucinda Forbes said. 'That will be all. Please close the door.'

She took a long, silent moment squeezing lime into her mineral water.

'I have some advice for you, Miss Powell. I hope you'll take it in the spirit in which it's offered.'

'I'll certainly try.'

'The best way for you and this Dr Andy Horner to stay out of prison would be to get that Vestcate deal going.'

Sharon felt eight different kinds of nervousness when she picked up the phone that evening and dialed Joe Mahler's number.

This time, finally, he answered. 'Joe Mahler.'

'Joe, it's Sharon – Sharon Powell.'

'Well hello.' His voice glowed. 'Nice to hear your voice.'

'Yours too. I've been phoning all afternoon.'

'I got your messages.'

Allegro, her cat, jumped into her lap. 'The hang-ups were mine too.'

'Sorry to be so elusive. I was on the road. Just got back. What's happening?'

'Joe, I had a talk with Harry Forbes' widow today.' She stroked Allegro along his spine and felt his whole body begin to purr. He was a black and white calico she'd adopted last month. 'She's the new CEO, and she's interested in your offer to back Sperilac.'

Joe didn't answer.

'She asked if the offer was still open. Is it?'

'Are you kidding?' Joe said.

'No.'

'Of course it's still open.'

In his room at the Holiday Inn, Eddie kicked off his shoes, lay down on the bed, and phoned his wife. 'I'm coming home tomorrow.'

'Excuse me while I turn cartwheels. What happened to the manhunt of the century?'

'The CEO was definitely a hit, but it looks to me like the wife did it.' Eddie had no idea if the line was secure, but what the hell. No one was naming names. 'He tripled his insurance a week before the murder. She's sole beneficiary and she got him to cut his daughters out of the will.'

'All that flying for nothing.'

'It wasn't for nothing. The cherry trees are in bloom, and the widow served smoked salmon at the funeral reception.'

'How did you get into the reception?'

'Followed the other cars from church and walked in.'

'You're terrible. I've missed you.'

'I've missed you too.'

'Will you be home in time for dinner?'

'Depends. What's dinner?'

'I was thinking of filet of flounder with a sauce veronique and wild rice and asparagus tip stuffing.'

'Serve the wild rice and asparagus on the side and I'll be home on the afternoon flight.'

'I'll stuff mine and leave yours on the side.'

'Deal.'

April 10

Sharon fixed her broadest smile to her face and strode into the CEO's office with a confidence she was far from actually feeling.

Lucinda Forbes and Joe Mahler were already at the conference table, mugs of coffee steaming at their elbows. A chubby-faced man with a bow tie and a revved-up voice was describing a presidential gaffe at a White House dinner. Joe was laughing politely and Lucinda Forbes was tapping a ballpoint on a yellow legal-sized pad.

'Sharon,' she interrupted, 'do you know Don Barnes, our lobbyist?'

Don Barnes rose and smiled without showing his teeth. 'Good to meet you, Sharon.'

Sharon took the fourth chair at the table. Joe flicked a smile her way.

'How far has the discussion got?' she said.

'Nowhere yet,' Lucinda said. 'We've been waiting for you.'

'Sorry.' Sharon noticed changes in the room: the moody little Corot landscape was gone, and a flashy piece of sixties pop art hung in its place. An enormous blue glass vase brimming with long-stemmed roses and baby's breath had been placed on the bar. 'I thought I was on time.'

'You are,' Joe said. 'Exactly on time. I'm early. But then, I'm the anxious one.'

'Exactly how anxious are you, Mr Mahler?' Lucinda asked.

'My partners and I think Sperilac is the investment opportunity of the decade. We don't want to miss out on it a second time.'

'Drug trials cost upwards of a hundred million.'

'I understand how you arrived at that figure, but I disagree with it.'

Lucinda lifted one eyebrow. 'Mr Mahler, I can assure you—'

'Realistically, we should be prepared to invest at least twice that amount. Possibly three times.'

Lucinda's face betrayed nothing. She began jotting rapidly on her notepad. 'At this point in time, Biochemtech can't invest a penny.'

'Vestcate doesn't expect you to.'

'Would it be too much to ask you what you *do* expect of us?'

'Biochemtech puts up the patent, the drug, the expertise. We put up the rest.'

'And is Vestcate doing this all as a good deed, or do you expect to recoup your investment?'

'We ask for fifty per cent of your royalties over the next twenty-five years.'

Lucinda's ballpoint stopped. 'You realize the patent on the active ingredient in Sperilac has only seven years to run.'

'I've done my homework, Mrs Forbes.'

'After seven years, we'll be competing with generic rip-offs. There'll be next to no profit.'

'Again, I disagree with your projections. Sperilac's profit margin will fall, but aggregate profits will rise.'

'How do you figure that?'

'The market for Sperilac has barely been scratched. For the next thirty years it'll be expanding. We'll have a seven-year head start penetration. When the patent expires, we'll drop our price *below* the generic level. That way we keep the lion's share of the market. We'll more than make up in volume what we lose per unit.'

'That frankly strikes me as an optimistic assumption.'

'A rising tide lifts all ships – and the demand for Sperilac will be just that.'

Lucinda snapped her ballpoint down. 'Biochemtech can assume no liability if you're mistaken.'

'Vestcate will take full responsibility for its assumptions.'

'You're saying there are others?'

'One other. I'd like to get this moving as quickly as possible. Given that we're dealing with an epidemic, I trust the FDA can be . . . induced to allow the old Phase One and Phase Two trial results.'

A silence passed.

'Inducing is Don's specialty.' Lucinda's eyes went to the lobbyist. 'Have you spoken to anyone on the FDA committee?'

Don Barnes nodded. 'I've sounded them out. Five out of the six votes think it would make sense and save valuable time to allow the old results.'

'And the sixth vote?'

'The sixth is holding out.'

'Who is it?'

'Thelma van Voss.'

Lucinda crossed her arms. 'She blocked us seven years ago. Is she going to block us now?'

'Time may have softened Thelma's opposition. For one thing, the

49

situation's a good deal more desperate now.' Don Barnes rattled off the worsening AIDS statistics, the various indices of public impatience with the FDA, the growing popular suspicion that the Administration, far from seeking a cure, was actually obstructing any hope of one.

Lucinda studied her fingernails, then her wedding ring.

'I can think of one sure way to change Thelma van Voss's mind.' Joe Mahler's smile was almost cunning.

Lucinda tipped her head. 'And what's that?'

'Sharon could show her the medical records of the Harvey Milk Clinic.'

Lucinda turned. 'Sharon?'

Sharon hesitated. Joe Mahler had put her on the spot. It would be a gamble, taking records of illegal underground trials to a government agency; admitting her own involvement. On the other hand, Sperilac worked. It would save lives. That was worth a gamble.

'I'm willing.'

After work, Sharon drove straight to the nursing home in Silver Spring, Maryland. She found her father in his room, in the final heat of a chess game with his next-door neighbor Millie.

'Hi, Millie. Hi, Dad.'

'Hi, honey.' Millie waved a captured pawn. 'Life treating you right?'

Lucas turned his wheelchair to the computer. Two severe strokes had left him unable to speak, but his mind was still agile and he had good use of his right hand. His fingers rapidly tapped keys and a glowing amber message unfurled across the screen: CIAO, GORGEOUS.

Sharon pulled up a kibitzer's chair and kissed the wispy white hair at the side of her father's head.

DID YOU BRING ME ANY CHOCOLATE BARS?

'I'm afraid not.'

GO GET SOME.

'Can't. Dr Johnson says they're bad for you.'

BULL.

'Dr Johnson's right.' Millie lifted her knight; carefully tapping each square, she moved it two forward and one left. 'Chocolate is high in saturated fat.'

THE ONLY THINGS HIGH IN FAT AROUND HERE ARE DOCTORS' HEADS AND YOURS, MILLIE.

'I didn't hear that.' Millie plucked up another of Lucas's pawns and added it to the collection of white chessmen on her side of the table.

'I've got some wonderful news,' Sharon said.

Lucas frowned at the chessboard, contemplating his options.

'I know exactly what he's going to do,' Millie said. 'Watch this.'

Lucas pushed his queen down the diagonal into Millie's knight.

'You don't have to be rough about it.' Millie lifted her knight and placed it on Lucas's side of the table.

'An investment syndicate wants to back Sperilac,' Sharon said.

Lucas's eyes flicked up at her. A scowl darkened his face. WHAT SYNDICATE?

'Their name is Vestcate.'

NEVER HEARD OF THEM.

'They're worldwide and huge.'

'I've heard of Vestcate,' Millie said. 'The *Post* had a column on them. They're worth billions.'

WHY ARE THEY INTERESTED IN SPERILAC?

'Because it's a great drug,' Sharon said. 'It will save millions of lives.'

GRANTED. BUT WITH ONLY SEVEN YEARS LEFT ON THE PATENT, IT'S A ROTTEN INVESTMENT.

'It's a terrific investment.'

THERE'S NOT ENOUGH TIME TO GO THROUGH NEW TRIALS AND RECOUP INVESTMENT.

'Haven't you heard of fast-track trials?'

SURE, AND I'VE HEARD OF SANTA CLAUS TOO.

'We're asking the FDA to accept the old Phase One and Phase Two results so we can go straight to Phase Three.'

THE FDA WILL NEVER ALLOW IT WITH THELMA VAN VOSS STILL ON THE COMMITTEE.

'Hey,' Millie said, 'is anyone around here playing chess?'

THELMA'S PALS ARE MAKING TOO MUCH MONEY OFF OF DRUGS THAT DON'T WORK. A DRUG THAT ACTUALLY DOES ITS JOB WOULD DRIVE THEM OUT OF BUSINESS. SHE'LL NEVER LET IT HAPPEN.

'If she blocks us,' Sharon said, 'Vestcate will take the case to the public through a media campaign. The FDA will have to yield.'

THAT WILL COST HUNDREDS OF MILLIONS.

'Vestcate believes in this drug, Dad, and so do I. One way or the other, we're going to beat the FDA this time.' Sharon hugged him. You sweet old man, do you know how much I love you? 'And that's a promise.'

I'M NOT GOING TO HOLD YOU TO IT.

'You just watch, Dad.' I'll be damned if I'll let you end your days believing the greatest work of your life was a failure. 'We go to the FDA tomorrow.'

'Lucas? I warned you.' Millie moved her castle. *Tap-tap-tap.* 'Check!'

April 11

Thelma van Voss waited in the smallest of the three hearing rooms at FDA headquarters. The chamber was oak-paneled, somberly comfortable, the air sweet with the smell of leather and lemon oil.

Two guards stood inside the double doors. Today's session was off limits to the press and public. Thelma had seen to that.

Three stacks of neatly aligned manila folders sat on the green baize conference table in front of her, each pile nearly four inches high. On top was a plastic binder. Through the clear cover red Xs marched down the margin beside lines of text. She really didn't need all the hard copy evidence; she prided herself on a memory that clutched to a fact with the tenacity of a hawk holding down a rabbit. Facts were weapons, and today Thelma was prepared for war.

The other five members of the board filed in. Thelma offered her sweetest smile to the chairman, Thayer MacLean. She hoped he did not see it as the grimace she sometimes noticed when she was trying to practice charm in front of a mirror.

The double doors at the rear of the hearing room opened. The guards admitted a man and a woman.

'Ladies and gentlemen,' MacLean cleared his throat and consulted his notes, 'we are here to consider allowing Forbes Biochemtech to continue tests on Sperilac, a drug that they assert to be effective in the treatment of AIDS. Our witnesses today are Dr Sharon Powell of Forbes Biochemtech and Dr Andy Horner of the Harvey Milk Clinic.' MacLean indicated each of them with a wave of his pencil.

The man's an idiot, Thelma thought. Doesn't he believe we can tell a Sharon from an Andy?

'Dr Powell, Dr Horner, please make yourselves comfortable at the table with us.'

Thelma studied the man and woman who sat across the table from her. She could see from Andy Horner's every-hair-in-place grooming, from the way he played with the push-button and clip of his ballpoint pen, that he was a man obsessed; she could sense he lacked the versatility to compromise, and as a result he was anybody's pawn in anybody's game. Sharon Powell was another kettle of kippers:

unconsciously striking, wealthy enough not to be bought, and too bright for anybody's good. Thelma suspected that somewhere, hidden behind that absurdly perfect face and figure, was an un-ladylike potential for brute force.

'Shall we begin our questioning?' MacLean asked.

Before any of the other members of the board could raise a hand, Thelma rapped her knuckle on a stack of folders.

'Mr Chairperson, I trust that most of you here will remember that it was I who blocked the Third Phase trials of the Sperilac tests,' she opened a notebook and pretended to consult it, 'seven years ago. My decision – which cost me weeks of agonizing – was based on Bio-chemtech's unconscionably sloppy paperwork.'

Thelma tried to shift her 300-pound-plus bulk in the government-issue swivel chair – without success. She felt as if she was being held in a giant fist that at any moment might get a notion to start squeezing. She steadied both feet against the floor.

'I've given over many hours examining the new material which Forbes has presented to us, and I am heartsick to tell you that we are wasting our time here today. I see no reason to change my position of seven years ago. I was opposed to this drug then and I am just as firmly opposed today.'

'But Sperilac works,' Sharon Powell said. 'And we have the proof.' She pushed a plastic binder of computer print-outs across the table at Thelma.

'I've already seen these.' Thelma shoved the binder back. 'Sperilac may do *something*, God only knows what, to gerbils and rhesus monkeys – maybe. There's no indication that it does anything to benefit human beings.'

With calculated rudeness, Thelma turned to MacLean.

'Mr Chairperson, I know that many on this board consider me too conservative. But may I remind you that while I was a lab technician, I was the sole voice in the Administration that spoke out against Thalidomide. Was I correct then?'

MacLean nodded. 'Yes, Thelma. You were right.'

'Do you remember my position on cyclamates? My *statistics* on cyclamates?'

'Thelma, Thelma.' Martita Rosenzweig sighed loudly, shaking her head. 'Your statistics dealt exclusively with rats.'

'Every one of my cyclamate rats grew tumors and died. *Every one of them.*'

'The Canadians,' Martita smiled, 'are using cyclamates on humans with absolutely no ill effects.'

'None that they're telling us about.' Thelma returned the smile. 'We all know about Canadian research.'

'I've looked at these reports.' Willem Hobbing pointed his folded glasses at Sharon's plastic binder. 'Thelma, with all due respect, there are clear indications that Sperilac works with fewer side effects than any of our presently approved therapies.'

'Oh sure, Biochemtech's Sperilac rats just sit there and nibble their kibble. How do we know they even contracted AIDS in the first place?' Thelma wagged a finger at Sharon. 'Sloppy, sloppy paperwork.'

'In my opinion,' Willem Hobbing went on, 'there are powerful indications that Sperilac may be wholly effective. I think we should allow Biochemtech to go on to Phase Three.'

A hum of assent went round the table.

Thelma glared. Hobbing did not drop his gaze.

'*Professor* Hobbing,' Thelma hissed, 'I've examined this so-called data, and what I've discovered is illicit experimentation on human beings done under the most shabbily arranged controls, at a clinic with *no accreditation*.'

With effort, Thelma wheeled her chair to face Sharon directly. She was having trouble catching her breath.

'What I see is an illegal conspiracy, opportunistic publicity-hunting, and a blatant attempt to undermine public confidence in this agency.'

Andy Horner sprang to his feet so violently that his chair slammed against the wall. 'And what *I* see is an ossified bureaucrat willing to let human beings suffer and die until she can figure out a way to make two and two equal five. We—'

'My father was a veterinarian,' Thelma shouted before MacLean could lift his gavel, 'and he used to say, "The more you stir a turd, the more it stinks." Well, Mr Horner, your little turd of a clinic stinks. And my guess is that somebody is going to get you closed down before you know what hit you. Real Americans don't like so-called doctors doing unsupervised experiments on human beings. You can get away with that stuff in Auschwitz, but not in the United States.'

'Thelma!' MacLean looked appalled.

'No!' she shouted. 'No, no, no! If we let Sperilac pass today, how do we expect to protect our citizens from all the other snake-oil vendors and alchemists and back-yard herbalists who'll be coming down the pike tomorrow? All Biochemtech has shown us with their so-called documentation is medical malpractice, reckless endangerment of human life, and an open defiance of the laws of this country. I can stop them here and now and I consider it is my duty to do so. I vote *no*.'

In the silence that followed, Andy Horner righted his chair and sank into it.

'That being the case,' Thayer MacLean said, 'I see no point in bringing this to a vote.' His lips twisted as if he was fighting back a powerful urge to say something he knew he would regret for the rest of his professional life. 'I apologize to you all.'

'Good.' Thelma braced to lift herself from her chair. 'Let's get some lunch.'

Sharon stepped out of the air-conditioned FDA building on to C Street. The afternoon heat was savage, a spring foretaste of summer. Her feet carried her with quick angry strides to the shade of a lone ginkgo tree. She yanked the cellphone from her purse, snapped it open, jabbed Lucinda Forbes' area code and seven digits into the keypad.

Lucinda answered before the first ring. 'What happened?'

Sharon took a moment to center herself, inhaling the blue of the cloudless sky, sighing it out again. 'We didn't make it this round. Thelma van Voss blocked us.'

A yellow district bus lumbered noisily past.

'Damn her.' Lucinda's voice darkened. 'That woman is making a serious mistake.'

Naturally, thought Thelma furiously, Thayer MacLean – the passive-aggressive little twit – had to take his own petty revenge. Claiming he had a meeting with the Secretary the next morning, he had ordered her to compose a draft report on the rejection of the Sperilac proposal. As a result, here she was stuck at her computer until nearly 11 p.m. She never got her lunch and her gastric juices were in turmoil.

It was 10:57 when the telephone rang. She snatched up the receiver.

'Thelma? What happened?'

She recognized the voice of the lobbyist for the company that manufactured the top-selling AIDS drug. Their drug happened not to work, and if Sperilac ever hit the market, their sales would plummet. Which was why they had slipped Thelma a nice little retainer under the table.

'Sperilac didn't pass. I saw to that.' She allowed herself a mirthless chuckle. 'They barely got a word in edgewise.'

'I've seen the results the Harvey Milk Clinic has been getting.' The lobbyist was obviously in a panic. 'If those figures are ever published, they'll destroy us. You've got to close that clinic down – fast.'

Thelma resented being told how to do her job. 'This isn't the time to discuss it. This line isn't secure. Everything's under control, so go get some sleep.'

Sighing, she ran a spell-check on the draft report, saved it to the hard disk, and did a print-out. She slipped the pages into a manila envelope, marked it 'Chairperson MacLean' and dropped it into her out-box.

She took the elevator to the parking garage and was delighted to see that her Lincoln town car sat just as pristine and undented as she had left it that morning in her handicap space. Moving around *was* a handicap. and the fewer steps she took the more energy she would save for the last chore of her day: late-night grocery shopping.

She slid into the driver's seat, gunned the motor, and wheeled out on to C Street. She could have sworn she heard a car turning out behind her. but a glance in the rearview mirror told her the avenue behind her was almost deserted. As sometimes happened when she worked too hard and too late and fueled herself with too much coffee, her nerves had gotten the better of her. She was imagining things.

She drove to Q Street, where traffic was heavier, and cut over to Wisconsin Avenue. She decided that she would stop at the Social Safeway on Wisconsin. All the ambassadors' servants shopped there and she had once seen Caspar Weinberger pushing a shopping cart for his maid. They would still be open at this hour, and their selection of cheeses was nearly as good as any in town. She would get some Gorgonzola and cream cheese and fresh fettuccine, and have herself a high cholesterol pasta orgy before she tumbled into bed. She owned an apartment in one of the District's most luxurious co-ops, the Westchester. She'd had the kitchen especially enlarged just this past year. and she looked forward to using it tonight. Cooking was Thelma's therapy. It rested her nerves and cleared her mind.

She pulled into the Safeway lot, saw that it was nearly empty, and steered into the handicap space closest to the entrance. She switched off the ignition.

Headlights flashed in her rearview mirror. She blinked, momentarily blinded. As she stepped out of the Lincoln, she saw a small sports car park at the far end of the lot. The parking lights winked off, but no one got out.

Odd, she thought. Lovers making out? A junkie shooting up?

Nowadays, who knew or cared? Certainly not Thelma van Voss.

She walked the twelve heavy steps to the automatic doors, took a shopping cart and aimed straight for the cheese counter.

Her mood brightened instantly. Such a selection! She loaded down with Brie, Gorgonzola, Stilton, Cheshire, and two plastic containers of homemade cream cheese awash with whey.

The fresh pastas were displayed across the aisle. She decided two packages of fettuccine and one of linguine ought to hold her.

She turned back toward her cart. A dark-skinned woman was staring inside it, inspecting her purchases. What nerve! Thelma thought.

'Excuse me.'

Apparently the woman didn't speak English. That figured.

Thelma tossed her pasta in, reached for the handles and steered the cart away. She saw that the fettuccine had mashed the Brie: it was oozing out the seams of its cellophane wrapper. Looking around to make sure no store employee saw her, she slipped the Brie back on to the shelf and replaced it with a new package.

As she pushed her cart to the check-out, she couldn't escape an impression that the dark-skinned woman was following her. She turned round and the woman was in line right behind her, grinning, holding a single carton of raspberry yogurt.

The check-out clerk rang up Thelma's purchases. They came to an astonishing $41.20 – so much for the administration's claims that the economy was sound.

The boy handed Thelma her change. 'Two bags please,' she said.

He repacked the groceries into two bags.

As she was counting her change, she accidentally dropped a nickel and a quarter. Quick as a salamander's tongue, the dark-skinned woman stooped and handed them back to her.

'Thank you.' Thelma dropped the coins into her purse.

The woman was staring at her.

What does she expect, Thelma wondered, a tip?

Thelma turned and hefted her bags. The electric door slid open at her approach. She stepped into the parking lot. And stopped.

The handicap parking spot by the door was empty.

That's not possible. Her heart thunked painfully against her ribs. Where's my car?

She scanned the lot and saw the blue Lincoln town car – twenty parking spaces away.

It couldn't have moved itself.

As she hurried toward the car, a plastic container of cream cheese dropped to the pavement in front of her foot.

God Almighty, what next?

A hand snatched the container up. 'Please.'

Thelma stared into the face of a dark-skinned young man who could have been the twin of the woman in the supermarket. 'Thank you. Could you put it in the bag?'

Instead of answering or putting the cheese back, he trotted alongside her. She wondered if he was some kind of stick-up artist or carjacker.

'Thank you very much.' Balancing both bags in one arm, she reached for the cheese. 'But I can manage by myself.'

There was a ripping sound. One of the bags split open under Thelma's arm. Plastic containers dropped and smashed.

Out of nowhere, two more young men were on their hands and knees, scooping up fresh fettuccine from the asphalt.

'No thank you.' Thelma backed away. 'I don't want it.'

The other bag tipped and fell. Scurrying hands snatched up packets.

'You can keep them,' Thelma screamed. 'I don't want them!'

Four young men crowded around her. Filthy hands held out sweating wads of Brie and Gorgonzola and Stilton and Cheshire.

There was no way of getting round them to her car. She thought of retreating into the Safeway, but she saw that two small dark-skinned women were cutting off that route of escape.

I'll flag a cab.

Heart pounding, lungs bursting, she attempted a lunge toward Wisconsin Avenue. Feet pattered behind her. Voices called in Spanish.

I'll stand in the street and wave down a cab.

A car turned into the nearly empty lot. Headlights strafed her. She held up her arms, shielding her eyes. A motor roared in her ears. A horn blared. Brakes squealed.

Voices seemed to be crying, '*Abolita! Abolita!*'

Her legs gave way and she was almost grateful for all the hands that caught her before her knees hit the asphalt.

April 12

A t 6:58 a.m., the phone beside Sharon's bed made a sound like a
dove cooing through gauze. She opened one eye. The sun was
casting a butter-colored ellipse on her bedroom wall.

She lifted the receiver just as Allegro sprang on to the bed.

'Hello?' She eased Allegro to the side. He began licking her
hand.

'Sharon.' The voice was male, manic, secretive. 'Don Barnes.' She
recognized Biochemtech's lobbyist. 'You awake?'

'Kind of.'

Allegro burrowed under the sheet. He liked dark places. She'd found
him meowing under an abandoned, stripped car, a shivering cat with
watery eyes. Good food, tetracycline, and tender loving care had
restored him.

'If you didn't happen to catch the early news on TV—'

'I didn't,' she said.

'The Park Police found Thelma van Voss at two a.m. this morning.'

Sharon sat up. 'What happened?'

'She committed suicide.'

'Oh no.' Sharon clenched her eyes shut.

'Shot herself.'

'That poor woman.'

'Bad news for her, good news for us. Needless to say, this brightens
the entire Sperilac picture. Considerably. God moves in mysterious
ways, right?'

It sounded like gloating and she didn't like it. 'Thanks for telling
me, Don. We'll talk later this morning, OK?'

Her feet searched for her slippers. Allegro rubbed insistently against
her shins, reminding her of priorities.

She changed the six bowls of water and scooped a can of Nine Lives
Tuna Treat into each of the six plastic feeders.

About a dozen cats charged. She saw that Sulk, the newest and littlest
of the lot, was not among them. She stepped over the feeding felines
and laid the telephone in the modem. She tapped Lucas Powell's phone
number into the computer.

Three rings. His computer picked up.

She typed quickly. *Dad, it's Sharon. Are you there?*

Half a minute went by. She loaded the coffee maker and set a saucer of milk over low heat just in case Sulk decided to make an appearance.

When she returned to the computer, a second line had typed itself on the screen below hers: AM I AWAKE, YOU ASK. BARELY. WHAT'S WITH THE UNGODLY HOUR?

A third line appeared: HELLO, ANYBODY THERE?

I just received important news. It looks as though the FDA will OK Sperilac for Phase Three.

A moment later the reply appeared: HALLELUJAH – BUT WHY THE HELL DID THELMA VAN VOSS REVERSE HER POSITION?

Thelma van Voss committed suicide last night.

I FIND IT HARD TO BELIEVE THAT A FORCE OF EVIL LIKE THELMA VAN VOSS WOULD KILL HERSELF.

The Park Police say she did.

THEY ARE NOT THE GREATEST AUTHORITIES.

The important thing is, we're free now to move forward with the double-blind.

IF ANYONE HAS THE FINANCIAL MUSCLE TO DO IT, YOUR INVESTORS SEEM TO. I LOCATED THEM ON NASDAQ, CHICAGO, TOKYO, AND SAN FRANCISCO EXCHANGES AND PARIS BOURSE. THEY MANAGE PENSION FUNDS FOR THREE STATES AND TWENTY-TWO MUNICIPALITIES – AND THREE FAR EASTERN COUNTRIES.

I thought I told you all that.

YOU TOLD YOUR OLD MAN NOTHING, BUT HE'S USED TO IT.

Just cut that out. I refuse to feel guilty before I've even had coffee.

WOULDN'T DREAM OF INSTILLING GUILT. FOR THE FIRST TIME IN SEVEN YEARS, I FEEL GOOD ABOUT SPERILAC. I THINK IT'S GOING TO REALLY HAPPEN THIS TIME.

After a night in the lab refrigerator, the culture tube was icy to Sharon's fingers. She loosened the screw cap and tipped one drop of the cloudy liquid on to the transparent specimen holder.

She waited a moment and gave the culture time to spread out and adjust to the warmer environment.

Clipping the slide to the stage of the microscope, she twisted the coarse focus adjuster. She could make out two thrashing rainbow-edged seahorse shapes. The culture was alive and well.

With a twist of the fine focus knob, the seahorses dissolved into two masses of wriggling pink filaments.

The telephone rang.

'Could you get that, Wendy?'

'Lab five. Wendy Johnson.'

Sharon lifted her face from the eyepieces and filled a dropper with a yellow dilute of activated iodine. She dripped two careful drops on to the slide and bent down to study the reaction.

'It's him,' Wendy whispered, covering the mouthpiece.

'Ask him to call back.' Magnified, the iodine was a bright, creeping orange. At the instant of contact, the filaments recoiled. It was the reaction Sharon had hoped for.

'He says it's important.'

Sharon brought her eyes up, blinked the lab back into focus and took the phone. 'Yes?'

'We need more.' Andy's voice sounded pressured, almost desperate.

'Already?'

'We had to Fed-ex some to Chicago.'

'How did Chicago hear about it?'

'Word's out. There are headlines in the underground press.'

'I'll try, but no promises.'

The outer vault door heaved open and Sharon slipped through.

Today the desk was piled high with computer print-out. Eyeglasses angled at the end of her nose, Helen Weller was busily filling the margins with fine-letter notations.

'Hi, Helen. Mind if I swipe some tetracycline for a friend with bronchitis?'

Helen jerked as if she'd been poked, then summoned a smile and a wink. 'Be my guest. Be Biochemtech's guest.' She entered the code on her computer keyboard. The barred doors swung open. 'Just remember to sign the log before you leave.'

Sharon stepped into the inner vault. She listened for Helen's footsteps and heard nothing but the rustle of paper. As she crammed Sperilac into the pockets of her lab coat, she saw that an entire new set of bins had been filled with the drug, enough to meet the needs of a large city on a long-term basis.

The log was open and waiting for her when she returned to the desk.

'How much?' Helen asked.

'Fifty capsules, standard dose.'

Helen didn't look up from her work. Sharon studied her. Somehow, her colleague seemed, well, less drab, less beige. For one thing, her hair was changing colour.

Could it be? Sharon thought. Could Helen have finally gotten herself a beau?

'I couldn't help noticing,' Sharon said. 'All those new bins are full of Sperilac.'

'Yes.' Helen flipped through her papers and did not look up.

'Isn't it taking a terrific chance to gear up this early?'

Helen threw her a quick glance. 'As no one in this whole outfit should know better than you, in today's world the pharmaceutical industry has to stay ahead of the curve. Biochemtech can afford the loss if anything goes wrong. If everything goes right, we're ready for immediate large-scale distribution.'

Sharon wondered. She'd heard rumors that the company was struggling with horrific cash-flow problems. 'All the same, it seems a little optimistic to increase production *that* much before Phase Three trials are officially approved.'

'Sharon, dear. I have some statistical work to do here that touches on a subject dear to both our hearts: drug distribution.' Helen's ballpoint tapped almost irritably on the stack of papers. 'I really don't have a single second for chitchat.'

Sharon felt dismissed and just a little hurt as she bent down and signed the log. Plunging her hands into her pockets to keep the bottles from rattling, she walked quickly through the outer door and toward the elevator.

Sharon stepped into Andy's office at the Harvey Milk Clinic and closed the door behind her. 'Are you the man who requested an illegal delivery?'

Andy looked up from a lab report. 'You're a life saver.' His white cloth jacket was rumpled and his tie was off to one side and she could feel agitation beneath the good cheer.

'This is all I could get for the moment.' She cleared a space among the papers and set the Sperilac bottles on his desk. 'Biochemtech seems to be gearing up for large-scale production.'

'That's good news.'

'It could be a problem for us if they start keeping closer inventory.

On the other hand, if they're planning to take Sperilac really big-time, they'll make give-away samples for doctors and hospitals – and nobody inventories those.'

'That would be the best of all possible worlds.'

'Anyway, these should keep a few customers healthy.'

The word 'customer' was a joke. The clinic didn't charge for its services; Andy and the staff drew their meager salaries from contributions.

'If you want to see a healthy, happy customer,' Andy said, 'take a look in the sun room. You won't recognize her.'

'Isabel?'

Andy nodded.

Sharon hurried down the corridor. The air smelled of rubbing alcohol and disinfectant and burnt coffee.

Isabel Mahler and her brother were sitting side by side on deck chairs. Isabel was staring through the glass wall at spring leaves swaying in the wind. Her eyes were alive; they shimmered like dark flame.

Sharon introduced herself. 'We met before. You don't remember.'

'You were asleep,' Joe said.

Isabel smiled and Sharon felt something stir through her like a warm breeze.

'It's good to see you smile,' Sharon said.

'It's good to have something to smile about,' Isabel said.

Her brother had a strange look on his face. Sharon couldn't tell whether he was holding back laughter or trying not to cry.

'What is it, Joe?' Sharon said. 'What's happening?'

He shook his head. 'How can I tell you what's happening when I don't know myself?'

Isabel rested her head against her brother's shoulder. 'Joe's happy, that's all. He's happy for me.' She raised his hand to her cheek. 'Maybe now I'll stop being a problem.'

'You're the one thing in my life that isn't a problem.'

Isabel kissed his hand and gave it back to his lap. 'Joe should have gone into diplomacy, don't you agree?'

'I could have sworn he had,' Sharon said. 'You should have seen him handle my new boss.'

'Lucinda contacted me this morning,' Joe said. 'She's scheduled a meeting with lawyers three days from now. Has she mentioned it to you and Andy?'

'No. She probably doesn't think it's any of Andy's or my business.'

'It *is* your business,' Joe said firmly. 'I want you both to be there.'

Sharon unlocked the apartment door, flicked on the light, and stepped over a meowing phalanx of cats and kittens who had gathered in the hallway, determined to charm their dinner out of her. She dumped a briefcase of reports and lab print-outs on the work table. The new cat, Sulk, was sitting on the answering machine, studying her with reproachful brown eyes.

She washed her hands and set a half cup of milk to heat in a saucepan. She poured Tabby Treat into six plastic feeders and stepped back as a horde of paws came thundering across the linoleum.

Sulk, she noticed, was not among them.

She tested the temperature of the milk on her wrist. When there was no chill left she carried the saucepan and an eye-dropper into the bedroom. Sulk watched her with a weary indifference. She filled the dropper and lifted his jaw.

Before she could squeeze, he leapt off the answering machine and bolted into the hallway.

She shrugged. 'Then you couldn't be feeling all that sick.'

Now that Sulk's belly wasn't covering the signal light, she saw that two messages had come in. She pressed *replay*.

'Hey, Sharon, Scheherezade is ready to come home.' It was Tommy Andrews, the vet, and he was talking about the mixed-breed homeless female who had followed Sharon in the supermarket parking lot three days ago. The animal had had an infected paw and heartbreaking blue eyes, which meant that somewhere in her tangled bloodlines there was a Persian ancestor. Sharon had adopted her, named her, and taken her to Tommy for shots and a complete check-up.

'She's borderline anemic, so you're going to have to feed her fresh liver for a couple of weeks.'

Uh oh, Sharon thought, there are going to be some jealous cats around here at mealtime.

'And she has worms and mites and a transient viral infection in the left eye. The good news is, she's negative for feline leukemia, and she's already been neutered.'

Good. One less worry.

'The shots are on the house, but I'll have to charge you for the antiviral. You'll have to keep her on medication for seven days and swab her ears. Pick her up any time tomorrow.'

The other message was from Helen Weller.

'Sharon, Helen. I didn't mean to snap at you at work today.' She sounded nervous and rushed and just a little stuttery. 'I was abominable and I'm embarrassed even to think about it. Could we have dinner and talk? Seems we haven't had an evening together in ages. Why don't you come over to my place and let me cook for you, say, the day after tomorrow?'

April 14

Eddie Arbogast was sitting in the patio, enjoying a late breakfast of Amy's homemade granola smothered in organic whole-milk yogurt. As he skimmed the *Miami Herald*, the letters FDA in a headline on the obit page snagged his eye:

'Thelma van Voss, fourteen years a director of the FDA, a Suicide.'

'Uh oh.'

Amy set down her coffee cup and glanced across the glass-top table at him. 'Uh oh what?'

'A sixty-four-year-old employee of the FDA blew her brains out in a Washington park.'

'So why's that uh oh?'

'Tell you in a minute.' Eddie slid the louvered door to one side and stepped into the den. He phoned District of Columbia information and asked for the number of the FDA.

'Thelma van Voss's office please. This is Edward G. Arbogast of the DEA, Miami division.'

'*Formerly* of the DEA,' Amy called.

'Yes, Mr Arbogast.' The voice on the phone was improbably pleasant. 'This is Thayer MacLean, Thelma van Voss's associate. How may I help you?'

'I'd like some information, please.'

Three minutes later, nodding to himself, pleased that his intuitions were on target, Eddie returned to his granola.

Amy watched him dubiously. 'Well?'

'Thelma van Voss was the single committee vote opposed to Sperilac. Now that she's dead, the drug's sure to be okayed for Phase Three trials.'

'You're acting as though this somehow makes a difference in your life.'

'A big difference. Sperilac is the drug they were talking about on the Mike Bosch tape.'

'Eddie, no.'

Eddie went to the bedroom and began stuffing socks and shirts into a suitcase.

Amy came after him. 'Don't you like your home, Eddie?'

67

'I love my home. But Mike Bosch is my retirement present to myself.'

'How do you know he's even involved?' Amy pushed his hands away from the suitcase, emptied it on to the bed and began again: shirts on the bottom, then underwear, then socks in the empty spaces. 'Last week you said the widow did it.'

'I was wrong. Widows kill rich husbands, but they don't rub out government officials – coke kingpins do. In nineteen ninety-two the Panamanian Minister of Education supposedly blew his brains out in a park. Turned out Mike's men pulled the trigger.'

'A gun, a park, and a government employee doesn't mean it's the drug cartel. Coincidences happen.'

'Not this time. Mike's crossed the line. No one's going to protect him now. He's murdered a director of a federal agency. If I can tie this killing to him, I've got him nailed.'

Eddie flew to Washington and dropped in unannounced on his friend Sam Schuyler of the District police. He figured unannounced was the strategy most likely to jiggle information loose.

Lieutenant Schuyler sat peeling two Di-Gels out of their wrapping. Eddie tapped lightly on the plasterboard partition. 'Got a minute for an old pain in the ass?'

The lieutenant looked up. A big grin lifted his sagging jowls. 'Eddie.' He came round the desk to clasp Eddie's hand. 'Four years, is it?'

'Five.'

'What the hell are you doing in town?'

'I'm on a case.' Eddie's shrug said it was small potatoes, hardly worth mentioning, certainly not worth elaborating.

'That so. I heard they put you out to pasture.'

'Not till the end of the year.' Casually, Eddie showed his credentials with their December 31st expiration date.

The lieutenant didn't even glance. 'Florida agrees with you, Eddie. You could lose a little weight, but your tan looks good. Goes with the gray.'

'You're looking good too, Sam.' Sam looked lousy, a stoop-shouldered balloon of walking dyspepsia with a nervous tic in the right eye. 'Tell the truth, the reason I dropped by, I could use some information.'

'If I got it, you can have it.'

'What have you got on Thelma van Voss?' Eddie spelled the name. 'She committed suicide on the P Street Beach night before last.'

'Friend?'

Eddie shook his head. 'FDA biggie.'

Sam whistled. He punched up a menu on his computer, cursed when the computer beeped at him, called up a file directory and cursored down the column to the Vs.

'She's not under van and she's not under Voss.' Sam pushed the help button. 'Know what? She's not ours. The Park Police handled her.'

Eddie couldn't believe it. 'A senior official of the FDA blows her head off and the Park Police handled it?'

'That's what it says here.'

Lieutenant Francis Curry of the Park Police, lean and hazel-eyed and obviously anxious to get home, stood tapping the earpiece of his reading glasses against his wrist. 'We weren't notified there was DEA involvement.'

'There may not need to be,' Eddie said.

Curry gave him the file and a desk in the corner.

Eddie opened the slender manila folder. He felt Curry's face aimed at him.

His eyes zipped down the two-page double-spaced report of the sergeant in charge.

Van Voss had been discovered after an anonymous phone tip. She was found sitting with her back against a ginkgo tree, her purse beside her, a Sebring and Wright pistol in her right hand, her car parked on the street eighty feet away. The purse held 187 dollars, three valid charge cards, a driver's licence, and her FDA ID.

The nurse examining the body had checked off options on a multiple-choice sheet, and that was the medical report. There had been no MD, no autopsy, and after twelve hours Thelma's body and car had been released to a nephew in Georgia.

When Eddie had worked in the District, in all cases of unexplained or violent death the rule had been to autopsy. Obviously, a lot of things had changed.

The ballistics report confirmed that the single .38 round that had ripped through van Voss's brain had been fired from the Sebring and Wright. Oddly, there was no mention of powder burns on van Voss's hand or head. It seemed even odder to Eddie that a gun with as much kick as the S&W would have stayed in the hand of a suicide instead of flying out on to the grass.

The Park Police detective in charge reported canvassing

householders, bars, and all-night convenience stores in the neighbor-hood: no one had heard the shot or seen any suspicious activity in the park between sunset and dawn.

Four black and white photos showed a thick-armed, open-mouthed woman in her sixties in a dark dress with a Peter Pan collar. She looked as though she'd leaned against a tree, smoothed her skirt, and fallen asleep at a midnight picnic. The flash camera exaggerated the spotless white of the collar. The black of the gun exactly matched the flat black of the evenly dyed, perfectly arranged coiffure.

That was the sum total of the investigation.

After twenty minutes Eddie closed the file and handed it back. He could feel Curry wanting to get him out.

'No autopsy?' he said.

'There was no reason,' Curry said, 'and the family didn't request it.'

In Thayer MacLean's dark, cluttered office on the eighth floor of the FDA building, Eddie asked questions and listened to answers.

'Thelma was a workaholic.' MacLean had forlorn gray eyes and a drinker's complexion. 'She was an effective administrator. Maybe a little compulsive about details.'

'Easy to work with?'

'I wouldn't go that far. She could be moody.'

'Depressed?'

'In retrospect, obviously – though no one around here ever had a hint she was thinking of taking her own life.'

'Was a suicide note found?'

'Not in her office.'

'Is her office the way she left it?'

'Pretty much.'

'Could I see?'

'No one's said it's off limits.' MacLean put on his jacket. Eddie followed him down a gray-carpeted corridor into a sunny corner office with shoulder-high potted palms and philodendra lining the windows.

'Thelma prided herself on her green thumb.'

'I can see why.'

On the desk, papers were neatly stacked in eight piles. Four thick books on antigen reactivity were propped between jade elephant book-ends. There were bronze holders for paperclips, staples, pens, stamps, and sour balls. A bronze cup held scissors and letter-opener.

The scissors looked odd. Eddie pulled them out of the cup and saw why. They were left-handed. He thought of that Sebring and Wright in van Voss's right hand. 'Was Ms van Voss right-handed or left-handed?'

'Left-handed.'

He dropped the scissors back into the cup. 'The desk has been searched?' He knew he was pushing it.

'It was searched and there was no note. Thelma was awfully busy that day.'

'You're saying she was too busy to leave a note?'

'Strange as this sounds, it would have been out of character. Suicide's a personal matter and Thelma was compulsive about keeping her private life separate from work.'

The wall behind the desk was half bookshelves, half mahogany file cabinets. The books were in alphabetical order. Framed degrees from Emory and Johns Hopkins and Michigan State sat on the cabinets.

'Michigan State was honorary,' MacLean said.

'The file cabinets were searched?'

'Everything was searched.'

'Even the books? Sometimes people leave notes in books.' Eddie pulled out a book on tumorigenesis. He riffled through the pages. No papers fluttered loose.

He felt MacLean sneaking glances at him, annoyed but cautious, trying to size him up without risking eye-to-eye contact.

'Would you say Ms van Voss was busier than usual the day she died?'

'God, yes. Four new drugs were coming up for preliminary hearings. Thelma insisted on being prepared. According to the building log, she didn't leave till after eleven p.m.'

'Was it like her to work that late?'

'Not usually, but there was a hearing that afternoon and it threw her schedule off.'

Eddie picked up another book at random. Parasites of the upper intestine. 'What did this hearing concern?'

'The usual, a new drug. Actually, it was an old drug trying to make a comeback. Look, is this relevant to your investigation? Because I've taken over half of Thelma's workload, and I'm running late.'

'I understand. What was the drug?'

'Sperilac.'

'Fights the AIDS virus, doesn't it?'

'Thelma didn't think so. Her last administrative act was to oppose Phase Three tests.'

'How much money rides on those tests?'

'At the moment it costs between one and two hundred million to bring a drug to market.'

'So when van Voss said no to Phase Three, she was costing some company approximately one hundred and fifty million?'

'Considerably more than that if you look at the market potential. A drug that cured AIDS would be worth billions. With Sperilac the stakes are even higher because the money has to be earned back faster. The patent only has seven years to run.'

'Can Biochemtech afford a risk like that, or is someone backing them?'

'I wouldn't know. The FDA looks at the drug, not the finances.'

Eddie didn't buy it. 'You must have an idea.'

'I heard talk an investment syndicate was putting up the money.' Resentment curled MacLean's voice. 'One of these jazzy multi-nationals with extra billions to park.'

'You don't by any chance remember the name?'

'Sorry.'

Eddie closed his notebook. 'There's only one other thing I need from you. Copies of your records on Sperilac.'

Seymour Chang, section manager of the Bell Atlantic telephone company for the District of Columbia and Northwestern Maryland, came round his desk and clasped Eddie's hand. 'Haven't seen you in – how many years?'

'Eight years,' Eddie said. 'The Grasso case.'

Seymour Chang had lost a fair amount of hair since then – scalp was showing through the careful comb-over. On the other hand, the furnishings in his office had improved: comfortable leather chairs, a seascape on the wall, an enormous partner's desk.

'I remember.' Seymour Chang gestured. 'Have a seat.'

'I appreciate your seeing me.' Eddie took the chair nearer the desk. 'And I appreciate any help you can give me.'

'What sort of help do you have in mind?'

'I need to look at some records and I need to monitor some lines.' Eddie took the list from his pocket and laid it on the desktop.

Seymour Chang studied the names. His eyebrows rose slightly. 'Wiretap?'

'If that can be done without too much trouble for you or your people.'

'No trouble if you have a court order.'

Eddie realized there might be a problem but that was a chance he had to take. 'The information we gather isn't going to be used in a trial. So the Supreme Court guidelines don't apply.'

'They apply to us.'

'For the time being, this is an unofficial request.'

'I understand. There shouldn't be any difficulty. I'll check and get back to you. What's your number?'

'They're repainting my office.' Eddie took out an old business card that dated from the year he'd been stationed in the District. He crossed out the work number and wrote down his number at the hotel. 'I've moved my files to the Holiday Inn, that's the easiest place to reach me.'

'You'll hear from me tomorrow before ten.'

'I appreciate it.'

Eddie took a taxi to the park area where Thelma van Voss was supposed to have killed herself. The P Street Beach was not precisely a beach, but a wooded area near a small stream that flowed into the Potomac just east of Georgetown.

Eddie asked the driver to wait. He got out of the cab and explored.

The park had its denizens, mostly male, and they struck Eddie as belonging to two groups: dopesters looking to score and gays cruising for sex. Night had scarcely begun and the joint was jumping.

He walked to the northern boundary and found Thelma's ginkgo. Somewhere in the dark two radios were tuned to different rap stations. A smell of marijuana hovered. He shone a penlight along the ground.

At first he thought someone had laid down a carpet to mark the spot of Thelma's last breath. He bent closer and saw that a two-by-six-foot area of earth, large enough for a human body to stretch out, had been freshly sodded that day.

April 14 – 8:30 p.m.

'**I**'m so glad you were free.' Helen planted a quick little kiss on Sharon's cheek and stood back from the door. 'We haven't had an evening together since – I forget when.'

Sharon stepped into the neat little apartment with its spinet piano and the fold-away table set with china and flowers for dinner. In the four years that she had known Helen, nothing in the living room had ever changed. 'Since January.'

'That long. I've missed you.'

'Me too.' Sharon sniffed. The air smelled of bolognese sauce – one of Helen's specialties. 'Something delicious is cooking.'

'We're having spaghetti. The sauce has to simmer.' Helen gestured nervously toward the sofa. She'd set out a bowl of hummus and a plate of crackers on the coffee table. 'Help yourself.'

Sharon plunged a cracker into the dip. 'Mmm. Homemade.'

'I remembered you enjoyed it last time. What can I get you to drink? Iced tea or ginger ale?' There was an edginess in Helen's voice. Her words seemed rushed. 'Or maybe something a little stronger?'

'Iced tea sounds great.'

Helen brought two brimming glasses decorated with mint sprigs. 'Here's to friendship. Sorry I was in a mood the other day.'

'You weren't in a mood. You were busy and I was being a pest.'

'You've never a pest.'

They clinked glasses.

Helen settled herself in the easy chair. 'How's your father?'

'Thriving. He spends half his life on the Internet. And he lets Millie beat him at chess.'

'He always was a gentleman.' Helen had known Lucas since before his stroke. 'Be sure to say hello for me. And the cats?'

'The cats are . . . cats.'

'How many now?'

'Ten or eleven. I've lost count.'

Helen's teeth came down on her lower lip. 'I don't suppose you . . .'

'You don't suppose I what?'

'I don't suppose you have a boyfriend yet?'

Sharon had to smile. Helen was such a well-intentioned blunderbuss. 'You always work around to the same question.'

'Because I hope one of these days you won't give me the same answer.'

'My life's exactly the same as it was last January. I have good friends, a great job, and an apartment full of cats. Why complicate things?'

'Friends and cats and work aren't enough for a young girl.'

'You're sounding like a mother.'

'If I were a mother, I'd want a daughter exactly like you.' Helen's eyes flicked up. 'And that's why I try to remind you what counts. Because one day you could wind up alone – and very sorry.'

'I could wind up like you, Helen, and you don't look sorry at all.'

'I'm not, but that's a different story.'

Sharon burst out laughing.

'What's so funny?'

Sharon shook her head. 'It's just that I was about to ask if *you* had a boyfriend.'

'Why in the world? *Me?*' Helen fiddled with a mint sprig. Sharon realized she'd hit a nerve: Helen was embarrassed. 'Don't you think I'm a little advanced in years for that sort of thing?'

'No, I don't. You look great – you've darkened your hair.'

Helen touched a hand to the side of her head. 'I was just experimenting with a rinse.'

'The experiment was a success. Who's the lucky man?'

'There's no man in particular.'

'You're holding out on me.'

'All right.' Helen leaned forward and set down her glass. 'I've met someone. But don't jump to any conclusions, it's nothing like that. I just want to look my best.'

'For him.'

'For me. It gives me confidence.'

'I think you're interested in him.'

'Not in the way you mean.' Helen was silent for a moment, thoughtful. She spread two crackers with hummus and offered one to Sharon. 'Do you still see your friend Andy?'

'Sure. Every week or so.'

'After a year, I should think you'd want to see him more often.'

'Helen, he's gay. I thought you knew.'

'Gay?' Helen shifted uncomfortably in the chair. 'Then why don't you see a young man who's not – gay?'

'You find one for me. Find me a man who's as smart and considerate and as funny as Andy and I'll marry him.'

'There must be plenty of attractive single men who aren't . . . you know.'

'I met one last month.'

'Really?' Helen brightened. 'What's his name?'

'His name's Joe.'

'Joseph. I've always liked the name. Tell me about him.'

Sharon tried to put her impressions together. There wasn't that much to tell. 'He's sweet and smart and he has dark hair and big dark eyes.'

'I think you like him.'

'I certainly don't *dis*like him.'

'What kind of work does he do?'

'Finance.'

Helen digested the information and nodded. Finance was acceptable. 'How did you meet him?'

'At Andy's clinic. His sister's very sick.'

'I'm sorry. That's a shame.'

'And he's very good to her. And I like that.'

'Has he asked you for a date?'

'Why should he?'

'Because you're a fine, beautiful young woman and he should have the brains to see it.'

'He's got a lot on his mind.' Sharon shrugged. 'Anyway, it's a professional relationship. He's the man who's backing Sperilac.'

'He might still ask you out. If you encouraged him.'

'Helen, do you realize how many years it's taken to get Sperilac this far?'

'Yes, I do. It's taken far too many.'

'And I'm not going to jeopardize the Phase Three trials – not this close to the end of the tunnel.'

Helen sighed strangely. 'If only you'd met Joe nine months ago.'

Sharon glanced at her. 'Why nine months ago?'

'Things might have been different.'

'What things?'

Helen ran her finger along the rim of her glass. An eerily high, pure note sounded. 'You won't always be young, Sharon. You won't always have the chances you're throwing away today.'

'Who's throwing chances away?'

'You had one unhappy experience and you've let it turn you into a nun.'

'That's nonsense. I was in love with a man, and he changed his mind – and I've forgotten the whole thing. Life goes on.'

'Does it?'

'Helen, believe me, I haven't taken the veil. There've been one or two times I've considered it, but I'm truly not nun material.'

Helen smiled almost sadly. 'I'd like to meet Joe.'

'You *are* a mother. And I love you for it. But let's talk about something else. You're wearing contact lenses, aren't you?'

Helen blinked. 'As a matter of fact, I am.'

'They look terrific on you. When did you get them?'

April 15

Eddie was halfway through a room service breakfast of synthetic-tasting scrambled eggs and limp bacon when the Gestapo pounded on the door.

Hitching up his bath towel, he padded across the carpeting. 'Who is it?'

A voice withered by cigarette smoke rasped five familiar syllables: 'Larry Lorenzo.'

'What is this, a bust?' Eddie opened the door. His smile faded when he saw the scowl on his old junior partner's face. 'You could have rung from downstairs. I'm not going to fly out the window.'

Lorenzo stood surveying the room, as cluttered with strewn documents as any college freshman's during final exam week. 'Seymour Chang of Bell Atlantic contacted us this morning. He said a DEA agent requested some taps yesterday. Seymour needed a confirmation.'

Right away Eddie knew he was in trouble.

'What the hell are you doing, representing yourself as an agent, asking for records and phone taps?'

'I've got unfinished business.' Eddie lowered his voice. 'Mike Bosch.'

'And *I've* got unfinished business. You.' Lorenzo closed the door and locked it. Still slim, still fit, he wore his dark hair pulled back into a ponytail that accented his narrow face and burning green eyes. Nonconformity was obviously one of the perks of middle management in today's DEA. 'You're retired, Eddie. You're not on assignment and you've got no right to represent yourself as DEA.'

'You're not hearing me.'

'No, Eddie, you're not hearing *me*. We both know the penalty for impersonating.'

'It's not impersonation till January first.'

'Don't give me technicalities.'

'Will you listen to me? I'm on to something major. You guys didn't catch it.' Eddie slipped his arms into a fresh shirt, stepped into underpants and trousers. 'Last month I found a tape and transcript in the agency files. The coke cartel is looking for a cure for AIDS. They've

78

murdered two American citizens – a drug-company CEO and an FDA director.'

'Jesus Christ, keep your cabin fever in Coconut Grove, don't bring it to us, we've got real world problems up here.'

'I'm not making this up. Give me five minutes and I'll prove it to you.'

Lorenzo grimaced.

'Larry, you owe me that much.'

'Five minutes.'

Eddie sat Lorenzo down at the writing table by the window. 'Coffee?' he offered.

'Why not.'

Eddie poured him a bathroom tumbler of the room service brew. He brought documents to the table, thumped them down.

Lorenzo stared at him a moment before picking up the Mike Bosch transcript. After a long skimming moment he turned to the investigating detectives' reports on Harry Forbes and Thelma van Voss. He examined a letter from Forbes to Thelma van Voss, dated seven years ago, stating Biochemtech would henceforward cease commercial manufacture of Sperilac. He studied a fax, dated last July, from Helen Weller, assistant to Harry Forbes; Ms Weller asked FDA permission to export 900,000 bottles of Sperilac to San Miguel de Bayamo, Sociedad Anonima, of Colombia. He studied another fax, dated yesterday, from Helen Weller, now assistant to Lucinda Forbes, asking permission to export another 900,000 bottles, again to San Miguel.

Tired eyes met Eddie's gaze. 'Would it surprise you to know we've seen these?'

'Then what are you doing about it?'

'We have no information linking any of this to Bosch.'

'Come on, Larry. The Colombian Supreme Court justices weren't cartel hits? The Panamanian Minister of Education wasn't?'

'Mike Bosch does not have a patent on these particular MOs.'

'Esme Rodriguez, the girl *you* people sent on to that yacht – you saw what Mike did to her?'

'So? He's an animal. What else is new?'

Eddie felt rage, sudden and irrational. 'What the hell has Mike Bosch got – immunity?'

Lorenzo flinched. His hands made a placating, stroking gesture. 'We're handling it – our way. We have over two hundred agents working full-time on Bosch.'

'And what are they doing besides drawing pay?'

'Believe me, there's an operation in place.'

'Don't give me operation-in-place. The agency's been trying to nail Bosch for twenty-five years and for twenty-five years he's been made of Teflon. I'm sick of it. I've got seven months before I'm officially retired. and I'm going to make a case against Bosch that sticks. I'm going to bring him in.'

Lorenzo looked at him with eyes that were almost pitying. 'If that's the way you want to spend your personal holiday, fine. I can't stop you. But don't bring the agency into it. Not if you love your pension. Am I clear?'

'OK, I see I'm going to have to lay some cards on the table.' Eddie set his coffee cup down on the chest of drawers. 'As a near retiree, I have one small advantage over you: I can go to the media and name names. With one appearance on *60 Minutes* or *Inside Edition*, I could score enough in book contracts and speaker fees so I wouldn't need my pension. The agency couldn't touch me. Do you catch my drift?'

'Bull.'

'Larry, we were both in Panama when Manuel Noriega was shipping two plane loads of coke a week into the US. That shit flew to US military bases on diplomatic visas. We know the agency set it up.'

'That was under orders from the CIA and the White House. And anyway the policy's been changed.'

'It would still make a helluva story in the media.'

Larry Lorenzo's eyes showed naked shock. 'You wouldn't go public.'

'I know every name on every falsified manifest. I was ground liaison for Operation Culebra, remember? And I seem to recollect you were my lieutenant.'

'You wouldn't do that to me, or yourself, or the agency.'

'Wouldn't I?'

'For Chrissake, Eddie, when we became agents we swore an oath. We signed an agreement.'

'I don't want to have to break that agreement.' Eddie took a long swallow of sour, lukewarm coffee. 'And if I get the right kind of cooperation from you, I won't need to.'

Larry rose and walked to the window and stared down into the courtyard. After a long, silent moment he turned. 'I'm not going to tap phones. That would go straight to the watchdogs.'

Eddie didn't answer. He let Larry's imagination do the work.

'I'm willing to share existing, non-invasive information but nothing that's going to attract attention upstairs.'

Eddie shrugged. 'Those parameters I can work with.'

Larry took out a notepad. 'Give me the shopping list.'

'OK. See the letters Helen Weller faxed to the FDA? Biochemtech is exporting Sperilac to San Miguel de Bayamo, Sociedad Anonima, of Colombia. Sociedad Anonima means it's a corporation. I need to know who owns it. I need to know if it's a front for the cartel.'

'I'll run a search.'

'I need to know if Forbes Biochemtech has outside financing for its Phase Three tests of Sperilac.'

'That's Treasury Department.'

'Don't give me that, Larry. You share a mainframe with them and Justice.'

'Computer time's logged, but I can try.'

'Does the agency know of any links between Helen Weller and the drug cartel? Any links between Sharon Powell or Lucinda Forbes and the cartel?'

'I'll see if we have files on them, but I may not be able to access the contents.'

'How soon?'

'I'm not a miracle worker.'

'You know how Mike Bosch moves. I need it last week.'

'I don't see why the indemnity should hold us up,' Lucinda Forbes said. Today the flowers in her office were rainbow-colored California calla lilies. 'We're agreed in principle, aren't we? We're men and women of good will. What more do we need at this point?'

'It has to be spelled out in the letter of agreement,' the lawyer for Biochemtech said. 'Phase Three trial participants will indemnify Biochemtech, its stockholders, officers and employees. I'm only thinking of you, Lucinda.'

'Think of me a little less, Harold.'

'Vestcate must also be indemnified,' the lawyer for Vestcate said.

Lucinda threw down her pencil. 'All right, we'll work out some form of mutual indemnification. That's easy and it doesn't have to hold us up now.'

The Vestcate lawyer disagreed. 'Vestcate will require indemnification from suits by the *participants*.'

'In the preliminary letter?' Lucinda seemed amazed. 'I thought the point of this meeting was to walk out of here with an agreement that allows us to get going.'

'Given the timetable you've shown us,' the Vestcate lawyer said, 'we'll be in trials before we have a contract.'

'I should hope so, the time it takes you lawyers to cross your ts.' Lucinda smiled and reached across the table and patted her lawyer's hand.

The face of the Vestcate lawyer remained grim. 'Vestcate needs equal protection.'

'Are we really concerned that participants might sue the backers?' Joe Mahler asked. 'Wouldn't the agreement between us and Biochemtech preclude that?'

'If there is a suit,' Vestcate's lawyer said, 'and there usually is, we're going to have to pay the legal costs. A limit has to be spelled out.'

'It seems peculiar,' Joe Mahler said. 'Regarding the participants as potential enemies.'

'But they are,' his lawyer said.

'I find that offensive,' Andy Horner said. 'The participants are risking their lives for the sake of this drug.'

'They're risking their lives for themselves,' Lucinda shot back. 'The waiting list isn't three thousand because these people love Biochemtech.'

'I'm sorry, did I miss something?' Andy Horner scowled. 'I wasn't aware we'd compiled a waiting list or even discussed how the participants will be selected.'

Sharon spoke up. 'There's a ready and willing population at the Harvey Milk Clinic.'

Joe Mahler nodded energetically. 'I agree. Harvey Milk made these trials possible, at considerable legal and medical risk. I think we owe them the recognition of using their people.'

'Three years ago,' Lucinda Forbes said, 'I'd have agreed wholeheartedly. But gay men are no longer the leading group of new AIDS cases. Addicts are. And therefore I'm running the Phase Three tests on an addict population.'

Andy Horner's jaw fell. 'Are you serious?'

'Of course I'm serious.'

'I think it's a *disgrace* to cut the clinic out of the trials at this point.'

'Sentiment is not the point,' Lucinda said.

'What is the point?'

'Speed. Going with an underground quasi-illegal corporation would snag everything.'

'I resent that.'

'The FDA is opposed to you. I asked.'

'You asked or you colluded?'

'Come on,' the Vestcate lawyer said, 'we're all adults. Let's act like adults.'

'In any case,' Lucinda said, 'it's done. I've arranged for Phase Three to be run at New Day Clinic. They focus on substance abuse, they're funded by a mix of private and public capital acceptable to the present administration, and they're excellent.'

Silence flowed through the room.

Joe Mahler cleared his throat. 'I'm disappointed. And I'll agree on only one condition. Sharon must be the director in charge of overseeing the trials.'

'Really, now.' Lucinda exhaled loudly. 'Sharon is a fine technician, and yes, her father developed the drug. But outside of one summer at Pizza Hut, I see no managerial experience on her résumé.'

'Sharon must oversee,' Joe Mahler said. 'That's Vestcate's one condition, and it's non-negotiable.'

It took another two hours to hammer out the wording, word process and revise the draft, and sign.

Riding down in the elevator, Andy stared glumly at the flashing floor indicator.

'Come on,' Sharon said. 'The important thing is to get Sperilac to the public as quickly as possible.'

'Biochemtech and Vestcate get rich, you get promoted, and I get the shaft. Excuse me if I feel a tad betrayed.'

She couldn't believe it: he was accusing her. 'I swear, Andy, I didn't know Lucinda was going to do that, and I had no idea Joe was going to—'

'Oh, sure, and you think babies grow under cabbage plants.'

The door opened and Joe Mahler was waiting in the lobby, a big happy grin on his face. He threw an arm round each of them. 'What say the three musketeers go celebrate our victory? It's on Vestcate.'

'No thanks.' Andy ducked free. 'It doesn't exactly feel like a red letter day for gay rights.'

'Come on, Andy. I got tickets for the Ballet Folklorico de Uruguay at the Kennedy Center – they're supposed to be sensational.'

'I said no thanks.' Andy turned and strode across the marble floor.

Joe stared in perplexity at the departing figure. 'I'm sorry he feels that way.'

'I see his point,' Sharon said. 'He put a year into Sperilac. Sixteen-hour days and tuna salad dinners.'

Joe shook his head. 'What about you? Care to come to the Kennedy Center?'

'I'd love to.'

April 15 – 6:20 p.m.

It sounded like a party roaring inside Mark Burgess's rundown wood frame house on Whittier Street, NE, but when the steel maximum-security door swung open, all Eddie saw was a wall of TV screens tuned to two dozen different channels.

The door slammed automatically shut behind him and the bolt slid home with a thud. Eddie tried to locate Burgess in the dimness. It wasn't easy. Sheets of Mylar covered the four windows, shutting out all natural light.

'Hey, Mark,' he shouted. 'I like your new home.'

The TV sets went mute. 'You're looking at the cerebellum of the Internet.' Mark Burgess, short and sinewy in his jogging clothes, threaded his way through electronic and computer equipment stacked ceiling high. 'You realize by stepping through that you're consorting with a convicted felon.'

'Doesn't surprise me. Where'd they send you?'

'Fairton Federal Correction Institute. Eight months of compulsory prayer, powdered eggs and reconstituted potatoes. The Federal Reserve security codes were wide open, so they blamed me. Your government's *smart*, Eddie, real smart.'

Eddie wasn't about to argue the point. 'Can you hack into the phone company computers?'

'C'm'ere.' Mark led him across the room. His hand swept toward a counter piled with blinking monitors. 'See that?' His eyes brightened with merry madness. 'I'm in.'

'I need incoming and outgoing phone calls at the office of Harry Forbes at Forbes Biochemtech, the week of March twenty-eighth. Incoming and outgoing calls at the office and home of Thelma van Voss of the FDA the week of April seventh. Incoming and outgoing calls at the Chevy Chase home of Harry and Lucinda Forbes over the last two weeks.'

'Spell those names and give me those addresses.'

Eddie spelled the names and the addresses.

Mark dropped on to a piano stool and punched keys on a console. Rivulets of print sped across eight monitors. A key froze them.

'You want hard copies?'

'Please.'

A printer clattered. Mark handed Eddie a thick stack of sheets.

Eddie put on his reading specs and scanned. He took out his ballpoint and drew lines under five of the numbers on the Forbes home print-out. 'Can you get me the names of these subscribers?'

Mark pointed to the nineteen-digit number underlined on the 2nd and the 11th. 'This isn't a phone subscriber. It came in from a French communications satellite. Ariane-IV. Privately owned.'

'Who uses it?'

'Businesses, mostly. My guess is these are E-mail. I'd have to hack into the Ariane records to find out who sent them – but one of my international speed chips is down.'

'What about the other four numbers?'

'Those are a piece of cake.' Mark accessed the phone company's reverse directory. '555-3456 is a cellular phone owned by Sharon Powell.'

Which meant Sharon Powell, the last appointment of Harry Forbes' and Thelma van Voss's life, had phoned the Forbes home ten minutes after seeing van Voss.

'555–2345 is a payphone. So are 555–4567 and 555–1357.'

'Where are those payphones?'

'1357 is in the Kennedy Center.'

Which meant someone in the Forbes home had phoned the Kennedy Center three hours before Harry Forbes' death and seven hours before van Voss's.

'2345 is Chevy Chase, Hallowell and Chestnut Street.'

Which meant the Forbes home had received a call from the scene of Harry Forbes' murder within minutes of his death.

'4567 is the P Street Beach area.'

And a call from the scene of van Voss's murder within minutes of *her* death.

Eddie's mind circled the data, drew connections. 'Thanks, Mark. I owe you.'

'No, Eddie, I owe you. If you hadn't put in a good word for me at the trial, I would have wound up serving eight years instead of eight months.'

Sharon and Joe sat in front-row center seats at the Kennedy Center. The Ballet Folklorico de Uruguay was more a circus than a ballet. Athletes in loincloths tumbled and leapt to the thunder of native drums; women in rainbow feathers materialized and vanished in flashes of stage lightning. At the climax a jaguar jumped through a flaming hoop.

It was an evening of nonstop, exhilarating turmoil, and Sharon's ears were still ringing when she and Joe stepped into the Terrace Restaurant at the Center.

The room was softly lit and their table had a view of yachts moored in the Potomac. Selecting the wine required a long, earnest conversation in French with the sommelier.

'How many languages do you speak?' Sharon asked.

Joe reflected for a moment. 'Restaurant French, bank German, a little quiz-show Spanish. And you?'

'I suppose I'm what the French called monophone. I can read scientific German, but I couldn't put a sentence together if my life depended on it.'

'Have you always been interested in science?'

'Ever since my mother died.'

'When was that?'

'She had uterine cancer when I was seven.'

'That must have been tough for you.'

'I was determined to find the cure. Dad already had his Nobel, and he couldn't even work the dishwasher. So I figured it would be a snap. It wasn't, and I didn't find a cure. There are days I can't even find the right test tube.' She spread a thin glaze of butter on a breadstick. 'What about you, Joe? What's your story?'

He shrugged. 'There's nothing interesting about me. No Nobel prizes in the family tree.'

'Nobelists can be pretty dull people. I frankly think my father's the most interesting of the lot.'

'I'd like to meet him.'

'He'd love to meet you.'

'Set it up.' Joe grinned.

She realized he'd changed the subject. 'Where were you born, Joe?'

'Miami.'

It surprised her that he was a native-born American. 'But sometimes you have a sort of—'

'Accent? English is my second language. My parents were Cuban refugees.'

'Cuban? Mahler's such a German name.'

He smiled. 'If you looked in the Havana phone directory the year before Castro came to power, half the names on the Avenida del Country Club were German.'

'Sounds pretty grand. Is that where your parents lived?'

He nodded. 'And they never let Isabel and me forget it. They'd had the best life could offer – mansions, servants, limousines, vacations in Europe – and it was snatched from them. My sister and I were children of the Cuban-American dream, determined to make it big and beat the Yankees at the game of success. We were going to win back everything our parents had lost.'

Sharon caught an edge of bitterness in Joe's tone.

'And then Isabel fell in with a drug crowd and got sick.'

'And you? How did you fall in with your finance crowd?'

'I think it happened when I won a scholarship to Harvard. The professors were unbelievably snide about capitalism. It made me furious, hearing that kind of talk after what Castro did to my parents. So naturally I became a rabid capitalist and went to Harvard Business School. Spent four years with Morgan Stanley and wound up working for Vestcate. I seemed to have a knack and in three years they invited me to become a partner.'

She wondered about Joe. There was something restless and questing in the eyes. 'Is it fulfilling?'

'It has its moments.' He raised his wine glass and clinked with hers. 'Once in a rare while there's an evening like this.'

Joe dropped Sharon off at her apartment building on Kentbury Drive in Bethesda. He kissed her on the lips; it was a warm, respectful, not completely chaste kiss.

'I loved the evening,' he said.

'Me too. Thanks. Don't get out of the car.'

She let herself into the vestibule. She heard him drive away as she was collecting the day's bills and junk from her mailbox.

There was a tap on the marble floor behind her. She turned and saw a man catch the door just before it shut.

'Ms Powell, could I have a word with you?'

She recognized the salt-and-pepper hair, the hard-focused hazel eyes: it was the man who had been staring at her at Harry Forbes' funeral.

'My name's Edward G. Arbogast.' His right hand held out identification. 'I'm an investigator with Aetna Life. According to police records, you were one of the last people to speak with Harry Forbes before his death.'

He was an older man, soft-spoken, but a kind of bulky power rippled from him, a readiness for violence, and she didn't like being alone with him in an unguarded vestibule.

'Do Aetna investigators conduct their interviews after one thirty in the morning?'

'If we have to.'

'I'm not a friend of insurance, Mr Arbogast. You're a key factor in the health cost run-ups that put coverage beyond the reach of sixty million Americans.' She turned toward the inner door.

'Insurance settlements like Harry Forbes' don't help. He tripled the benefits to his widow a week before he died.'

She frowned and turned back. 'How does this concern me?'

'You spoke with Thelma van Voss the day of her suicide. You spoke with Lucinda Forbes the same day.'

'I happen to work for Lucinda Forbes. We had business with Thelma van Voss at the FDA. Now if you'll be good enough to excuse me—'

'Just a moment. Please.' There was urgency in his voice. 'After your meeting with Harry Forbes, a ten-second call was made from his home to a payphone in the Kennedy Center. After his death, a three-second call was made *to* his home from a payphone on the street where he was murdered.'

It took her an instant to see what he was saying. She felt something cold as a block of ice in her stomach. 'This doesn't concern me.'

'But it does, Ms Powell. On the day of Thelma van Voss's suicide, you made a two-minute cellular call to Lucinda Forbes' home.'

'As I just got through telling you, she's my employer.'

'Thirty seconds later, a ten-second call was made from the Forbes home to the same payphone in the Kennedy Center. After Thelma van Voss's suicide, a three-second call was made *to* the Forbes home from a payphone in the park where her body was found.'

'What is it you want from me, Mr Arbogast?'

'I need to know what you discussed when you met with Harry Forbes.'

'That information happens to be confidential. Now if you'll excuse me. I'm beginning a new job next week and I have a lot of preparation to do.'

She unlocked the inner door to the lobby. There was nothing she could have done if he'd pulled a gun or jumped her.

The door clicked shut and she hurried to the elevator. She didn't glance back.

April 17

'Half of you have been randomly assigned to the Sperilac group. That means you'll be given one hundred and fifty milligrams of Sperilac daily.'

Sharon stood on the dais in the lecture room of New Day Clinic, addressing the three hundred participants who had been selected for Phase Three. Tinted state-of-the-art sealed windows cast a beer-colored glow across her audience.

'The rest of you have been assigned to the placebo group. You'll be given sugar pills. Until the trial has ended, neither you nor the doctors will know which of you is receiving which.'

'Will anyone know?' someone shouted.

'I'll know.' Sharon smiled. 'But I promise not to tell.'

It was a grim audience, caught in a grim predicament. No one smiled back.

'Before you take your pill today, your blood will be drawn to give us your baseline values. For the next six months you'll come to the clinic every day for medication and blood work. It's imperative that you keep your appointments.' Her eyes swept the overcrowded rows of folding steel chairs. 'Are there any questions?'

A hand shot up.

'Yes, the lady in the third row.'

'What about side effects?' She was a weathered-looking woman with a rasping voice. 'A friend of mine was on that other AIDS drug, and it almost killed her.'

'I understand your concern. Several of the AIDS drugs currently being tested and used have toxic side effects. Sperilac doesn't.'

The questioner's face became skeptical. 'Have you tried it?'

'No, I haven't.'

'Then how do you know?'

'In earlier trials, the only harmful side effect reported was a slight headache. And that was a single patient who was subject to migraines. Furthermore, under the rules of the double-blind, you only have one chance in two of being assigned Sperilac. Anyone else? The gentleman in the fifth row.'

An overbuilt, red-headed man in jogging clothes rose to his feet. 'Is it OK to take steroids?' He held himself as though his shoulders ached. 'Because I'm competing for the Mr East Coast title.'

'Sperilac doesn't interact with steroids, anabolic or otherwise.'

'Then it's OK?'

'It's not OK. I'm sorry. Body-building steroids skew your hormones and compromise liver function. You're going to have to give them up for the duration of the trial.'

'Shit.' The body-builder shot her a murdering look and dropped back into his seat.

A hand went up at the back of the room. 'What's this about permission to autopsy?'

'You mean the consent form.' Sharon drew in a deep breath. 'That's a precaution. In the unlikely event that any of you should die during the course of the trial, we need to know the cause.'

'Has Sperilac ever killed anyone?'

'No. Sperilac went through exhaustive Phase One and Phase Two testing seven years ago. There were deaths on the placebo side of the trial, but not a single person taking Sperilac died. If anything, Sperilac is more likely to keep you alive.'

Afterwards, in her newly painted office, Sharon shared tuna sandwiches and diet Cokes with Jack Arnold, a co-worker and MD.

'Some of the trial members seemed a little resentful,' she said.

'Not surprising. They're walking around with a terminal disease. You're not.'

Sharon hated mainstream medicine's attitude that a diagnosis of AIDS was tantamount to a death sentence. 'No one's proved that AIDS is always fatal. There've been documented recoveries. Maybe not in the *Journal of the American Medical Association*, but they're on record.'

'Hey, relax. I'm not the enemy.' He smiled. 'And I wasn't talking about AIDS.'

She looked at him in bafflement.

'Addiction kills too – or didn't you know?' He lobbed his empty can into the waste basket. 'Come on. I want to show you something.'

He led her down the corridor into the west wing. 'This morning in that auditorium you met the cream of the New Day crop.' He stopped at a door with mesh-reinforced Plexiglas panes. 'Take a look at the other half. Have you ever seen the inside of a detox ward?'

She shook her head.

He slipped a card key into the door. 'After you. Don't worry, they won't hurt you. These aren't the violent ones.'

Sharon gripped the door handle and pulled the door open. A smell of chemical disinfectant gushed out, so strong that she had to fight back a gag reflex. They stepped into an enormous room with barred windows and peeling wallpaper and stained carpeting. The door locked itself behind them.

She looked around her and blinked in disbelief.

Young men and women in various stages of dress and undress sat listlessly on dilapidated sofas and chairs, or huddled in corners, or prowled the aisles pawing at their throats, perspiring and wrapped in blankets. Several of the men pulled aimlessly at their crotches, as if they were trying to relocate some pleasure zone in their bodies that they had mislaid.

Not a single eye turned in their direction. Not a single person spoke. The only voice was a TV set tuned to a softly chattering talk show.

Sharon sniffed. The air was stagnant with cigarette smoke and the unbelievably acrid stink of unwashed socks. The combination was lethal.

'You can always tell a junkie,' Jack Arnold said quietly. 'Their feet smell.'

'These are heroin addicts?'

'And cocaine, and pills, and designer drugs. We've even got two or three old-fashioned alcoholics. You name it, someone here's hooked on it.'

A boy who couldn't have been older than seventeen lay crouched and motionless on the floor. Dried vomit had dribbled down his T-shirt.

'Is he alive?' Sharon bent down to touch his arm.

'Oh, God! No!' The boy jerked away and rolled himself into a ball. 'Please, please, don't. It hurts.'

She snatched back her hand and looked at Jack for reassurance.

He shrugged. 'His skin is sensitive. You hurt him.'

'I'm sorry,' she apologized. 'I didn't know.'

The boy didn't answer.

She turned to Jack. 'I didn't know.'

'And now you do. Seen enough to get the idea?'

'I think so.'

Jack unlocked the door. They returned to the corridor.

'Why's the door kept locked?' she asked.

'So they won't run off and get high again. We can't begin treatment till the drugs are cleaned out of their systems. That takes two to ten days.'

'But they can leave any time they want, can't they?'

He shook his head. 'The majority are sentenced to detox and treatment instead of jail. As a matter of fact, some of them were sentenced to the Sperilac Phase Three trial.'

'You're kidding.'

He shook his head. 'Remember the woman who asked you about side effects – she was up for dealing coke. The court gave her a choice. Two years in jail or six months here playing Sperilac/placebo monte.'

Sharon didn't like the sound of it. Mortality among ex-convict addicts was double the average for addicts who hadn't served time. And the average for non-convict addicts was 80 per cent higher than for people with AIDS who weren't addicted. Statistics like that were bound to cut into Sperilac's success rate. 'How many of our trial participants are ex-cons?'

'I don't know how ex you could call them – a lot are in and out of jail two, three times a year.'

'How many are in the trial, Jack?'

He shrugged. 'Wouldn't surprise me if it was fifty per cent or so.'

'Are any of them still using drugs?'

'At a rough guess, no more than a third.'

She couldn't believe the figure would be so high. 'If they're in rehab, why so many?'

'Just because a judge sent them here doesn't mean they want to stop. Seventy per cent of our business comes from repeat clients. We're not complaining.'

The phone rang at 3:30.

'Sharon Powell. Can I help you?'

'This is Melissa Miller, Andy Horner's assistant at the Harvey Milk Clinic. I know it's your first day down there, and I'm sure things are pretty crazy, but we need more Sperilac right away.'

It irritated Sharon that Andy had dispatched his assistant instead of talking to her himself. 'Could I speak with Andy, please?'

'I'm afraid he's on another line.'

Sharon knew the phones at the Harvey Milk Clinic – there was no other line. 'I'll hold.'

In a moment, Andy came on the line. 'Yes, Sharon.'

'Andy, it's not my fault Lucinda Forbes is a small-minded

opportunist. You and I have been co-workers and good friends for over a year. If you need more Sperilac, I'd appreciate your asking me for it yourself.'

'OK. I'm asking you myself.'

This is going to be a three-month snit, she realized. At least. 'They keep track of the drugs here. I'll have to get it from Biochemtech. Can you wait till this evening?'

'I guess I'll have to.'

Click.

The Biochemtech employee parking lot was emptying out as Sharon switched off her ignition. She greeted the building guard and headed down the corridor to the storeroom.

A stranger was seated at Helen Weller's desk, eyes shadowed blue, hair tied in a blonde chipmunk tail.

'Is Helen sick today?'

'Helen won't be back for two weeks.' The young woman dog-eared a page of her paperback mystery. 'She's taking a short vacation to South America.'

'South *America*?' Sharon was astonished. 'When did she decide on that?'

'I have no idea.' The young woman smiled. 'I'm Irene from publicity. I'm sitting in for Miss Weller, but I've never met her.'

'I'm Sharon Powell.' Sharon showed her company ID. 'I wonder if you could help me. I need some Amitol.'

The smile became embarrassed. 'I'm afraid I don't know the stock that well.'

'That's all right. If you could just let me in, I know where to find it.'

Irene entered a command on the computer keyboard. The vault bars hummed and swung back.

Sharon went straight to the Sperilac.

She opened a bin. The shelves were empty. She looked in the next bin. Empty again. She searched eight bins. Just days ago they'd been heaped with Sperilac. Today there wasn't a single bottle of it.

'Are you OK in there?' a voice called.

'Sorry to take so long.' Sharon nudged the bars shut behind her. 'I couldn't help noticing the Sperilac bins are empty. Has it been moved?'

'It's been shipped.' Helen's replacement slipped into her jacket. 'Demand's way up, what with the Phase Three trial.'

That didn't make sense to Sharon: how could there be demand

before the trial was completed? 'Where was it shipped to?'

'That I couldn't tell you.' The young woman switched off the computer. 'But apparently everybody's ordering.'

It was dinnertime in the nursing home. Sharon found her father seated in front of the MacNeil Lehrer news hour, dentures clicking determinedly on a drumstick.

'How's the chicken?' she asked.

He made a face.

'I stopped at Biochemtech after work.' She lowered the volume on the TV and pulled up a chair. 'Last week there were eight bins full of Sperilac. Today there's not one bottle in the entire storeroom. Helen Weller has taken a two-week vacation to South America and her replacement said all the Sperilac has been shipped. Is that possible before it's been approved?'

Lucas wiped his hands on a paper napkin and swiveled toward the computer. IT COULD HAVE BEEN AN INTERNATIONAL SHIPMENT. DRUGS DON'T ALWAYS NEED FDA APPROVAL TO BE SHIPPED TO FOREIGN COUNTRIES.

'But what country would buy an untested drug in that quantity?'

I AGREE, IT SEEMS A LITTLE PECULIAR. LET'S SEE WHAT THEIR RECORDS SAY.

Lucas tried to hack into the Biochemtech computers. He couldn't make a connection.

YOU'D THINK SOMEWHERE IN A COMPANY OF 3,000 SOMEONE WOULD HAVE LEFT A COMPUTER RUNNING.

'Company policy is to power down before you go home.'

DO ME A FAVOR – CAN YOU GET TO HELEN WELLER'S DESK AFTER HER REPLACEMENT HAS LEFT FOR THE DAY AND TURN HER COMPUTER BACK ON?

It was karaoke night at the Silver Spur Bar and Grill. A blue-haired matron in a spangled vest was lip-synching a moronic song that Eddie Arbogast was glad he'd never had to listen to before. She kept losing her cowboy hat and drunken hands kept Frisbeeing it back on to the stage.

'Our records show no file on Helen Weller or Lucinda Forbes or Sharon Powell.' Larry Lorenzo spoke just loud enough for Eddie to hear across their corner table. 'If any of them had any connection to the drug cartel, they'd show up in our computers.'

A man in a sombrero joined the cowgirl for verse two. Voices roared approval. A paper streamer flew through the air and a bottle shattered against a wall.

'San Miguel de Bayamo is a church in Gurana, Colombia. No links to the drug cartel.'

Eddie frowned. 'Why export half a ton of an untested pharmaceutical to a church in Colombia?'

'Some churches run hospitals.'

Eddie didn't buy it. His mind rotated the problem, searching for another angle. 'Did you find out if Biochemtech has a backer for Sperilac?'

'I looked into that. The Phase Three Sperilac trials are being bank-rolled by Vestcate. They're being run on an addict population at a clinic called New Day. Your friend Sharon Powell is listed as trial director.'

'Hold it. Back up a minute. What the hell is Vestcate?'

'They're an international investment syndicate.'

'Legit?'

'The Treasury Department deals with them.'

'Doesn't prove anything. The Treasury buys its paper from an indicted felon.'

Larry Lorenzo shrugged.

'Find out if that church is affiliated with any hospital.' Eddie lifted the pitcher of Rolling Rock and refilled Larry's glass and his own. 'And take a look at Vestcate's cash flow. I want to know if any comes from the drug banks in Miami and Cayman and Liechtenstein – or winds up there.'

'Jesus, Eddie.' Larry's voice was fed up. 'The agency logs our computer time. This stuff relates to no ongoing investigation. It'll stick out like a charitable deduction on Leona Helmsley's tax return.'

'You used to be pretty good with computers back in our Panama days. I'll bet you can arrange for it not to stick out.'

It was almost 1 a.m. by the time Eddie returned to his hotel room, and the voice-mail light was blinking on the telephone. He dialed for the message.

'Hi, Eddie, it's just me.' Amy sounded a little put out. 'Just calling to see how you're doing. You certainly are out late. Hope it's going OK. Love you.'

April 19

In her office at New Day, Sharon slid the tube containing trial member 232's blood into the Baker System 9000 hematology machine. Bright amber options appeared on the black screen. She entered the codes for chem screen and serology.

With a whirring sound, the black console digested the sample. In a moment the readings appeared.

AST was 112 and ALT was 153 – twice normal.

Sharon frowned. Why so high?

She glanced at the other enzymes to see if she could find a clue. All were within normal range.

GGTP and alkaline phosphatase ruled out liver damage. Sedimentation rate ruled out infection.

Medication was a possible culprit, or tumor involvement. Or 232 could be a fluctuator, up today, down tomorrow. Oscillating enzyme levels were common in people with AIDS.

She pressed the *print* option.

The machine spat out a ribbon of paper covered like an ATM receipt with 232's stats. She paperclipped it to his chart and made a notation to monitor his AST and ALT.

Jack Arnold rapped on the door. 'Have you seen the NIH's latest on drug abuse and mortality rates?'

'Not this week's.'

'Shame on you. Don't you believe in keeping abreast?'

'It's going to take three to six months for those stats to reflect our work.'

'I quote. "In January of this year, some surprising comparisons emerged between the AIDS mortality rates of four classes of drug abusers: cocaine addicts, heroin addicts, amphetamine abusers, and alcoholics." ' He offered her the latest National Institutes of Health newsletter. 'Read it. Blow your mind.'

She waved it aside. 'That has nothing to do with Phase Three.'

'Ye of little faith.'

'And little time to chat. I'm working, Jack.'

'You'd work better with reagents.' He pointed to the blinking yellow light on the hematology machine.

'Damn. Where are they kept?'

Jack opened the cabinet under the machine and brought out the half-gallon container. 'May I do the honors?' He tipped the spout toward the tank and poured till the light went off. He recapped the container and backed out the door, salaaming.

'You must have made a wonderful sophomore, Jack.'

'That I did. Dean's list.'

She glanced up. 'By the way, something seems to be affecting two thirty-two's liver function.'

He looked at her blankly. 'Two thirty-two?'

'Myron Ebarts.' Participants in the Phase Three trial had been randomly assigned identification numbers. While the numbers would eventually be useful for guarding identities in the published reports, at the moment they added a cumbersome layer of pointless confusion. The resident staff of New Day knew their clients as names, not numbers. The issue that had to be kept blind wasn't who was who, but who was on Sperilac. That information could only be accessed through a password file, and only Sharon knew the password. 'You'd better check for tumors and review his medication.'

'Will do.'

Sharon opened the refrigerator. The next tube in the rack was trial member 233.

The payphone rang with a jangling sound, like a fighting cock attacked by a dentist's drill.

'Fernando!' a voice screamed across the rehearsal hall.

Fernando de Larra completed his spin and stepped out of the line of dancers. He negotiated his way through eighty wheeling, catapulting bodies. The music could have been bullets slamming into the dancers, picking them up, whipping them around in the air, tossing them down again. Fernando had toured three seasons with the Ballet Folklorico, and ethnic music definitely was getting noisier. The racing, pounding dissonances made him wonder which would wear out first: the dancers' cardio-vascular systems or the rehearsal piano.

He caught the swinging receiver. 'Hello?'

'Fernando?' The voice was Spanish.

He covered one ear and answered in Spanish. 'I'm listening to you.'

'Flowers for Lou Kmiotek.' The voice spelled the name with its insane clash of consonants.

Fernando replaced the receiver. As he turned he caught reflections leaping in the floor-to-ceiling mirror. He also caught a glimpse of himself. To the average eye Fernando might have seemed tall and sinewy, especially in his work-out leotard, but he had a dancer's eye and he judged himself unforgivingly.

Lose weight, he told himself. Three pounds. At least.

His gaze flicked past the dancers, searching for Emelina Luna. He saw her. Even with that overbuilt monkey of a partner, the girl moved like sweet water flowing over pure rock crystal.

'Emelina!' he called, cupping his mouth. 'Emelina Luna!'

She looked his way and took an uncertain step toward him.

He nodded: yes, you.

As she moved through the crowd, he could see she was a tough kid. She had speed and determination, and there was thunder in those ballet- and karate-trained limbs.

'I have something for you,' he said in Spanish.

She tossed her head, flipping the black braid with the green feather woven through it. 'A solo?'

A smile stole across his face. 'A very demanding solo. Come with me and I'll show you.'

He took her to the men's changing room. They were both dancers, and Latin. They had no false modesty. He opened the combination lock and searched through a carton on the floor of his locker.

He handed her a map of the District of Columbia. 'We're here.' His finger pointed to the Kennedy Center, circled in red. 'And this is where you're going.' He pointed to Logan Circle, also circled in red. 'The building is called New Day Clinic. It's a sort of hospital.'

There were three hundred alphabetized manila envelopes in the carton. He withdrew the envelope labeled *Kmiotek*, opened it and handed her a photograph.

'This man will be leaving the building shortly after four forty-five. You will follow him.'

'There we are.' The red-headed nurse removed the needle and snapped a Band-Aid over the tiny puncture in the crook of Lou Kmiotek's left arm. She labeled the tube and dropped it into the holding rack. 'See you tomorrow, Mr Kmiotek. Same time, same place.'

'You got a date.' Lou rolled down his shirtsleeves and slipped into his seersucker jacket. 'May the Higher Power be with you.' He made a V sign and strode through the waiting area. Aside from the technicians, he was the only man in the clinic who was wearing a jacket.

No self-respect, he thought. Look at those lugs – T-shirts, tank tops even.

In Lou's book, a person who wasn't interested in looking his best wasn't interested in being his best, and if you weren't interested in being your best, your sobriety wasn't worth a Canadian dime.

He glanced at an emaciated young woman with jittering fingers and the bloodshot, jaundiced eyes of a heroin addict who'd just shot up. The skin of her left arm was ulcerated and scabbed and he recognized her as a speed-baller, an addict who shot cocaine with her smack because coke gave temporary energy and the illusion of being in control of the addiction. The poor bimbo had obviously wound up hooked on coke too, and now she was suffering acute coke bugs – the sensation of lice crawling under the skin that caused cokeheads to scratch their own flesh to shreds.

She should be in detox, Lou thought, and here she was in maintenance, adding methadone to all her other problems. Lou shook his head. There but for the grace of God . . .

Lou had never done methadone; he'd opted to kick his heroin habit cold turkey, and stayed sober with the help of New Day's weekly one-on-one and group counseling. Workmen's Disability picked up the tab. He'd been clean two years and eleven days, knock wood.

Not like half the nitwits around New Day, who enrolled because it was the only way they could get welfare, and who were still doing dope. He'd seen them dealing in the men's room; once he'd even seen a kid shoot up in the stall with the door open. No self-respect.

Lou stepped into the sunlight of Logan Circle and hurried to the Metro. It was rush hour, and the train was jammed, and since he had a thing about crowds, that was a chore for him. The mobs in the Red Line supermarket were just as bad; they drove him to a rage that reminded him of his manic-depressive days before he went on Prozac: instant, explosive, and intoxicating.

It had taken Lou twelve months in Narcotics Anonymous to understand that anger was a deadly drug, too.

God grant me the serenity . . .

At the check-out counter, the bag boy dropped his jar of wheat germ and broke it. Lou had a blinding impulse to smash the fat-assed halfwit. He fought it by cycling NA mantras rapidly through his mind: This too shall pass . . . Keep it simple . . . Let go and let God . . .

The four-block walk from DuPont Circle to 1718 P Street, NW, helped him cool off. He felt almost serene as he put his key in the outer lock.

'Excuse me.' A young, bewildered-looking Latina stopped him before he could open the inner door. 'I have papers from the White House for Mr Jenkins who lives here.' She held up an attaché case. 'Are you Mr Jenkins?'

A single black braid hung over her shoulder with a parrot feather laced through it. She looked a little too exotic to be a courier.

Lou shrugged; with this administration, anything was possible. 'What's Mr Jenkins' first name?'

'Mr Brian Jenkins. He is very important.'

Lou surveyed the sateen blouse, the sandals, the handwoven skirt. No way was this a White House courier. More likely a phone-order hooker. Lucky Mr Jenkins.

'Sorry,' he grinned, turning the key. 'You'll have to ask at the desk.'

He opened the glass door. She scooted in after him, still staring at him expectantly.

'Go to the reception desk.' He pointed. 'Adolfo can help you.' He hefted his groceries and headed toward the elevator.

Pushing the button for three, he tried to recall if maybe he'd met a Brian or a Jenkins at the apartment house Christmas party. That tall guy from Archives . . .

He stepped off on the third floor and walked down the green-carpeted hall, past neighbors' shrieking TVs and garlicky cooking smells. He stopped at 3-H. Bracing his groceries in one arm, he slipped the apartment key into the lock.

He felt a hand on his arm.

'You are not Mr Jenkins?'

He practically jumped out of his skin. 'Jesus!'

She must have come up the emergency stairwell. She'd had to have run to beat him to the floor.

'Honey, I'm not interested. *Yo no estoy interesado*, capeesh?'

He shoved the door open with his shoulder.

Moisture from the pint of ginger tofutti was seeping through his fingers, and he could feel brown paper about to separate. He made a dash for the kitchen. Three feet from the counter, the bag broke like a Mexican pinata. Tangerines, limes, non-fat low sodium cookies, celery and free-range chicken breast spilled across the linoleum.

'Damn!'

He turned on the cold water and threw fruit into the sink. As he stood rinsing celery under the faucet he realized something was wrong: he hadn't heard the apartment door shut.

He turned.

She stood two feet from him, baring her teeth like a lunatic chimpanzee.

'Now just one fucking minute!' he shouted.

She slammed the attaché case into his face. Caught off balance, he skidded on spilled milk and hit the floor.

She leaped on top of him. An overpowering smell of vanilla flooded his nostrils.

He had only a split-second glimpse of what she held in her other hand. And then the needle caught him under the left ear.

Eddie jigged in distress, trying to find which way his Holiday Inn card key was meant to fit into the door.

He'd spent the afternoon poring over maps of the provinces of Colombia, revving himself with seven cups of coin-machine coffee. Even though he'd relieved himself in the men's room at the National Geographic Society, his bladder was bursting again.

The card key finally worked. Eureka. He shoved the door open and made a diagonal dash for the bathroom.

Standing there, staring back into the darkened bedroom, he saw the message light blinking on the phone. He washed his hands, flicked on the lamp, and dialed 8 for voice mail.

'Hey, Eddie,' came the bubbling speed-enhanced voice, 'it's Mark Burgess, hacker to kings and retired DEA champs. Got something I think is going to interest you very much. Call me. I'm not going anywhere.'

Eddie called. 'What have you got?'

'Ten after ten this morning, guess what? Another call from the Forbes home to that payphone in the Kennedy Center.'

Eddie didn't like it. People's vital signs had a way of flatlining whenever the Forbes home rang that number. 'Any way you can find out where in the Center that payphone's located?'

'I knew you'd ask, and I have the answer. Isn't the Internet grand? The phone's backstage in the second floor rehearsal area. Practice room A.'

At 6:15 she saw Helen Weller's replacement leave the Biochemtech building, brisk in her stone-washed jeans and plaid shirt.

Sharon stepped out of her car and crossed the parking lot.

'Liking your new job, Sharon?' the guard asked.

She smiled at him. 'Hi, Frank. The new job's great.'

The air-conditioning inside the building raised goosebumps on her arms. The corridors were almost deserted. She took the elevator and hurried to the storeroom door. Looking over her shoulder, she saw no one. Heard no one.

She slid her passcard into the slot. There was a click and the motor drive hummed to life. The steel door swung open eighteen inches, giving her five seconds.

She angled herself sideways and slipped inside.

Light from the corridor fell in a parallelogram across Helen's desk and computer, reaching as far as the vault bars. Otherwise, the room was pitch dark.

The motor began humming again. As the door closed, the light narrowed and she realized she didn't know where the light switch was. Her eyes raked the steel walls.

There was a thud, and now she was in blackness.

She slid a hand along the wall, exploring at shoulder level, then above, then below, and then, beginning to feel panic, with both hands. There had to be a switch.

It suddenly occurred to her: maybe not.

She clapped her hands. Lights snapped on blindingly in the ceiling. After several seconds her pupils adjusted.

Her eyes searched the computer surface, found the power button. She pushed it. The computer buzzed and clicked and a moment later a blinking C prompt appeared on the monitor screen. Ready for business.

She was startled by the sound of a deep, humming motor. The storeroom door swung inward.

A guard peered in. 'Help you, miss?' he challenged.

'No thanks.' She stepped back into the corridor. 'I want some Amitol samples.'

He barely moved aside for her. 'Could I see your ID?'

A smell of clove mouthwash hovered. She dredged the wallet out of her purse.

He examined her driver's licence, her charge cards, her company ID. 'The custodian has gone for the day.' He handed the wallet back. 'You'll have to come tomorrow.'

'Thanks. I'll do that.'

*   *   *

103

When Sharon reached the nursing home, Lucas had eaten only the tuna in his tuna salad plate: a pile of chopped celery and onion and green pepper remained at the side of the plate.

'You didn't finish your dinner.'

SOME SADIST IN THE KITCHEN LIKES TO FEED ME RAW VEGETABLES.

'Raw veg is good for you. Chock full of vitamins.'

YOU'LL CHANGE YOUR MIND ABOUT BEING CHOCK FULL OF ANYTHING WHEN YOUR BOWELS ARE 78 YEARS OLD.

'I see your point.' She dropped into a chair. 'Helen Weller's plugged in.'

WHAT'S HER EXTENSION?

Sharon consulted a scrap of paper. 'Five seven five five.'

Lucas modemed into Helen's computer. For the next ten minutes, hunched over the keyboard, squinting and silent, he explored inventory and sales and shipping records.

She felt his finger on her arm. He motioned her attention to the screen.

She scanned columns of print. In the two weeks preceding the Phase Three trial, Helen had authorized the manufacture of 1.8 million 100-pill bottles of Sperilac; each pill was 150 milligrams.

Lucas called up sales. He scrolled past page after page. Not one bottle, not one tablet of Sperilac had been sold – ever.

'What happened?' Sharon scowled. 'They didn't dump it all in the Potomac.'

THEY GAVE IT AWAY.

'Come on.'

NOT JOKING.

Lucas called up the shipping files. Sharon read over his shoulder.

Last July 30th, when there had been 20,197 bottles of Sperilac in stock, 1,800,000 additional bottles had been ordered from the manufacturing department.

WHAT DO YOU KNOW ABOUT THAT ORDER?

'Nothing. It doesn't make sense.'

The records showed that on August 21st, 1,800,000 bottles had been sent to San Miguel de Bayamo hospital in the province of Gurana, Colombia.

'That's not possible. There's no way two million bottles of Sperilac could have been in and out of that storeroom without my noticing them.' Sharon thought back. 'Wait a minute. I was on vacation the week of

104

August seventeenth. They must have arrived and gone out while I was in Colorado.'

KNOW ANYTHING ABOUT THAT HOSPITAL?

'Never heard of them.'

SOMEBODY MUST KNOW THEM. AND LOVE THEM. THEY WERE NEVER INVOICED AND THEY NEVER PAID.

The 20,093 bottles of Sperilac remaining in stock had dropped by November 20th to 19,983. By January 22nd, that number had dropped to 19,871; and by March 20th to 19,766.

INVENTORY SEEMS TO BE SHRINKING BY 50 BOTTLES A MONTH.

'That's me – I usually managed to smuggle out about a dozen a week.'

GOOD GIRL.

On March 31st, another 1,800,000 bottles were ordered.

KNOW ANYTHING ABOUT THIS ORDER?

Sharon frowned. 'It's too early and much too large to be New Day.'

On April 16th, 600 bottles were sent to New Day Clinic, leaving 19,081 in stock.

THERE'S YOUR NEW DAY ORDER – CHICKEN FEED COMPARED TO WHAT SAN MIGUEL IS GOBBLING UP.

On April 17th, 1,800,000 bottles of Sperilac were received from manufacturing; the same day, 1,819,081 bottles, the entire stock, were sent to San Miguel de Bayamo hospital.

NO INVOICE THIS TIME EITHER.

Sharon nodded. 'That's explains where all the Sperilac went. The only thing I don't understand is why?'

HOW OFTEN DOES FORBES BIOCHEMTEC TAKE INVENTORY?

'Once a year.'

WHEN?

'The end of June.'

THEN THESE SHIPMENTS WERE VERY NICELY TIMED. APPARENTLY THERE'S A LITTLE MORE TO YOUR FRIEND HELEN WELLER THAN YOU SUSPECTED.

'Come on, Dad, I know her. She's not a crook.'

NOT ON YOUR SCALE, I'LL GRANT. YOU MAY BE PRETTY HANDY AT PILFERING FROM THE STOREROOM, BUT WHEN IT COMES TO GRAND LARCENY AND BRAZEN CHUTZPAH, I'D SAY HELEN HAS YOU BEAT HANDS DOWN.

'That's completely unjustified. I'm sure there's some simple explanation.'

YOU BET. THE SIMPLE EXPLANATION IS, SHE STOLE CLOSE TO THREE AND A HALF MILLION BOTTLES. DEPENDING HOW THE COMPANY SETS THE PRICE, THAT'S UPWARDS OF HALF A BILLION DOLLARS. I'LL LAY YOU TWENTY TO ONE THESE SAN MIGUEL PEOPLE DON'T EVEN EXIST AND FORBES BIOCHEMTECH NEVER SEES HELEN WELLER'S FACE AGAIN. AND NEITHER WILL YOU.

April 20

Sharon began phoning Lucinda at 9:10 in the morning. At 9:50 Lucinda finally answered.

'Lucinda, I hope this is a tempest in a teapot, but what do you know about one million eight hundred thousand bottles of Sperilac manufactured last July thirtieth?'

'*What?*' Lucinda's voice was a slow rising arc of astonishment. 'Last *July?*'

'And another one million eight hundred thousand bottles manufactured March thirty-first?'

'That's impossible.'

'And shipped free of charge to San Miguel de Bayamo Hospital in Gurana, Colombia.'

'What? Who? Where?'

Sharon repeated the name and spelled it.

'Harry never authorized a shipment that size and neither did I. Where did you get this information?'

'From Helen Weller's computer.'

'Then her computer's flipped out. I'll have a talk with Helen right now.'

'I'm afraid you won't be able to. Helen's on vacation. In South America.'

'Then how did you get into her computer?'

'My father hacked in. It's a long story.'

'Save it. Let me check into this and I'll get back to you.'

Eddie peered through the window in the door of practice room A. For the life of him he couldn't see a telephone.

Sound carried, though. A ballet master shouted beats; a pianist pounded; eight dozen dark-haired, dark-eyed young men and women in leotards jumped and spun and ran and turned cartwheels. The floor shook with thundering feet.

It looked to Eddie more like a football scrimmage than dance – too many collisions, too little synchronization – but what did he know about ballet or folklore or Uruguay?

'Excuse me.' A stagehand wheeled a rack of costumes past: flamboyant eye-popping concoctions of fruit, fur, foliage and feathers.

'Hey, fella,' Eddie called, 'is there a public phone around here?'

The stagehand shouted back: 'Downstairs.'

'*Perdona.*' A gorgeous little mocha-skinned girl wearing parrot's wings and a braided banana leaf wriggled round him. The door swung shut and Eddie's eyes followed her.

Shrugging on a bustle of flamingo feathers, she crossed to the window. An elaborate monkey-skin and orchid headdress hung from a hat peg on the wall. She lifted it to her head and Eddie saw that the hat peg was a telephone.

He could see he was going to have a problem: access.

A schedule was posted beside the door. He noted the hours. Ballet Folklorico had the rehearsal space from 9 to 1; that afternoon, the touring company of *Pal Joey* had the hall from 1 to 5.

Lucinda Forbes slammed her electronic passcard into the slot. As the vault door groaned open, a startled and mousey-looking secretary jumped up from her desk.

'I'm Lucinda Forbes.'

'Yes, Mrs Forbes.'

'I need your computer for a moment.'

The girl stood aside.

Lucinda called up the Sperilac records and winced. She raced through Helen Weller's correspondence with Thelma van Voss of the FDA, word-searched for Sperilac, and found two faxes. She noted discrepancies in Helen Weller's export requests totaling close to two million bottles.

Giving away those 3,600,000 bottles of Sperilac is theft, thought Lucinda, but lying to the government about it, and leaving evidence of the lie, is suicide.

Returning to the manufacturing record, Lucinda altered the August figure of 1,800,000 to 900,000, the figure Helen had faxed to the FDA. She did the same with the March figure. She repeated the operation with the August and March shipping figures. Next, she deleted any and all back-ups of the original files and entered the command to back up, and backdate, the files she had just altered.

Finally she printed out all available information on San Miguel de Bayamo Hospital in Gurana, Colombia. She ripped the paper out of the printer and jammed it into her pocket.

She turned and read the name off the secretary's ID tag. 'Irene.'

'Yes, ma'am.'

'What did you just see me do?'

'I didn't quite understand it, ma'am. You're awfully good with that computer.'

'You saw me do nothing.'

Irene blinked. 'Yes, ma'am.'

'In fact you didn't even see me here today.'

'Yes, ma'am.'

'You wouldn't happen to have Helen Weller's vacation address?'

'I'm sorry, I don't.'

Neither did anyone else Lucinda had questioned in the company.

'To tell the truth, I don't even know Miss Weller.'

Lucinda gritted. 'Obviously none of us did.'

'Beg your pardon?'

'You can have your computer back. Would you buzz me out?'

The door lumbered open and Lucinda squeezed through.

When Eddie returned to the practice room at 5:15, the population was down to four. Two dancers were rehearsing a Fred and Ginger routine. A singer belting out a *Pal Joey* number was getting riffed under by her pianist.

Eddie stepped through the door, Mr Cool, and sauntered to the payphone. He dropped a quarter in, dialed six digits, had a nice talk with himself. The dancers ignored him. The singer and the pianist ignored him. His eye traced the phone line. Ten feet from the window, it vanished into the baseboard.

He went into the men's room next door. No one at the sinks, no one at the urinals. A cloying synthetic fruit smell hovered. Eddie wished the people who decided these things would go back to camphor.

He peeked under the stall doors. Empty.

The phone line came through the wall in the third stall and climbed up into a duct. He stuck a voice-activated pin bug into it, down low behind the toilet.

Since the transmitter only carried ten feet, his problem now was where to hide the micro-cassette recorder.

He decided to fasten it under the second sink with duct tape.

As she was shutting up her office for the night, Sharon noticed that one member of the Phase Three trial hadn't shown up today – 187.

She looked up 187 in the password file: Lou Kmiotek. She accessed the clinic clientele records and found only a home number listed for Lou Kmiotek, no work phone.

She dialed the number. No answer. She let it ring, thinking a machine might pick up.

After ten rings she hung up. She stuck a post-it note to the computer screen, reminding herself to check into L. Kmiotek.

She turned off the light, called goodnight to Jack Arnold, and hurried to her dinner date with Joe Mahler.

Joe had asked Sharon to meet him at Le Lavandou in Chevy Chase, an old country house with exposed beams and brick walls, with crystal on the tables and menus in French. It was the sort of place that made Sharon realize how very seductive the comforts of money could be.

The maître d' led her across a softly chattering room of hairdos and diamonds and bare tanned shoulders. Joe had reserved a corner table. In his conservatively cut dark Italian suit and gray-on-gray power tie, he looked like the youngest, handsomest mogul in the Fortune 500.

'Sharon. Great to see you.' He kissed her on the cheek and she felt like a teenager.

'You should have told me we were dressing. I'd have thrown on my Barbara Bush pearls.'

'These are my work clothes,' Joe said. 'I came straight from a meeting.'

At eight o'clock in the evening, it sounded like a white lie.

'Late meeting?'

'Early. In Seattle. I flew back. I didn't want to miss our date.'

She stared at him, putting the pieces together. 'Private jet?'

He seemed embarrassed. 'Vestcate's jet. All the partners have the use of it. That's five hundred and sixteen of us, you couldn't call it private.'

'I read profiles about people like you in the Sunday magazines.'

'I've never been profiled.'

'I bet you have a home in Palm Beach.'

'It's not really a home, two bedrooms and a patio on Primavera Way. It's just an investment, nothing fancy.'

'And you're a personal friend of the President and the Speaker of the House. And you handle investments for Liz Taylor and David Letterman.'

'I've never met the Speaker. And I don't discuss clients. And to tell the truth, I'm a little uncomfortable in a pigeonhole.'

'Sorry.' She realized she was being defensive and more than a little unfair. It wasn't Joe's fault she'd gotten so caught up in work there hadn't been time to go home and change. And on second glance, she saw that not all the women in the restaurant were wearing designer originals. Only about half of them.

'Joe, could I ask you a personal question?'

'If you don't mind a personal answer.'

'How do you feel about cats?'

'Cats?' He cocked his head to one side and studied her a long moment. 'Some of my best friends are cats.'

'Do you own any?'

'We used to own three. But with Isabel's immune problems, we had to give them away.'

Sharon understood. Pets carried parasites and viruses, like toxo-plasmosis, that were harmless to healthy people but could destroy an immuno-compromised person.

'It broke Isabel's heart.' Joe sighed. 'Mine too.'

'I'm glad you said that. Because I'm a cat person.'

'That's terrific.' Joe grinned. 'How many do you have?'

'Between ten and twenty. It varies. I run a sort of halfway house for strays. I get them healthy and place them in loving homes. So when Isabel's well again, and you're looking for new cats, come visit me. One of mine might decide to adopt you.'

'I'll bet you're great with cats.'

'I enjoy them. They understand me.'

'You mean you understand *them*.'

Joe caught the waiter's attention and nodded toward the bucket beside the table where a bottle of champagne was cooling.

'You're an understanding person, Sharon. It's the very first thing I noticed about you. Would it embarrass you if I told you how very much you've meant to me these last weeks? Things would have been pretty hopeless without you.'

Instinctively, she deflected praise. 'Joe, I'm a sucker for admiration but I didn't invent Sperilac.'

'But you made it accessible to the AIDS underground and that saved my sister's life. Her viral activity is down eighty-five per cent.'

Suddenly she understood the champagne and the four-star restaurant. It was a celebratory dinner. 'Joe, I'm so happy. That's wonderful news.'

A cork popped and iced Piper-Heidsieck spumed into two crystal flutes.

'To Isabel,' she proposed.

'To recovery.'

They clinked glasses.

He was thoughtful. 'Has anyone on Sperilac ever cleared the virus completely?'

'Maybe six per cent. In about eighty per cent the virus becomes inactive. No one's figured out why.'

He nodded. 'Maybe the Phase Three trials will tell us.'

Helen Weller's hand moved quickly across the sheet of Varig Aeronaves do Brasil stationery.

'People were dying, terribly and needlessly. I made what seemed at the time the only possible decision. Circumstances may have changed, time will tell, but too late for me to alter course.' The plane banked sharply and the pen drew a jagged loop up through the word 'Brasil'.

Looking through the window, Helen made out a nocturnal sea of dark green and black, of barely discernible tropical foliage floating on the mystery of the jungle. The skyline of Bogota, edged in light on its mile-high mesa, loomed up without warning.

Varig Airlines charter flight 43, nonstop from Dulles Airport, glided past the capital city of Colombia. Two minutes later it settled on the runway and bounced toward the terminal.

Water instantly began collecting on the window. Helen peered through the drips and streaks. The searchlit area around the terminal was barren. Flame-throwers had burned away every plant and bulldozers had flattened every hillock, destroying any spot where life could conceal itself.

Wars have been fought here, Helen mused. They're still being fought.

The plane bumped to a sudden, total stop. The hatch opened and a handsome young steward escorted Helen down the metal stairway on to the tarmac. She allowed him to kiss her hand: an extravagant farewell gesture perhaps, but not all that extravagant when you considered that she had been the sole passenger on the 4,000-mile flight.

She hitched the belt of her new raincoat a notch tighter and followed him to the rear of the plane. Workers unloaded eight gigantic crates on to a motorized cart.

The crates lumbered through the huge double doors of the terminal. Helen followed the cart. The steward walked behind her, holding the customs manifest.

Three officials removed their caps at her approach.

She recognized them from last time. 'Good evening, gentlemen.'

Lieutenant Julio Gonzales took her passport, gave it a cursory glance, and handed it to Sergeant Jose Rivera. Rivera stamped it and returned it to Helen. The whole process took less than fifteen seconds.

Captain Luis Mendoza, a man with a waist as ample as his smile, reached for the steward's clipboard.

'Welcome to Colombia, Señora Weller.' Mendoza's English was smeared with an accent that challenged Helen's ear.

'It's good to see you again, Captain,' Helen smiled.

He studied the manifest. 'And what have you to declare this time?'

Helen straightened her spine. In her new high heels, she was three inches taller than any of these portly little men and she knew the advantage her height gave her. 'The same as last August. I bring you medicine.'

'Of course.' He stamped the papers on the clipboard, tore off the master copy, and returned the carbons to the steward. 'You are a physician, Señora Weller? Or a missionary perhaps?'

'Not a physician, and not exactly a missionary.' She smiled. 'I'm a scientist. I represent the manufacturer of this medicine. I ensure that it's delivered to those who need it.'

'Then you will not be returning to North America as before?'

'Not immediately. This time I fly inland with my cargo.'

The two other customs inspectors were busy applying stamps and labels to the crates.

'If the señora will permit me, it is most laudable for a woman of your elegance and charm to undertake such an arduous task when you without doubt have a lonely lover awaiting your return.'

If this was sexual harassment, Helen Weller was all for it. The little inspector had been far less courtly last August. She suspected he was responding to the eye shadow and the dye job. Money well spent.

'You are much too gracious and your tongue too sweet.'

Captain Mendoza flushed, doffed his cap, and gave a little bow. 'Might I ask what this medicine cures?'

'We hope it cures la SIDA.'

Mendoza flinched. 'Señora, you are a saint to bring this boon to us.'

On the tarmac behind her, a two-prop cargo plane taxied toward the motorized baggage cart.

'Pleasant as this is, Captain Mendoza, I must continue on my journey. Would you be able to give us some assistance?'

'Of course, señora. Of course.'

Captain Mendoza barked an order in Spanish. Ten men ran toward the crates and began hoisting them on to the prop plane. Helen watched closely to be sure that the boxes were not jostled or bumped.

Finally the hatch was sealed.

'Captain Mendoza,' Helen handed him a thin, blue, airmail envelope. 'Would you be kind enough to mail this letter for me?'

'But of course, señora.'

'I'm sorry I have no postage.'

He waved away the dollar bill that she offered. 'It is my pleasure, señora.'

With a helping hand from the captain, Helen climbed the little ladder into the cockpit.

The young pilot, seated behind the controls, flashed her a blinding smile. 'Good evening, señora. My name is Juan.'

'Good evening, Juan.'

'Señora Weller,' the steward called, 'good luck!'

The engines revved for take-off.

Captain Mendoza waved his cap. 'God bless you, Señora Weller! I will mail your letter tonight!'

Helen fastened her seat belt and waved to the men outside.

The plane gathered speed.

Yielding to a kind of voluptuous fatigue she had not experienced since adolescence, she closed her eyes and settled back. Her fate was in the lap of God, and it would be a long flight over the jungle into the deep green savagery beyond.

April 21

W ith only the slightest wobble, the propeller-driven aircraft settled on to the landing strip and taxied toward the electric golf cart where Miguel Bosch waited in the whitening dawn. Long jungle shadows spread across the runway, and he regretted that it was just bright enough for Señora Weller to see the fifty men with machine pistols lining the tarmac.

In this part of the world – his world – a show of strength was simple protocol. It was expected by friends, enemies, and servants alike. But what would she think of a man who needed an army to welcome a visitor bearing gifts? He wondered if she would take it for weakness on his part, or perhaps even fear.

As soon as the plane came to a stop, Indians in ragged khaki shorts swarmed over it, tearing open the hatches and hefting the crates from the cargo hold. They looked like army ants gutting the corpse of a dragonfly.

'A bit much for our lady librarian, don't you think, Mike?' Bertolt Devereux swung his legs out of the cart. 'All that naked manhood might send her into a swoon.'

The sniping remark troubled Bosch, for it showed that Devereux was still jealous of Helen Weller. In nine short months she had proved herself more useful to the cartel than Devereux had in two decades. And, unlike Dev, she'd requested no remuneration. Bosch hoped Dev, for his own sake, would have the good sense not to force the cartel to choose between them.

The Indians raised the entrance to the cockpit. A towering flame of a woman allowed herself to be lifted and passed to the ground.

Bosch watched with amazement that approached disbelief. Helen Weller's crimson raincoat blistered against the azure and emerald background of vine and forest. Before he could move to greet her, she was striding toward them. She had darkened her hair – that he saw at once. And her glasses were gone.

Helen Weller had changed. Decidedly.

'Helen!' Bosch grabbed her by both shoulders and studied her. 'You grow lovelier by the second.'

And it was true. She had plucked her eyebrows into ebony circum-flexes. The lenses in her eyes made them a brilliant blue. The fawn-and-gray hair had turned deep mahogany brown, twisted into a crown of braids. She had become regal.

'And you, Miguel, grow more near-sighted by the instant. But that was a sweet thing to say.' She seized the initiative and planted a soft kiss on his cheek.

To his horror, he felt himself blush.

Helen quickly extended her hand toward Bertolt Devereux. 'Mr Devereux. We met last July on Miguel's yacht and two weeks ago at Harry Forbes' funeral. Are you still with Bertolt-Bienvenue Pharmaceuticals?'

'Miss Weller.' Devereux slid his hand in and out of hers like a snake through a coil of rope. 'How very nice to see you looking so well. And yes, I stay put – more or less.'

Somehow Miguel Bosch did not like the tone of that.

'Helen, Bertolt, let's have some breakfast.'

Bosch directed his guests into the golf cart and steered them along a trail twisting through the forest. As they rounded a curve, a sprawling single-story white building came into view. It stood in a fresh clearing where no grass yet grew. Hewn letters over the doorway declared it to be the Hospedal de San Miguel de Bayamo.

The golf cart whizzed past a loading platform that stretched out from the shadow of the western wall. Dozen of Indians, naked muscles straining, wrestled crates into the interior.

'What on earth . . . ?' Helen cried.

'Later.' Bosch chuckled. 'After we've fed you.'

The cart climbed a rise. They came to another clearing in the jungle. 'My house,' Bosch said.

Bosch's house, as he well knew, shone like a jewel, the stucco a blinding topaz in the early morning sunlight. Its angled wings and ells surrounded a pool shaped like a capital B, with two coral and concrete islands filling the holes in the letter. Waterfalls and cascades ran from the jungle in tamed streamlets, splashing into the pool. Fountains flowered and surged from the islands.

In every direction, there bloomed huge, violent-hued plants that appeared capable of yanking themselves out of the terraces and planters and fighting off a cohort of jaguars. Hummingbirds, tiny gems of iridescent green and blue, flitted about them like gnats.

Bosch prided himself on this beauty, this excess of color. And yet this morning, for some reason, he felt it was insufficient, too pallid to contain this woman in the flame-colored raincoat.

'Lovely,' she said. 'You've done very well with the gardens.'

Her remark deflated Bosch, as if his garden – which he certainly had never intended as tribute to her when he designed it a decade earlier – was lacking some essential ingredient.

'Well, I think it's damn beautiful,' Devereux asserted, seeming to sense that any display short of reverence would be ill-received by their host. 'Most beautiful thing I've ever seen.'

They disembarked from the cart and walked to a glass-topped table on the patio. Indian servants scurried to lay out salvers of eggs, bowls of jellied calf's feet and thin-sliced deep-fried plantain, saffron rice dotted with green and red pepper and olive, roast chicken, shrimp flown in from the Gulf of Mexico, platters of iced fresh guava and papaya and mango and soursap, steaming pitchers of coffee and chocolate and hot milk.

Miguel Bosch believed in excess.

'Please,' he said. 'Take off your coat. In a very short time it will be much too hot to wear it.'

Helen allowed him to pull the raincoat off her shoulders. He almost gasped at what she wore underneath: a simple dress, tailored to complement her slender frame but figured with a Paisley print that was ten times as exotic, a hundred times more striking than anything in his gardens. There was not a color around her, from the sunrise beating against the house to the flowers and the hummingbirds, that wasn't already contained in that fabric.

Bosch wondered what instinct had told her to wear a garment that turned the best he could offer into a dim image of her own taste.

One of the Indians hastened to help her seat herself at the breakfast table. Another scurried to pour her *café con leche* – two spouts of coffee and hot milk aimed simultaneously into a huge earthenware cup.

'What can we offer you?' Bosch said. 'I don't know if you are suffering jet lag, but perhaps you would like a steak? Or a simple flan?'

'No, nothing special.' Helen waved a hand in dismissal. 'Just a little bit of everything. I'm starved.'

'A little bit of everything' would fill several plates, but Bosch gave the order and the Indians dashed back and forth, keeping her fed while the two men picked at their scrambled eggs and mango.

Is this woman testing her appetites, Bosch wondered, or demonstrating them?

As she pushed away her last platter, Devereux asked her, 'How was your trip?'

'Much pleasanter than my first trip. But that layover in Bogota is a waste of time.' She stifled a yawn with the back of her hand. 'If you'd expand your airstrip to accommodate jets, I could be here six hours faster, with no exposure to officials outside the States.'

'I prefer to keep the airfield inconspicuous,' Bosch said.

'You're treating Sperilac like an illegal drug. Which it is not.'

'I see no harm in caution.'

'Was it cautious to fly nine hundred thousand bottles on an unregistered plane that the Mexicans shot down? Or were you thinking like criminals?'

'Would you care for more guava?' Bosch offered. What she said was true, and the truth annoyed him. 'Or guayanaba?'

'Thank you, no. It's a good thing I doubled that order or we'd have lost eight precious months.'

'It's lucky you were able to bring the rest down on a commercial flight. And so quickly.' Bosch smiled his most diplomatic smile. 'You bring us luck. You *are* our luck.'

'It wasn't luck,' Helen said. 'It was planning. Now tell me. How is our experiment going?'

Bosch was grateful for the change of subject. 'Let me have the pleasure of showing you. I believe our scientists have finally discovered the optimum proportions.'

As they walked through the corridors of the Hospedal de San Miguel de Bayamo, it struck Helen how little Spanish was spoken by the staff. Doctors, nurses and orderlies all seemed to be chatting in English or German or Russian. She reflected that Miguel Bosch must be using enormous cash reserves as a suction to drain the last brains out of eastern Europe.

Bosch led them through laboratories, sunrooms and lounges. Occasionally he paused to speak to a staff member in low whispers.

'Very good,' he inevitably concluded in English. 'All very good indeed.'

They strolled through wards and individual treatment rooms. Freshly waxed floors and brightly painted walls sparkled. Every bedside table held a huge vase of flowers from the house gardens. Every bed was made up, sheets taut and crisp.

And every one of the beds was empty.

'It's superb,' Helen finally volunteered. 'Better than I'd dared hope. But I thought you'd have some patients for me to see.'

Bosch chuckled. 'Oh yes. Patients.'

'No hospital would be complete without them,' Devereux said.

'We just have trouble keeping track of ours.' Bosch smiled at the confusion on Helen's face.

They descended a flight of polished wooden stairs. The sound of shouting voices and stamping feet and splashing bodies grew almost deafening.

Electrically controlled double doors parted. A smell of clean human sweat and chlorine and wintergreen gusted out.

They stepped into an enormous glass-roofed gymnasium. A low wall divided a swimming pool from basketball and badminton and volleyball courts. Indian boys and girls hurled themselves off diving boards, bounced on trampolines, batted shuttlecocks, their toned muscles straining and gleaming.

A few cuddled on mats in corners, and the boys caressed the budding exposed breasts of the girls. Bosch hoped that Helen would not be shocked by the obvious sexual arousal of so many of the young men. He could explain it, but he hoped she would not ask.

'Absolutely remarkable,' Devereux said. A couple of boys in a tangle of limbs rolled off their wrestling mat and tumbled past. 'How long have they been like this?'

'Twenty, twenty-one days,' Bosch said. 'Three weeks seems to be sufficient. No exceptions.'

'Who are these children?' Helen said.

'Our patients,' Bosch answered.

'My God.'

Bosch watched her reach for her throat as if to clutch something. Her hand closed on empty air. The gesture gave him pleasure.

A man with an impish face approached. His hair was as white as his lab coat, and he wore a stethoscope round his neck. 'Well, Señor Bosch,' he had a thick Slavic accent, 'have we got it right, or have we got it right?'

Bosch made introductions. 'Dr Plovinko, I'd like you to meet our honored guests and colleagues from North America, Dr Weller and Mr Devereux.'

Plovinko gave Devereux a quick courtesy bow. He took Helen's hands in both of his. 'You have come as a savior, doctor. I hope you will love San Miguel de Bayamo as much as I—'

119

Bosch cut him off. 'Señora Weller still has much to see.'

It was less than ten minutes by helicopter from the hospital to the laboratory complex. The construction was so new that the bulldozers and felled trees and heaps of unplaned earth had yet to be removed. Sidewalk forms were in place between the seven buildings, waiting for the concrete to be poured.

'And now,' Miguel Bosch said, 'the special surprise. Our factory.'

'Factory?' Helen stared at the cinderblock buildings, at the armed guards stationed every ten paces. A premonition of betrayal fanned through her. She took off her high heels and made the little leap from the helicopter to the ground.

Bosch steadied her elbow as she landed. 'We're still in a somewhat basic state at the moment.'

She stepped back into her shoes. Heels had been a bad idea.

Bosch led his guests down a path through piles of debris and mud. 'The complex will, of course, be entirely camouflaged from the air.'

Two soldiers guarded an electronically controlled door. They saluted.

Bosch pulled two cards from his breast pocket. He opened the door with one and handed the other to Helen. 'This is yours.'

Puzzled, she took the card and followed him through the entry.

Inside the building, masked technicians moved from vats and retorts to distilleries and encapsulating machines, checking computer screens and gauges and dials.

Helen gaped. Great God in heaven, this operation was bigger than Forbes'! 'What have you done? Set up your own Sperilac lab?'

'And it's all for you, my dear Helen.' Bosch smiled. 'Would you like to see it?'

She swallowed her shock. Instinct warned her to be careful. 'You don't need *any* of this.'

'Ah, but we do,' Devereux said. 'Within the very near future, the FDA is going to forbid the export of Sperilac to any foreign nation. You'll no longer be able to bring it into Colombia. We'll have to make it on the premises.'

'That's nonsense.'

'Let's step in here, please.' Bosch motioned. 'We need privacy.'

They entered a chamber that was clearly an uncompleted conference room. Half the walls were paneled in mahogany. Half were naked cement. There were no windows. Bare fluorescent fixtures hung from the unfinished ceiling. Ventilators blew in cool air tinged with the smells of plaster and paint.

A large black walnut table dominated the center of the room. Eighteen matching black-cushioned chairs had been placed round it. Except for a telephone and a slide projector, the gleaming tabletop was bare.

'I apologize that the conference room isn't finished, but at least we're in a secure space here.' Bosch directed Helen to the chair at the head of the table. He and Devereux took the seats beside her.

'You were born to sit in that chair,' he said.

Helen bit back rage. This man actually thought he was charming her.

Bosch pushed a button on the telephone. Two Indians brought coffee, cookies and, incongruously, a strudel.

Bosch turned to Devereux. 'Explain our situation.'

Devereux waited until the Indians had left the room and closed the doors behind them.

'As I said,' he began, 'it will soon be a federal offense to dispense, transport, or manufacture Sperilac in the US. All current stocks will be impounded. The FDA will declare the drug toxic.'

Helen was incredulous. 'Am I hearing things?'

'Please,' Miguel Bosch said. 'Let Dev finish.'

Devereux traced a figure in the dust on the walnut table. 'Depending how quickly the government decides to call off the trial, up to fifty per cent of the patients in Phase Three are going to die. It will be discovered that the dead patients have been those taking Sperilac.'

'That's ridiculous!' Helen cried. 'Sperilac is no more deadly than aspirin!'

Devereux smiled. 'The patients aren't going to die from Sperilac.'

In the next instant of silence, Helen understood. 'Don't do this. Don't even think it.'

He ignored her. 'Naturally, we'll use an untraceable agent: succino-choline. Bertolt-Bienvenue manufactured it as an insecticide. In sufficient concentration, it's very effective on human beings as well.'

Helen pushed her chair back. 'Two innocent lives have been lost already, isn't that enough?'

Miguel Bosch arched an eyebrow. 'You consider Harry Forbes and Thelma van Voss *innocent*?'

'All right, maybe they were crooks, but they weren't *killers*! Why do you think I joined with you. To end the dying! And now you want to kill a hundred and fifty *more*?'

'Let's not get over-dramatic,' Devereux suggested. 'One hundred and fifty is the maximum figure. The actual number could be as few as five. Depending how quickly the FDA chooses to become alarmed.'

Helen leapt to her feet. 'Señor Bosch, in the name of heaven, *don't do this!*'

Bosch stared at the tabletop and sighed. 'My dear Ms Weller. We live in the real world. We must face some bitter economic truths. We can amortize our costs in a timely manner only if Sperilac is declared illegal in the United States.'

'Have I lost my mind or have you?'

Bosch smiled. 'We're all quite sane. Dev, why don't you explain the economics?'

Devereux had moved from the table and was dimming the overhead fluorescents. The room sank into a claustrophobic artificial dusk. He returned to his chair and flipped on the projector. A white square glowed on the cement wall. With a click, a chart appeared. Two lines crossed: one red, rising in a smooth curve; the other black, describing an Alpine slide to the lower right-hand corner.

'The red line is our projection of cures if Sperilac goes into general accessible distribution. As you can see, AIDS will become as extinct as smallpox. But the black line shows what happens to the cartel's income if Sperilac is approved for conventional distribution in the United States. We'll be out of business.'

'That's ridiculous,' Helen said.

'Let me clarify,' Devereux said.

Another slide blinked on to the wall.

'AIDS treatments are currently being marketed at a cost to the patient of eight thousand dollars a year. The patient dies after an average of three years – or twenty-four thousand dollars – of therapy. Sperilac, on the other hand, requires only thirty to one hundred and eighty doses to stabilize or cure the patient. Assume the maximum protocol, one hundred and eighty doses. Assume Sperilac passes its Phase Three. The American health industry can maintain present earnings only by recouping twenty-four thousand dollars from every one hundred and eighty tablets of Sperilac. A single tablet of one hundred and fifty milligrams will therefore be priced at a minimum of one hundred and thirty-three dollars. This doesn't factor in additional costs imposed by druggists, bureaucrats, and all the usual health-care piranha lining up at the trough. The price could easily go as high as two hundred dollars.'

Helen drew in a long breath and exhaled. As a scenario in

pharmaceutical greed, it was fantastic but all too familiar, all too credible. She had only to think of the price of cancer therapies, or the two dollars that a three-cent aspirin cost in the average American hospital.

'Fewer than a third of those who need Sperilac will be able to get it. The cartel's pool of customers will thus continue shrinking exponentially.'

Devereux clicked to another chart. A green line arced upwards.

'But if Sperilac is delivered through the cartel, *exclusively*, the cost of manufacturing the drug will be more than offset by the increased life expectancy of the customer pool. Profits will triple within four years.'

'In other words,' Helen said, her voice somber, 'you plan to turn Sperilac into another street drug.'

'A street drug that *heals*.'

'And which you monopolize.'

'Why not, so long as it's available at a price anyone can afford?' Devereux returned the lights to their normal level and shut down the projector. 'Aren't we entitled to some return on our investment?'

'You've made no investment! I stole the drug for you!' Helen's fury surged to the surface, coating her brain like a field of lava. 'The idea was to save *lives* not to maximize profits! You're no better than the drug companies!' She hated the tears that streamed down her cheeks, and it mortified her that Miguel Bosch should see them. But she could no longer control herself. 'You could have had the decency to tell me your intentions at the beginning!'

'Decency?' Bosch gave a low chuckle. 'You wouldn't have joined us. We needed you then. We need you now.'

'I will not participate in this . . .' she struggled for the right word, 'this massacre. It's an affront to God's will.'

'*God*, you say?' Bosch touched Helen's bare arm. 'My poor, dear lady, if there were a God, could there be drug addiction? Could there be AIDS? Could there be a Miguel Bosch?'

She whirled and slapped him across the face.

Silence fell like the blade of a guillotine.

She stared at her hand, astonished, as though it had acted without her will.

'This is hopeless.' Devereux moved toward the door. 'Mike, isn't there another option? Why don't I call someone in here to tidy this up?'

Bosch stroked his cheek, looking at Helen with an expression that was a peculiar combination of sadness and amusement. 'I think we should give this lady some time to reflect on her decision.' He reached into his breast pocket and offered a handkerchief.

Helen turned toward the wall.

'You have one hour to decide,' Bosch said. 'You can remain with us to manage the manufacture of Sperilac. Or you can refuse. But whatever your decision, you will not be leaving here.'

Helen clenched her eyes shut. 'You're going to kill me. Why not come out and say it?'

'I have no desire to kill anyone,' Bosch said. 'But sometimes circumstances force me to hard choices.'

'Señor Bosch.' Helen faced him. 'Eight years ago the media reported that you lost a daughter to AIDS.'

Bosch's face turned white. 'What does Rosa have to do with this?'

'Everything. You established a foundation in your daughter's memory. Last May I sent a letter to that foundation. I knew I was putting an end to my career, but innocent people were dying and I had faith in your humanity as a father.'

Bosch nodded. 'It was a wise and beautiful letter. You told me about Sperilac. You said it was being blocked. You suggested we join forces.'

'And you invited me to your yacht.'

'I still remember that evening.' Bosch smiled. 'You were wearing unattractive eyeglasses, but you had the fire and vision of a goddess. Have you forgotten? You spoke of willingness to take great risks.'

'I *have* taken great risks.'

'And now you must decide whether you dare to take the greatest risk of all.'

Mike Bosch opened the door of the conference room. As he and Devereux stepped out, Helen turned her head and saw two guards with automatic weapons standing in the corridor.

'One hour,' Bosch said.

The door closed and Helen heard a bolt slam shut on the other side.

April 21

A t 9:07 a.m. Eddie was in the shower. At 9:08, naturally, the phone rang. His soap-slicked hand caught it on the fifth ring. 'Hello?'

'Wow. Practice makes perfect. I knew I'd catch you in if I kept trying.'

'Amy. Hi.' Guilt stirred.

'Did you get my messages?'

'Thanks. Yeah. I got them. I've been meaning to call, but I've been getting in late from work and I didn't want to wake you.'

'Don't worry about waking me, I don't sleep much when you're not here. You know me, never happy unless I'm worrying. I figured you must be busy or I'd have heard from you.'

'Yeah, it's going OK, I've got some leads.'

'It's been a week, I'm not surprised. When do you think you'll be coming home?'

'Hard to say. I'll let you know. How are things down there?'

'The pool filter clogged. A lizard got in. It's OK now. The girls missed you at bridge. I miss you.'

'I miss you too, honey. I can't say much on the phone, but I'll be in touch, OK?'

'I love you.'

'Same here.'

He had stepped back into the shower and gotten the hot water just right when the phone rang again. He grabbed a towel and made another sloppy dash.

'Sleeping late?' He recognized the voice of his hacker friend Mark Burgess.

'Nothing so exciting.'

'Thought you'd want to know. There was another call from the Forbes house to that payphone. Three minutes ago.'

In the heat waves rippling up off Virginia Avenue, the John F. Kennedy Center had all the glamor of a giant cement packing crate. Up on the second floor the boys and girls of the Ballet Folklorico were at it early, doing their careening, out-of-control thing.

Eddie ambled into the men's room, saw he had the place to

125

himself, and removed the micro-cassette under the sink.

Sitting in his rented blue Chevy Caprice, he played the tape. A fine mist of white noise spooled out of the speaker. He fast-forwarded and tried again. More mist.

He realized he'd goofed. It was a dud tape, one of the repackaged jobs that swindlers sell as new, with too little metal left on the strip to magnetize. He felt like smacking himself on the side of the head. He was an idiot not to have checked the tape before he used it.

He wasn't going to make the same mistake twice.

He slipped a new tape into the player and tested, 'One two three, how's it sound?' and when he pressed *replay* his voice came back, clear and irritable.

He returned to the men's room. He had to wash his hands for seven minutes before he was alone. And then he inserted the new micro-cassette.

Helen glanced at her watch. Her heart thumped painfully against her ribs when she saw that the hour was nearly up.

The conference room possessed the stillness found only in houses that have never been lived in. Behind her an air-conditioner labored softly. Somewhere in the distance she could hear the faint barking of a dog.

The first stirrings of panic beat in her blood. Not because she faced death – that was the least of her fears. Nor because she dreaded pain – to endure undeserved agony was to know Christ more nearly.

But with all her heart she believed God had brought her to this place to use as His willing servant. Yet after an hour's pacing and worrying, she still could not see what He wanted of her.

So Helen did the only thing she could. She dropped to her knees.

Dear Lord, accept the gift of myself, what I am, where I am, who I am. I can offer you no more. I am an imperfect vessel for your grace, but I plead with you to make me an instrument of hope to those forgotten and unloved souls who are dying of this plague.

Something was missing. Helen lifted her head and tried to clear her brain, to open her spirit.

Perspiration poured down her face. A hot wind blew under the door along the floorboards. An insect buzzed and clicked against the ceiling over her head. There was a scrambling noise in the wall, as though a jungle creature had wandered in and couldn't find its way out again.

Oh Heavenly Father, I am frightened of Miguel Bosch. I fear that I may fail you because I do not see what it is you require of me. Yet, in your wisdom you have put me at this man's mercy. He, too, is your child, and for all his sins, an object of your love and compassion. I pray for him. I pray for those who are in his service, that they may know your power, your light, your mercy and your goodness.

As she formed these words in her mind, Helen felt the lightning flash of a thought that was not her own: you are beautiful. Use your beauty to make my world beautiful.

Nothing could have startled her more. Never had she thought of herself as a beautiful woman, merely as presentable or at best distinctive.

She had asked for no sign, yet as she heard the bolt on the door slide back, a lightness seemed to lift her. In absolute peace and assurance, ready for any demand the Lord might make of her, she stood.

The door opened and Miguel Bosch entered the conference room. 'Have you said your prayers?' he asked, irony thick in his voice.

Helen now recognized him as part of God's plan, and she discovered in her heart a place for this man. Perhaps he would kill her. Perhaps not. It did not matter. She was where God had brought her.

'Yes. I've prayed.'

'And what did you pray for?'

'I prayed for you.'

They contemplated each other a long moment in silence.

'You broke a cross necklace on my boat.' Bosch's eyes were sly. 'Do you remember I said I'd have it fixed for you?'

'Of course. I remember all your promises.'

'I'm terribly sorry.' He reached into his breast pocket and drew out an oblong black velvet box. 'It was quite past repair. I had to replace it. Please accept this as a token of my gratitude for all that you have done, and a pledge of my hopes for our future collaborations.'

Helen took the box and opened it. Inside lay a diamond-encrusted crucifix on a choker of matched pearls. Large emeralds marked the five points of Christ's wounds.

She could not imagine its value. She wondered if he had burgled the Hermitage for it.

'Please.' Bosch's voice was insistent, pressing. 'Accept this gift.'

Helen let her fingers touch the pearls, the diamonds, the emeralds. They were cold, like theorems waiting to be warmed by a human pulse. As she lifted them they flashed a sparkle into the gray smoke of Miguel Bosch's sunglasses.

127

She stared into those glasses. In her mind she saw a corridor lined by doors, some opening with shining opportunity, others slamming with darkest loss.

'I accept.'

'Sorry to drag you to Georgetown,' Lucinda Forbes apologized.

'No trouble,' Sharon said. In fact it was a damned nuisance, but Lucinda had sounded almost crazed on the phone.

'I've spent the last two hours round the corner at the Colombian Embassy. The Ambassador says – strictly off the record – that the town where Helen sent the Sperilac is a drug cartel stronghold.'

They were sitting at a corner table in a small French restaurant. Sunlight fell through the iron grillwork of the window on to roses in a crystal vase.

'Helen sent the Sperilac to a *hospital* in Gurana,' Sharon said.

'The Ambassador says that hospital is a suspected coke-processing plant.'

To Sharon it sounded like CIA disinformation. 'What on earth would the coke cartel want with Sperilac?'

'Plenty. They're into drugs and Helen Weller's in with them.'

'I find that awfully hard to believe.'

'Of course it's hard to believe. Helen spent twenty years deceiving us. Look at this.' Lucinda pushed aside a salad plate and slapped documents down on to the table. 'Two faxes asking FDA permission to export nine hundred thousand bottles of Sperilac. No one authorized those requests. Yet she implies she's acting for Harry. And for me. And look at these shipping orders.' More documents snapped down. 'She didn't send nine hundred thousand, she sent one million eight hundred thousand – two times. Why did she lie? Because a million or more in a nine-month period would have required an export licence, which would have required a review, which would have scuttled her whole plan.'

Sharon felt something she couldn't put a name to. Common sense told her Lucinda's data were probably sound, but instinct told her they were also incomplete. 'All right. Maybe Helen did everything you say.'

'There's no maybe to it.'

'But she didn't do it for money. She didn't do it for herself.'

Lucinda's scowl tightened. 'At this point I frankly don't see that the why of it makes one iota of difference.'

'It makes all the difference in the world. The reason Helen Weller sent those three million bottles to Colombia – '

'Three and a half million.'

' – is the same reason I smuggled a dozen bottles a week to Andy Horner's clinic. People were dying. A cure existed and no one was getting it. Helen did what she did because the situation struck her as evil.'

'Evil?' Lucinda seemed to ponder. 'Do you mean she discussed this with you?'

'Of course she didn't. But I know her, and if she did something this desperate it was because she wanted to send Sperilac where it would save lives.'

'And so she sent all those pills to one teeny hospital in the middle of Timbuktu?'

Sharon shrugged. 'Love has led a lot of people astray.'

Lucinda took another swallow of champagne, leaned back in her chair, and blew out air. 'You call it *love*?'

How do you explain to a person like Lucinda Forbes that love is a spectrum, that it encompasses everything from passion shared with a spouse to a touch on a child's hand to a dime dropped into a beggar's cup? How do you explain that any thought or deed that links us caringly to another human being is blessed?

'If I ever get to heaven,' Sharon said, 'and Helen Weller isn't there, I'm going to picket.'

'Then you've got your work cut out for you. And so has Forbes Biochemtech. Thanks to Helen Weller, we've lied to the FDA – twice. We've violated federal export regulations – twice. And traded with known international felons – twice. Forget the financial damage she's done the company, the *legal* damage alone could destroy us. If the government knew, they'd shut us down tomorrow.'

'Then it all depends how carefully the regulators check the June audit.'

'Hopefully none of this will show up in the June audit.'

'But the records—'

'The records have been modified.'

Sharon understood. 'Then what's the problem?'

'The problem is you and your father. You know everything.'

For an instant Sharon couldn't speak. 'That's ridiculous. My father's not going to tell the government; neither am I.'

'And you're not going to tell Vestcate either. Neither one of you. In fact you're not going to tell *anyone*.'

'Are you asking us to lie?'

'I'm *telling* you to lie. Or keep your mouths shut. Whichever comes more naturally. Because one word could sink Sperilac for good. And I don't think you or your father would want that.'

Wordlessly, Sharon gathered up her purse.

Lucinda touched her wrist. 'And Sharon, it goes without saying, if Helen contacts you, you *will* for all our sakes let me know immediately.'

At four in the afternoon, Sondra Cass sneaked out of the house in Kalorama to get her blood work done at the New Day Clinic.

The nurse drew her blood, Band-Aided the puncture, and handed her a pill.

Sondra studied the gel capsule, a smooth dove-gray in the creased pink of her palm. 'Wonder if this is the real thing.'

'You'll know in six months.' The nurse handed her a Dixie cup of water and watched to make sure she swallowed. As though Sondra might hide the pill in her cheek and spit it out later and sell it to a dealer, the way some of the methadone patients did.

'How've you been feeling since the Phase Three trial began?'

'Me?' Sondra shrugged. 'Fine.'

The nurse made a check on a printed form. 'Any dizziness, rashes, nausea, headache, or other side effects?'

Sondra shook her head.

'Are you still taking your hypertension medication?'

What do I look like, Sondra wondered, an idiot who'd skip the medicine that keeps her alive? She smiled. 'Yes, ma'am.'

'You're not taking any other medications or recreational drugs?'

What's this white bitch thinking, all black women shoot skag? 'No, ma'am. Not me. Clean and dry seven years.'

'Way to go, Sondra. See you tomorrow.'

'Yes, ma'am.'

Sondra hurried past apathetic faces in the waiting area and pushed through the revolving door into the afternoon sunlight.

'Hey, grandma.' A mean-looking one-legged Latino approached her. He moved faster on those crutches than most runners on two legs.

'You talking to me?'

'Sure am.' He had a cross-stitched scar on his neck and barely healed needle tracks on his arms. 'You got any meth to sell?'

Sondra didn't know which made her want to laugh more, the notion that she was taking methadone or the notion that she'd sell it. 'Sorry.'

'I'm paying six dollars.' He smiled and two steel teeth glinted. 'More than you'll get on Thirteenth Street.'

Sondra recognized those teeth. She'd seen this kid in the clinic, sitting in the waiting room. 'I've seen you. You're in the maintenance program.'

'Oh yeah? So report me.'

'With all the troubles you got, why you want to be dealing dope?'

Sondra raised her arm and signaled a passing taxi. As she climbed into the rear seat, the end of a crutch smashed against the door.

'*Cabrona tortillera!* Go screw yourself!'

By the time the taxi got Sondra back to Kalorama, the house was in an uproar.

'Why, if it isn't Sondra Cass.' Fiona McFadden DuPont Pullman, America's former Ambassador to Austria, stood in the kitchen door slathered in face cream, her hair in curlers and a chiffon snood. 'How kind of you to get your fat African ass back to work.'

Uh oh. This promised to be one of Miss Fiona's more spectacular public breakdowns. Sondra felt a tightness in the region of her heart. Mustn't get excited, she reminded herself.

'Do I or do I not,' Miss Fiona shrieked, 'pay you seven hundred dollars a week plus social security?'

'You do, ma'am.' Sondra wasn't sure about the social security. She took it on faith that it would be there when her hypertension finally forced her into retirement.

'Then can you please get these lunatics under control, or am I going to have to call nine one one?'

The fourteen cooks, flown in, charter, from Vienna, didn't look like lunatics to Sondra. They stood serenely chopping, stirring, slicing, and stuffing.

'Not them,' Fiona Pullman cried. 'The *waiters*!'

In less than an hour and a half Fiona Pullman was giving a reception for Austria's Ambassador to the United States. The Vice President and his wife Trixie were expected. Fourteen senators, eighteen ambassadors, sixty-five members of the House, and assorted honchos from the White House and other, larger homes in Washington and surrounding suburbs had all sent their acceptances.

'I'm comin', honey.' Sondra eased past a pastry chef decorating a tray of profiteroles. 'Hold your horses.'

The two women embraced. Although they were miles apart in what the world would call social station, they had much in common: too many husbands, a taste for disastrous lovers, and an inexplicable love for each other. Sondra Cass and Fiona Pullman had shared gossip, residences, and troubles for eighteen years, and one little rotten reception wasn't going to tear them asunder.

'Sondra, I am going to kill, murder and slay Bertolt Devereux. Come out here and see what his little amigos have done to the buffet table. The forks are where the knives should be, the napkins have disappeared, and I think they've pocketed all the spoons.'

'Baby,' Sondra reminded, 'I told you not to let Mr Devereux hire our extra help for tonight. So what if he's a good dancer, so what if he runs Bertolt-Bienvenue Pharmaceuticals; doesn't mean he can run a kitchen. And just because he keeps asking you to marry him, doesn't mean he knows where to find decent waiters for a *real* party. He's just a powder puff in wingtips.'

Fiona groaned. 'I'm still greased up like a pig, my hair is a shambles, and I've got a seamstress upstairs sewing on my dress.' Her crisp British inflections negated two decades' attempts to cross the Atlantic. 'Sondra darling, could you, *would* you get these South American revolutionaries into some semblance of order and, *please*, do something about that table? Let's at least get the forks, knives and spoons out where they can be found.'

'I'll handle it, honey.'

Shaking her head, Fiona Pullman shoved her way through clusters of idle Hispanics in white jackets and swooped up the staircase.

Sondra squared her shoulders and marched into the dining room. 'All right, you no-good wetbacks,' she shouted. 'Listen up! We got a party to give, and I'm gonna give a party or report every blessed one of you to the Immigration Department!'

April 21

Shortly after five, Sharon reviewed her records and saw that for the second day running Lou Kmiotek had failed to show up at the clinic. She phoned his number.

Again there was no answer.

As she set the phone back in the cradle, it rang.

'Sharon Powell, may I help you?'

'It's Lucinda. Lucinda Forbes.' Sounding furious. 'I don't suppose you've spoken to your pal Andy Horner?'

'Not since last week.'

'I just had a call from his lawyers. Do you know what that imbecile's doing? He's suing to block the Phase Three trials.'

For a moment Sharon was too stunned to answer. Clicks and buzzes and ghost conversations seemed to crowd in on the line.

'Are you there?' Lucinda said.

'I can't believe it. What are his grounds?'

'Anti-gay discrimination, if you please. As if there weren't any gays at New Day.'

'I don't know. Maybe there aren't.'

'I hope you have some influence with Mr Horner.'

'At this point I frankly doubt it.'

'Get some. Because I'm counting on you to persuade him to drop that suit.'

'I'll do my best, but—'

'Because if *anything* interferes with these trials, your two asses will be in federal prison for theft of Sperilac. And I'll see you get the max. Am I clear?'

'Crystal.'

The phone slammed down.

Sharon dialed the Harvey Milk Clinic. A woman answered.

'Could I speak with Andy Horner, please? This is Sharon Powell.'

'I'm sorry, Andy just left for the day.'

Premonition flickered through Sharon like the shadow of a diving condor. Harry Forbes blocked Sperilac. Thelma van Voss blocked Sperilac. And now Andy . . .

She ran to her car and tore out of the parking lot. At the first intersection she tried to veer round a truck. Her right wheel struck a parked jeep.

The truck driver leaned on his horn and shouted, 'Die at home, will ya? You're blockin' traffic!'

A block from Andy's house she saw his green Toyota. She honked and waved but he didn't look in her direction.

By the time she reached the driveway he was stepping through the front door with a bag of groceries.

'Andy!' she screamed.

The door slammed shut.

She ran across the lawn.

What happened next was so sudden that her mind had no time to process it. She heard a deep *whoomf* and felt it at the same time. The sound picked her up like a wave of surf and flung her to the ground.

There was a crackling and shattering of glass. A hailstorm of broken panes rained down on her bare arms and the windows of Andy's house thrust out beating wings of smoke. Roof shingles and splintered beams blew into the air.

'Andy!' She pulled herself back to her feet and ran screaming toward the conflagration. 'My God, Andy!'

The kitchen wall fell back on to the lawn. Smoke thundered up and a sheet of roaring flame bisected the sky.

Horns blaring, sirens yowling, three city fire rigs came screaming west. They took the turn swaying and careened on to Andy's lawn.

Yellow-slickered firemen leapt down and attacked the inferno with hoses and axes. Ambulances and cop cars piled up in the street. A crowd gathered. Cops pushed them back.

Sharon waited, shell-shocked and coughing, beyond the police barriers. The air crackled with flying embers and blazing wood fragments and radio feedback. An oily smokescreen fanned out low over the street.

She saw two firemen lurch out of the smog. They were carrying a black body bag on a stretcher. She stumbled past the barrier.

'Excuse me. Sir.' She had to shout. 'Andy Horner was a personal friend of mine.'

One of the firemen shook his head. 'I'm afraid you wouldn't recognize what's left.'

They pushed the stretcher up into an ambulance.

'What caused the explosion? Do you have any idea?'

'Could be he forgot to clean the filter in his hot water heater.' The fireman wiped grime from his eyes. 'Sediment could've clogged the line, boiler overheated and exploded. Happens more often than you think. Or it could've been something else.' He shrugged. 'Bomb squad's looking into it.'

Fiona Pullman glided through the rooms of her mansion, resplendent in a dead archduchess's amethyst choker and a black lamé cocktail dress that was, by her own appraisal, a knockout.

'Fiona, absolutely stunning.' The director of the National Gallery planted a kiss on her cheek.

'Thanks, Brad.' She squeezed his arm. 'Do be an angel and say hi to Rosemary Carter, she's looking lonely over there.'

Fiona surveyed the mobbed, giddily celebratory living room. So far one senator had fallen down, whether because of senility or over-indulgence was anybody's guess. The Vice President's wife had spilled her plate of food only once, perhaps a record. The Austrian Ambassador, who had thoughtfully made a pass at every woman over fifty, was now working on Janet Reno.

Fiona felt a glow of satisfaction. After all the hassle and panic and madness, the party was a success.

'Madam Ambassador.'

A hand touched her elbow. She recognized the Brazilian surgeon who'd done her face-lift and the First Lady's.

'Yes, Doctor . . . uh, doctor.' She smiled.

'I think your presence is required in the kitchen.'

Across the sea of chattering coiffures, Fiona spotted the Ambassador from Turkey. Now *there* was a real raconteur, a scandal factory! She began to move ever so smoothly away from the dour-faced surgeon. 'I'm sure my housekeeper has everything under control.'

The hand on her elbow tightened. 'Forgive me, Madam Ambassador, but the problem *is* your housekeeper.'

Fiona slammed her champagne flute on to a passing tray and angled her way through her guests into the kitchen. A circle of rented waiters and their assistants stood gawking at something on the floor by the refrigerator. Low, fearful voices buzzed in Spanish.

Fiona felt a stab of panic: what had they done now? Dropped the *mousse au cassis*?

She pushed aside starched white jackets and strode to the scene of the disaster. She looked down and froze.

Sondra Cass lay splayed on the linoleum, tongue bulging from her face. eyes staring in terror as if they'd seen a giant rat scuttling across the ceiling.

'You stubborn old *ox*!' Fiona threw herself beside the unconscious body. 'Didn't I *tell* you to take your hypertension medicine?'

She instantly regretted the outburst. Redirecting her rage, she windmilled her arms.

'Clear a space, you idiots. Can't you see she needs air?'

In a softer, gentler tone she cooed reassurance: 'It's all right, darling, you just relax.' She slapped Sondra's cheeks, rubbed Sondra's wrists, pressed her ear to Sondra's bosom and listened for the heartbeat.

And heard only silence.

In that instant she knew her truest friend had left her forever.

Fiona McFadden DuPont Pullman threw back her head and released a howl of grief and fury. It was a scream so loud that five rooms away, in the study where Van Gogh's 'Lilacs' hung, the prisms in the chandelier tinkled in sympathy.

By the time Sharon reached the nursing home, her father was glowering at the late night news. Reflections of speeding cop cars and jabbering news anchors flickered in the lenses of his eyeglasses.

She rapped lightly on the open door. 'Sorry to bother you. Can I come in?'

He muted the sound. YOU LOOK LIKE THE ONE WHO'S BOTHERED. WHAT'S THE MATTER?

'I need to talk. I guess I need your advice.'

GLAD TO OBLIGE. HAVE A SEAT.

She pulled up his old wood chair with the MIT insignia.

In a quiet voice that sometimes trembled, she told her father about the man from Aetna Life, about the questions he'd asked and the evidence he'd presented.

WHAT EVIDENCE?

'The day that Harry Forbes died, and the day Thelma van Voss died, a few hours before it happened . . .' Her thought wriggled away and she felt a *whoomf* go through her.

HELLO, ARE YOU THERE?

'Before they died, there were phone calls from Lucinda Forbes' house, to the Kennedy Center.'

WHO IN THE KENNEDY CENTER?

'A payphone.' It had sounded so damning when he'd said it, and it sounded so damned inconclusive when she said it now.

136

THE SAME PAYPHONE BOTH TIMES?

She nodded. 'And right *after* they died, someone made calls from payphones near where they died – to the Forbes house.'

Her father gazed at her and seemed to chew that one over a while. His hand returned to the keyboard.

IS THAT ALL, OR IS THERE MORE?

'Today . . .' She sat absolutely still, blinking back tears. 'Today Andy's lawyers told Lucinda he was going to sue to stop the trials. I thought of what happened to Forbes and van Voss, and I went to warn him to be careful, and . . .'

A moment passed before she could go on.

'His house blew up.'

Her father looked at her, unsurprised, and she tried to recall how many years it had been since she'd last seen surprise or shock or fear in those eyes.

'They brought Andy out in a bag. He's . . .'

I'M VERY VERY SORRY.

'He was one of my best friends.'

I KNOW. NOW DON'T GET MORE UPSET THAN YOU NEED TO.

Her father wheeled unsteadily to the door and closed it and wheeled back.

PHARMACEUTICALS ARE A BILLION-DOLLAR INDUSTRY. THE STAKES ARE HIGH. PEOPLE WILL DO A LOT OF THINGS TO GET AN EDGE. I FRANKLY DOUBT MANY WILL GO SO FAR AS MURDER, BUT THEY'LL ALL SURE AS HELL LIE.

'I'm sorry, Dad. I'm not following.'

HOW DO WE KNOW THIS MAN FROM AETNA IS REALLY FROM AETNA? HOW DO WE KNOW WHO HE IS? WERE THOSE PHONE CALLS REALLY MADE? ALL YOU HAVE IS HIS WORD.

'Why would he lie to me?'

I'M ONLY GUESSING, BUT I CAN THINK OF REASONS. HE COULD WANT TO SET YOU SQUABBLING WITH LUCINDA AND ACCUSING HER.

'Why?'

AS A WAY OF DERAILING THE PHASE THREE TRIAL.

Sharon stared at him. 'Why?'

BECAUSE MAYBE HE'S BEING PAID BY THE OPPOSITION. A LOT OF PHARMACEUTICAL GIANTS WILL LOSE BIG IF SPERILAC EVER COMES TO MARKET.

'It seems – complicated.'

NOT AS COMPLICATED AS LUCINDA FORBES KILLING EVERYONE WHO OPENS THEIR MOUTH AGAINST SPERILAC. SHE'D BE SHOOTING HER OWN FOOT OFF. LUCINDA'S A DREADFUL WOMAN. BUT NOT A DUMB ONE.

'Her husband tripled his insurance before he died. She was sole beneficiary.'

HOW DO YOU KNOW? THE POLICE ARE SATISFIED THE DEATHS WERE ACCIDENTS. UNLESS YOUR MAN FROM AETNA HAS SOME PRETTY COMPELLING PROOF OTHERWISE, I'D TRUST THE COPS. AND GO GET A GOOD NIGHT'S SLEEP.

Shortly before midnight, Eddie and Larry Lorenzo sat in a Korean strippers' bar at the raunchy end of New York Avenue, trying to hear one another over the amplified Oriental hoochie-kooch music that bing-bonged from ceiling speakers.

'Vestcate is clean,' Larry said. 'Swiss corporation, chartered in Zurich. They don't deal with any banks in Miami or Cayman or Liechtenstein. I found zero links to the drug cartel or any money-laundering outfit – and believe me, I looked.'

Larry claimed they needed noisy meeting places in case anyone tried to record their conversations. But watching the way he belted back his fifth beer and sake, Eddie had to wonder if he didn't have other reasons too, like trouble with his wife or a fondness for getting stinko.

'What about San Miguel and hospitals?' Eddie said. 'Did you find any?'

'San Miguel de Bayamo is affiliated with two hospitals. One's in Medellin; it's seventy-five years old. They're rebuilding.'

Eddie was thoughtful. 'When I was on my last South American tour, Mike Bosch was processing his coke at a lab four miles north of Medellin. It pretended to be a hospital. The Colombian army blew that hospital off the map.'

'I remember.' Larry nodded somberly. 'It almost brought down the government.'

'It's the same hospital, isn't it?'

Larry shook his head. 'My information doesn't go that far.'

'Come on, Larry, you know it's the same.'

'If you know so damned much about what I know, how come you need to ask me?'

Larry seemed more than a little drunk, and Eddie wasn't about to argue the point.

'Where's the other hospital?'

'The other's in Gurana.'

'Gurana?' Eddie was incredulous.

'For that part of the world, it's considered state-of-the-art.'

'You need a magnifying glass to see Gurana on the map. What the hell is a hamlet in the jungle doing with a state-of-the-art hospital?'

'Maybe Gurana's growing.'

'Or maybe something's growing in Gurana. Where did Mike Bosch relocate after you blasted him out of Medellin?'

'Damn it, Eddie, what makes you think I'd have access to that kind of information in an ongoing investigation?'

'In other words, he moved the works to Gurana.'

'We don't know for sure.'

'Don't give me that, Larry. If your spy satellites can tell a dime on the pavement from a penny, they can tell the difference between a magnetic resonance imager and a coke factory.'

'All we have is raw data.'

'Give it to me raw then.'

'One informant says Bosch went a mile deeper into the jungle. Another says he pulled up stakes eleven months ago and moved the whole operation.'

'Where to?'

'Paraibo, northern Peru.'

'I doubt it very much. Bosch doesn't own enough of Peru. He moved his headquarters to Gurana.'

'You don't know that, Eddie.'

On a stage three feet from their table, a doll-faced teenaged girl with shaved pubes slowly stripped down to a dime-sized bikini. Pink-gelled follow spots thrust through layered cigarette smoke and tweaked her tiny bare nipples.

'Is drug money backing the Ballet Folklorico in Uruguay?' Eddie asked.

Larry focused bleary eyes. 'Backing who?'

'The Ballet Folklorico. Over at the Kennedy Center. The opera house attraction.'

'Drug money does not, as a rule, back cultural events.'

Eddie nodded toward the girl. She was stepping out of her bikini. Beneath her glaze of smack and coke, he could see she was terrified.

'Don't tell me drug money isn't backing *this* cultural event.'

The girl swung the bikini over her head and let it fly. Customers cheered and stamped.

'See if you can find out who's paying for the Folklorico.'

Larry didn't take his eyes off the girl. 'Come again?'

'Find out who's paying to bring the Ballet Folklorico de Uruguay to Kennedy Center.'

April 22

At 9:12 Eddie left a clean, pre-tested micro-cassette under the men's room sink and took yesterday's cassette down to his car. Driving along L Street, he listened to the catch.

The calls were mostly outgoing, mostly disappointing: shouted orders for deli take-out, screaming phone-ins to answering services. Stamping feet and tico-tico piano in the background.

But then there was an incoming call in Spanish.

'*Fernando?*'

'*Momentito.*'

'*Ola – Fernando le escucha.*'

'*Flores para Sondra Cass.*' The voice spelled the name.

Later, another call came in Spanish.

'*Fernando?*'

'*Momentito.*'

'*Ola – Fernando le escucha.*'

'*Flores para Andy Horner.*' Again, the voice spelled the name, and this time also gave an address.

Eddie double-parked at a payphone on M Street and called his pal Lieutenant Sam Schuyler over at District Police.

'Sam, what can you tell me about a guy called Andy Horner, address two oh oh three River Street? Ten to one he died yesterday.'

'Sharon Powell. May I help you?'

'Yes, Miss Powell. This is Edward Arbogast again of Aetna Life.'

Silence.

'Remember when we first spoke, I told you calls were made from the Forbes home to a Kennedy Center payphone just before Harry Forbes and Thelma van Voss were killed? Yesterday there were two more calls from the Forbes house to that phone. The messages were, "Flowers for Sondra Cass" and "Flowers for Andy Horner". I don't know who Sondra Cass is, but I have a hunch you do. And after last night's TV news. I think we can both figure out what "flowers for Andy Horner" means. I take it he was somehow involved with Sperilac?'

Silence.

'You may not realize who you're involved with – or maybe you're beginning to. There's no reason for them to treat you any better than they did Forbes or van Voss or Horner. You're in trouble, Miss Powell. I can help you – and you can help me. Think about it. My number's five five five, one five eight nine.'

'Mr Arbogast.' Sharon Powell's voice burnt with white-hot indignation. 'I'm going to tell you exactly what I think of you and your tactics. Your opportunism, your readiness to exploit human tragedy for your own money-grubbing ends, are beyond belief. And I want nothing to do with you.'

Sharon slammed down the receiver and resolved to put Mr Arbogast and his alarmist insinuations out of her mind.

And found she couldn't do it.

So she phoned the local Aetna office and asked to speak to Edward Arbogast's supervisor. A lady in Personnel said that no one by that name was employed in the District office.

'Then could you tell me where his home office is?'

'This is with reference to . . . ?'

'He's been harassing me.'

'I'm very sorry to hear that, ma'am. One moment please.' There was a click, followed by a hundred bars or so of an elevator music arrangement of 'My Funny Valentine', and then the voice was back. 'No Edward Arbogast is employed at any Aetna office in the United States or Puerto Rico.'

'You're sure?'

'I'm positive, ma'am. I just checked our national personnel roster. Possibly he's employed in France or Spain?'

'No, he's definitely here in the United States.'

'Then he's misrepresenting himself as an Aetna employee.'

'Thank you.'

Sharon hung up and sat wondering. If Arbogast doesn't work for Aetna, then what the hell is he after? And why on earth does he think he can get it from me?

But she had more pressing problems than reading the mind of a conniving con man. Such as a complete review of blood stats to date.

She saw that Lou Kmiotek was still a no-show – three days running. And today another trial member had failed to come in for blood work and medication – trial participant number 73, Sondra Cass.

She phoned Lou Kmiotek's home number.

Ten rings. Still no answer, still no answering machine.

She phoned Sondra Cass's number. As she dialed, the thought popped into her head, how did Arbogast get hold of Sondra Cass's name?

A machine picked up. 'Hi. This is Sondra.' A warm, maternal voice. 'I can't come to the phone right now but I sure do want to hear from you. At the sound of the beep please leave your name, phone number, and any brief message. I'll return your call as soon as possible. Peace be with you.'

A wobbling, up-and-down car alarm type of beep.

'Miss Cass, this is Sharon Powell at New Day. I noticed you missed your appointment today. If there's any problem, could you contact me?'

She left her number.

Sharon drove at a crawl past the ruin of Andy Horner's house. A six-foot wood fence had been erected and plastered with red-letter warnings: KEEP OUT ORDER OF DC FIRE DEPT. She parked three blocks away, took the flashlight from the car trunk, and walked back through slow drizzling rain.

The fence was a crude quick job: wood posts had been sunk into the ashes of Andy's lawn and two-by-four crossbeams slapped across. Planks and plywood had been hammered on with thick-headed nails. Big Mac wrappers and Coke cans testified that sightseers had already started coming by.

Sharon stepped round a row of scorched dogwood and searched the fence for an opening. Halfway down the driveway, out of sight of the street, she found a three-inch gap. She worked both hands into it and tugged.

At first the plank refused to budge. She braced her knees against the fence and sucked in a deep breath and pulled with all the power she could muster.

Black dots swirled in front of her eyes. Gradually, with excruciating slowness, the plank began to yield. The nails suddenly let out a tortured-cat squeal and the plank popped loose.

She caught herself before she fell back. Laying the plank on the ground, she realized she had a splinter in the heel of her palm.

Can't be helped.

Now, with more room to maneuver, she was able to get both arms round the next plank. In three minutes she wrestled it loose and had an opening large enough to squeeze through.

This dress will be a rag. Oh well.

A stench of wet ashes and chemical fire extinguisher hovered. She waved her hand in front of her face, clearing the air of particles.

She shone her flashlight through the gaping kitchen wall. The sink, suspended by its pipes, had survived. The refrigerator stood on a narrow ledge of floor. Beside it the dishwasher door had twisted like the open mouth of a scream. There was a plate inside, unharmed.

Through a criss-cross of fallen beams she could see a pit where the kitchen floor stopped.

She looked up to make sure there was no roof left to fall down on her. Nothing but particles of ash floating in an evening sky.

She leaned into the broken wall and aimed the flashlight down. A charred skeleton of a staircase descended to a concrete basement. She played the beam beneath what had been stairs. A shape rose in the midst of the rubble. A cylinder of blackened steel.

The hot water tank. Intact.

Her heart gave a thump against her ribs. If Andy's boiler is still standing there, how could it have caused the explosion?

Something creaked behind her. She turned.

'Hey.' A scowling man in a DC patrolman's uniform was watching her through the fence. 'You ripped this board off?'

'The owner was a friend of mine.'

'Would you come over here, please.'

She climbed back over fallen timbers. 'I was looking for some remembrance I could keep.'

'Can I see some ID, please.'

She stepped through the opening and handed him her wallet.

He studied it a moment and handed it back. 'You should be a little more careful, Ms Powell. That fence was put up for a reason. People get hurt prowling around explosion sites.'

The drizzle had stopped, leaving the overcast evening ten degrees warmer than before. Eddie and Larry Lorenzo and two thousand families with kids strolled past the bear enclosure at the National Zoo. Eddie found it hard to believe that just last week one of these cuddly lumbering beasts had had a homeless woman for dinner.

'Let's hit the birds.' Larry seemed antsy about something. The crowd maybe. 'Birds make more of a racket. It's easier to talk there.'

The Brazilian *Papagalli amarilli* were shrieking.

'Who's backing the Ballet Folklorico?' Eddie said.

'There are three backers,' Larry said. 'The US government, the Inter-American Fund of the Rockefeller Foundation, and the Friends of San Miguel de Bayamo.'

Ah ha. 'Tell me about these friends.'

'It's a *sociedad anonima* chartered in the Cayman Islands.'

'Fascinating. A humble little Colombian church bankrolls ballet and has a fund-raising arm incorporated in the hot-money haven of the western hemisphere.'

Larry stared into a cage. Creatures the color of fire and jade preened on a trapeze bar. 'You like these parrots?'

'They beat the strippers in that joint last night.'

'Say, are you irritated about something?'

'I'm irritated about Mike Bosch. He blew up the home of a young doctor last night. The doctor happened to be inside.'

'Where was this?'

'On a quiet residential street eight miles from DEA headquarters.'

'If Bosch was involved, it's funny I didn't hear about it.'

'I suppose funnier things have happened.' Eddie drew in a breath, let it out, and strolled on to the peacock cage. 'I wonder where Mike Bosch is right now, this moment. That hospital in Gurana? Buenos Aires? New York? Paris? The District?'

Larry shook his head. 'He's not here.'

'How do you know he's not?'

'Believe me, I'd know if he was.'

Eddie smiled. 'But would you tell me?'

'What makes you think I wouldn't?'

'Maybe you don't trust me. Or maybe you don't want me to nail Bosch. You could be saving him for yourself.'

'You're right about one thing. The way you're seeing Bosch under every toadstool, I'd have to be crazy to trust you. You're losing it, Eddie. But do I have a choice?' Larry glanced at his watch. 'I gotta run. Promised my wife I'd be home. It's my kid's birthday.'

'Congratulations to the kid. How are you celebrating?'

'We're going to the new Disney movie.'

Eddie waved. 'Enjoy.'

That night Eddie bought a balcony seat to the Ballet Folklorico. There must have been over three thousand parents and kids in the Kennedy Center, going bananas over every acrobat and juggler and dancing jaguar that spun across the stage.

145

When the lights came up in the intermission, Eddie bought the souvenir program and found the names and photos of all 120 members of the troupe. He returned to his seat and started with Adelaide Azulano and worked his way straight through the alphabet to Gregorio Zapata.

There were three Hernandos in the troupe, and two Armandos, but there was only one Fernando.

His last name was de Larra, and in his photo he had a hawk nose and a widow's peak and gleaming black eyes that made him look like a comic-book Spanish inquisitor. According to the program he danced the part of Sacred Frog in Act Two.

The frog costume and make-up made Fernando unrecognizable, but like many of the cast, he had fast feet and fast hands. Not to mention astonishing accuracy throwing maidens, flames, and knives.

The audience gave the company a standing ovation.

Driving back to the Holiday Inn, Eddie reviewed the pieces. Someone in the Forbes home was phoning Fernando de Larra during company rehearsal and ordering flowers for people who later turned up dead. From the look of him, Eddie could believe Fernando was a killer; he could believe the whole troupe were killers. And they were financed by Friends of San Miguel who were looking very much like friends of Mike Bosch.

Which left only one missing link. Mike Bosch, like an Italian prince of the Middle Ages, reserved the absolute power of the death decree. The kill orders had to originate with him. So how was he contacting the Forbes home?

It was the kind of question Eddie didn't care to discuss over the telephone. He skipped his Holiday Inn turn-off and swung round to Mark Burgess's place on Whittier Street.

Tonight the party sounds behind the steel door were actual, not virtual. Mark was entertaining a coven of fellow hackers and tried to interest Eddie in a slice of magic mushroom quiche.

'Thanks,' Eddie said, 'but I can't stay.'

'Come on. Your outlook needs changing.'

'Maybe next time.' Eddie drew Mark toward the kitchen where Jefferson Airplane's greatest hits were pounding a little less deafeningly. 'Mark, do you remember Lucinda Forbes' incoming phone records – those two pieces of E-mail she received from a French satellite hook-up?'

'Sure I remember.' Mark nodded. 'Ariane–IV.'

'Can you find out who the caller was?'

'I'd have to hack into their billing records in Paris. When do you need the information?'

'Asap.'

'How's tomorrow morning?'

April 23

At 10 a.m., Mark Burgess opened his front door in his bare feet, grinning. 'Found what you wanted.' He beckoned Eddie over to a color monitor, called up Lucinda's incoming phone traffic and scrolled to April 2nd. The afternoon of Harry Forbes' murder.

He cursored to the 19-digit satellite number. 'Turns out that was an E-mail message sent from a cellphone hook-up in Belen, Colombia.' He split the screen and scrolled the bottom half to April 11th. The night of Thelma van Voss's suicide.

The same 19-digit number showed up.

'And so was that. The reason they had to use the satellite was, there's no phone company at the moment in that part of Colombia.'

Mark brought up a new file in the top half of the monitor. Eddie sat there, staring at the words 'Société-Satellite Ariane–IV'.

'This is Ariane's billing file.' Mark cursored down. 'As you can see, the time was paid for by the Friends of San Miguel de Bayamo. Who turn out to be a Cayman Islands corporation.'

Eddie nodded. 'And where's Belen?'

Mark cleared the screen and brought up a map of north-western Colombia. He zoomed in on a black triangle that the cartographer had planted on the Aguila River. The triangle was labeled 'Belen'.

Eddie frowned. 'Is that cellphone *physically* in Belen?'

'Not necessarily.' Mark pushed a button. A forty-mile zone around the town turned purple. 'It can be anywhere in this area.'

Eddie leaned forward and squinted. 'Can you enlarge that?'

The purple area expanded to fill the screen.

Now Eddie could see the lettering on the neighboring town more clearly. 'What do you know. Gurana.'

Mark's head turned. 'Mean something to you?'

'It's certainly beginning to.'

April 27

Through the wall of trees and vines, the ringing of the morning Angelus signaled Mike Bosch that it was time to catch the helicopter to the labs. He was bemused by Helen's insistence that her workers begin the day with Aves and Paternosters, but it seemed an effective means of maintaining discipline. Since she had instituted the daily pauses for prayer, there had been no inter-tribal stabbings or blow-dart poisonings, and her crew treated her serene authority with a deference that was close to reverential. The Indians referred to her as *la santa*, 'the holy woman', and many joined her for noon rosary in the little room she had fitted out as a chapel.

At a moderate cost, Bosch had been able to procure from the local bishop a priest who served as live-in chaplain, saying a daily Mass and leading the prayers. The priest had arrived with an Indian concubine and two squalling children, and Mike had no doubt that was the reason he'd come so cheap.

Mike fastened his seat belt, straightened his tie, and felt himself a contented man as the helicopter lifted off to take him to breakfast with Helen. And why shouldn't he be contented? Thanks to Helen Weller, production was up, profits were up; the cartel's future had never looked brighter or more assured.

He had only one frustration: Helen had not allowed him to sleep with her.

Mike Bosch found her attitude incomprehensible. In his world, love-making between a man and a woman was the equivalent of a handshake between men; it sealed the relationship and testified to both parties' good faith. No woman had ever before refused him – not when he'd been a boy, and certainly not now when he ruled two continents.

'We'll see,' she had said, pulling away from his embrace. The memory of those two words still stung. 'Maybe when we know one another a little better.'

And thus it was that Mike Bosch, who could have any teenager or beauty queen or film star he wanted, found himself in the humiliating position of being rejected by a middle-aged woman. A beautiful woman, admittedly – in her own odd way; but old enough to be his wife. Yet she had become indispensable to him. And so only one course remained open to him, to swallow his hurt pride and persevere.

She had refused to set foot in his hacienda, insisting that a small residence be set up for her at the labs. Within twenty-four hours of frenzied carpentry, he had supplied her with a seven-room air-conditioned apartment, staffed by two cooks, five maids, a hairdresser and a masseuse, not to mention six guards working three eight-hour shifts. The guards doubled as spies, reporting to him on her activities.

She had none except work, prayer, and sleep. And meals with Mike Bosch.

As the helicopter lowered on to the pad near the laboratory complex, he saw Helen standing in an aquamarine dressing gown by a table on her patio. Her hair was loose, hanging in waves over her shoulders.

He jumped down from the 'copter. He strode down the walk toward her, arms open. She stepped forward to receive a kiss on the cheek and a swift embrace. Just as swiftly, she disentangled herself.

'I thought we'd have omelettes this morning,' she said. 'Sound agreeable?'

'Whatever appeals to you, *querida*.'

The newly sodded lawn sparkled in the morning dew, but the excavations for her pool were scarcely underway. Mike regretted the ugliness of the open pit that greeted her every time she came outdoors. He could see a huge dead snake lying in a puddle at the bottom of the dig. He would have to do something about that.

He waved his hand, and the pilot staggered forward bearing a head-high heap of beribboned boxes.

'What's all this?' Helen's smile was broad and expectant.

The boxes were labeled Dior and Chanel. They were a test. Mike wanted to see if Helen Weller, in her heart of hearts, was a nun or a woman.

Helen pulled lids and tissue away to reveal dresses and gowns and lacy undergarments. 'Oh, Mike.' There was a tiny suggestion of reproach. 'This is too much. You shouldn't have.'

But she was pleased; he could hear it in her voice, see it in her eyes.

'You brought so little when you joined us, I thought we should do something about your wardrobe. If anything doesn't please you, say so, and I'll have it returned. And if you have problems with the fit, we have seamstresses here.'

She held each article up and studied her reflection in the glass doors leading to her rooms. 'You're much too kind.'

She bent and kissed him, this time on the lips. He let his hands hold her waist, just for a second.

A woman, he decided. Thank God, there's hope.

She pulled slowly away. 'But whatever am I going to do with all this out here in a rainforest?'

'A *rainforest*?' He pretended anger at the choice of words. 'My dear lady, this is our Garden of Eden, and I am planning to give a ball, a fiesta to celebrate your arrival.'

'Inviting the neighbors over for a barbecue?' Her smile was wry and dubious.

'There'll be some business associates, of course, and I thought that since you're becoming so essential to us, it would be a good idea for them to meet you.'

Helen sat down and cut into her omelette. It oozed sour cream and unsalted gray caviar, flown refrigerated from the Caspian. 'I won't play hostess.'

Bosch was shocked. 'But you'll make yourself known, mingle with the wives?'

'I'll make myself known all right. Do you realize your projected production and distribution figures for Sperilac are completely out of whack? You've grossly underestimated the manufacturing potential and the need for transport. Your accountants are myopic: they haven't thought for a moment about anything but shady deals on street corners in the States. Don't you people realize that we'll be able to export the drug *legally* to Europe and the Third World?'

Helen spread fresh Normandy butter on a croissant that had been baked twelve hours earlier in Marseilles.

'So while "the neighbors" are chomping down on broiled monkey and charred iguana, I'll clarify the situation. I'll tell them what we need and what they'll be expected to provide. Before they leave, we'll either have their assurance of cooperation, or you will have cut them out of the cartel.'

Bosch was not merely stunned, but a little frightened too. 'But Helen, you can brief me to do this. For you to do it yourself isn't, well, just isn't . . .'

Her eyes met his. 'Just isn't what?'

He felt his tongue stumble. 'You have to understand, we're old-fashioned down here. To a Latin male, women's lib is an aberration of the *norteamericanos*. It isn't your place to say such things.'

'But that's where you're wrong, Mike.' She carefully set her fork down on her plate. She aimed a dazzling smile at him. 'Of *course* it's my place. Now be a darling and pass me another croissant.'

April 30

For Sharon, the turning point came the morning of the fourteenth day when she reviewed the cumulative blood stats. She almost knocked over her chair dashing into the hallway to knock on Jack Arnold's door. 'Jack, have you looked at viral load counts?'

'Not for a few days. Anything interesting?'

'Check out the aggregate.'

He punched up a file on the computer. The Phase Three program tracked daily percentage change in individual viral loads. It also tracked a medically meaningless but statistically significant quantity, the percentage change in aggregate viral load of all three hundred Phase Three participants.

'Well, well, well. Seems to be nosing down, except for that little blip last Thursday.'

'It's down seventeen per cent in the last four days. And two-thirds of that's in the last two days. It's dropping faster each day.'

Jack cocked his head. 'I wouldn't go that far. Two days do not a trend make.'

'Oh yes they do, and a damned hopeful one. As the concentration of Sperilac builds up in the blood, the viricidal effect increases exponentially.'

'Easy there, big girl. Viruses are unpredictable little critters, and we've got five and a half months to go.'

'Check individual viral loads. Participant two fourteen.'

He tapped the figures into his keyboard and pressed *enter*, and 214's chart flashed up on the screen.

He whistled softly.

'Take a look at participant eighteen. Look at one five two.'

'Wait a minute, wait a minute.' He pressed *enter*.

Again, he whistled.

'Participants two seven nine, sixty-seven, and one thirteen.'

Jack stared at the screen a long, head-shaking moment. 'Wow.' He spun round in his swivel chair. 'Wow wow wow.'

'Six of our participants are within ten percentage points of clearing the virus.'

'And wouldn't it be a laugh if they were all on the placebo side.'

The breakdown by Sperilac and placebo could not be accessed without the password. Sharon knew the password, but the doctors did not.

'Come on, Jack. Results like that? There's not a chance.'

'Don't be so sure.' He steepled his hands over his white jacket. 'I've seen some fantastic results from placebos in double-blind trials. Sometimes I think placebos hold the answer to this disease.'

'Know what I think, Jack? I think you've had your hopes dashed so often you've forgotten *how* to hope.'

'Then teach me. Please. Is it anything like wishing on a star?'

'Has anyone ever called you an ass?'

'My fiancée.'

'Marry her. She understands you.'

Sharon locked her office door and called up the password file: 214, Raquel Balmer, and 18, Pam Gault, and 152, Audrey Goodman were all on Sperilac. She scrolled down the column. So were 279, Booker Kincaid, 67, Tim McJoyce, and 113, Molly Verba.

She stared at the glowing screen.

She wanted to clap her hands, dance on the desk, call a press conference. *It's working!*

And then she noticed the two names and numbers on the post-it stuck to the side of the computer: 73, Sondra Cass, and 187, Lou Kmiotek. She frowned.

Participant 73 was on Sperilac too. And so was 187. And both had been missing for a week.

She phoned Cass's number and got the answering machine again. 'Ms Cass, it's Sharon Powell at New Day. I haven't heard from you in a week. I hope you're planning to keep your appointment today.'

She broke the connection and dialed Lou Kmiotek's number.

'Hello?' At long last. An answer. A man.

'Mr Kmiotek, this is Sharon Powell at New Day.'

'Yes.' The tone was odd, as though he didn't know what she was talking about.

'Have you been sick or out of town?'

'Why do you ask?'

'Because I hope you're planning to keep your appointment today.'

'I'm sorry. Mr Kmiotek can't come to the phone right now.'

She bit back annoyance. 'When *can* Mr Kmiotek come to the phone?'

'You're his doctor?'

'No, not his doctor. I'm overseeing the trial for a new drug and Mr Kmiotek is one of the participants.'

'Ms Powell, I'm Detective John Abernathy of the District Police. It might save time if you came over here. Tell me where you are, and I'll send a squad car to pick you up.'

Luckily, Eddie heard the phone before he stepped into the shower. He turned off the hot water, crossed to the phone.

His Holiday Inn bedroom was littered with Mark Burgess's print-outs: Lucinda Forbes' home phone traffic, satellite time used by the Friends of San Miguel cellphone in Belen, numbers in the DC area that the Friends had contacted, and the traffic to and from those numbers. Eddie was barely halfway through the arduous, eye-killing work of collating.

He sat on the edge of the bed and lifted the receiver. 'Hello?'

'Guess what.' The voice on the phone was Mark's. Manic. 'The Forbes house called that payphone twelve minutes ago.'

The door to Lou Kmiotek's apartment was open. A smell of ammonia hovered, not quite blotting out a stench of rotted meat. A young patrol-woman blocked Sharon's way.

'Sorry, ma'am. Off limits.'

'Detective Abernathy wanted to speak to me.'

The patrolwoman whispered to a man in a rumpled blue jacket. He had a high-domed head, tanned as though he spent time outdoors. He glanced at Sharon with weary brown eyes and nodded.

The patrolwoman came back. 'Detective Abernathy will be with you in just a moment.'

He was speaking with a heavy-set woman in jeans. Beyond them a lattice of sunlight and shadow dappled the wall-to-wall carpet. Sharon tried to piece together what was happening.

'There've been people in the building soliciting for wildlife,' the woman was saying. 'I saw one of them at Mr Kmiotek's door.'

'You saw someone soliciting Mr Kmiotek for wildlife?'

'Sometime last week. It was one of those native Americans they send around.'

'How do you know?'

'The way she dressed. Feathers in her hair.'

'A native American woman with feathers in her hair. Did you get a look at her face?'

'She was looking at him, not me. I was taking my garbage to the incinerator. I wanted to have a word with her. The wildlife people put pamphlets under the doors and the last one had skinned baby seals. It upset my children and I wanted her to stop. But by the time I got my garbage dumped, she was gone.'

The detective didn't answer. He moved to the window and stood gazing across the courtyard.

Sharon stepped forward. 'Lieutenant, I'm Sharon Powell.'

He turned and looked at her blankly.

'From New Day Clinic. We spoke on the phone.'

'Right.' The detective's expression changed. 'You were testing a drug on Lou Kmiotek?'

'And on three hundred other people.'

'Could this drug have made him drowsy or caused him to lose consciousness?'

'There's no record of Sperilac's ever doing that to anyone. Why? What's happened to Mr Kmiotek?'

'He's dead.'

It was as though he'd reached out and slapped her. For a moment she couldn't even react.

'How did it happen?'

The detective pointed. She looked through the kitchen door. An enormous gray pile of bills and junk mail sat on the counter. An inch of water covered the floor.

'Downstairs neighbor had a leak in her ceiling. Janitor used his passkey. The sink was running and Kmiotek was on the floor.'

'Where is he now?'

Sharon followed the detective down a narrow hallway to the bedroom. The smells of ammonia and rot grew stronger. The dead man lay white-faced and staring on the bed. It must have been a horrible, panicky death.

A set of wind chimes moved gently in the breeze of the opened window.

'Do you know if he had any health problems?' the detective said.

'I know of one. We're testing Sperilac as a cure for AIDS.'

'Kmiotek had AIDS?'

It seemed to her the detective recoiled.

'He fitted the Center for Disease Control's definition. But he wouldn't just drop dead. AIDS doesn't work like that.'

Abernathy squatted to shine a penlight under a chair. 'Something happened, and it happened suddenly.'

'This may not be relevant, but . . .' New Day's clients by and large are drug addicts. A number of them are still active.'

'Drugs.' The detective glanced at her. 'Could be that.'

'He signed a release allowing us to have his body for autopsy.'

The detective shook his head. 'Sorry. A situation like this, the law requires us to autopsy.'

'Could you let me know the results?'

'Glad to.'

Eddie's left hand steered the wheel of the Chevy Caprice. His right hand brought a styrofoam cup of Burger King coffee to his lips: lukewarm, plenty of milk, and very sweet, exactly the way he liked it.

On the seat beside him, the tape recorder reeled through the last twenty-four hours' catch. It was mostly the same as yesterday's: deli orders and answering service checks.

And then one incoming call in Spanish.

'Fernando?'

'Si, Fernando le habla.'

'Flores para Jimmy Santos.'

Eddie slammed on the brakes and pulled over to a payphone and called Sharon Powell. Today he got her voice mail.

'Ms Powell, this is Eddie Arbogast again. I hope to hell you're picking up your messages. Does the name Jimmy Santos mean anything to you? If he's connected in any way to Sperilac, please contact me immediately. Because he's in trouble.'

April 30 – 4 p.m.

Jimmy Santos watched the technician struggle to find a working vein, plunging and replunging the syringe into his needle-tracked arm.

'Mercy, what have you done to your circulatory system?'

'It's hiding.' Jimmy grinned. 'It's afraid I might put some coke into it.'

The technician, a young pock-marked blond-haired male nurse named Tommy who moonlighted at New Day, gave a little shudder. 'Ever think of sex as a substitute?'

'Tried it.' Jimmy laughed. 'It'll do in a pinch. But for the real big bang, it's coke or nothing. Makes sex seem like one of God's afterthoughts.'

'Heroin?'

'Only when I feel the urge to wobble around and bump into walls. Naw, I don't use that shit.'

'Crack?'

'Not enough oomph. That's for junior high school kids.'

'Bingo,' Tommy said. 'We're in.'

They both watched as the vacuum syringe slurped full of Jimmy's blood.

'All right.' Tommy slapped a label to the test tube. 'This will hold the vampires till sunrise.'

Jimmy pressed the cotton pad on to his arm till the bleeding stopped.

The technician applied a Band-Aid, then snapped off his rubber gloves. 'See you tomorrow at the same time? Four?'

Jimmy winked. He liked the little faggot, despite some sour memories of Tommy's brethren back in his prison days. But hey, this was a free country, right?

Jimmy put on his cap and sauntered down to the men's room. He needed to take a piss real bad. As he washed his hands he glanced in the mirror and saw a kid lying on the floor in a half-open stall. Curious, he pushed the door open.

The kid had passed out with a needle jammed into the ugliest, spindliest, most ulcerated arm Jimmy had ever seen on a living human being. The syringe was full of blood.

'For fuckin' out loud. Hey, asshole.' Jimmy kicked the body.

The kid mumbled something; a whitish froth pulsed out between his chapped lips. Satisfied that he wasn't going to wake up, Jimmy rolled the body with his foot. He lost interest when he saw that someone had beaten him to the wallet. He saw, too, that the kid had wet himself. It was just beginning to stink.

Jimmy could imagine the scenario. Some bleeding heart judge had sentenced the kid to New Day; the kid had come into the john to shoot up one last time for auld lang syne before detox.

Jimmy spat in disgust. Fucking animal, doing smack in a public place. What kind of idiots was the world producing?

He dried his hands and found the janitor. 'Check out the men's room. There's a mess in there needs cleaning up.'

Pushing through the revolving door into the late afternoon sunlight, Jimmy looked right and left before he ventured down the street. Always had to check out the scene: you might run into somebody you owed money to. Never knew how long your credit would hold out before they slammed a brick into your head or pulled a knife.

Although his skin was white as a baby's first meal, Jimmy had cultivated a black man's street swagger, a pendular rocking of the torso from the pelvis, the legs taking lo-o-ong strides. He strutted down 13th Street until he came to the Metro station by Hecht's department store. He took the red line train two stops to Farragut North and headed for the upstairs porn movie house over the Greek restaurant.

The movies were all straight, the floor show gay. So the audience was mixed. But they could be fun, and there was always the possibility he'd pick up a few bucks for letting some guy give him a feel during the dancing boys or bouncing girls.

He bought his ticket. Tripping and groping his way into the darkened theater, he took a seat one in from the aisle.

Cindy Buff, his number-one favorite skin-flick starlet, was performing on-screen with a man sporting a shlong the size of a rolling pin.

God, Jimmy wondered, how do they ever get into those positions, much less hold them?

Six on-screen orgasms later, he felt a pressure on his armrest and the spider tickle of fingers tracing up his thigh.

'Hold on, chum. That's twenty bucks.'

The fingers withdrew. They returned crackling a crisp bill.

Jimmy flicked a Bic and made sure it was a twenty. Alongside it the hand held the fattest joint he had ever beheld in his life.

He looked up into the liquid black eyes of a smiling Latino.

'OK, *compadre*. Get it hard and it's all yours.'

He lit the joint just as Cindy's on-screen partner stood her on her head and with fast jack-hammering thrusts began driving her into the mattress.

Jimmy inhaled and held his breath.

Jesus, this must be pure Oregon sinsemilla.

Sinsemilla and something else. Talk about ecstasy – he could feel his soul peeling away from his bones, leaping free.

'*Zoweee!*' he cried. Barely noticing as the hand slid away from his fly. Slumping down and not noticing at all as his companion left his seat.

There's got to be a mistake.

Sharon pulled to the side of Kalorama Road, an area of the nation's capital so moneyed that by comparison Georgetown was a teeming Third World ghetto. She took Sondra Cass's address from her purse: 3805 Kalorama.

Her eye scanned manicured façades with house numbers veiled under ivy or shadowed by huge porticos. This was the 3700 block.

She slipped into gear and steered round a bend. Ahead of her, a pillared Greek-revival mansion rose among hundred-year oaks on a landscaped hill. Brass numerals had been fixed to the stone wall: 3805.

She steered slowly into the drive and up to the ivied portico.

A black man was carefully trimming the ears of a boxwood topiary rabbit.

'Excuse me.' Sharon stepped out of the car. 'I'm trying to locate a woman by the name of Sondra Cass.'

He edged back the brim of the straw hat. 'You want to talk to Miz Pullman.' The shears pointed.

She turned and saw that the front door had opened. A grim-faced woman with enormous blonde hair and triple pearls stared at her. Just last week Sharon had seen the very same face, smiling, in the pages of *Vanity Fair*. She recognized America's former Ambassador to Austria.

'Are you from Good Will?'

'No, I'm from New Day. I'm looking for Sondra Cass. She gave this address.'

'I'm afraid we've promised all her things to Good Will. They seem to be late.'

'I'm not here about her things.'

'No?'

'I'm overseeing a drug trial at the clinic, and Ms Cass has missed her appointments for a week.'

'Then *you're* the messages on her answering machine. Come in. Please.'

Sharon stepped into a coolness that smelled faintly of honeysuckle.

'I'd rather Hiram didn't overhear everything. What sort of clinic? Hypertension?'

Following Fiona Pullman down a corridor of open doors, Sharon had the impression of Van Goghs and Cezannes flashing past.

'New Day rehabilitates substance abusers.'

'Really? Sondra never told me she had a drug problem.'

They entered a small room with a Picasso harlequin staring mournfully from over the fireplace. Fiona Pullman dropped into an overstuffed chintz chair. She motioned Sharon to sit.

'Would it be possible to speak with Ms Cass?'

'I'm afraid not. Sondra died a week ago.'

'*Died?* How?'

'She dropped dead in the kitchen.'

'Do you have any idea what caused it?'

'Stress. She was taking medicine for hypertension. I was giving a reception that night; the house was in an uproar. It was too much for her, poor dear soul.' Fiona moved objects on a table – a small jade Buddha, a silver-framed photograph of a child on a white donkey. She stared at them, dissatisfied. 'What sort of drug were you testing on her?'

'We hope it cures AIDS.'

'Sondra never told me she had AIDS either.'

'She may not have. The only requirement for the trial is a positive antibody test.'

'I suppose she kept it to herself because she didn't want me worrying about her.' The tip of Fiona's finger traced figure eights on the arm of the chair. 'She had a lot of backbone. She never wanted to be a burden to anyone else.'

'I'm sorry to have to bring this up, but Ms Cass signed a release.'

Fiona's pale blue eyes registered confusion. 'A release?'

'Allowing us to autopsy. Where's the body?'

Fiona shook her head. 'They wouldn't let me have her. I'm not a relative. Sondra and I were together eighteen years but it didn't seem to matter.'

'Who wouldn't let you have her?'
'The District Medical Examiner's Office.'

At the porn theater above the Greek eatery near Farragut Square, a Korean sat dozing in the box office. A patron rapped a quarter on the ticket window, trying to catch his attention.

'Hey, do you people know you got some sort of dead guy blocking the aisle in the seventh row?'

After two hours arguing with the District Coroner's office and achieving absolutely nothing, Sharon returned in a rage to New Day. The voice mail light on her phone was blinking.

Eddie Arbogast's message only made her mood worse. Without thinking, she scribbled Arbogast's phone number and beeper on a piece of scratch paper.

When she saw what she'd done she did a double take. Why should I trust a con man?

She ripped the sheet from the pad, balled it and tossed it into the wastepaper basket.

On the other hand . . .

The name Jimmy Santos meant nothing to her. She checked her computer files and found he was trial participant 94, the very first name under S. He showed close to 28 per cent reduction in viral load over the past five days.

She went into the password file. Santos had been assigned Sperilac.

She pulled the waste basket into the light and foraged till she found the crumpled paper with Arbogast's numbers. She smoothed it out, folded it, and carefully tucked it into her wallet.

She knocked on Jack Arnold's door.

'Hey, Sharon.' He swung his loafers off the desk. 'What's up?'

'We've had two deaths – Lou Kmiotek and Sondra Cass.'

Jack's smile became a gaping O. 'Damn. What happened?'

'No one knows yet. I should have the autopsies some time tomorrow. Do your files show any other deaths?'

Jack called up the files. 'Nothing so far. But with an addict population, mortality is going to run higher than—'

'Anyone sick or in an accident?'

'No one.'

'You're sure? There's no mention of anything happening to James Santos?'

'James Santos?' Jack shook his head. 'He's alive and well in these files – knock wood.'

'His name is Fernando de Larra.' A fake Tiffany lamp cast a dull red glow over the photo that Eddie had scissored from the program. 'He's at the Kennedy Center with the Uruguayan ballet. The Forbes home phones him when there's a kill order.'

Larry Lorenzo pulled the photo round the salt and pepper and across the table. 'And then what?'

'And then someone dies.'

'This guy's killing them?'

'Or passing the order on. Does it matter? They're dead, he's an accessory.'

'You have proof?'

'Hey, fellas.' The blonde waitress was hovering about as subtly and as gracefully as a gunship helicopter. 'There's a five-dollar minimum in the booths. Per person.'

Larry's hand covered the photo.

'Tuna salad, toasted rye,' Eddie said. 'Diet Pepsi. Is that five bucks?'

'That's four seventy-five.' The waitress had a husky, smoker's voice.

'Then give me two Pepsis.'

She waited for Larry, tapping a pencil against her pad.

'Give me a Scotch on the rocks.'

'No liquor. Rolling Rock, Bud, Bud Lite, Tuborg.'

'Rolling Rock. Diet salad special.'

Larry waited for her to collect the menus and go.

'You have proof this Fernando person's involved?'

Eddie nodded. 'Tapes of the calls. They're in Spanish, but his name and the victims' names are clear as a bell.'

Larry straightened his tie, smoothing it down over his striped shirt. 'You have authorization for the tap?'

Eddie couldn't believe it. 'Cut it out, Larry, who the hell's side are you on?'

'The same side as you, but we have a little nuisance called rules.'

'For Chrissake, US citizens are getting killed. They whacked a pharmaceutical CEO and a top-ranking director of a federal agency. Mike Bosch has stepped over the line, way over.'

'In other words, no authorization.'

'OK, no authorization. But believe me, no one's going to complain, because this time you can make the charge stick.'

Larry glanced at him. '*I* can make it stick?'

'You'll get the credit, why not?'

Larry had that look on his face of waiting for a buzz bomb to explode. 'So what do you want from me?'

'I want you to surveil Fernando, round the clock.'

'Come on, Eddie.' Larry's eyes were weary under drooping lids. 'I can't just assign three agents. It's got to relate to an ongoing case.'

'So lie. It won't be the first time.'

Larry didn't bother to answer.

'You can pick Fernando up tomorrow morning at the Kennedy Center, rehearsal room A.'

Larry tucked the photo into his wallet. 'I'll see what I can do. But you're putting me in a situation.'

'One other thing.'

Larry flicked him a murderous glance. 'I'm listening.'

'We need to know Mike Bosch's physical whereabouts at the time the E-mail was sent from Belen to the Forbes home.'

Larry's fist hit the table. Salt and pepper and Tabasco sauce jumped. 'If I go near those surveillance files, my ass is right in the line of fire.'

'And if we're this close to nailing Bosch and you let him get away, your ass *isn't*?'

Larry looked at Eddie. He closed his eyes. He turned his face toward the ceiling. 'What the hell are you planning to do, Eddie?'

Talking with Larry Lorenzo lately made Eddie feel like an old tomcat toying with a favorite ball. 'I want Bosch. I'll do whatever I have to.'

'I mean to *me*. What the hell are you planning to do to *me*?'

'Whatever I have to.'

Eddie pushed open the hotel room door, punched on the TV, and dropped into a chair. He unlaced his shoes and massaged an aching bone in his foot.

The phone rang. As he lifted the receiver he saw the voice mail light blinking. Two calls.

'Hello?'

'It's been two weeks and two days, Eddie. Tomorrow's a new page in the calendar. Want me to put your things in a trunk and ship them up there?'

Damn. He'd meant to phone this morning. 'Sorry, honey. It's taking a little longer than I planned.'

'Could you give me an estimate? Because Dottie wants to have us to dinner and I've been putting her off.'

'It depends on a lot of things.'

'Who's with you? Sounds like Tom Hanks.'

'Just the TV.' He reached and turned down the volume on the late night movie. 'Look, I can't really talk on the phone, but I'm finally getting the cooperation I need, and . . . we're going to be seeing some results in the next few days.'

'Speaking of results, did you see in the news, the FDA found eighteen billion dollars of cocaine in a dolphin at Marina del Rey?'

'They've used everything else, why not a dolphin?'

'You sound tired. Are you getting enough sleep?'

'I'm OK.'

'You're eating enough?'

'I'm eating fine.'

'Take care of yourself. I want you back.'

'I'll be back. That's a promise.'

'I'm holding you to it. G'night. I love you.'

'Me too.'

Sharon scooped the day's catch of mail out of her mailbox. Riding up in the elevator, she noticed that one of the envelopes had been addressed by hand and carried a Colombian stamp and a Bogota postmark. There was no return address.

She ripped it open and drew out a sheet of Varig Aeronaves do Brasil stationery.

April 20.
Dear Sharon,

I don't know when, if ever, we'll meet again. By the time you receive this – or certainly by the end of June inventory – you will have learned what I've done. Don't judge me too harshly. People were dying, terribly and needlessly. I made what seemed at the time the only possible decision. Circumstances may have changed, time will tell, but too late for me to alter course.

At this point, Helen's pen had drawn a curve up through the word Brasil in the letterhead. It looked accidental; something must have nudged her hand.

I have many regrets. The greatest is that I couldn't explain to you. Or say goodbye.

My love to you and Joe – I hope it works out for you both. Remember me in your prayers.

Helen.

Sharon let herself into the apartment. Cats swarmed at her feet. She stepped over them, hurried to the telephone, and tapped Lucinda's number into the keypad.

'Forbes residence,' a male voice answered. She had a feeling it was the houseboy.

'Could I speak with Lucinda Forbes, please?'

'I'm sorry, Mrs Forbes went to the theater this evening and hasn't returned yet. Could I take a message?'

What on earth am I doing? Sharon asked herself. Helen is my friend. If Lucinda wants her scalp, let her track it down herself. 'No. There's no message.'

'Who shall I say phoned?'

'No one.'

May 1

A t ten in the morning, Sharon sat in her New Day office scowling at
a fax of Lou Kmiotek's autopsy.

The medical examiner had found needle marks on the thighs,
suggesting Kmiotek was a long-time diabetic. Blood analysis had
revealed trace amounts of cocaine and insulin.

Liver normal, spleen normal, kidneys normal.

She searched to see what the pancreatic exam had yielded. There
wasn't any.

The examiner suspects diabetes and doesn't examine the pancreas?
Where did this guy get his MD?

She flipped to the last sheet.

Death was not due to insulin shock, sugar overload, or cocaine
poisoning. The examiner's verdict was that Kmiotek's system had, for
reasons unknown, given out. Lou Kmiotek had simply stopped breathing.

She punched up Kmiotek's file. In the box 'Have you ever been
diagnosed with diabetes?' he had ticked NO.

She sighed. We're going to have to do our own autopsy.

Her mind flashed a worst-case projection: turf war with the police.
Relatives challenging the consent to autopsy that Kmiotek had signed.
Lawyers jumping into the act, smelling big pharmaceutical bucks . . .

She cleared the screen of Lou Kmiotek and stood. Her back cracked.

She dropped her head, let her arms hang from her shoulders.
Exhaling, she slowly curled forward till her spine was fully extended
and her fingertips were just touching the floor. Keeping the knees
unlocked. That was important. Never lock the knees.

The fax began beeping.

Refusing to be hurried, she reversed the process, slowly bringing
herself back to standing, vertebra by vertebra.

A coil of paper was working its way out of the fax machine. She
plucked up Sondra Cass's autopsy.

The examiner had discovered a needle mark on the outer left upper
arm. Heart arteries clogged solid with plaque and cholesterol. Liver
pre-cirrhotic. Aneurysm in left kidney. Trace amounts of cocaine in the
blood.

167

The examiner concluded that death had not been due to cocaine poisoning or heart or kidney or liver malfunction. Sondra Cass's respiratory functions had simply, of their own accord, stopped.

Sharon checked the signatures to see if the two autopsies by any chance were the work of the same examiner. They weren't.

She stared at her own left arm. Rotated it. Frowned. If you were injecting cocaine, would you shoot into the *outer* side of the upper arm? How could you even reach it?

The phone rang. She lifted the receiver. 'Sharon Powell. How may I help you?'

'Good morning, Ms Powell.' A male voice, familiar but not immediately placeable. 'This is Detective John Abernathy, we met yesterday at the Kmiotek apartment.'

'Good morning. Thanks for faxing me the autopsy.'

'My pleasure.'

'I thought it seemed a little inconclusive. What was your feeling?'

'Haven't had a chance to look at it. The reason I'm calling, there's a guy down here in one of the cells says he's gotta see you. Name of Tim McJoyce.'

'Wants to see *me*?' Something told her she'd seen that name in print. She couldn't recall where and she certainly didn't know the man.

'He says you're his doctor.'

'He's mistaken, I'm not that kind of doctor. I don't have patients.'

'He says you're treating him at New Day Clinic.'

'One minute please, Lieutenant.'

She brought up the file. Tim McJoyce, Phase Three participant number 67, was indeed a member of the trial. He was on Sperilac and he was one of the six who had almost cleared the virus.

'Is Mr McJoyce hurt?' she said.

'Not too bad. It's his friend that got hurt.'

'I'll be right down. What's that address?'

A steel security door crashed shut behind them. A bolt slapped home.

Detective Abernathy followed the guard down a corridor of steel cages. Sharon followed Detective Abernathy. They walked a gauntlet of unshaved faces, hating eyes. The air had a sick smell of unbathed bodies and take-no-hostages disinfectant.

The guard stopped at the last cell on the right.

A sinewy little man bolted up from the cot. 'Dr Powell?'

'Mr McJoyce.'

He thrust a beefy hand through the bars. 'Everyone calls me Tim.'

The guard unlocked the door and swung the bars halfway open. Sharon stepped through.

'I'll be back for you in ten minutes,' Abernathy said. 'If you need me before then, you'd better start screaming your head off.'

She smiled. 'Thank you, Lieutenant.'

The bars swung shut.

'You take the cot.' Tim McJoyce placed an open newspaper delicately across the toilet and sat.

Suddenly she recognized him. 'You're the man who asked me about steroids.'

He nodded. 'Once a substance abuser, always . . . Right?'

'What happened? They say you got into a fight.'

He pounded fists on the thighs of beltless jeans. 'You got time for the real story?'

'I've got time, sure.'

'You know the Glass Slipper? It's a bar over on Pennsylvania Avenue near Twenty-first Street. Five blocks from the White House.'

'Sorry. I don't go out much.'

'It's a place to pick up gypsies.' He saw the blank look on her face. 'Show dancers go there – touring companies from the Kennedy Center. I go there because I'm into physical fitness.'

'I can see you are.'

Tim drew in a deep inhalation. His chest expanded to twice its size and tiny vertical rips appeared in his T-shirt. 'I admire the human body and when I make love I don't want these toothpicks the media try to pass off as women. Give me a female with glutes and thighs and a little definition and a rib cage and – you follow my drift.'

Sharon nodded.

'Most dancers have great bottoms – all that leg work. Most are underdeveloped up top, so when a dancer has it all, I notice. Well, in came this mob of kids, chattering and giggling in Spanish, every one of them carrying a dancer's tote bag, every one of them built like a little circus pony.'

'Little circus pony' was obviously high praise in Tim McJoyce's book.

'Turned out they were from the Ballet Folklorico de Uruguay. I can't *habla* much besides *como esta* and *mucho gusto*, but this real cute little kid started coming on to me. Pointing to things and saying the Spanish name and I'd say the English, and she'd laugh and hug me. Tells me her name is Rosario but I can call her Rosie.'

A triangle of tongue moistened Tim's upper lip.

'Rosie has everything that turns me on. Plus long dark hair, and big brown eyes, and a smile like a light bulb in a bowl of cocoa. She starts talking about *vamos a casa* – and it's not five minutes till we're out of the Slipper and into a cab.'

A scowl came over his face.

'I get her home and right away she's critical. I have a small place, and a lot of weight-lifting equipment, and maybe it isn't the most romantic environment. So who's she making love to, me or my apartment, right? But she has this attitude, pouting and pulling back and pointing at my weights and *no no no, no puedo.*'

He mimicked the voice of an exasperatingly coy little Latin-American girl.

'Well, I manage to coax her over to the bed. Then she wants to go to the john. She's in there a half hour. Running water, flushing toilets. "Rosie, what the hell's going on in there?"

'"Momentito, momentito." Giggle giggle.

'*Momentito* turns out to be Spanish for please wait a half hour.

'Out she comes, finally. Wearing my bathrobe – cute. Dragging that tote bag. She hops up on the bed. Hands all over me. Undresses me. She wants to play a game. Sure, Rosie, I'll play a game.

'She blindfolds me – she never tied blindfolds for any junta because I can see right under. When she thinks I can't see, out from the tote bag comes a loaded syringe. A whole cc of liquid in that mother. She pops off the cap, squirts a drop in the air, and then she comes after me.

'I'm off that bed in one half a second and she's running after my bare butt. giggling – "Coca-*eena*! Coca-*eena*! Tee-mee! Tee-mee!" Like it's birthday cake and we're going to have us a party.'

Tim blinked. His eyes misted and his voice thickened. 'I've been clean and dry thirty-seven days, and I fought for my sobriety, and I'm not going to give it up for a pony ride on coca-eena.'

'Of course not.'

'So first things first, right? I knock the syringe out of her hand and I throw her and her clothes out of my apartment. She's banging on the door. screaming in Spanish, like this is breach of promise. Christ, I let her keep the bathrobe!'

Tim socked one hand into the other.

'So she goes to the neighbors, screaming and weeping, and the next thing I know, cops arrive and this is domestic partner abuse and a real mean female Latina cop cuffs me.'

'Did you mention the cocaine to the police?'

He shook his head. 'Rosie would have just said it was mine and they'd have turned it against me.'

'They didn't search your apartment?'

'I wouldn't let them in. Rosie was out in the corridor, and they didn't have a warrant. So they dragged me down here.'

'Where's Rosie now?'

'Someone from the Uruguayan Embassy came over and faster than you can say CIA, she was out of there.'

'I'm going to get you a lawyer.'

'He'd better be a fast worker. This place is giving me drug signals.'

'Can you remember what happened to the syringe?'

Tim had to think for a moment. 'It's in the trash basket in my bedroom.'

'I'd like you to authorize the custodian to turn your house keys over to me.'

One sticker on Tim McJoyce's apartment door warned that his property was protected by Top Dog Security. It had been placed just low enough for a dog to read.

The other sticker warned that the owner contributed to the Police Athletic League and the precinct kept an eye on the premises.

Sharon twisted the key in the lock. Nothing resisted her, nothing jangled. So much for Top Dog and PAL.

The door opened into dusty dimness. A faint rancid smell of un-washed clothes hovered. She let the door tap shut behind her.

Her foot sent a dumbbell clunking over bare floorboards.

The studio apartment, ground floor on a narrow courtyard, received no more daylight than the bottom of a well. She flicked a light switch. One bare light bulb went on in a ceiling fixture of four. Now she could see cracked walls and sagging door frames and a burglar grate on the window with work-out clothes hung to dry.

A home gymnasium shared space with a tangled fold-out bed. Cloth-ing had been tossed everywhere. She stepped around dumbbells and barbells and peeked under T-shirts and jockey shorts and finally lifted the sweatshirt that covered the waste basket.

She emptied the basket on to the bathroom floor. She picked care-fully through health-bar wrappers and junk mail and banana skins.

A three-inch needle winked on a 1cc disposable syringe. She held the chamber up to the light and saw that it was three-quarters full. The solution looked like a 3:1 dilute of hepatitic urine.

She cocooned the needle in toilet paper and tucked the syringe into her purse, then scooped the papers and banana skins back into the basket.

As she crossed to the door, she noticed a Ballet Folklorico tote bag on the floor by the fold-out bed.

Curious, she emptied it on to the sheets. She sifted through dancer's work-out clothes, a pair of danced-through toe shoes, sandals, a Spanish-language newspaper, half a wrapped sandwich, and a small bundle of papers fastened with a rubber band.

She snapped the band loose.

The bundle included a map of Washington, with the locations of the Kennedy Center and New Day Clinic circled in red. And a fax photograph of Tim McJoyce, full face, an ID mug shot. His home address was neatly printed beneath, along with the address of New Day Clinic and the hour of his appointment yesterday.

Sharon returned to the lab at Biochemtech and emptied the syringe into a half-liter sterile steel chamber. She fitted the chamber to the centrifuge, pressed *start*, and pushed the r.p.m. up till she could see a fine mist of purified water clouding the Plexiglas lid.

She opened a plastic catheter and drew off the water vapor.

Pressing *stop*, she let the centrifuge spin itself to a standstill. She lifted the lid and aimed the beam of a tensor lamp down into the bowl.

Concentric rings of trace minerals descended in order of increasing molecular weight – a fine white line of zinc, a pale yellow line of copper, a frighteningly thick gray band of lead.

Next came a ring of a white powder.

She transferred a tweezer pinch of the substance to a slide and fixed the slide to the microscope.

She peered through the eyepiece. At every magnification, she saw inert white crystal.

She touched the damp tip of a litmus stick to the powder. The stick developed a bright blue spot: alkaloid.

She returned her attention to the chamber. Just below the white alkaloid was a ring of reddish powder. She studied a pinch under the microscope and made out another inert crystal.

Dampening a second litmus stick, she again touched the tip to the powder. This time the stick came away with a purple dot: acid.

Toward the bottom of the bowl were the heaviest elements of all. They formed a continuous band, black shading to dark green.

A glance under the microscope told her that these were fragmented amoeba and protozoa – colonies of cryptosporidia and E. coli and Escherichia nana. From the sheer density of parasites it was obvious that this had been no lab mixture; instead of distilled water, some amateur scientist had taken water straight from the tap, and the tap had obviously been leeching from a sewer. Though nothing short of a DNA check on the crypto could establish where the mix had been made, her guess would be somewhere in the tropics where population was dense and sanitation was lax.

She tweezed a small amount of the white crystalline powder on to the stage of the spectroscope. She shut the chamber and zapped the powder with the helium-cadmium laser.

Vaporized particles streamed up. As the scope read their light spectra, chemical symbols popped up on the screen: H, C, O, N. Hydrogen, carbon, oxygen, nitrogen. And then the ratios – 21, 17, 4, 1.

She called across the lab. 'Hey, Wendy, what's cocaine, H21 or 31?'

'C17-H21-NO4.'

'Looks like we got us some injectible cocaine plus a little red mystery.'

She put the spectroscope stage in a bowl to rinse and slid a clean one into place. She tweezed a speck of the red powder, shut the chamber and zapped.

The symbols popped up: H, C, O and then again H, C, O. And then the ratios: 40, 24, 5 and 6, 4, 4.

Obviously, two molecules had bonded together too strongly for a piddling lab centrifuge to spin them apart.

'What's got twenty-four carbon atoms, forty hydrogen, five oxygen?'

'Cholic acid,' Wendy called back.

'What's it used for?'

'Your stomach uses it for digestion.'

'And what's C4-H6-O4?'

'Succinic acid. Used in manufacturing perfume.'

'This makes no sense at all. Why would anyone mix a batch of cocaine, cholic acid, and succinic acid?'

'If the acid molecules are bonded, you have succinocholine. It's a lethal poison.'

'Why mix cocaine and a lethal poison?'

'I dunno. To kill a cocaine user?'

That made sense. 'Wendy, what do you know about succinocholine?'

Wendy had to think for a moment. 'It was developed by Bertolt-Bienvenue as an insecticide. Unfortunately, when it contacted human skin it interfered with chemical transmission along nerve synapses. They had to recall it. Later it was okayed as a tranquilizer and local anesthetic in veterinary medicine. And as a means of putting animals to sleep.'

'How does it work?'

'In vertebrates, at low doses, it blocks the function of intestinal nerves. At high doses it depresses the central nervous system. Breathing stops.'

'Would it show up in an autopsy?'

'I doubt it. It metabolizes pretty fast. Once it enters the bloodstream, I doubt you could even isolate it.'

Sharon grabbed the phone and tapped in the number of the pathologist who had done Lou Kmiotek's autopsy. 'Dr Magsaysay, this is Sharon Powell of New Day Clinic.'

'Yes, Miss Powell.' A polite voice, faintly accented, faintly impatient.

'You autopsied one of our patients, Lou Kmiotek?'

'That's correct.'

'Could you check all puncture marks on the body and see if there's any residue of succinocholine on the skin?'

'Succino*choline*?' Amazement lifted his voice.

'That's right. Succinocholine.'

Next she phoned the pathologist who'd done Sondra Cass.

'Dr Whitney, would you check all puncture marks on Sondra Cass's body?'

'There are an awful lot of those.' A sigh came over the phone. 'Are we talking fresh punctures or old?'

'It would be the most recent puncture. Could you see if there's any external residue of succinocholine?'

Two hours later, Sharon had her answer. She called an emergency meeting with Joe Mahler and Lucinda Forbes.

'It'll have to be at the house,' Lucinda said.

May 1 – 3:15 p.m.

'Two patients on the Sperilac side of the Phase Three trial have been murdered.'

'*Murdered?*' Lucinda Forbes stared at Sharon with startled green eyes.

'And an attempt has been made on the life of a third.'

'Murdered *how*?'

'With injections of succinocholine.'

There was a soft rapping at the living-room door. Lucinda's hulking young manservant wheeled in a dessert trolley.

'Succino-*what*?' Lucinda said.

The cart jingled to a stop in front of Sharon's chair. The manservant's graceful hands offered sherbet and butter cookies. She declined the sweets and took a glass of iced tea. 'Succinocholine. It's a veterinary poison.'

'Who'd use dog poison on human beings? It seems awfully crude and amateurish, doesn't it?'

Sharon felt uneasy discussing the matter in front of the servant. Lucinda, obviously, did not.

'Not as crude as you'd think,' Sharon said. 'It acts instantly.'

The manservant's dark brown eyes were remote, as though he barely understood or cared what they were discussing. It occurred to her he might not understand English beyond a few elementary household commands.

'And it's untraceable,' she added. 'It didn't even show up in the police or county autopsies.'

'Then how do you know it was used?'

'It left a residue on the skin at the puncture site.'

Lucinda was thoughtful. 'Is it difficult to get hold of?'

'Hardly. Bertolt-Bienvenue manufactures it in thirty-eight countries and anyone with a veterinarian's licence can buy as much as they want.'

Lucinda stood and went to the window and stood gazing out at the landscaped lawn. 'But who'd go to such lengths to sabotage a Phase Three trial?'

'I can think of a few people.' Joe Mahler, lanky and handsome in the easy chair, helped himself to tea and cookies. 'If the FDA okay Sperilac for wide-scale use, it'll upset the earnings of five leading pharmaceutical houses. So if we're thinking of market share as the motive, there's no shortage of suspects.'

Lucinda frowned. 'You've been watching too much television. People in the pharmaceutical business may bend a few rules, but they don't murder.'

'What about Tuskegee?' Joe said, referring to the infamous federal medical experiment where twenty-eight black men had been allowed to die of untreated syphilis.

'That was the government,' Lucinda said, 'not the industry. And anyway that was years ago.'

'Mrs Forbes, ma'am?' The servant had wheeled the cart to her chair.

She returned to her seat. 'No one wants my pear sorbet?' Her voice was plaintive.

'It's a little close to dinner,' Joe said.

'*My* dinner's not for hours.' Lucinda took tea, cookie and sherbet. She set the plate on a carved rosewood table. 'Thank you, Key. I'll ring when we need you.'

The manservant pushed the trolley from the room. The door closed soundlessly behind him.

'Ethically,' Sharon said, 'we have no choice. We've got to report the murders to the police.'

Lucinda looked at her in astonishment. 'Why?'

'*Why?* So the police can put a stop to them.'

'What makes you think they can do that? Go to the police, and you'll accomplish one thing only: you'll force the FDA to close the trial down. A great many men and women with AIDS will die and Joe Mahler's investors will lose their shirts. Sperilac will never come to market, and who will that help? None of us.'

'What alternative do we have?' Sharon said. 'We can't just continue the trial as if nothing had happened.'

'I disagree,' Lucinda shot back. 'We can continue and we must.'

'That's insane.' Sharon slammed down her glass. 'How in the world do you expect to—'

'You say the police autopsied and didn't find a thing. Have you told anyone else about this succino-what's-it?'

'Not yet.'

'So who's to be the wiser?'

'Everyone will be the wiser when more trial members are killed.'

176

'Then we'll make sure they're *not* killed.'

'And how are you planning to accomplish that?'

'We continue the trial under airtight security.'

Sharon's eyes swung to Joe, appealing for sanity.

'That's not a bad idea,' Joe said quietly. 'Let's talk about it.'

'I wonder,' Sharon said, 'if Lucinda quite realizes what airtight security would entail?'

'Of course I realize. It would require feeding and housing two hundred and ninety-eight trial members plus staff. It would mean keeping them under round-the-clock guard for another five and a half months.'

'That's only the beginning,' Sharon said. 'It means trial-members with jobs wouldn't be able to work. Those with families wouldn't be able to see them. Under those circumstances, I doubt even two dozen would opt to stay on.'

'If we paid them enough,' Joe said, 'I bet they'd all stay on.'

Sharon looked at him. 'You're not serious.'

'Why not?'

'Because that would cost your investors millions of dollars.'

'My investors are hoping for profits of *hundreds* of millions.'

'Joe's absolutely right,' Lucinda said. 'We've got a major problem, a challenge to the very survival of Phase Three, and we're not going to solve it by thinking small or thinking ordinary or thinking negative.'

'Since when is it small or negative to be concerned about people's lives?'

'You're concerned about two people's lives, and Joe and I are concerned about the lives of twenty million.'

'I wonder if Joe's partners will share that concern.'

'I'll get on the phone right now,' Joe said, 'and start sounding them out.'

Dr Jack Arnold, blond and melon-plump, was standing at the drink machine in the corridor at New Day. He dropped three quarters into the coin slot and pushed buttons for *no ice* and *diet Slice*.

'Sharon.' He turned as she hurried past. 'That fellow you were asking about? Jimmy Santos?'

She stopped. 'What's happened?'

The machine dropped a waxed cup into the door. Fizzing spouts of syrup and soda intermingled.

'He died yesterday.'

She put a hand behind her and felt for the wall. 'How?'

'Dropped dead in a porn theater.'

Arbogast's message came back to her. *Does the name Jimmy Santos mean anything to you?*

'What was the cause of death?'

'Autopsy hasn't turned up anything.' Jack brought the polka-dot cup carefully to his lips and sipped. 'He just stopped breathing.'

'That's the third one who "just stopped".'

''Scuse me?'

'I have to take care of something. Talk to you later.'

She stepped into her office and shut the door. She dug through her wallet and found the piece of paper with Arbogast's two numbers. She phoned the hotel first. 'Ed Arbogast, please.'

After five rings a recorded voice told her the party she wanted was not in their room. She left a voice mail message. 'This is Sharon Powell at New Day Clinic. I'm calling at,' she angled her wrist, 'four thirty-five. Please contact me. It's urgent.'

She phoned his beeper number and left the same message.

Seven minutes later her phone rang. She snatched up the receiver. 'Sharon Powell. How may I—'

'Eddie Arbogast. What's happening?'

'Mr Arbogast, I'll be candid with you if you'll be candid with me.'

'OK.'

'Are you calling from a cellphone?'

'No, I'm at a payphone.'

'I checked with Aetna and you don't work for them. Who are you working for?'

There was an instant's silence before he answered. 'The government.'

'Which agency?'

'It'd be better if we discussed that face to face, not on the phone.'

'Where did you get the names Sondra Cass and Jimmy Santos?'

'That's another point we'd better save for face to face. I take it you know them.'

'They were members of the drug trial we're running.'

'You said "were". Past tense.'

'That's right.'

'What happened? Did they drop out of the trial?'

'Not exactly.'

'Are they alive?'

She didn't answer.

'I was afraid of that. What about Abbie Lewis and Frank Kerouac and Tim McJoyce? Do you know any of them?'

At the name McJoyce, she felt a fist clench in her stomach. 'Mr Arbogast, you've admitted you lied to me once. How do I know I can trust you now?'

'All right. Just tell me this. Do you have any idea where any of these people are now?'

'Why do you ask?'

'Because they're in danger.'

'Tim McJoyce is perfectly safe.'

'Can you make sure he stays safe?'

She thought about it. All she had to do was not pay his bail and he'd stay in jail. 'He'll stay safe.'

'What about Lewis and Kerouac?'

Sharon swiveled to the computer and called up the password file. She saw that Abbie Lewis and Frank Kerouac were both participating in Phase Three, both receiving Sperilac. There was a sudden dryness in her throat.

'Hello,' Arbogast said. 'You still there?'

'I'm still here.'

'Do you have any idea where Lewis and Kerouac are? Do you know if they're safe?'

She called up another file and saw that Lewis and Kerouac had checked into the clinic fifteen minutes ago and were both getting their blood work done. 'They're safe for the moment.'

'That means they're at the clinic.'

'Mr Arbogast, you say you work for the government, but I have no proof of that.'

'Keep them there till five after five. Can you do that?'

She didn't answer.

'Miss Powell, I'm on the same side as you.'

'That's what you say now, but two weeks ago you said you worked for Aetna.'

'Unless you want to keep losing your trial participants, you're going to have to trust me.'

'And supposing I do, what happens at five oh five?'

'You'll walk Lewis and Kerouac out the main entrance yourself.'

'Why?'

'Because I know you and I don't know them.'

'What's going to happen to them?'

179

'They'll be taken into protective custody by a government agent or agents – and yes, Miss Powell, the agents will have appropriate ID.'

At the corner of 17th and K Streets, a hot breeze whipped traffic soot into Eddie's eyes. Blinking hard, he pressed down the switch hook of the payphone and got a fresh dial tone. He dropped another quarter into the coin slot and tapped in the direct line Larry Lorenzo had given him at DEA headquarters.

'Lorenzo.'

'Hi. It's your nemesis. I need you to arrest two guys by the name of Abbie Lewis and Frank Kerouac.'

'What's the charge?' Larry's tone was long-suffering.

'Drug possession. You'll have to plant the coke on them.'

'*Why*, Eddie?'

'To get them behind bars where they can't be murdered. They'll be leaving New Day Clinic at five after five sharp. I'll meet you in Logan Circle in front of the clinic at five.'

May 1 – 5:05 p.m.

At 5:05 Eddie and Larry were sitting in Logan Circle in an unmarked Chevy Majestic belonging to the DEA. Larry was tapping a finger on the dash and chewing gum to block the craving for nicotine. The front seat smelled like spilled root beer.

Across the street a sluggish line of pickets paraded signs in front of the New Day Clinic: WOMEN AND MINORITIES ARE NOT GUINEA PIGS! END HUMAN EXPERIMENTS! TUSKEGEE WAS ENOUGH!

At 5:06 the automated glass doors slid open. Sharon Powell, crisp in a white lab smock, stepped on to the sidewalk. Two men in rumpled work clothes sauntered alongside her. One wore a Prozac baseball cap and the other had a nose ring.

'That's them.' Eddie pointed a low finger. 'The two lowlifes walking with the young blonde woman.'

Lorenzo picked up the radio mike: 'The two guys with the blonde.'

Four men in business suits burst out of a parked car. Two of them flashed IDs. Sharon glimpsed the letters DEA on one of the badges.

'Abbie Lewis? Frank Kerouac?'

Kerouac's face was a white moon of shock.

'You're both under arrest. Please come quietly.'

Sharon stepped back and watched it happen.

Lewis tried to argue – 'You're making a mistake, I swear!' – and Kerouac tried to run through the line of pickets.

One of the agents caught Kerouac's arm and slammed him against the car. Two agents, one at each shoulder, hurled Lewis into the back seat. The fourth cuffed Kerouac and pushed him in behind Lewis. Two doors slammed.

A white mini-van careened to the curb. The U-turning DEA car almost rammed it. The rear door flew open. Three men jumped down to the pavement with mini-cams. A TV SWAT team.

'Excuse me.' A woman thrust a mike into Sharon's face. 'Do you work at New Day Clinic?'

'At the moment, yes.'

'What can you tell us about tests of the controversial new AIDS drug, Sperilac?'

181

'That test hasn't been completed.'

'How many unexplained deaths have resulted so far from Sperilac?'

'Sperilac has never—'

'Excuse me.'

On the sidewalk ten feet away, an African-American woman with her blonde wig pulled back in a bun was swinging her picket at a white woman in a tailored suit. They were screaming names, earrings flying in the wind.

Two dozen other pickets joined in. A flying Chicken McNuggets sandwich caught Sharon in the shoulder. She ducked back into the clinic.

'You OK, hon?' A male nurse handed her a paper towel.

She rubbed at the stain on her smock. 'What's going on out there?'

The nurse pointed at the TV in the waiting area.

On the 30-inch screen, pickets were swinging and garbage was flying.

'This is Cappie Dominique, live at New Day Clinic.' The woman who'd interviewed Sharon raised a forearm to fend off a flying Coke can. 'The scene here is tumultuous as rumors of unexplained deaths and unauthorized autopsies sweep through a community already devastated by budget cutbacks and medical shut-downs.'

'I don't believe it.' Sharon strode down the corridor. She flung open the door to her office. Two strange men were searching her desk. 'Who the hell are you and just what do you think you're doing?'

'Federal marshal, ma'am.'

'I'm sorry, Ms Powell.' The other man handed her a warrant. She recognized Thayer MacLean of the FDA. 'Truly sorry.'

She tore through a three-page lump of 'heretofores' and 'insofars' with her name and New Day's and Biochemtech's typed in the blanks. 'Why?'

'We've had reports that three trial participants have died.'

'That had nothing to do with Sperilac.'

'I sincerely hope not. We'll have to examine your records.'

'Be my guest.'

'Naturally, we're suspending Phase Three till the committee has a chance to evaluate the evidence.'

'There's nothing to evaluate.' Sharon threw the warrant down. 'You *know* Sperilac works. You've seen the Phase One and Phase Two results.'

'Phase One and Phase Two have nothing to do with this.'

'The dead people were killed with succinicholine in an attempt to sabotage the trial and I can show you proof.'

She went to close the office door.

Eddie Arbogast's foot was in the way. 'Ms Powell, I'd like you to meet my friend Larry Lorenzo of the Drug Enforcement Administration.'

They sat in a deserted corner of the Old Black Magic Coffee Shop.

'Sorry I lied.' Eddie laid a Drug Enforcement Administration ID on the table.

Sharon looked at it, then back at him. He seemed five to ten years younger than his photo. 'What do you want from me?'

'Same thing I wanted two weeks ago. Information.'

The waitress brought their orders. 'Peppermint tea?'

'For me, please,' Sharon said.

The waitress handed her a cup.

Eddie measured three teaspoons of sugar into his coffee. He added a generous splash of milk. 'What did you and Harry Forbes discuss in that last meeting?'

'Sperilac.' She sipped and decided to let the tea cool. 'I had an offer from a company called Vestcate to back new trials. He turned it down.'

Eddie glanced at Larry. Larry sat silently spreading butter on his bran muffin.

'What was Andy Horner's connection to Sperilac?'

'He was about to bring suit to stop the Phase Three trial.'

Eddie glanced again at Larry. 'Then Forbes and Horner were both blocking the drug. The same as Thelma van Voss.'

Sharon nodded. 'Very much the same.'

'According to FDA documents, nine hundred thousand bottles of Sperilac were exported to South America last August. Another nine hundred thousand were exported four days ago. What can you tell us about those shipments?'

Sharon hesitated. 'Nothing.'

'Who authorized them?'

'The officer in charge of inventory and shipping. Helen Weller.'

'Why'd she do it?'

'My guess is, people were dying and the hospital needed the Sperilac and she didn't want to risk having a permit denied.'

'What hospital?'

'San Miguel de Bayamo in Gurana, Colombia.'

This time it was Larry who glanced at Eddie.

'How much do you know about that hospital?' Eddie asked.

'Personally? Nothing.'

'Some people think it's a cocaine factory run by the dope cartel.'

'Helen Weller is not a criminal.'

'Where is she now?'

'I don't know. She left the country when the second shipment went out.'

'How did San Miguel pay?'

'No one paid.'

'Then you're wrong about Weller. She's in with the cartel.'

Sharon drew in a deep breath and slowly exhaled. 'You seem to have all the answers.'

'Some of them.'

'Then let me ask *you* a question. Why are you interested in the murders of Phase Three trial members?'

'Because they're drug killings. So were Forbes and van Voss and Horner.'

'How do you know?'

'Ever heard of a man called Miguel Bosch? Better known as Mike?'

'Vaguely. Isn't he some kind of international criminal?'

'He's an international criminal and I want him. I've been wanting him for twenty-five years, and before I turn in my badge, I'm going to get him. Which means time's running out. He runs the biggest drug cartel in the western hemisphere.'

A memory flickered. Sharon recalled a PBS documentary four or five years back – montages of peasants harvesting coca crops and stirring processing vats, an altar in Medellin with votive candles burning to Our Lady of Drug Hitmen, telephoto shots of a gray-haired Don Juan yachting in a Cayman harbor.

'Mike Bosch is also rumored to run San Miguel de Bayamo hospital.'

'Rumors don't prove anything,' Sharon said.

'Not by themselves.' Eddie stirred his coffee. 'But last July an agent was surveilling a meeting on Mike Bosch's yacht. The name Sperilac turned up on the tape.'

Sharon's eyebrows shot up. '*Sperilac?*'

Eddie nodded. 'Putting the pieces together, it sounded like Mike was looking for a cure for AIDS.'

'That's crazy.'

'I thought so too, and then I realized, AIDS is wiping out Mike's clientele. His business is way down. Sperilac cures AIDS, right? Mike thinks Sperilac can save his business.'

'That's absurd.'

The Solution

'Is it?' Eddie took a photo from his wallet. It had obviously been clipped from a larger black-and-white glossy. It showed a yacht moored in a harbor after dusk, men in blazers sitting with drinks on the deck. A woman stood at the railing, her back toward the group, staring out at the camera.

'An agent took this photo of Mike Bosch's yacht, the night they discussed Sperilac. We identified everyone except the woman. Recognize her?'

Sharon looked and swallowed. She didn't answer.

'It's Helen Weller, isn't it?'

Sharon didn't deny it. 'But that doesn't mean she's working with them.'

'Of course not, maybe it was just a social visit. Except for one little fact: last August a South America-bound cartel plane crashed in Mexico. An agent found the label from a bottle of Sperilac in the wreckage.'

'One label doesn't mean—'

'Sperilac implies the involvement of Helen Weller. Helen Weller implies the involvement of Sperilac. They're what we call mutually confirmatory.'

'Maybe government agents think that way, but—'

'Forbes and van Voss were standing in the way of Sperilac, right? They died, right? And you know what? Their deaths were identical in MO to drug cartel hits in Colombia and Panama.'

'But that doesn't prove—'

Eddie held up a finger, silencing her. 'Phone records showed that before Forbes and van Voss were killed, calls were made from the Forbes home to a payphone in the Kennedy Center. That payphone is in the room where the Ballet Folklorico de Uruguay is rehearsing. A group called the Friends of San Miguel de Bayamo are funding the ballet. The dancers aren't Nureyevs or Barishnikovs, but they're fast, and strong, and they're good knife-throwers. I tapped that phone.' Eddie thunked a micro-cassette player on to the table. 'Here's what turned up.'

He pressed *start*.

Sharon listened to the soft Spanish voice. *Flores para Andy Horner. . . Flores para Sondra Cass . . . Flores para Jimmy Santos . . . Flores para Abbie Lewis . . . Flores para Frank Kerouac . . . Flores para Tim McJoyce.*

'Those calls were made *before* the murders. Flowers for every one of the victims. Plus the three who haven't been killed yet. They're hit orders.'

185

Sharon frowned. She remembered the Ballet Folklorico tote bag in Tim McJoyce's apartment and the map with New Day Clinic's location circled. 'And the calls came from Lucinda Forbes' phone?'

Eddie slapped down a sheath of AT&T print-outs. 'Every damned one of them.'

Sharon shook her head. Something wasn't computing. 'But if Mike Bosch killed Forbes and van Voss and Andy Horner for trying to *block* Sperilac, why turn round and kill Kmiotek and Cass and Santos? He's scuttling the trial.'

'He wants Sperilac to have its trial and he wants it to fail. *He wants Sperilac banned.*'

'I don't understand.'

'How long does Sperilac's patent have to run?'

'Seven years.'

'There's only one way you can keep a monopoly on a drug that's past its patent. The US government has to declare it illegal.'

'You mean like narcotics?'

Eddie nodded. 'Exactly.'

Sharon stared a moment at the phone records. She reached into her purse and yanked out her cellphone. She tapped in Lucinda Forbes' home number.

A young man answered. 'Forbes residence.'

Sharon stiffened. It was the voice on Eddie Arbogast's tapes.

'May I speak with Lucinda Forbes, please?'

'May I ask who's calling?'

'This is Sharon Powell at New Day.'

'I'm sorry, Mrs Forbes isn't home at present. Would you care to leave a message?'

'Could you please tell Mrs Forbes that as of a half-hour ago, the FDA has closed down the Sperilac trials?'

'I'm sure she'll be very sorry to hear that.'

Sharon broke the connection. 'The name of the man who made those calls is Key. I don't know his last name. He's Lucinda Forbes' houseboy.'

Larry set down his coffee cup. 'Want me to take him in?'

'No way.' Eddie shook his head. 'He's not calling those hits on his own, he's relaying orders from his boss. We'll leave Key right where he is. Larry, I want you to put him under surveillance. Monitor his phone calls. He's going to lead us straight to Mike Bosch.'

Sharon frowned. 'What makes you think Bosch will need to contact him again? The Phase Three trial's dead.'

Eddie shook his head. 'Not dead enough.'

'I don't follow.'

'Why's Mike interested in Sperilac? Because it works. But he's in trouble if the trial records *show* that it works.'

'But that's exactly what they show. Six trial members have almost cleared the virus.'

'You think Mike Bosch is going to let the FDA find that out and verify it?'

'How can he stop them? The FDA have the power to seize our records any time they want.'

'He can't stop the FDA from getting the records, but he can stop them from getting the people. That's where he's going to need his friend Key.'

Sharon understood. Chair legs shrieked as she pushed back from the table. 'I have to get rid of those records.'

'Not so fast.' Eddie reached over and touched her hand. A fatherly, calming touch. 'Chances are, Mike Bosch has been in your computer from day one. Assuming those six people are still alive, they need protection and they need it *now*.'

He turned.

'Larry. I need airtight security for Sharon Powell and six trial members. Set it up with the Willard Hotel. No one's to know who they are or where they are. Armed agents on guard twenty-four hours a day. No one gets near them.'

Larry groaned. 'Eddie, you keep acting as though I have a magic wand.'

'Either you have a magic wand, or I have a long talk with *Inside Edition*.'

For a tenth of a second, Larry's eyes winced shut. 'OK. I'll set it up. How long will you need the guard?'

Eddie glanced toward Sharon.

She ran it through her mind. 'I have to get passports, air tickets to Amsterdam . . .'

Eddie arched an inquiring eyebrow. 'What's in Amsterdam?'

'The International AIDS Conference. If I can just get those six men and women up on that stage, the world will see that Sperilac works – and this mess will be over for once and all.'

'You'll need photographs for the passports.'

'We have photographs in the clinic files.'

'What about proof of citizenship?'

'I'm willing to swear they're American citizens.'

'Are they? All six of them?'

'I'm pretty sure they are. I'd have noticed if the files said they weren't. Anyway, the assistant Under-Secretary of State is an old Princeton pal of my father's. He once got me a passport in two hours and I had no documentation except a vaccination certificate. When I explain the situation, I know he'll help.'

'How long do you figure it will take you to get all that done?'

'Just to be on the safe side, you'd better give me thirty-six hours.'

'Thirty-six hours.' Larry pushed up from the table. 'You got it.'

May 1 – 6:10 p.m.

W hen Sharon and Eddie returned to New Day, the pickets and TV people had vanished. Silence had settled like dust on the corridors; marshals pushed carts of seized manila folders.

Locking her office door might have drawn attention, so Sharon asked Eddie to stand guard. She dialed Lucas on the modem. While the connection clicked through, she tore through the hard copy Phase Three registration files and removed the mug shots of Balmer, Gault, Goodman, McJoyce and Verba. But where the hell was Kincaid?

There was a beep, and Lucas picked up. The words GREETINGS! L. POWELL HERE appeared on the computer screen.

Sharon finally found Kincaid attached to Kennedy's registration. She slapped his photo on to the stack and swiveled round to the computer keyboard.

Hi. Dad. It's Sharon. How would you feel about being accessary to a felony?

THAT'S THE MOST EXCITING OFFER I'VE HAD ALL DAY.

I want to copy six files to your computer and delete them from mine. OK by you?

ABSOLUTELY.

Hands moving rapidly through the blue-green glow of the monitor screen, she entered the command to copy the files into her father's computer.

A progress report appeared on the screen:

214: BALMER RAQUEL COPYING
18: GAULT PAM COPYING

Eddie turned and warned in a low voice, 'Company.'

Jack Arnold leaned into the half-open door. 'What are you doing in the dark, Sharon?'

She stood, blocking the monitor. 'Just tidying up some old files.'

152: GOODMAN AUDREY COPYING
279: KINCAID BOOKER COPYING

189

'Jack, this is my uncle Ed Arbogast – Jack Arnold. Uncle Ed's with Aetna Life.'

Jack thrust out a hand. 'Pleased to meet you.' He took three steps into the office. 'I just wanted you to know, Sharon, I think it's a crime what the FDA's doing.'

He peered curiously over her shoulder. She moved to keep herself positioned between him and the monitor, trying to make it seem like a casual shifting of weight.

67: MCJOYCE TIM COPYING
113: VERBA MOLLY COPYING
6 FILES COPIED

'Sperilac's a good drug,' he said, 'and one of these days it's going to actually get to market.'

'Thanks, Jack. I've loved working with you.'

'And I've loved working with you. G'night.' He vanished into the corridor.

She quickly entered the command to delete the files.

A question appeared: ARE YOU SURE YOU WANT TO DO THIS? ENTER YES OR NO. ANY REPLY BUT 'YES' WILL ABORT COMMAND.

'He's back,' Eddie warned softly.

Jack's round face hovered in the doorway. 'And Sharon, if there's anything I can do to help, any affidavits or depositions – '

She entered the word *yes*.

' – just ask.'

'Thanks, Jack. I appreciate it.'

Her hard drive began clicking.

Jack's eyebrows arched. 'Say, you're really busy.'

Another message appeared: 6 FILES DELETED.

'Cleaning house?'

She shrugged. 'Taking care of some personal mail I didn't want to leave in the hard drive. Why should the FDA know about my home equity troubles?'

He chuckled. 'I understand.' He waved and was gone.

She lifted the receiver and tapped in the number of Joe Mahler's cellphone. 'Joe, it's Sharon.'

'I've been able to reach exactly three partners.' Joe sounded ragged and stressed. 'A phone satellite's down. This is going to take me all night.'

'There isn't time. We've got to talk right away, and not over the phone.'

Sharon aimed the Mazda toward the Dupont Circle turn-off. 'The FDA has closed down the trial.'

Joe's mouth hung open in disbelief.

'Someone told the media about the deaths. We've had pickets and TV at the clinic.'

'That's awfully fast.' Joe frowned. 'Who knew? There's only you and me and Lucinda. Unless you told someone else?'

'A girl I work with at the lab might have figured something out. But I doubt it. I have a hunch Lucinda's houseboy was eavesdropping.'

'Her *houseboy*?'

Sharon nodded. 'So here's the situation. In sixteen days on Sperilac, six members of the trial have almost cleared the virus.'

Joe whistled softly. 'They're doing better than Isabel.'

'Faster,' Sharon said. 'Not better. Now if we can round up these six and get them to the Willard Hotel, Eddie Arbogast has arranged for them to have an FDA guard until we can fly them to Amsterdam. We'll present them at the AIDS conference as a living demonstration that Sperilac works.'

Joe's eyes were dancing. 'Bypass the opposition and go straight for the touchdown.' He grinned. 'I like it. When do we start?'

Eddie spoke up from the back seat. 'We have to round them up fast, and we can't use the phone. If the wrong people find out what we're doing, we're *all* dead.'

Lucinda Forbes was entertaining seventeen guests at a seated dinner when the butler leaned down and whispered in her ear. 'Phone call, ma'am.'

'Honestly, Wheelock.' She spoke in a lowered hiss. 'Just take the message.'

'It's Mr MacLean of the FDA. He says it's an emergency.'

She laid her spoon beside the plate of perfectly saffroned *bisque aux crevettes*. She turned to the Swedish Ambassador and then to the Director of the FCC. 'Would you excuse me, gentlemen?'

Diamonds jingling like wind chimes in a gale, she hurried to the library. The receiver lay on the table beside the phone. As she picked it up she could hear troubled breathing.

'Yes, Mr MacLean?' Her tone communicated irritation.

'I apologize for contacting you at this hour.'

'I have guests, Mr MacLean. Please be brief.'

'I realize you're not in the line of command of the Phase Three trials, but Sharon Powell seems to have disappeared and so have several of the files. There are three hundred participants listed as taking part in the trial, but there are only two hundred and ninety-four individual patient files in the computer. Six files seem to have vanished.'

'Which files?'

'214 – Raquel Balmer; 18 – Pam Gault; 152 – Audrey Goodman; 279 – Booker Kincaid; 67 – Tim McJoyce; 113 – Molly Verba.'

'I can't say I've ever heard of a single one of those individuals.'

'I didn't expect you would have.'

'Then why are you phoning me?'

'Because I hope you have a back-up set of files.'

'I don't have any of the Phase Three files, Mr MacLean. I'm linked to New Day and I can access Phase Three through Sharon's computer, but if she doesn't have the files, there's no way I can get them for you.'

'Can you think of any reason they'd be removed from the New Day computer?'

'I doubt very much they were removed, Mr Forbes. Mislabeled, perhaps.'

'How could that have happened?'

'When you send armed agents on a Gestapo raid, when you handle honest men and women with all the courtesy you'd reserve for serial killers and bombers of federal office buildings, there's bound to be a little confusion. I'm sure as soon as the dust settles the files will turn up. Now if you'll excuse me, my guests are waiting.'

In his mistress's study, receiver pressed to his ear, Key quickly jotted down the six names and numbers on a piece of paper. The sound of a click was followed an instant later by the flat hum of the dial tone. He replaced the receiver and crossed the room.

His feet made no sound on the blue and jade Persian rug.

Lowering himself into Lucinda Forbes' custom-built ergonomically efficient work chair, he switched on the computer. When the system had booted, he entered the command that accessed the Phase Three files at New Day.

He called up the directory of trial participants and verified that the Balmer, Gault, Goodman, Kincaid, McJoyce, and Verba files had been deleted. Next he verified that no back-ups of the missing files existed.

Finally he called up the personnel roster of the Phase Three trial. He copied down the name and Bethesda, Maryland, address of Dr Jack Arnold, chief medical director. He lifted the telephone and tapped the seven digits of Dr Arnold's number into the keypad.

There were two rings and then a male voice. 'Hello?'

'Dr Arnold?' Key suspected that Booker Kincaid was the name of a black man, so he deepened his voice. 'This is Booker Kincaid, one of the patients in the Sperilac trial?'

'Yes. Mr Kincaid.' Dr Arnold's tone was perplexed.

'I'm sorry to bother you, but I'm having a reaction. I went to the emergency room, and they say it's the Sperilac.'

'What kind of reaction?'

'I'd like to discuss it with you personally – before we bring lawyers into it.'

'Lawyers?'

'I could be at your place in five minutes.'

There was a split second's hesitation, and a sigh. 'All right, come on over.'

May 1 – 8:20 p.m.

S haron drove slowly down V Street, searching for Pam Gault's address. Black youths in watch caps and hooded jogging jackets slouched at intersections and muttered into cellular telephones. They were obviously spreading the word that three whites were prowling the area in a green Mazda.

Second-story curtains fluttered as though caressed by ghosts. Old women were half visible in shadowed windows, watching, telephones at their ears, hands over mouthpieces.

It was a neighborhood that had gone well beyond decay. On home after home, paint peeled from loose aluminum siding, fake brick shingle façades scaled away from weathered wood. Chain-link fences surrounded litter-strewn lawns. Every home had a Dog to Beware of, and a sign announcing the fact.

A silence hung over this zone, a sense of hope abandoned.

This is the real Washington, Sharon thought. Not the Mussolini-modern white marble and granite buildings in the center of town. Not Georgetown. Not Kalorama. The muscle may be elsewhere, but this is the heart. And it's beat is slow, strong, and inaudible to any but the trained ear.

'Forty-one twelve.' Joe Mahler pointed to a house near the corner of V and 10th Street. It stood next to a lot filled with abandoned and well-autopsied automobiles. 'There.'

Sharon pulled to the curb and cut the motor.

Eddie was out of the car first. Sharon and Joe followed. Eddie pushed open the squeaking gate.

The house was unremarkable, but like its neighbors it was showing irreversible signs of age and neglect.

A tall black man loped round the corner of the building and blocked the way to the porch. 'You folks huntin' for somethin'?'

Out of the corner of her eye, Sharon could see two more men, shadows in shadows, standing behind a diseased evergreen. 'I need to talk to Pam.'

'Pam?' The man in front of them chuckled. 'You said *Pam*?'

'It's for her own protection.'

'I don't know no Pam round here needs no protection.'

The two shadows moved slightly closer.

'Look. Pam knows me. If you'll get her, or tell me where I can find her, she'll see me.'

Joe reached into his pocket and pulled out three ten-dollar bills. 'If this would help . . .'

'Do it twice more, and maybe we have something to talk about.'

Eddie struggled getting out his wallet. He produced three twenties.

The two shadows moved into clear view, large black men. They took up positions next to their colleague.

He divided the cash with them. 'That's just fine. You stay here. My friends will keep you company while I see if anybody round here heard of Pam.'

'Tell her it's Sharon Powell from New Day Clinic.'

'I'm T-Bone,' the man said. And trotted up the steps into the house.

At the end of a dim, cracked hallway, a rickety wood staircase with a broken banister led to the second story. T-Bone took the steps two at a time. On the landing, bright light shone in a shaft from under a closed door. Two men with automatic pistols stood guard.

T-Bone exchanged nods.

On the other side of the door, Pam Gault, a tall barefoot black woman in a floor-length smock, stood keeping an eye on the employees in her crack shop.

The room was silent as rigor mortis. A long table stretched from one end to the other. Working with razor blades on plastic cutting boards, twenty men and two women sliced small chips from golfball–sized chunks of hard yellow material. Rapid hands slid the chips into little glassine envelopes and sealed the envelopes over Bunsen burners.

Pam calculated there was about thirty-five thousand dollars' worth of crack on that table. She expected to process and package at least twice that amount before morning.

In a far corner, a third female employee monitored boiling Pyrex saucepans on a gas stove.

Except for rubber gloves and white nose-and-mouth filter masks, every man and woman in the room was stark naked.

Nakedness was an employee rule in Pam's shop. It served two purposes: with no pockets, nobody took home any free samples; and if anyone tried to consume any product on the premises, he or she would show visible signs of sexual arousal.

Pam glanced down the row of crotches and was satisfied that nobody was enjoying anything they shouldn't.

195

There were three knocks on the door, followed by two. T-Bone's signal. Pam slid the bolt and opened the door a crack. 'Yeah?'

T-Bone's face was three inches from hers. He spoke in a lowered voice. 'People to see you.' His breath was a blast of anchovy pizza.

'What people?'

'The white girl in the green Mazda. She's got two friends with her. Says she's Sharon Powell from New Day Clinic.'

Pam grimaced in annoyance. The last thing her operation needed was an interruption. She had twenty runners paying her six bucks a rock to take her crack to dealers all over the city; the dealers would give them eight dollars a rock and sell it for ten. Everyone was waiting – runners, retailers, customers. One thing Pam had learned in this business, you don't let your marketplace down.

'Yeah, I know her. What does she want?'

'She says she has to talk to you.'

Pam sighed. She stepped on to the landing, locked the door behind her, and followed T-Bone downstairs, where she waited in the hallway while T-Bone went outside. In a moment the screen door slammed, and T-Bone led a white woman and two white men into the house. Pam recognized Sharon Powell but not the others. She glanced up over her shoulder towards the guards. 'Tourists,' she joked. 'The rest of the busload is outside waiting to see the monuments.'

The two guards smiled, but they didn't laugh.

'Who's watching the Mazda?' Pam said.

'Deep Freeze is watching,' T-Bone said.

'I appreciate your seeing us,' Sharon Powell said. 'These are my friends Eddie Arbogast and Joe Mahler. We need to talk to you about—'

'Take off your clothes.' As Pam gave the command, she let the smock slide off her shoulders. Heavy-breasted and wide-hipped, she wore nothing underneath. 'All of you.'

'Why?' Sharon was visibly jolted. 'What is this?'

'House rules. Just to make sure you ain't wearin' a wire. You can leave your panties on.'

Hesitantly, Sharon began to undress. She folded her clothes and found a relatively dustless area at the foot of the stairs where she could leave them. The two men stripped quickly and matter-of-factly, as if they were about to take a shower. They put their clothes into neat piles.

'Shoes too. And you two guys drop your shorts.'

The men obeyed.

Pam evaluated their endowments. Not too bad for white men. 'OK,

196

you can pull 'em up.' She pointed to Eddie. 'You with the law?'

He gave her a thin smile. 'Formerly.'

'It shows. You got a belly on you that is pure police issue.' She turned to Sharon. 'So what's on your mind, honey?'

Sharon explained.

Pam guffawed. '*Amsterdam?*' She folded her arms and cocked her head. 'Let me explain something. This here is my place of business. Every time I leave it, I wind up ten, twelve thousand dollars poorer. So I don't think I'll be flying across the Atlantic.'

'We need you with us to prove that Sperilac works,' Sharon pleaded. 'Just a few days out of your life and you could help save hundreds of thousands of lives.'

'I wish I could, honey, but the answer's no.'

'But they're killing people. You're on the list. You've *got* to come with us for your own protection.'

'Protection?' Pam Gault let out a whoop of laughter. 'Honey, you're looking at the most protected bitch in Washington. I got watchers on every corner within six blocks of here. Somebody call and tell me a police car cruisin' too close, I can fold this place in two minutes and we be scattered down every alley in the 'hood. Some strange dude stroll up the street, some new car show up, I know somebody comin'. Like you. My folks phone up and say two white men and a white girl in a car with no special licence plates drivin' around the 'hood, and we check out the plates. My gramma and my Aunt Lucy does that from a phone in the attic. T-Bone got six men downstairs besides the two you saw. There be seven more men with guns in this house. We got the neighbor lady listenin' to the police band for interestin' talk. I got protection hidin' in corners where there ain't no corners.'

'Without Sperilac,' Sharon said, 'you'd still have AIDS. Don't you feel you owe us *anything?*'

'Sure I do, and I'm grateful.' Pam patted Sharon's arm. 'You want Amsterdam, baby? One of these days I'll be able to buy it for you, show you how grateful I am.' Her face hardened. 'But not now.'

Sharon shuddered.

'Baby,' Pam said. 'You catchin' a chill. We best get you back in your clothes and out of here.'

Outside Pam Gault's building, the early moon was a crescent smear in the hazy evening sky. A child shot down V Street on a clattering skateboard.

The green Mazda waited at the curb, magically untouched.

'I'll sit in the back,' Joe volunteered.

Sharon slid into the driver's seat.

Eddie angled his wristwatch to the glow of the dashboard lights. 'This is taking much too long.'

Sharon turned the ignition key and pumped the engine to life. 'What do you suggest?'

'We'll save time if we split up.'

Jack Arnold's neat Georgian brick home sat atop a hill on Kentwood Drive. Behind the foliage of rhododendron and sycamore, a Tiffany lamp glowed in a downstairs window.

Key pressed the doorbell. A round-faced man wearing a National Symphony Orchestra T-shirt opened the door and squinted into the dimness. 'Mr Kincaid?'

Key realized Arnold had no idea what Booker Kincaid looked like. He held out a hand. 'Dr Arnold. Thanks for seeing me.'

'Please come in. Excuse the state of the house.'

Jack led him into a fanatically neat study. Book bindings stood at the exact edges of shelves. A computer monitor glowed on a spotlessly uncluttered desk.

'You mentioned an emergency.' Jack's tone was annoyed but cautious. 'What's the problem and how can I help?'

Reaching beneath his jacket, Key drew a .38 Smith and Wesson semi-automatic from the holster under his left arm.

For a moment Jack just stared at the gun, too shocked to say any-thing. And then a gargling sound sputtered from his throat. 'Wh-what's going on? What do you want?'

'Information on six members of the Sperilac Phase Three trial: Raquel Balmer, 214; Pam Gault, 18; Audrey Goodman, 152; Booker Kincaid, 279; Tim McJoyce, 67; Molly Verba, 113. I want you to tell me why Sharon Powell deleted their files.'

'D-d-deleted? She wouldn't do that.'

'But she has, doctor. See for yourself.'

Jack sat at the computer. With fumbling fingers he accessed the New Day computer and tried to call up the files. And couldn't. And tried to call up back-ups; and couldn't. 'You're right, they're gone.' His eyes glistened with fear and perplexity. 'Come to think of it, I did see her deleting some files this evening . . .'

'And I'm asking you why.'

'I don't know.'

'Come on, doctor. *Think*. There's something about those six that makes them important. What is it?'

'There are three hundred men and women in the trial. Do you expect me to memorize their files?'

Key drew the 6-inch Symington-4-12 silencer from the holster under his right arm. With two twists he fitted it to the gun barrel. 'I need information, doctor, not sarcasm.'

Jack's forehead was sweating like a beer glass. 'What are you going to do to me?'

'I hope I won't have to do anything. Now why don't you just think back over your conversations with Dr Powell. Try to remember if she ever discussed those six patients with you. Apparently some detail about them escaped your attention, but it didn't escape hers. Did she ever mention anything odd or noteworthy about them? Anything they had in common?'

'Wait a minute . . .' Jack blinked rapidly. 'She did mention something . . . but it was crazy, obviously a statistical artifact. Their viral loads . . .'

Key clicked off the safety. 'What about their viral loads?'

Jack's jaw trembled. 'In t-two weeks on Sperilac, their v-viral loads seemed to . . .'

'Will you please complete your sentences, doctor? Their viral loads seemed to *what*?'

'Seemed to have almost vanished.'

'And what does that mean, when a viral load almost vanishes?'

'She was extrapolating from fluctuations in the data. You have to understand, statistics by themselves, ripped out of context, are clinically meaningless.'

Key sighed. 'What did Sharon Powell *think* it meant?'

'She thought Sperilac worked and those six people were the proof.'

'Ah ha. Thank you, doctor.' Key held the gun absolutely steady. 'That's exactly what I needed to know.'

'You're welcome. Now would you mind putting that d-damned gun away?'

'Not at all.'

But first, Key fired a round into Jack Arnold's forehead.

May 1 – 9:30 p.m.

The address was one of those featureless white brick apartment buildings that look as if they were designed by a Department of Housing laser printer. There was no answer when Sharon pushed Raquel Balmer's buzzer, so she pushed three others.

'Who is it?'

'Pizza.'

Some hungry soul buzzed her in.

She found a scrawled note taped to the door of 3-D: 'Hal – I'm at the Whale. Raq.'

Down the corridor, an old woman was trying to punch the contents of a paper bag into the incinerator.

'Excuse me,' Sharon called. 'Is there a place around here called the Whale?'

The old woman made a face. 'R Street. Out the door, take a left, and hold your nose.'

Sharon found R Street, but it was five minutes before she found the Whale, tucked halfway down a dead-end alley. A stenciled sign in the window announced 'Amateur Night'.

The place was half filled. She sat on a bar stool. The air-conditioner blew a smell of beer and stale smoke.

'What'll it be?' The bartender had red hair surrounding a balding pate.

'Rolling Rock, please.'

He thumped a mug and a sweating bottle in front of her.

She slid a ten toward him. 'You wouldn't know a lady by the name of Raquel Balmer?'

He jerked a thumb toward the stage. 'In person.'

Up in the spotlight, a man and a woman were singing '*Cuando Calienta el Sol*' in Spanish. With the electric keyboard and mechanical drum back-up, their voices sounded urgent and naked, not quite together and not quite sure of the key. The man was short and chubby but he had a huge tenor. The woman, almost six feet tall, had a long store-bought blonde fall and enhanced breasts, and her consonants popped through the mike like firecrackers. She hit a climactic high

200

note that blotted out the tenor and triggered a squawk of feedback.

A moment's silence hung in the air and then the singers kissed and hugged and the audience realized it was over. Applause spattered, perfunctory but polite. The woman paused for a moment, looking around the room for someone she didn't see, and then she stepped down as gracefully as her too-tight silver skirt would allow and went and sat alone in a booth.

Sharon took her Rolling Rock and sat opposite her. 'Raquel Balmer?'

Raquel lit a cigarette, blew out smoke, and nodded.

'I'm Sharon Powell.'

'I know.'

'Could I offer you a drink?'

Raquel thrust a braceleted wrist into the air and snapped her fingers. A waitress's head turned. 'Hey, Angie. Double Dewars on the rocks.'

'That was quite a rendition.'

'Puh-*leeze*. I only do it because my therapist tells me to.'

Raquel's drink came. They clinked Dewars and Rolling Rock.

'I saw you on TV.' Raquel stared at her. 'Looks like you got yourself some trouble.'

'Which is why I'm here. How would you like to fly to Amsterdam?'

'Amsterdam? Why?'

'You'll get five hundred dollars a day, all expenses paid.'

'What's the catch?'

'You have to come with me now to a hotel and you have to agree to stay sequestered till tomorrow evening.'

Raquel's face turned cagey. 'And then?'

'You and four other Phase Three trial members will be presented to the AIDS conference in Amsterdam as proof that Sperilac works.'

Raquel's eyes showed surprise, flecked with something very much like relief. 'Does that mean my blood work was good?'

'Very good. How about it?'

'Who's going to be at this conference?'

'Representatives of the World Health Organization; doctors and researchers from all over the world; pharmaceutical manufacturers; people with AIDS; ten thousand men and women from a hundred and fifty nations who have an interest in finding the cure.'

Raquel shrugged. 'Sounds cool. I'll go. Assuming I have anything to wear.'

* * *

Key sat at the computer in Lucinda Forbes' study, tapping into Sharon
Powell's cellphone record. He scrolled down the column, noting repeat
calls. The number 555–7800 showed up three times today.

He split the screen and accessed the telephone company's reverse
directory.

The cursor glided down the numerical column: 7797 – 7798 – 7799
– and bingo, he had it: 7800.

The cursor slid across the screen to the name of the subscriber: *KLM
Royal Dutch Airlines*.

He called up Sharon's Mastercard transactions. Only today she had
charged $7,860.80 at the Golden Eagle Travel Agency.

He worked his keyboard magic and scrolled through the KLM mani-
fests. Plunging an electronic finger into the pie, he pulled out his plum:
on the 8:30 flight from Dulles to Amsterdam tomorrow evening, Sharon
Powell and the six others were booked together, all on her credit card.
She was spending close to eight thousand dollars to fly Balmer, Gault,
Goodman, Kincaid, McJoyce and Verba to Amsterdam.

He tapped out the command to hard copy the flight data.

While the last printer went to work, he engaged the modem and
called an overseas number. He typed in the E-mail message: 'Six trial
members on Sperilac have almost cleared the virus. Sharon Powell
believes this proves Sperilac works. She has made plane reservations
for them and herself to Amsterdam departing Dulles tomorrow at 8:30
p.m. What do you want me to do?'

After sixty seconds, he entered the code to retrieve messages.

The response was waiting: 'They must not reach Amsterdam. Include
Sharon Powell in your arrangements. Termination of problems essential.
Repeat. Essential.'

He heard the door open behind him. He quickly cleared the screen of
E-mail, but it was too late to stop the printer.

'Just what do you think you're doing in here?'

He spun round.

Lucinda Forbes strode across the carpet, eyes blazing. 'How dare
you monkey with my computer!'

'I was only . . .' Key's mind flailed. 'Making sure the printer had
enough toner.' He leaned down to the printer, snatched out the pages,
and ripped them into ribbons.

'What did you just tear up?'

Instinct shouted in him: *waste this bitch*. His fingers flexed,
strangler's fingers, hungry for that jeweled neck, but he forced his hands

to stay at his side. He gloved his voice in meekness. 'I was only looking for games.'

'You were looking for games *in my computer*?' She slapped him. She had to stand on tiptoe, but she did it. For a woman of 115 pounds, she could muster astounding force. 'You were snooping. I will not abide spies in my own home!'

He took two stumbling steps backward and collided with the Aubusson settee.

'Who are you working for? Merck? Pfizer?'

Lucinda Forbes wouldn't have been half so furious if Key hadn't been such a damned good servant. Since last July, when Bertolt Devereux had recommended him as a houseboy, Key had made himself indispensable in hundreds of ways. Squeezing her morning orange juice exactly the way she liked it, with a *soupçon* of rind. Pre-sorting her mail. Taking over the household for an entire month when the butler had been too arthritic to manage. Handling the arrangements for Harry's funeral.

And now he turned out to be not a godsend but a sneak.

'Are you working for Bertolt-Bienvenue?'

'I work for you, Mrs Forbes.'

'Not any more. Pack your things and have your butt out of this house in fifteen minutes.'

'I'm sorry if I've offended you.' He pulled himself to his feet. 'I never intended—'

'Fifteen minutes or I'm calling the police.'

He shot her a look of 200-proof venom and left the room.

Anger was exhausting and now Lucinda Forbes was exhausted. She went to the bar and poured herself a Cutty Sark on the rocks. And then another. They didn't help, but that was what she did.

The sound of a car revving wildly broke into her annoyance. She lifted an edge of the window curtain just in time to see Key's blue Datsun tear out of the garage.

He didn't even pack his things.

Curious now to know what he'd been doing in her files, she sat down at the computer and tapped the instruction to display the contents of the hard disk. She saw that the most recent file had been created only three minutes ago.

She called it up.

It appeared Key had unintentionally saved an E-mail exchange when he cleared it from the screen. She read it twice, once quickly and then, as the shock seeped in, a second time. Her eyes narrowed at the sentences, 'Include Sharon Powell in your arrangements. Termination of problems essential.'

For an instant the world seemed to shrink to a tunnel with those words glowing at the far end.

She phoned Sharon's home number. After three rings the answering machine cut in.

'Sharon, it's Lucinda. If you're there, pick up.'

Silence.

'Sharon, it's urgent. Contact me the minute you get this message.'

She phoned Sharon's voice mail at New Day and left the same message.

May 1 – 9:40 p.m.

Joe Mahler heard them from down the street: voices chanting in low, rapid unison. He checked the address one last time before entering the wood-frame tenement.

A hand-lettered sign was taped to the inner door: 'Booker Kincaid / Western Buddhist Center / Apt. 3A / PLEASE DO NOT RING.'

As he climbed the creaking stairs his ear began to distinguish syllables – '*Nam myoho renge kyo . . .*'

A sign taped to the door of 3A asked all visitors to remove their shoes. Three dozen pairs lined the hallway: wing tips, high heels, work boots, sneakers, sandals. He placed his at the end of the row and opened the apartment door.

The chanting surrounded him now, but the room was dark and still, like the surface of a lake on a calm night. His first impression was that it was empty, that the voices might be some kind of recording.

Candles placed on windowsills cast a flickering light on bare blue walls. As his eyes adjusted he saw dozens of men and women sitting on the floor in lotus position, facing the eastern wall.

The leader of the chant, a black man with dreadlocks, wearing a white Buddhist robe, lifted a soft mallet and touched a suspended gong. A shivering hiss passed through the air.

Joe leaned toward a young Oriental girl and whispered, 'Excuse me. Where can I find Booker Kincaid?'

Without opening her eyes, she tipped her head sideways, expelling a rush of syllables in unison with the others: '*Shakemitsi bushu.*' He had the impression she'd heard him, and her head seemed to be indicating the far side of the room.

He tiptoed across.

A man with open eyes sat pressing his fingers into a pyramid.

'Excuse me,' Joe whispered. 'I'm looking for Booker Kincaid.'

'*Busha-mitsi tasha-mitsi.*' The head nodded toward a bamboo-curtained doorway.

Joe stepped into a kitchen. A bald-headed black man stood stirring a three-gallon vat over a low flame. A soothing smell of herbs and barks and mint floated up.

'Booker Kincaid?'

The man smiled very slightly, as if in recognition of an irony. 'And who are you, brother?'

'My name's Joe Mahler. I'm a friend of Sharon Powell, from New Day.'

'And how can I help you?'

He let Joe explain, watching him with interested brown eyes. All the while he rotated his neck back and forth, as if seeking some internal adjustment.

When Joe finished, Kincaid said, 'Just a moment.'

He stepped through the curtain and returned with a young woman. 'Sarah, this is Joe Mahler.'

She nodded, eyes downcast.

'I have to go to Amsterdam, Sarah. Will you take care of the tea?'

Kincaid touched Joe's arm. They tiptoed to the hallway and recovered their shoes.

'Tell me something,' Joe said going down the stairs. 'Those words that they're chanting, what language is that?'

'No language. The words are meaningless.'

Joe was astounded. 'Meaningless?'

Kincaid nodded. 'Don't you think it's truer than a philosophy that explains the world? We do.'

Key located Raquel Balmer's name on the panel, pushed the buzzer, and waited.

No one answered.

Picking other residents at random, he jabbed another six buttons.

A staticky voice came over the intercom: 'Who is it?'

'Gas man.'

'You know what time it is?'

'You got a leak in your cellar. Emergency.'

'Jesus Christ.'

There were two loud clicks and the door swung inward.

The elevator indicator pointed to seven. Key bounded up the service stairs, two steps at a time.

He could hear a TV through the door of 3-D. He pressed the door bell.

No answer.

He knocked.

Still no answer.

206

Possibly Raquel Balmer had fallen asleep in front of the TV, though he wondered how she managed with that cacophony of gunshots and squealing brakes.

He glanced to the left and then to the right, making sure the corridor was empty. He took out his semi-automatic and slipped the silencer on to the barrel.

He fired a single round into Raquel Balmer's lock. The sound was no louder than a foot stomping down on a balloon of water. The lock leapt out of the door like a surprised toad. Inside the apartment, a carpet muffled its fall.

He eased the door open. The room was dark. He slipped inside and closed the door behind him. He stood quietly, composed himself, let information enter his senses.

The TV threw a splash of flickering blue across the empty sofa. The sound of canned mayhem covered his footsteps.

In the kitchen, a faucet dripped on a stack of dishes. The refrigerator wheezed and sighed, laboring like a patient on an artificial respirator.

He crossed to the bedroom and flicked the wall switch.

The bed was still made up: pink satin throw pillows, Barbie dolls, and a stuffed baby leopard with Maybellined eyelashes. Jackets and sweaters lay scattered on the tasseled spread. A silver skirt was draped over the rocking chair. The closet door was open and a nylon stocking trailed out of a bureau drawer.

Key forced himself to take a deep breath. He crossed to the bathroom. He had a good idea what he would find.

He snapped on the light.

She had taken her toothbrush.

'*Mierda!*'

'This is the offer.' Sharon spoke through the bars of Tim McJoyce's cell, voice lowered in deference to prisoners who might be sleeping. 'I'll pay your bail. In addition you'll receive five hundred dollars a day plus expenses.'

'Sounds illegal.' Tim McJoyce winked. 'What do I have to do?'

'Come with me now to a hotel in downtown Washington.'

'Right now?' He grinned and tipped his head sideways. 'With you?'

'Right now. With me. Is something not clear?'

'How many days am I supposed to spend with you in this hotel?'

'You'll be sequestered with four other trial participants till tomorrow evening.'

'And then?'

'And then you'll all fly with me to Amsterdam.'

'What's in Amsterdam?'

'The International AIDS Conference. You five are going to be the proof that Sperilac works.'

Tim McJoyce reflected a moment. 'Amsterdam's got to be a better place than this cell.' He shrugged. 'OK. I'll do it.'

'I'll be right back.' Sharon went to the end of the corridor and rang the bell.

Almost three minutes passed before a key turned and the security door swung open. A heavyset cop hustled a drunk through.

She went to the front desk. 'I want to pay Tim McJoyce's bail. Cell four oh nine.'

The duty officer gave her a look. 'Funny hour to be paying bail.'

She opened her purse and peeled two bills off the roll of hundreds and another fifteen off the twenties. 'My money's dead serious.'

He counted the five hundred dollars and gave her a receipt. He picked up a telephone.

Ten minutes later he shoved a manila envelope across the desktop.

Tim McJoyce ripped it open and stuffed his wallet into the pocket of his faded denim jacket.

'And don't forget this.' The duty officer handed him a summons. 'Superior court. Four weeks.'

'We'll be there,' Sharon said.

Key was breathing hard from the three-story climb. He pushed opened the door. The chanting voices grew louder. '*Taka-mitsi shaka-bushu . . .*'

He looked around the darkness.

'Help you, brother?' someone whispered. A tall, broad silhouette rose out of the dimness and blocked his way.

'I'm looking for Booker Kincaid.'

A finger gestured to lower his voice. 'There's a sign outside. It says take off your shoes.'

'I'm not staying,' Key whispered.

'You sure aren't if you don't take off those shoes. Leave 'em in the hallway.' The man said nothing more. He just waited, staring into Key's eyes. Candlelight seemed to spread like an aureole around his head.

Key went back into the hallway and slipped out of his shoes. As he stepped over the doorsill, the texture of woven straw mats pressed through his socks.

'You interested in Buddhism, brother?'
'I'm interested in Booker Kincaid.'
'Why's that?'
'Because I have a message for him.'
'I'll give him the message.'
'I have to give it to him personally.'
'That's a shame, brother, because you just missed him.'

May 1 – 11:40 p.m.

'**M**y name's Arbogast,' Eddie shouted into the staticking intercom. 'I need to talk to you about the New Day trial.'

'You know what time it is?'

'I'm sorry. But this is an emergency.'

At that moment a young man came into the vestibule tugging a miniature white poodle on a leash. 'Come on, Fluffums, you've had your excitement for the day.' He smiled at Eddie. 'And so have I.'

Eddie caught the door behind Fluffums and went into the lobby. Audrey Goodman's apartment, 1-F, was at the end of a long dim corridor. He rapped lightly. 'Ms Goodman?'

A TV was making late-night talk show noises.

He rapped again, louder. 'Ms Goodman?'

The door snapped open and an unbelievable stench of cat urine hit him like a fist in the face. A snarling mouth appeared above the safety chain. 'You got ten seconds.'

'If you'd let me in it might be easier to talk.'

'And it'd be a whole lot easier to walk off with the TV and the microwave.'

He opened his wallet and held it up to the crack. 'I'm a federal employee.'

'So's my ex-husband and he's in jail.' The chain clattered loose and Audrey Goodman held the door open eight inches. 'Careful you don't let the cats out.'

He squeezed through. Five cats attacked his trouser leg and a sixth decided his shoe was an emery stick.

'So talk.' Audrey Goodman, dark-haired and wary-eyed and shapeless in a faded bathrobe, must have believed his heart was on the right, because that was where she was pointing her revolver.

He took a deep breath and explained the situation.

Audrey Goodman didn't interrupt. She didn't react. She gazed at him with a kind of fixed contempt, as though he was a drunk in a bar feeding her a long, boring, predictable line.

When he mentioned five hundred dollars a day she took a step backward and caught the arm of a chair. On the table next to it, a bottle jiggled. He couldn't see the label but he realized that whatever it was, she had most of it in her.

When she lifted the phone he had a hunch she was calling 911. But she dialed four digits too many. 'Talia, it's Audrey. Yes, I know the time.'

She held the receiver away from her ear and silently mouthed, '*Yak-yak*.'

'Talia, the reason I'm calling, my mother's had another stroke. She needs me. I won't be able to come in to work for the rest of the week.'

'*Yak-yak*.'

'Thanks, I owe you.' She dropped the phone into the cradle and tossed the gun on to the sofa. 'Amsterdam.' She lingered over the pronunciation, as though she could taste the word. 'Hey, whatever your name is.'

'Eddie.'

'Do me a favor while I pack, there's some dry food for the cats in the kitchen.'

'What about water?'

'They use the toilet.'

Key pressed his ear to Tim McJoyce's door and heard absolute stillness.

He glanced around the shadows of the deserted hallway. Ignoring the PAL and Top Dog Security stickers, he slid his Mastercard into the crack between the lock and the doorjamb. The latchbolt clicked.

He ducked quickly inside.

The hall light caught a huddled shape on a fold-out bed and then the door clicked shut.

He took a moment to explore the wall and locate the electric switch. He slipped the silencer on to the gun barrel. Taking aim at the bed, he flicked the switch.

And realized he was aiming at two pillows and a tangle of sheets.

Frowning, he surveyed the pulleys and bars of a home work-out center. Barbells, dumbbells, and dirty clothing were strewn across the floor.

He kicked a T-shirt out of the way and snapped on the bathroom light. A limp-bristled toothbrush rested in a tumbler on the sink.

He sat on the corner of the bed, weighing his options.

His eye caught movement on the mattress. He looked closer.

A tuna sandwich lay in the valley between pillows, and a cohort of cockroaches were having a fiesta.

He realized Tim McJoyce had not been home for at least twenty-four hours.

* * *

Sharon could hear the Verba family from down the corridor. Toppling furniture. Thrown shoes. Treble voices screaming.

She knocked at the door of 6-B: steel, fireproof, regulation Department of Housing and Urban Development.

The door opened, and a little girl whose head barely reached the safety chain stood gazing up at her.

'Is your mommy home?' Sharon said.

The girl turned. 'Are you home, Mommy?'

'Who is it?' a used-up voice shot back.

'Tell your mommy it's Sharon Powell from New Day.'

Footsteps thumped. An adult hand undid the chain.

'What do you want?'

Sharon stared into a mass of fiery hair, a numbed mask of a face that had yet to lose its last layer of baby fat.

'Molly Verba?'

A tired nod.

'I'm sorry to bother you at this hour, I realize it's late.'

'It's never late around here.'

'Could I come in for a moment?'

'Careful you don't get run down. We have a few meteors in here.'

The place seemed crowded with children scurrying and whirling, and shrieking and wheeling and dancing. It was a shock to count heads and realize there were only three. Still dressed, they were all of different races, and all bore a marked resemblance to their mother.

The littlest had seized the TV remote and the others were trying to grab it from her.

'We're having cocoa. Want some?'

Sharon shook her head. 'No thanks.'

'Why don't you sit down, I'll only be a minute.'

Sharon surveyed plastic chairs. Wood-crate tables. Walls hung with liquor store calendars and children's crayoned drawings. A 36-inch Sony Trinitron leaping from channel to channel.

She sat on an orange plastic chair contoured like a bus seat and watched Molly pass cups of hot chocolate to the three children. Within seconds, two of the unbreakable cups were on the floor.

'Shewana, you clean that up.' Molly dropped into a blue plastic chair that vibrated a little under her weight. Weary pale blue eyes turned toward Sharon. 'What's the matter?'

'Actually it's good news. It's about your health.'

212

The eyes were dubious. 'You're here because you got good news?'

'There's a little more to it than that.' Sharon explained the situation.

'No way.' Molly shook her head. 'I have to pick up my benefits in person, Thursday, ten a.m. sharp. If I'm not there, I lose my benefits. I have three kids to feed, I can't afford to lose my benefits.'

'You'll only be gone four days.'

'Four days, four years, same difference. Who'll take care of the kids?'

'Don't you have a relative?'

Molly grunted. 'You're looking at the only relative I trust.'

'Maybe a neighbor would help out?'

For a moment Molly didn't answer. Her eyes were calculating. 'The lady upstairs charges thirty dollars a day.'

'We'll pay your expenses.'

'Per kid. In advance.'

Sharon took the money from her wallet.

'And food's extra,' Molly said.

Day was already a faint pink smear in the eastern sky when Key found the dilapidated house on V Street. As he opened the squeaky gate, a tall, hooded black man stepped out of the shadow and blocked his way.

'Help you, bro?'

'I have to speak to Pam Gault.' Key laid on a Trinidad accent. 'It's urgent.'

'And what makes you think she lives here?'

'Because this is the address she gave the clinic.' Key handed him a print-out of the addresses of the nine trial members whose names began with G. He had circled Pam's.

The man flicked a cigarette lighter and studied the print-out. His eyes came back to Key. 'And what's so urgent?'

'Ms Gault's last test shows she's at risk for a metastasizing sarcoma.'

The man's face was skeptical. 'The other doctor was here a few hours ago – she didn't mention no sarcoma.'

'Dr Powell hasn't seen these results. They came in twenty minutes ago.'

The man glanced at his watch. 'You fellas sure work around the clock.'

'Look, Ms Gault needs to change her medication now, and I mean within the next two hours, or she faces a bone-marrow transplant. Now if you want to take responsibility . . .'

'I ain't takin' responsibility for no bone marrow. But Pam left ten, fifteen minutes ago.'

'Then where can I find her?'

May 2 – 5:25 a.m.

S ome deliveries Pam Gault made herself, either for old customers, or rich customers, or customers who let her share a joke or two with them. This morning she had three deliveries. Two were United States senators. The third was a nice elderly white man named Higgins, a retired teacher who had been introduced late in life to the joy of crack by a pixie-witted student.

For obvious reasons, bald-headed old white men were better off not paying calls on Pam so, for a consideration, she made the delivery. Higgins never bought fewer than twenty bags, never failed to tip, and never failed to share.

Pam liked Mr Higgins.

She went up the three front steps to the entryway of the luxury condominium and rang the desk.

'Yes?'

'Pam to see Mr Higgins in seven one oh.'

'Oh, right. You're expected. I'll buzz you in.'

The lock on the door sprang and Pam strode to the elevators and pushed the button for the seventh floor.

At 710, she started to knock but realized that the door was already standing slightly ajar. She pushed it wide, stepped in and looked around the living room with its carved wood tables and track-lit Hockneys.

No sign of Mr Higgins.

'Yoo hoo. Honey? It's Pam.'

Then she saw him – tied, blindfolded, and gagged, lying on his stomach on the couch.

'What the fuck—'

The door slammed behind her. She wheeled and saw a big angel-faced lug blocking the way. Mexican or Indian to judge by the Aztec nose.

'I have a message for you, Pam,' he said.

With a single fluid movement she had the straight razor out of her garter, flipped open, and ready for action. 'Nobody sends me messages here, Spick.' She crouched and slashed the air between them in a swift glinting arc, letting him know she meant business.

215

'This time they do.' From inside his jacket, he pulled a discreet little semi with a very large silencer. He fired once and shattered her brain.

Sharon and Joe stood in the lobby of the Willard Hotel saying goodbye. He was taking an early flight to Amsterdam for the first day of the AIDS conference.

'Are you sure you wouldn't rather I stay with you and take the later flight?'

She shook her head. 'I have top protection – DEA marksmen. You can't get safer than that.'

'I'm still going to worry about you.'

'Worry about Sperilac. Get over to that conference and start boosting it.'

He pressed a small pale blue Tiffany shopping bag into her hands.

'What's this?' She peeked beneath the tissue and saw a stack of freshly printed hundred-dollar bills.

'You've been spending a lot of your own money lately. Vestcate pays all expenses, remember?'

'Joe, I don't need it.'

'You never know when it may help keep you and those little dope addicts alive.'

'What are you trying to make me, a kept woman?'

At that instant, something in his face was funny and touching and vulnerable. 'Did I ever tell you I think you're one of the bravest, most terrific human beings I've ever met?'

'No, you never told me.'

'Well, you're not terrific. You're absolutely sensational.'

She pulled back and stared into his eyes. Brown, liquid, adoring eyes. She felt a pain in her chest, like glass cracking.

'And I've thought so ever since day one, when you walked into that sunroom and saved my sister's life. And mine.'

'I didn't save anyone's life,' she said.

'We'll argue this later. I have a plane to catch.'

He kissed her quickly on the lips. And then he vanished through the revolving glass door.

Sharon stepped into the elevator and pressed seven. For the next thirty-six hours, the management of the Willard Hotel had agreed to keep the seventh floor empty except for six guests and their guards. Vestcate was paying $250 a night for each of the forty rooms on the floor – a total of $40,000 for the thirty-six hours.

She stepped out, nodded to the three dark-suited men from the DEA, and went to room 712. The five trial members who were going to Amsterdam had gathered for breakfast and briefing.

'As you know,' Sharon said, 'you're here under guard now because we want to get you to Amsterdam alive. The threat is real. Two of our trial members and possibly a third were killed with poisoned cocaine. An attempt was made on Tim McJoyce's life with poisoned cocaine. So if any of you are holding cocaine, the chances are damned good that you're holding poison. I'm going to ask you to hand it over right now.'

Five shocked faces stared at her.

'You think I'd be holding that shit?' Booker Kincaid said.

'Are you?'

'Hell, no.'

'I don't let drugs near my body,' Tim McJoyce said.

Which left Raquel Balmer and Molly Verba and Audrey Goodman, three pairs of evasive eyes and fidgeting feet.

'Ladies?' Sharon said.

It was Raquel Balmer who broke the silence. 'OK, so I'm holding. Is personal use a crime?'

'Crime isn't the issue. If you want to do coke while you're in rehab, that's between you and New Day. I just don't want you getting poisoned.'

'I've been getting coke from my dealer for ten years and he's never poisoned me yet, why's he going to start now?'

'Are you saying you won't give me the coke?'

'No way.'

Sharon turned. 'Audrey?'

'I'm holding a little,' Audrey Goodman said. 'But I feel the same as Raquel. I trust my dealer.'

'Molly?'

'Eight hours cooped up in a jet?' Molly Verba shuddered. 'No *way* I'm going to make this trip without coke.'

'Then the three of you have to let me analyze that coke and make sure it's not poisoned.'

Groans went up.

Sharon played her trump. She opened Joe's little blue Tiffany bag and lifted off a sheet of tissue. 'I'll pay ten times street value – non-refundable – for the loan of your stashes.'

217

* * *

Key came up the creaking steps of the old stairwell into the flickering fluorescent light of the hallway. He stood for a moment, breathing hard, and listened at the door of 6-B.

Some kind of murder-a-minute, shoot-'em-up, blow-'em-up was blasting on the TV. Cars screeched and bullets rattled and music pounded. He heard something else too, the live sound of feet jumping, of furniture falling over.

He rapped on the door.

A child opened it. Her blonde afro barely came up to the safety chain. He could see two other children whirling and leaping behind her.

'Is Mommy home?' he asked.

A slow, mischievous grin lit the little face. 'Mommy's gone to Holland.'

At twenty-five after seven, Sharon crossed an almost empty employees' parking lot and stepped into the Biochemtech building.

The guard smiled. 'Hi, Sharon. Nice to see you back.'

'Nice to be back, Frank.'

'You're starting bright and early today.'

'You know how it is. Lots to get done.'

She went directly to the lab. Not surprisingly, she was the first to arrive. She flicked on the overheads and the air-conditioner, started the coffee, and went straight to her work station.

She poured two inches of distilled water into three retorts. She dropped Balmer's cocaine into the first, Verba's into the second, Goodman's into the third.

Clamping each retort over a gas burner, she set the air and gas regulators to bring the water to just under boiling: hot enough to dissolve the cocaine, but not so hot as to vaporize any element.

When the dissolution was completed, she poured her first sample, Balmer, into the centrifuge, and set it spinning. Very gradually she pushed the speed level up to the top r.p.m.

A rush of vapor clouded the Plexiglas lid. She opened the catheter and drew off the water.

After three minutes she pressed *stop*. The chamber slowed and finally whined down to a standstill. She lifted the lid and peered inside.

Since she'd used purified water, there were no trace minerals today or pulverized protozoa. But there were three clear bands: two crystalline white and almost touching; below them, separated by an empty 10-millimeter zone, a ring of faint yellow.

She tweezed a sample from the higher white band, placed it in the spectroscope, and gave it a millisecond blast of laser.

Vapors streamed past the scope and the chemical symbols for cocaine popped up on the screen.

No surprise there.

She repeated the process with a sample from the second white band. If this second crystalline powder were succinocholine, and she suspected it was, the read-out would be two linked molecules, $C24$-$H40$-$O5$ bonded to the far less massive $C4$-$H6$-$O4$.

Instead, the screen showed a single, completely different molecule: $C12$-$H22$-$O11$.

Frowning, she reached for Wendy's organic chemistry desk reference and thumbed through the $C12$ compounds.

Lactose. A disaccharide.

That stood to reason: street dealers cut cocaine with milk sugar, right?

Then if there was any succinocholine present, it had to be the third ring, the faintly yellow powder.

She tweezed a sample into the spectroscope and zapped.

Letters and numbers popped up on the screen. They made absolutely no sense to her. They certainly were no form of succinocholine. She ripped through the desk reference. What the reference said made even less sense.

Some contaminant must have gotten into the sample. Perhaps from the tweezers.

She took a fresh pair from the sterilizing chamber, tweezed another smidgin of yellow into the spectroscope, and re-zapped.

She stared at the screen: up came the identical letters and numbers. She couldn't believe it.

She repeated the analysis with the Verba sample and the Goodman sample. The cocaine in both was virtually identical with Balmer. The lactose was higher in Verba and lower in Goodman, but the spectroscopic analysis of the baffling yellow powder was exactly the same as in Balmer.

She puzzled for a moment, and then she did what she normally did when she was stymied: she booted the computer, laid the telephone receiver in the modem, and phoned her father.

It's Sharon. Are you awake?

I AM NOW.

I'm trying to analyze some street cocaine samples and I can't. She described her dilemma.

ARE YOU SURE YOU HAVEN'T MADE A MISTAKE? ALL THREE SAMPLES ARE *POSITIVE* FOR ETHYLATED SULFONAMIDE?

Sharon reviewed her results: *All samples are positive.*

TEST THOSE SAMPLES FOR ZINC SULPHIDE AND POTASSIUM CARBONATE.

May 2 – 8:10 a.m.

C hoosing at random, Key pressed four buttons that weren't Audrey Goodman.

A cantankerous voice staticked back over the intercom. 'Yeah?'

'PepCo. Gotta read the electric meter.'

'Christ Almighty.'

The lock released with a buzz.

Key located the Goodman apartment, 1-F, at the end of a long, poorly lit corridor. He pressed his ear to the door and heard voices. A man and a woman. When he heard the *Good Morning America* theme he realized it was the TV.

He slipped his Mastercard into the doorjamb, found the latch, and tried to slip it. The latch slipped all right, but Goodman had thrown the deadbolt, and it wasn't about to budge.

Key glanced behind him, making sure none of the neighbors were up and about. He slipped the silencer to the semi and shot a round into the bolt.

He nudged the door open, squeezed inside, quickly shut the door.

He paused for a moment, looking around him. The living room was dark. He could see the reflected flicker of the TV on the bedroom wall. He stepped quietly across the scatter rugs and peered through the half-open door.

A spill of unsteady blue light caught five or six cats huddled on the bedspread. On the table beside them, the light on the answering machine was blinking.

Key crossed the room and pressed the *replay* button.

'Honey, it's Audrey.' There was something gray and melancholy and possibly a little slurred about the woman's voice. 'If you should happen to get back today, could you do me a favor? Fix me up with a few dimes of shake and some works – put it in an envelope and drop it off at the Willard Hotel, Room 702. Thanks, you're saving my life. Love you much, kiss kiss.'

The rapping on the door was insistent and loud.

Audrey lowered the volume on Regis and Kathie Lee. 'Who is it?' she demanded.

221

'Delivery for Audrey Goodman,' a slightly accented voice answered.

Audrey rushed to the door, undid the safety chain, turned the bolt and flung wide.

A sweet-faced young woman stood in the corridor holding a padded manila envelope.

God bless him, Audrey thought. He scored!

'Sign here, please.' The young woman handed Audrey a lined sheet of paper on a clipboard.

Audrey scratched her name across the paper and took the envelope. 'Just a second, hon.' She fumbled in her purse and handed the young woman a dollar bill. 'Thanks. You saved my life.'

The young woman smiled and vanished.

Hands trembling, Audrey closed the door and rushed across the room to the bed. She tore open the envelope and shook out the contents: a blue-point syringe and twelve little half-inch square glassine packets of shake.

She filled the syringe with water from the bathroom sink, then emptied three of the tiny bags into an unused ashtray. She squirted half the syringe into the powder, shot the rest on to the carpet, and used the plastic needle guard to stir the cocaine till it dissolved.

Laying the syringe next to the ashtray, she dug through her purse and found a crumpled pack of Marlboros. She tore a piece of filter off one of the cigarettes and dropped it into the liquid to screen out any undissolved chunks.

With the focused attentiveness of a medieval monk illuminating a manuscript, she drew the gold liquid through the soaked filter back into the syringe.

Now to find a working vein.

'I feel like a root-beer float!'

'You just hold that feeling, baby.' Hopping on one foot toward the bathtub, Booker Kincaid struggled out of his jockey shorts.

Inside the tub, Raquel Balmer kicked her legs, whipping the bubble bath into a froth of suds.

Booker splashed in on top of her. She glided beneath him for an instant. He pulled her up to the surface and kissed her long and hard on the mouth.

She broke away to catch her breath. 'My my. I've never done it in a bathtub before.'

'It's good.' He lifted her so she was straddling him. 'Slick and slippery all over.'

'Oh my.' She tipped her head back and closed her eyes. 'My oh my.'

'Told ya it's better without coke.'

'I was blind but now I see.'

A shadow fell across the tub. Booker's head whipped round.

A dark young man in a waiter's jacket stood beside the sink.

'What the hell's going on?' Booker demanded.

Raquel quickly folded her arms over her breasts.

The young man wore his long dark hair in a ponytail and he was plugging a toaster into the outlet over the shaving mirror. He smiled at the lovebirds. 'Breakfast.'

'Fuck it,' Booker shouted. 'We already had our breakfast!'

'Chef's surprise.' The young man tossed the toaster into the tub.

Sharon combined the yellow crystalline powder from the Balmer sample with 20ccs of distilled water. She heated the mix in a retort, keeping the temperature just below boiling till the powder was liquefied.

Using a dropper, she measured three drops of the solution into a Petri dish of zinc reagent; she then measured another three into a dish of potassium reagent.

Both reagents were clear, colorless liquids.

The zinc reaction was almost instantaneous: the dish turned bright red.

She tapped the message into the computer: *Positive for zinc sulphide.*

Lucas's astonishment flashed on to the screen: YOU'RE SURE?

Absolutely. No question.

WHAT ABOUT POTASSIUM CARBONATE?

I'm waiting for a reaction.

The potassium reagent remained clear for almost two minutes.

I think we've got a negative.

At 2 minutes and 30 seconds, two small blue spots appeared in the mix.

Wait a minute. Something's beginning to happen.

The blue quickly spread to cover the surface of the dish.

Positive for potassium carbonate.

ASTONISHING.

What does it mean?

ONE STEP AT A TIME. LET'S NOT JUMP TO ANY CON-CLUSIONS BEFORE ALL THE EVIDENCE IS IN. TEST YOUR NEXT SAMPLE.

Sharon transferred the yellow crystalline powder from the

Verba sample into a fresh retort. She dripped three drops of the Verba solution into the zinc reagent. The Petri dish turned an instant, bright red.

Sample two is positive for zinc sulphide.

AND THE POTASSIUM?

She dripped three drops into the potassium reagent. Two minutes went by. Then three.

It's not reacting.

GIVE IT ANOTHER MINUTE.

At 3 minutes and 47 seconds a single small blue dot appeared at the corner of the dish. Two seconds later, at the opposite side of the dish, a second dot. Over the next twelve seconds the circumference gradually filled in with dots.

I'm getting a reaction at the edge of the dish.

THAT'S A POSITIVE.

What's going on?

LET'S JUST MAKE SURE. TEST THE LAST SAMPLE.

Sharon took a paper cone containing the yellow crystalline powder from the Goodman sample. Carefully tapping the paper, she tipped the powder into a clean retort. At 2 minutes and 35 seconds two small blue dots appeared a little to the right of the center of the dish.

I'm beginning to get a reaction.

GIVE IT A LITTLE MORE TIME.

Blue tentacles reached from one dot to the other, then swept an arc out to the circumference. Blue fanned across the surface of the dish.

Sample three is definitely positive.

FRANKLY, I'M ASTOUNDED.

Would you let me in on it please?

THERE'S SPERILAC IN EVERY ONE OF YOUR SAMPLES.

Sharon just sat there, staring at bright red dishes and bright blue dishes, tapping a pen against the knuckle of her left thumb, trying to put it together in her head and not quite managing.

I don't get it. How in the world could there possibly be Sperilac in street coke?

I CAN TELL YOU PART OF THE HOW. JUDGING FROM THE CONCENTRATION, IT MUST HAVE BEEN PUT IN AT THE SOURCE.

Sharon's co-worker Wendy came finger-snapping into the lab, pulled off her Walkman earphones, and surveyed the countertop. 'What the bejeezus is going on here?'

'Sorry about the mess.' Sharon typed, *So long, Dad, gotta go. Talk to you later*. She disconnected.

'Are you running a designer drug boutique?'

'Just checking the ingredients in a compound.' Sharon set the dirty bowls and retorts in the sink.

'What's the matter, don't they have a lab over at New Day?'

'Not with the equipment we do.' Sharon opened her purse and handed Wendy a set of apartment keys. 'I hate to ask on such short notice, but could you do me a favor? I have to go away for four or five days. Could you take care of the cats for me?'

May 2 – 9:40 a.m.

Being locked up in some frigging hotel was not the kind of stimulation Tim McJoyce needed to keep his mind on his program. He had done nine sets of abdominal crunches, one hundred and fifty squats, and now he began his push-ups.

He hated push-ups. If only he'd had the foresight to bring his barbells. Oh well . . .

'One day at a time, one,' he recited. 'One day at a time, two. One day at a time, three . . .'

He could feel the sweat rolling off his chest and buttocks. When he was alone, he preferred to work out naked. He felt it was more natural, gave his pores a better chance to eliminate bodily toxins.

Someone knocked on the door. He ignored the sound.

'One day at a time, twenty-one. One day at a time, twenty-two.'

The knock came again. 'Your breakfast, sir,' a muffled voice called from the hallway.

'I've had my breakfast, thirty-six,' Tim shouted. 'You've got the wrong, thirty-seven, room.'

He thought he heard something click, but he didn't even turn his head to investigate. He was going to get through this routine without interruption if it killed him.

A voice above him froze him in mid-body lift. 'Mr McJoyce keeps himself in excellent condition.'

'Yes,' another voice answered, 'the señor has done a fine job of body-sculpting.'

Still more voices concurred.

The sweat on Tim McJoyce's body suddenly felt like ice. He started to roll over, but just as he shifted his balance, half a dozen hands grabbed him by the calves and buttocks and shoulders. He felt a wire slip round his throat and slice into his gullet.

Molly Verba came out of the bathroom toweling her hair, humming 'Love Makes the World Go Round'. She felt clean and relaxed and energized. What luxury to be able to soak in a tub without having to hear wailing children or share space with a flock of rubber duckies!

226

'Ms Verba?' a voice asked.

Molly pulled the towel from in front of her face and was surprised to see an olive-complexioned woman standing in the middle of her bedroom. She wore a maid's uniform and she held out a huge bouquet of flowers.

'How pretty!' Molly cried. 'For *me*?'

'For you.'

Life just seemed to be getting better and better. Molly stepped toward the bouquet. She pushed aside ferns and calla lilies and spider mums and bent down to sniff a purple-and-orange bloom with white speckles that she'd never before seen in her life.

Concealed in the daisies, roses, and carnations, the maid held a four-ounce atomizer. As Molly inhaled, the maid gave five brutal squeezes in fast succession.

Coughing and gagging, Molly took a stumbling step backward. Her leg buckled beneath her and she fell to the carpet.

The bouquet followed, misting her nose and mouth and eyes and respiratory passages with an odorless, tasteless 75 per cent solution of succinocholine.

At the KLM Royal Dutch Airlines office on K Street, Sharon waited in line with growing impatience. The woman ahead of her was trying to exchange Delta frequent flyer miles for a trip to the Dutch West Indies.

'I'm sorry, ma'am,' the ticket agent told her for the third time. He was a young man, well-groomed and imperturbably good-natured. 'But as I've explained, we don't honor Delta frequent flyer.'

'I'm sure I saw an ad—'

'We've never honored Delta frequent flyer. If I could make a suggestion, you might have better luck with your own travel agent.'

'What the hell kind of airline are you? Your ads say you're caring.'

'Yes, ma'am.' He peered round her shoulder and beckoned. 'Next.'

Sharon eased up to the counter. The woman was still grumbling and jamming travel brochures into a Radio Pacifica tote bag.

'You're holding seven reservations for me. They've been paid for.' She laid her Mastercard down on the countertop. 'Sharon Powell.'

The clerk called up her record on his computer.

'Yes, Ms Powell. Flight 48 direct to Amsterdam, departing Dulles at eight thirty tonight. We show reservations for Ms Balmer, Ms Gault . . .'

Sharon wondered if it was absolutely necessary to read off all six names. She glanced behind her to see who was listening. Three men and a woman stood in line, all of them placidly involved with their newspapers.

'. . . Ms Verba,' the agent concluded, 'and yourself.'

'Pam Gault has changed her plans. Could you cancel her reservation? I'll only need the other six tickets.'

'Certainly.' The agent printed up six tickets and slipped them into six separate folders. 'Your travel agent will be holding your reimbursement. You and your party should plan to be at the airport two hours before take-off. With passports.'

Sharon slid the tickets into her purse. 'Thank you.'

'Have a good trip, Ms Powell. Enjoy Amsterdam.'

Sharon picked up a cup of hazelnut mocha from a take-out coffee shop and returned to her parked car. Sipping with her left hand, working the cellphone with her right, she checked her voice mail at the clinic.

Lucinda Forbes had left six messages in tones of mounting hysteria. 'Contact me the minute you get this message. Urgent.'

Sharon phoned the Forbes home. An answering machine told her Mrs Forbes could be reached at her office number.

Sharon phoned the office.

'My God,' Lucinda groaned, 'I've been going nuts worrying about you. Where have you been?'

'Busy. Sorry.'

'Listen, are you OK?'

'More or less.'

'Because last night I discovered an E-mail exchange in my computer. My houseboy Key turns out to be some kind of – well, let's not get into *that*. He knows you deleted the files of six patients on the Sperilac side who've almost cleared the virus. He knows you're taking them to Amsterdam tonight.'

Sharon listened with a sense of unreality. In front of her blinking eyes, traffic and pedestrians moved placidly down F Street.

'And he's been ordered to kill you all.' The voice in her hand seemed to come from an alternate universe far, far away. 'Sharon, are you there?'

'I'm here. I heard you.'

'Whatever it is you're planning, they know all about it. Maybe you should reconsider.'

Sharon twisted the key in the ignition. 'I've got to go now.'

'Sharon, would you mind telling me what's going on?'

'Sorry, there isn't time.'

* * *

She ran up the steps of the Willard Hotel. The lobby was crowded with people drifting and chattering. As she hurried toward the elevators, the desk clerk called to her.

'Ms Powell? Ms Powell!'

She circled back to the marble-topped counter.

'We have an urgent message from one of your party.' He thumbed through a tall stack of slips. 'Ah yes. Here we are.'

Sharon unfolded the piece of pink message paper. The handwriting was unfamiliar: 'Need some advice on an important matter. Please come to my room. Audrey.'

She frowned. 'Miss Goodman brought this down, or phoned it down?'

'Phoned it down, ma'am. No more than forty-five minutes ago.'

Sharon picked up the house phone and asked for room 702. After five rings the operator cut back in. 'Ms Goodman doesn't seem to be answering. Would you care to leave a message?'

'No thank you.' Wondering what in the world could have gone wrong now, Sharon hurried toward the elevators.

The lobby was filling with clusters of dark-haired, sleekly attired men and women wearing Chilean Arts and Trade Delegation convention tags. At the entrance to the Peacock Walk, a long hallway covered with carpet resembling flamboyant plumage, an elaborately lettered sign announced 'Welcome Ambassador de Miros/Bienvenido Embajador de Miros'.

Sharon stood impatiently punching the *up* button. When the door finally opened, a crowd of suntanned faces chattering exuberant Spanish swept past her.

She stepped into the elevator and pressed 7.

Just as the doors were closing, a man in a seersucker suit darted on board. 'Seems to be Pan-American day around here.'

Sharon nodded. 'I believe there's a trade delegation show.'

'I thought Latin America was supposed to be an economic disaster zone. Looking at the jewels on some of these babes, you'd never know it.'

The elevator stopped on seven and Sharon got off.

She walked down the deserted corridor with a sense of something amiss. It wasn't until she reached Audrey Goodman's door that she realized what was bothering her: there were no guards. The three men from the DEA had vanished.

She raised her hand and knocked on 702. 'Audrey.'

No answer.

She knocked harder, almost pounding this time.

The door swung open. Sharon took one step and stopped.

Audrey's feet were still on the bed. The rest of her lay sprawled in a tangled spill of bedsheets on the floor. Her eyes were wide open, staring toward the door. Her mouth gaped. It was a strange, happy kind of gaping. Her face was a deep cyanotic blue.

A syringe hung out of her inner left elbow.

Sharon stepped back into the hallway and closed the door. She knocked at Molly Verba's room.

Again, no answer. Again, unlocked.

Molly lay beside the coffee table, stretched beneath a blanket of fresh cut flowers. Sharon knelt beside her and felt the left wrist for a pulse.

There was none.

She ran across the hallway to Booker Kincaid's room. The door swung open at the first knock.

'Booker?'

No answer. Her eye swept from bed to bureau to closets.

She sniffed. A smell of something burning hovered in the air. At the same time she was aware of a sound like a hissing radio.

Yet the television set was dark.

The bathroom door was half open. She could see a trickle of light blue sputtering against the white tile wall. As she crossed the room, the static grew louder.

'Mr Kincaid?' she called out. 'Booker?'

She smelled something cooking. She knocked and peered round the door and saw who it was.

A bitter, involuntary surge of coffee pushed up from Sharon's stomach. Choking back the instinctive urge to vomit, she wheeled and dashed into the hallway.

Tim McJoyce's door swung open at the first touch of her knuckles. Tim lay stark naked on the carpet in a pool of congealed blood. His head, in a wire loop, had been twisted back until it clung to his neck by a celery-stick-thin skein of cords and bone. Blood had spattered as far as the window and the ceiling.

Sharon felt her knees giving out. She gripped the doorknob.

As she turned back toward the hallway, a figure glided out of Audrey Goodman's room. She recognized the angelic eyes and huge upper body of Lucinda Forbes' manservant Key.

'Ms Powell.' Key spoke in an almost conversational tone, and he held a silenced semi-automatic pistol in his right hand. 'I have no wish to hurt you.'

He was waiting for me in Audrey's room, she realized. If I'd gone in, I'd be dead too.

'Let's discuss this calmly, shall we, Ms Powell?'

She saw the door marked *exit* and she dove for it.

May 2 – 10:50 a.m.

S he slapped a hand on the railing and ran down toward the floor
below. Her shoes tapped on each steel step, sending out a click that
triggered an avalanche of answering clicks.

Blood was beating so violently in her temples that the image of the
stairway trembled before her eyes.

Above her, the door slammed open. Pursuing feet clattered.

She darted a glance over her shoulder.

The form of a man scuttled across the landing in a half crouch, arms
extended before him, backlit by light washing in from the hallway.

There was a sound like a fist slamming into a mound of wet dough.
A bullet whined by her ear and pinged off the wall.

Her foot completely missed the next step.

She lunged forward, took a skidding fall down three steps, barely
managed to catch the steel handrail. Momentum flung her on to the landing
and into the wall. She spun round, seized the doorhandle and pulled.

She shot into the sixth-floor corridor, sped past closed doors with
'Do not disturb' signs and doors with room service trays on the floor.
She could see from the floor indicator that one of the elevators was
climbing from the ground floor and another was descending from ten.

She pushed the *up* button and the *down*. Behind her, the stairwell
door slammed open. Footsteps thudded down the carpet. One elevator
had reached 3 and another had reached 7 and the third was still sitting
in the lobby. She pushed the buttons again.

The *up* button dissolved under her finger and a bullet dug into
plaster.

The *down* elevator opened. A wall of well-dressed bodies parted for
her. She turned and faced the door. Key was running toward her, shoving
the gun into his jacket.

The door whooshed shut.

Around her, voices chattered cheerfully in Spanish. Words like *linda*
and *divina* and *superba*.

The floor indicator dropped to 5. Then 4. The door opened.

A gray-haired lady with a walker hobbled toward them. 'Hold it,
please! Going down!'

232

Someone pressed the *open* button.

'Thank you very much.' She squeezed in next to Sharon. 'Lovely day,' she said, 'don't you think?'

Halfway down the corridor, the door to the stairwell flew open and Key came skidding into the hall.

Sharon jabbed the *close* button. The door closed, then jerked open again.

'It's my walker,' the old lady said. 'I'm sorry.'

Sharon yanked the walker into the elevator and pushed *down*.

'Wait a minute,' the old woman said. 'Can't you see that young man wants the elevator?'

Key was fifteen feet away, too winded to cry out, one arm flailing.

Sharon kept her finger on *down*. The door shut.

The old woman tsk-tsked. 'Young lady, you must be in a terrible rush.'

'You don't know how terrible.'

The floor indicator dropped to 3. Then 2. Then L.

The doors opened. The lobby was filled with Chileans waving flags and champagne glasses, whooping to one another in Spanish. The press of sweetly scented bodies almost knocked Sharon back into the elevator. Using all her weight and strength, she held out her arms and forced her way through the crowd.

Over her shoulder, she saw a second elevator open. Towering over the shorter passengers, Key scanned the chaotic festivities. His eyes locked on hers.

Moving with brawny authority, he shoved people out of his way. He was quicker at cutting through the mob than she was, and in seconds he was at her side. The gun pressed through his jacket pocket into her ribs. 'Keep calm and do as you're told.'

'Like hell!' she shouted.

Startled heads turned. A ripple of shock flashed through the crowd.

Snatching a champagne glass from the hand of a jolted bystander, she plunged it full force into Key's face. She could feel the shards sink into the skin under his right eye. He gave a howl and flailed his left arm in an attempt to fend her off.

She struck again, driving the shattered glass this time into his jaw.

'*Cono!*' Blood sprayed from Key's mouth. Cocktail dresses and Italian suits recoiled. '*Puta!*' He whipped the gun into the open.

Panicked Chileans stampeded.

Sharon brought her knee up hard and swift into Key's groin, then wheeled and ran.

The mob poured through the glass hotel doors, down the steps and out on to Pennsylvania Avenue.

A black limousine double-parked at the curb flew the Israeli flag on its front fenders. Sharon yanked open the passenger door, hurled herself into the back seat, snapped the lock down.

'I demand political asylum!'

Key lunged through the crowd and hammered his gun butt against the safety glass.

'Take me to your Embassy!' she screamed.

The chauffeur took one look at his passenger, then pulled into the traffic and picked up speed, as if this was the sort of thing he did two or three times every day.

In a reception room off the main entrance to the Israeli Embassy, Sharon and the junior attaché sat facing each other in hard-backed chairs.

'Ms Powell, as interesting as your story of mass murder at the Willard may be, I am afraid that the government of Israel can take no official position other, of course, than regret.'

He was a handsome young man with neatly coiffed brown hair and beautifully manicured nails. He had said his name was Ari Kalim.

'You are perfectly welcome to remain here on Israeli soil until we can procure a police car to escort you to some other haven.' He smiled hopefully. 'Perhaps protective custody with the Justice Department?'

'Absolutely not.'

'Then we have a problem. I'm afraid we can't offer you further use of the Ambassador's automobile.' Ari Kalim allowed himself a wry, thin smile. 'He happens to need it himself.'

Sharon reached across the space between them and placed her hands on top of his. 'Mr Kalim, I know I was followed here. I need some way of getting out without being seen.'

'I can arrange for a special taxi.' Ari Kalim gently shifted his hands and took Sharon's in his. 'After dusk would be best. The taxi will arrive at an entry not visible from the street. The driver will be one of our people. He can see you safely to wherever you want to go.'

'Thank you.'

'I must warn you, however,' Ari Kalim's face darkened, 'if any question arises in the future over your presence here, you understand that we shall say we expelled you from the Embassy.'

'I understand. You're very kind. If I could ask one last favor. May I use your phone?'

'Of course.' He reached sideways and slid the telephone across the desktop. 'Dial nine for an outside line. And press the green button for privacy. Now if you'll excuse me, I'll make arrangements for your cab.'

Ari Kalim left the room and closed the door behind him. Sharon lifted the telephone receiver, dialed nine, pressed the green button, and dialed Eddie Arbogast's number. It rang three times.

'Arbogast.'

'Eddie, it's Sharon Powell.'

'Why are you whispering?'

'They've been murdered. Every one of them. Balmer and Goodman and Verba and—'

'When?'

'Some time this morning while I was at the lab.'

'Where the hell was the guard?'

'I don't know. When I got back to the hotel, the hall was unguarded.'

'Christ. Something's happened to Larry.'

'He could have been on the hit list too.'

'What hit list?'

'Last night around midnight Lucinda discovered Key using her computer. She found an E-mail exchange. Key was ordered to kill the six trial members who'd almost cleared the virus. He was also ordered to kill me.'

'Are you safe?'

'For the moment. I'm at the Israeli Embassy.'

'Good. Stay there till you hear from me. I'll trace that E-mail. Only one person could have given that order – Mike Bosch himself. What's your phone?'

She gave him the number. 'And you'd better take my cellphone too. Just in case.'

'Just in case what?'

'In case I'm not here.'

'Why wouldn't you be there?'

'I might think of something.'

'Like what?'

'Like some way of saving Sperilac.'

'If you want my advice, you'll stay right where you are. Save yourself, and there'll be plenty of time later to save Sperilac.'

Eddie broke the phone connection and dialed the number of his hacker friend Mark Burgess.

Edward Stewart

Mark's machine answered, manically. 'Hey, good-looking. You have reached the warren of Mark Burgess, philanthropist, philosopher king, and world traveler. If you need a war fought, a revolution started, or an assassination solved, press *one*. If you need a tiger tamed, a virgin converted, or your computer security verified, press *two*. If you wish to speak to me personally, get in line at the sound of the beep and pray.'

Today Mark's *beep* was discordant chimes banging the first bars of the national anthem.

'Mark, you there? It's Eddie.'

Mark cut in with a click. 'Whithersoever thou needest me.'

'Sorry to keep pestering you.'

'No one I'd rather be pestered by.'

'Lucinda Forbes' computer received some E-mail last night. I need the sender's phone.'

'What time was this?'

'Around midnight. That's approximate.'

'Close enough. You got it.'

'Thanks, Mark. I appreciate it.' Eddie broke the connection and dialed Larry Lorenzo's direct line at work.

Two rings. A kind of hiccup in the second. No answer.

Two more rings. Still no pick-up. Not even an answering machine.

Eddie tapped a finger on the receiver. It seemed odd – in a federal office there should be *someone* to pick up. Or at least voice mail.

That buzz with the curious hiccup came again. He frowned, realizing there must be some kind of ring-activated bug on the line, tracking incoming calls even when there was no pick-up.

But that didn't make sense, the DEA phone system was state-of-the-art bug proof; no one could monitor it except the DEA themselves.

He lowered the receiver to the cradle, got out the phone directory, and looked up Larry's home number.

He dialed. There were four rings. No pick-up, no machine. It struck him as odd that there was no one in Larry's office or at his home.

And then he heard that same little hiccup, and he knew something was wrong. He could see a federal agency running a random security check on their own lines, but not on Larry's home phone.

He broke the connection and dialed the central DEA switchboard.

'Drug Enforcement Administration.'

'Larry Lorenzo, please.'

'Could you spell that name?'

Eddie spelled it.

'One moment, please.'

A burst of elevator music shot over the line – 'Raindrops Keep Falling On My Head' – and then a female voice was saying, 'Larry Lorenzo's line, may I help you?'

Where were you two minutes ago? he wondered. 'This is Eddie Arbogast. I'm trying to get hold of Mr Lorenzo.'

'Would you hold one moment, please, Mr Arbogast?'

There was a click, and more 'Raindrops', and a sudden drop in volume that told Eddie they were tracing the call, and then she was back, apologetic.

'I'm sorry, but Mr Lorenzo had to step out. This is Connie Robbins, his assistant. He asked if there's any chance you could come down to the office?'

Eddie didn't buy it and he didn't like it. Someone was in bad trouble, and it had better not be him. 'What time?'

'Mr Lorenzo will be free in half an hour.'

May 2 – 1:20 p.m.

From the blue Datsun parked twenty feet west of the main entrance of the Israeli Embassy, Key watched the outs and ignored the ins.

It was interesting how the flow was never even. People came through the door in surges. A burst of schoolchildren. A burst of middle-aged men in yarmulkes. A burst of cops. All chattering.

And then a lone woman wearing a raincoat shot out of the door. Her head was down; dark glasses hid her eyes; a dark kerchief wrapped her hair.

On a sunny day like today Key could see a reason for the sunglasses. But there was no reason for the raincoat. He smelled a disguise.

Heels clacking, long legs scissoring space, the woman passed within three feet of him.

'Ms Powell,' he said through the open driver's window. Not calling, just conversational. In his lap, his hands fitted the silencer to the gun barrel. 'Sharon. Hi.'

She stopped. Not frightened, not even startled. Baffled. She lifted the dark glasses. Her skin was pale brown, her eyes black.

Sour disappointment flooded Key's stomach. Right height, right stride. wrong race. Not Sharon Powell.

For a moment she was looking straight at him, mystified. 'Did you speak to me?'

He shook his head.

She shrugged, as though dismissing a voice she'd imagined, and continued on her way.

Eddie asked the people at the DEA a simple question; at least he thought it was simple. 'Would you tell Larry Lorenzo that Ed Arbogast is here?'

'What department is Mr Lorenzo with?' the young lady at the reception desk asked.

'Enforcement. He's expecting me.'

Though she hadn't asked for his ID, he showed it anyway, thinking it might speed things. It didn't. He took a seat and stared at the gray hi-tech walls and waited. DEA headquarters was a place of ringing phones, beeping faxes, agents charging down corridors like cardiac resuscitation teams. Faces were grim and macho, especially the women's.

Especially the face of the woman striding toward Eddie. 'Mr Arbogast, we spoke on the phone. I'm Connie Robbins, Larry's assistant.'

'Larry's a hard man to get hold of.'

'Isn't he. Would you come with me?'

He followed her down a twisting corridor, past a glittering state-of-the-art cafeteria and conference room and auditorium. She knocked on a half-open door. 'Mr Arbogast to see you, sir.' She stood aside.

A man who was not Larry Lorenzo rose from behind a desk, hand extended. 'Good to meet you.' He crossed the room and shut the door.

'I didn't catch your name,' Eddie said.

'Tom Wynant. Larry's boss.' Wynant had the weatherbeaten complexion of a man who'd bagged his share of guerrillas in Peru and his share of lunchtime martinis too. He gestured toward a leather armchair. 'Have a seat. Care for some coffee, soft drink, something stronger?'

'No thanks.' Eddie remained standing. 'Actually, I came to see Larry.'

Wynant dropped into a chair. 'If you don't mind my asking, what's your connection with Larry?'

Do I have to pass an interview before they let me see the guy? 'We worked together back in the eighties.'

'Where was that?'

'Florida and Ecuador.'

'Any particular reason you're looking for Larry now?'

Why do I feel this man is grilling me? 'Happened to be passing through town, haven't seen him in a while, thought I'd find out how he's doing.'

'When did you last see Larry?'

Eddie's instincts warned him to shade the truth: 'Three, four years ago – we ran into one another in Seattle.'

'I take it you're not a close friend.'

'How close is close?'

'Were you aware that Larry was working for the drug cartel?'

Silence rolled in.

'No, I wasn't aware of that.' Eddie sat down. 'I thought he was working here at the agency.'

'He was. That was the point. We wanted the drug cartel to think they'd turned him.'

'Sting operation?'

'That was the intention.'

'How long's this been going on?'

'Two years.' Wynant was looking straight at Eddie.

'Really.'

'Last night Larry flew an assignment to the Bahamas. He was carrying sensitive documents, and he never arrived.'

'What happened?'

'Turns out he made an unscheduled change of planes in Miami, flew to Mexico City, changed passports and changed planes again and made a connection to Bogota.' Wynant moved an ashtray on his desk and aligned it with the edge of his blotter. 'Day before yesterday, his wife and kid flew to Paris on vacation. From Paris they made an unscheduled flight straight to Bogota.'

'Bogota.' Eddie nodded, playing for time, trying to make sense of it, making sense of it and realizing he'd been royally taken.

'Larry ever mention the name Malcolm Evans?'

'Not that I recall. Why?'

'That's the name on the Cayman account he transferred his funds to yesterday. There's over four million dollars in that account. It's also the name on his new passport.'

A mouse squeaked in Eddie's pocket. 'Excuse me.' He pulled out his beeper. Mark Burgess's phone number, complete with area code, glowed in the read-out window.

'If that's an important call,' Wynant said, 'feel free to use my phone.'

'Thanks. It's nothing.' Eddie slid the beeper back into his pocket.

Wynant was watching Eddie closely. 'So we have good reason to believe that for some time now, Larry Lorenzo's primary allegiance has been to the drug cartel. He's been acting as their agent, not ours.'

'Hard to believe,' Eddie said. 'You never know, do you?'

'Never.' Wynant leaned forward to tap a code into his phone. The door buzzed and two men in dark suits stepped into the office, unsmiling and line-backer huge.

Wynant made introductions. 'Agent Robert Donahue, Agent Richard Farrell, meet Agent Edward Arbogast. Turns out Ed's a friend of Larry Lorenzo's, just dropped in to say hi. He may be able to shed some light.'

Eddie glanced at his watch. 'Could you give me some idea how long this is going to take?'

Wynant smiled without humor. 'It all depends on you.'

It was almost 5 p.m., and Sharon was pacing the reception room in the

Israeli Embassy, when suddenly she remembered Jack Arnold and his NIH mortality stats.

She tried to recall what he'd said, something about AIDS deaths among cocaine addicts, heroin addicts, and amphetamine and alcohol abusers. *Blow your mind*, he'd said.

Her thoughts began racing. If there was Sperilac in street cocaine, AIDS deaths among cocaine users should be lower than other groups, and if the National Institutes of Health had published mortality rates, the government's own statistics would prove Sperilac worked.

She punched Jack's work number into the telephone. Four rings.

Pick up, Jack.

At the fifth ring his voice mail cut in. '. . . And I'll return your call as soon as possible.' *Beep.*

'Jack, it's Sharon. Remember that NIH report on the AIDS death rate among addicts? I think it was the April nineteenth newsletter. Is there any chance you can find it again?'

But even if he could find the report, she realized, that doesn't put a physical copy in my hands.

'Never mind, Jack. Sorry to bother you.'

She broke the connection and leafed through her address book. Afternoon sun beamed through leaded windowpanes, catching golden petals in a vase of chrysanthemums.

She dialed her father's neighbor Millie at the nursing home. There were seven rings with interminable silences between.

Please be there, Millie. Please.

And then the familiar, 'Uh huh?'

'Millie, it's Sharon.'

'Hiya, toots. Let me turn down the TV. OK, now I can hear you. What's up?'

'I've got to talk to my father but I don't have a modem or laptop. Can you relay messages?'

'Sure thing.'

For forty-five seconds the phone was singing faint dial-tone melodies, and then Millie was back. 'Your father's right here. I'm putting him on the line. Hold on. Here he is.'

She recognized the sound of her father's breathing.

'We've had a disaster, Dad. The FDA has closed down the Phase Three trial. Five of the six patients who'd almost cleared the virus have been murdered. There's still one slim chance I can save Sperilac, but I need your help.'

* * *

Lucas Powell listened, nodded gravely, and handed the receiver back to Millie. He turned his swivel chair to face the computer. His age-speckled hand moved rapidly, tapping out his reply.

YOUR DAD IS READY ABLE AND WILLING.

Millie angled her reading glasses to the tip of her nose and leaned forward. 'The old bastard says he's ready, able and willing. I believe him. Hold on, here he is.'

She gave the phone to Lucas.

'Here's what I'd like you to do,' Sharon said. 'The National Institutes of Health publish an electronic edition of their AIDS mortality newsletter. There's an article in the April nineteenth issue. It compares cocaine and heroin addicts, and amphetamine and alcohol abusers. Can you see if the AIDS mortality among cocaine users is lower than the other groups?'

Lucas handed back the phone and typed a message on his computer.

CAN DO.

'He says he can do it,' Millie said.

It took Lucas almost four minutes to locate the April 19th newsletter and call it up. He entered the command to search for the word *cocaine*. A river of print glided up on the screen and stopped. The cursor stood blinking beside the phrase *cocaine addicts*.

He beckoned to Millie.

She read from the screen into the telephone. '"In January of this year, some surprising comparisons emerged between the AIDS mortality rates of four classes of drug abusers: cocaine addicts, heroin addicts, amphetamine abusers, and alcoholics. For the third consecutive month, the death rate among cocaine users dropped. At present trends, persons with AIDS who smoke or inject cocaine are fourteen per cent less likely to die of their condition than persons with AIDS who do not abuse drugs, and an astonishing sixty-one per cent less likely to die than persons with AIDS who abuse heroin, amphetamines, or alcohol."'

Millie was silent for a moment.

'OK, here he is.' She handed the phone back to Lucas.

'I need a hard copy of that article,' Sharon said. 'I also need hard copies of the AIDS mortality stats for cocaine addicts for the past six months, so could you print them out? I'll be by to pick them up later today. Thanks, Dad. I know I'm a nuisance but I love you.'

Sharon knew exactly what she had to do. Heart thumping, she

242

squinted at a number she'd scrawled in the margin of her address book. Was that a four or a nine?

She decided this was not the sort of call to make on an embassy phone, so she tapped the digits into the keypad of her cellphone. She tried four first.

A deep male voice answered. 'Yeah?'

'Could I speak with Pam Gault?'

'Pam ain't here.' The voice sounded stressed.

'Look, she knows me.'

'She knows a lot of people.'

'This is Sharon Powell. From New Day Clinic. I was there last night with two men friends.'

'Oh yeah. I remember you. This is T-Bone. How can I help you?'

'I need to buy something from you.'

'What do you want?'

'I need at least twenty bags. More if you can get it. Ten crack, ten pure.'

'You *crazy* talking like that on the telephone, lady.'

'Sorry. This is an emergency.'

'You must be in a bad way.'

She ignored the chuckling insinuation. 'I'll be coming in a cab right after dusk.'

'Don't bring anybody with you. Pull up in front of the house. Stay in the car. I'll come to you.'

'Thanks, T-Bone.'

She broke the connection and dialed Eddie Arbogast's hotel. There was no answer. She dialed his cellphone. He didn't answer the cellphone either.

May 2 – 7:30 p.m.

Shortly after dusk, Ari Kalim appeared in the doorway. 'We have your taxi. Are you ready?'

Sharon rose. 'Ready.'

He motioned her to follow. Three other male members of the Embassy staff joined them, one each side of her, another behind. They passed through several corridors, down a short flight of stairs, and out the kitchen door.

Beyond boxwood-lined paths and dogwood trees, she could see a dark alley behind the Embassy. A taxi waited, its headlights doused.

Shielded by her four escorts, she quickly crossed the garden. An electrical gate in the hedge buzzed wide at their approach. Ari Kalim held the taxi door.

She slid into the back seat. 'I don't know how I can thank you.'

Ari Kalim smiled charmingly. 'For what? The government of Israel is always happy to provide transportation for a distinguished American scientist. Perhaps some day you can do a favor for us.' He slammed the door behind her. '*Shalom*.'

Without turning on its headlights, the taxi began to slide through the alley.

'V and Tenth Street, Northwest,' she said.

'Yes, madam.'

She studied the taxi driver's delicate profile and deep mocha skin. According to the license displayed on the dashboard, his name was Solomon Barandi. She recognized the last name as Ethiopian.

She glanced at her wristwatch. Barely an hour and a half till take-off. 'Please hurry.'

'Of course.'

As the cab slid to the curb, the street seemed darker and the houses more ragged than Sharon remembered them. The street light in front of Pam Gault's building had been shot out since last night. No other cars were parked on the block.

A hulking form trotted down the sidewalk. As he bent down by the passenger window, she recognized T-Bone. He signaled her to roll the window down.

'I got you twenty-five bags. That's three hundred dollars straight money. If you wasn't a friend of Pam's, no way I'd do this for some white woman I barely ever seen before. The extra fifth's my tip.'

Sharon didn't have time to quibble. She pulled four one hundred dollar bills from her purse and passed them out the window.

T-Bone took the bills and formed his lips into a silent whistle. He reached into the car and dropped a Zip-Loc sandwich bag at her feet. 'Can't make no change.'

'Keep the rest as a bonus.'

'Thanks. Now get out of here.'

'Wait a minute.' She lifted the baggie off the floor and saw the twenty-five glassine envelopes nestling at the bottom. She slipped them into her purse. 'Have you heard from Pam since last night?'

T-Bone didn't answer, but the concern on his face was obvious.

'Then if I were you, I'd start looking for her. I think she's in trouble.' She rolled up the window.

Solomon Barandi turned his head. 'Where to now, ma'am?'

She gave him the address of the nursing home.

In Lucas Powell's neat, gray-walled room, the click of chess pieces seemed carved out of silence. Sharon rapped on the half-open door. 'Who's ahead?'

'Your dad thinks he's letting me win.' Millie transferred one of Lucas's pawns to her collection of hostages. 'But I'm winning on my own.'

Lucas swiveled in his chair. Amber letters came up on the computer screen.

SHE EXAGGERATES.

'I wish I could stay and watch, but I've got a cab waiting.'

Her father's eyes flicked up alertly.

WHERE ARE YOU GOING?

'Amsterdam.'

WHY?

'Long story. I'll tell you all about it when I get back.'

DON'T GET YOURSELF KILLED.

'No way. Were you able to get those documents?'

Lucas reached into a desk drawer and handed her a thick manila envelope.

'I knew I could count on you.' She planted a kiss on his forehead. 'God bless you.'

'Hey.' Millie's fist, wrapped round a bishop, froze in mid-air. 'Doesn't the old bag get anything?'

'You're an angel.' Sharon's lips brushed Millie's cheek. 'I'd be sunk without you.'

Millie squeezed her hand. 'Send a postcard. No windmills.'

Sharon hurried down the corridor and out the side entrance. Her taxi had vanished.

But I told him to wait!

She was about to go back and borrow Lucas's phone when a horn sounded lightly, three times.

She saw the cab on the far side of the street. As she crossed and slid into the back seat, the driver turned the key in the ignition. The motor growled smoothly to life.

'Where to now, miss?'

She settled into the back seat. 'Dulles Airport, please.'

'Any particular way you want me to go?'

'The fastest.'

Keeping her eye on the back of Solomon Barandi's head, she opened her purse. Quietly extracting the glassine envelopes, she began to tuck them one by one into the cups of her brassiere.

Before checking in, Sharon went to a magazine store and bought a twelve-dollar Kennedy Center tote bag and enough magazines to give it the bulk of carry-on luggage.

The KLM clerk examined her ticket and passport. 'Any luggage?'

She placed the tote bag on the scale. 'I'll be carrying this with me.'

'You're certainly traveling light.' He handed her the boarding pass. 'You should be boarding in twenty minutes. Have a good flight.'

She found a seat in the waiting area and settled down with a copy of the *New Yorker*. Speakers overhead announced imminent arrivals. Imminent departures. A voice paged a George MacAdam.

Suddenly she felt a prickling on her skin, a slight spilling warmth. She had an overpowering sense that someone was watching her.

She peered over the top of her magazine. The waiting area had filled. Piles of baggage had appeared, like mushrooms after a downpour.

Across the aisle, facing her, a thin-faced man with spectacles and bow tie studied his boarding pass. Three seats down, an enormously fat man with jet-black hair unwrapped a package of Tums.

A voice announced that KLM Flight 48, nonstop to Amsterdam, would be boarding in fifteen minutes.

Sharon turned a page and tried to concentrate on the movie review. She couldn't. After a moment she let the edge of the magazine slip away from her fingers.

The fat man was watching her. He was wearing a mustard-colored tie. When he saw she was looking at him, his eyes ricocheted away.

Sharon's mind circled the data. Am I being paranoid?

She sneaked another glance. This time the fat man was ready for her, eyes buried in a paperback thriller, face smooth and blank, betraying nothing.

I'd rather be paranoid than sorry.

Dropping her *New Yorker* into the tote bag, she rose and crossed the concourse. A chicly coiffed Air France ticket clerk smiled at her. 'May I help you?'

'When's your next flight?'

'Where to, madam?'

'Anywhere.'

The clerk gave her a wondering glance. 'That will be Paris. Departing in fifty minutes.'

Sharon charged a one-way fare on her American Express card. She did not trade in her Amsterdam reservation.

Under fluorescent lights, rows of Paris-bound travelers waited with newspapers and magazines. Sharon sat and opened her *New Yorker*.

'You wish to trade in your Amsterdam ticket?'

She glanced up. A dark-haired, slightly stooped woman with thick eyeglasses seemed to be arguing with the ticket clerk.

'I can't refund cash,' the clerk told her. 'You'll have to take a voucher for the difference.'

'OK. Just give me the voucher.'

The woman took a seat in the row behind Sharon. She had no carry-on luggage.

Sharon glanced round behind her. The woman quickly averted her eyes.

She's watching me.

Sharon rose and crossed the concourse to Lufthansa. The schedule board behind the clerk showed a departure to Frankfurt in forty minutes.

'Frankfurt, please.' Sharon laid down her American Express card. 'One way, coach.' She did not trade in her Paris or Amsterdam flights.

A voice announced that KLM Flight 48, nonstop to Amsterdam, was now boarding.

She took a seat against the wall that allowed her to see the other passengers. Directly across the aisle, a pleasant-faced woman was wiping chocolate ice-cream residue from her little boy's face. A Rastafarian sat with eyes closed, feet tapping to music playing through his Walkman earphones. A studious young man studied a copy of the *Journal of the American Medical Association*. In the concourse beyond them, a man wearing a mustard-colored tie hurried toward the Lufthansa counter. Sharon recognized the obese, dark-haired man who'd been watching her at KLM.

Lifted on a jolt of panic, she folded her magazine. She didn't think he'd seen her yet. She rose and crossed to the passenger promenade, scanning shop windows. A blinking neon sign announced drugs and beauty aids.

'Check your bag, ma'am?'

Sharon handed her tote bag to the teenaged sales clerk. She grabbed a shopping basket, searched the hair shelves and found a bottle of spray-on instant frost. Two pink plastic barrettes. Bobby pins. A blue kerchief.

At the eyeglass counter she found a pair of half-tinted non-prescription harlequins.

As she joined the line at the cash register, she noticed that the stoop-shouldered woman with thick eyeglasses who'd been watching her at Air France was standing at the greeting card rack.

May 2 – 8:53 p.m.

Eddie Arbogast dropped a quarter into the payphone and tapped in seven digits.

Two rings. Then: 'Ciao. You have reached the home office of Mark Burgess, psychotherapist, leveraged buy-out strategist, and stand-up comic.'

The wind blowing down Whittier Street wafted a lung-scorching blast of auto exhaust.

'If you wish to speak to me personally, get down on your knees at the sound of the beep and pray.'

'Mark, are you there? It's Eddie. Damn. Don't tell me I missed you.'

There was a click and then Mark's voice. 'You sure took your sweet time. I called you seven hours ago. You said this trace was urgent.'

'It is urgent. I got tied up with some agency stuff. What did you find out?'

'The party who sent the E-mail to Lucinda Forbes' phone was calling from the Doelen Hotel in Amsterdam.'

'Christ, he's in *Amsterdam*?'

'Who's in Amsterdam?'

'Never mind. Thanks, Mark. I owe you.'

Eddie broke the connection. He dropped another quarter into the slot and dialed the number at the Israeli Embassy that Sharon Powell had given him. After three rings a man answered.

'Israeli Embassy, security. Ari Kalim speaking. How may I help you?'

'Could I speak with Sharon Powell, please?'

There was an instant's silence. And then: 'I'm sorry, Sharon Powell is no longer here.'

'But I told her to wait. What happened?'

'We were forced to expel her.'

'*Expel* her? Where did she go?'

'I'm sorry, I have no idea.'

There was a disconnect, followed by a dial tone. Eddie stood a moment, looking across the Washington skyline at the scarlet bloat of the setting sun. He dug into his pocket for another quarter, dropped it into the coin slot, and dialed Sharon Powell's cellphone.

She was laying her purchases down on the counter when the cellphone began ringing in her purse. She apologized to the clerk and pushed the answer button. 'Hello?'

'Sharon? It's Eddie.'

'I tried to reach you.'

'I got tied up in conference. Sorry.' He was yelling over traffic. He sounded rushed and agitated. 'How come you left the Embassy?'

'I thought of a way I may still be able to save Sperilac.'

'What are you planning?'

'I'm flying to Amsterdam.'

'Oh, Christ. Where are you?'

'Dulles International.'

'Sharon, don't get on that plane. Mike Bosch is in Amsterdam, he'll try to kill you.'

'That's a chance I'm going to have to take.'

'What are you, crazy?'

'Maybe.'

'Do me one favor.'

'That depends.'

'Wait for me.'

'If you can get here in time, fine.'

'Which flight are you taking?'

Sharon's eye went to the greeting card rack. The woman with thick glasses was holding a birthday card, her tongue curled over her lip in apparent concentration; but her eyes were fixed on Sharon. They quickly flicked away.

Sharon knew right away, didn't even have to think. *She's following me.*

'I can't talk now.' She broke the connection. She slapped down her American Express card. The clerk rang up her charges.

A voice on the overhead speakers announced, 'KLM flight forty-eight to Amsterdam; boarding for take-off, gate twenty-three.'

The clerk scooped her purchases into a plastic shopping bag. She hurried to the women's room and locked herself in a stall. Working quickly, she pinned her hair up with bobby pins and barrettes, hid it under the kerchief, checked the results in her compact mirror. She carefully arranged three curls so they showed and saturated them with spray-on frost, ageing herself a good fifteen years.

The bathroom door opened, then shut with a soft, air-braked slam. Silence fell like the drop of a blade. There were three sharp clacks of high heels on tile.

Through the crack in the door, Sharon caught a glimpse of the stooped woman with thick glasses. She was bending down, checking for feet beneath the stall doors.

'Last call,' the voice on the speaker announced. 'KLM flight forty-eight to Amsterdam is now boarding for take-off at gate twenty-three.'

Sharon silently lowered the toilet lid and stood on the seat.

The heels clacked by. A moment later, the bathroom door slammed again.

Sharon slipped on her harlequin glasses and stepped out of the stall.

A young girl was peering agonizingly into one of the mirrors. 'Excuse me,' she called as Sharon hurried by. 'Can you see if there's a green contact lens in my eye or in this sink?'

'Last call,' the voice on the speaker repeated. 'KLM flight forty-eight to Amsterdam; boarding for take-off gate twenty-three.'

Sharon studied the girl's blinking eye; studied the sink. 'I'm sorry, I don't see anything.' She was about to drop her shopping bag into the trash basket when she felt something blunt and metallic press into her back.

'Just be quiet,' the girl said, 'and you won't get hurt. We're going to turn round and go back into that stall.'

Sharon turned round and blasted the girl's eyes with spray frost.

The girl cried out. The gun clattered to the tiles. Sharon kicked and sent it spinning into the stalls. The girl lurched into a sink. Hands flailing, she opened the faucets and splashed handfuls of water into her eyes.

Sharon lunged for the door.

She moved as fast as she could without actually breaking into a run. Her reflection raced her in the plate-glass wall. The woman with thick glasses and the fat man with the mustard tie stood anxiously conferring at the Lufthansa counter. Neither seemed to notice the white-haired matron with unflattering harlequins hurrying toward KLM.

The agent was about to close gate 23. Sharon thrust out her boarding pass.

The agent detached a portion of the pass and handed back the rest. 'Nick of time,' he grinned.

Sharon stepped through the gate. She placed her boarding pass inside

Raquel Balmer's ticket. As she boarded the aircraft, she handed the ticket to the steward.

'You're in seat R-7, Ms Balmer.'

Bagless and breathless, Eddie Arbogast gripped the edge of the KLM counter. 'Has the flight to Amsterdam left yet?'

The agent shot him a commiserating look. 'A half-hour ago, sir.'

'What's the fastest connection I can make to Amsterdam?'

The agent punched up a schedule on the computer. 'You could fly Air France to Paris, departing in half an hour. There's a connecting KLM flight to Amsterdam forty minutes after arrival.'

'Where's Air France?'

The agent pointed. 'Right over there, sir.'

May 3

T he glowing hands on the bedside clock read 3:15, so Miguel Bosch
knew that whatever it was that had awakened him, it wasn't the
alarm.

The telephone gave its peculiar European gargle. He pulled himself
upright in bed and reached for it.

'Bosch,' he said.

'Niewendam.' Kees Niewendam, a former assistant director of Inter-
pol, had been Mike's West European operations chief for the last seven
years. His voice was grim. 'KLM has just confirmed that Sharon Powell
is on board flight forty-eight to Amsterdam.'

Mike Bosch felt his heartbeat quicken and his face fill with heat.
'*Mierda.*'

'She'll be landing at Schiphol Airport in five hours. What do you
want us to do?'

'I don't want Sharon Powell reaching Amsterdam. *Take care of her.*'

The door to the adjoining bedroom opened. A long rectangle of light
speared its way across the room and the bed. Helen Weller, a green silk
dressing gown over her shoulders, stood silhouetted in the doorway.

'It could be complicated,' Niewendam warned.

'It's your job to handle complications. And I don't want any more of
them.' Mike slammed the telephone into its cradle.

Helen moved to the bedside table and switched on the light.

'What's happened?' Her eyes were grave as she seated herself on the
bed next to him.

'Nothing.' Bosch reached out and patted her hand. 'A minor
annoyance.'

'It couldn't be so minor if they phone at this hour.'

Bosch straightened his pillows, and sighed. 'It's been taken care of.'

Helen put her head on Bosch's shoulder. 'Who are you talking about?'

He reached over and cupped her breast. 'Business.'

She placed her hand on his and held it there. 'You said "take care of
her". You shouted it.'

He forced a chuckle. 'You certainly have an imagination. I said "take
care of *it*".'

The discussion made him uneasy. She had spoken to him about Sharon Powell, and he knew she regarded the girl almost as the daughter she'd never had. Sharon's death would, of course, desolate her. And doubtless complicate her feelings toward him.

'Are you telling me the truth, Mike?'

Bosch pulled his hands away from her and groaned. 'Helen, please. I'm running a business. Sometimes it may seem to you I carry privacy to an extreme, but it's natural you would think that. You're *norteameri-cana*, I'm a Latin.'

'How can we work together if you shut me out? All I want to do is help you.'

'You've been a wonderful help, my darling, but when no help is needed, please, don't offer it.' He stole a look at her and didn't like the expression on her face. 'Now go get some sleep. We have a lot of sightseeing to do tomorrow.'

Helen rose from the bed and began to move back to her own room. She glanced back at him. 'You were talking about Sharon, weren't you?'

He started. 'Sharon?' He forced a smile. 'Sharon *Powell*? What gave you that crazy idea?'

'I heard you say her name.'

'You were dreaming.'

'Mike, don't hurt her.' Her voice had darkened. 'Don't ever hurt her.'

'You're imagining things. Go to sleep, my darling.'

She stared at him a long, questioning moment. 'I'll see you tomorrow.' She closed the door behind her.

Bosch lay in the dark, wondering.

No, he decided. Never leave a problem like Sharon Powell dangling. Remove it surgically, like a cancer, before it spreads. Besides, it's a sign of weakness to rescind an order.

KLM flight 48 from Dulles International arrived at Amsterdam's Schiphol Airport at 8:05 a.m., exactly on schedule. Sharon deplaned with three hundred other under-slept passengers.

The immigration officer took her passport under the glass partition. He glanced at two pages of entry visas and exit stamps that it had taken her six years to accumulate. He studied her photograph and compared it to her face.

She could see that the babushka and glasses and gray forelock confused him. She took off the glasses and kerchief, removed the barrettes, and shook her head to let her hair fall down.

Again, he compared photograph and face. He scowled. 'Will you be staying with us long, Miss Powell?'

Outside the booth, a woman wearing a nun's veil and round eye-glasses turned her head at the sound of the name Powell.

'I'll be staying four or five days.'

'Are you here on business or pleasure?'

She hesitated. 'A short vacation.'

'Will you be traveling elsewhere in Europe or will you return directly to the United States?'

'I'll be returning directly to the States.'

The immigration officer stamped her passport, slid it under the glass window, and waved her on.

As Sharon stepped out of the booth, she almost bumped into a nun with her face buried in a pocket map of Amsterdam.

'I'm sorry,' she apologized.

'Quite all right.' The nun lowered the map and smiled. She had a dead eyetooth, and she spoke English with the Oxbridge accent that all northern Europeans seemed to acquire in grade school. 'My fault.'

Sharon hurried down the corridor past shimmering duty-free boutiques.

The nun gave her a ten-second lead and followed. She slipped the map into the pocket of her jacket. Her hand remained in the pocket.

Sharon bypassed the crowd at the baggage carousel and went straight to customs.

The customs officer touched his cap politely. 'Good morning, miss.'

'Good morning.'

A red-headed man with a wheeled suitcase got in line behind Sharon. The nun got in line behind the man. She drew her hand out of her pocket but kept it close to her jacket. She was holding a small blue syringe. She held it like an unlit cigarette, partly hidden in her palm. Her thumb nudged the blue plastic cap off.

At the sound of something plinking on the concrete floor, the red-headed man glanced at the ground and frowned.

'Have you any luggage?' the customs officer was asking.

Sharon shook her head. 'None.'

The officer gave her a questioning glance. 'Have you anything to declare?'

The nun edged her way round the red-headed man. Her eye was fixed to the outer curve of Sharon's left buttock, and she was still holding her right hand close to her side. Her fingers gave a preparatory flex.

255

'The only thing I have to declare,' Sharon reached into her blouse and removed a small glassine envelope, 'is twenty-five grams of cocaine.'

The red-headed man recoiled, knocking the nun backward.

The astonished officer examined the glassine envelope. He lifted his telephone and shot off a quick volley of Dutch, all the while eyeing Sharon with utter disbelief. He replaced the receiver. 'Will you come with me, please?'

The canal smelled faintly of decaying vegetation, and the wake of passing boats lifted and rocked the restaurant barge where they sat. But Mike Bosch ignored these distractions and ate with raw gusto, rapidly forking sausage and eggs into his mouth, sopping up the juices with his croissant. Helen Weller sipped at her coffee, eyes squinting in the reflected sunlight from the water.

Bosch speared a chunk of sausage on the prongs of his fork. 'You're awfully quiet.'

'Am I?'

'You know what I think?'

'No.' Helen turned an expressionless face toward him. 'Tell me what you think.'

'I think you're still upset over that dream of yours.'

'Upset over a dream?' Her gaze slid back to the water. 'No, I don't think so.'

'Then why are you brooding?' Something almost pitiable edged into Bosch's voice. 'You should be happy today. We've accomplished so much. We deserve a celebration.'

Helen did not answer.

On the table beside the peppermill, Bosch's cellular phone rang. He picked it up. 'Bosch.'

'Niewendam,' the voice said.

Damn, Bosch thought. His operations chief would not be phoning again unless something else had gone wrong. He pressed the receiver close to his ear, sealing off any leakage of sound. 'Well? Did you get the data?'

'Sharon Powell is either the craziest woman alive or the smartest.'

'What makes you say that?'

'Our operative couldn't get her.'

'Why not?' Bosch snapped.

Helen stared at him, brows furrowed as though she was trying to read the other half of the conversation from his face.

'Because she'd had herself arrested for smuggling cocaine.'

A fit of coughing took Bosch. He cleared his throat and pretended to watch a tour boat chugging past. 'Then you'll have to keep trying till you get through.'

'Don't worry, we'll get her. We have her under surveillance right now.'

'I'm counting on you. Keep me advised.' Bosch lowered the telephone. He wiped his lips with a napkin.

'What was that all about?' Helen's fingers tapped on the edge of the table. 'Good news or bad?'

'No news at all. They're having trouble locating some data I need for tonight.' Mike tossed down his napkin.

'What sort of data? Maybe I could help.'

'I told you, we're not working today.' Mike rose. 'I have an idea. Let's visit the tulip market. Unless you'd rather see the diamond market?'

The passenger ahead of Eddie, a Frenchwoman, flashed her travel documents at the official behind the glass partition. A hand waved her through.

Eddie opened his wallet and showed his DEA credentials.

The official wrinkled his brow.

'I wonder if you could help me locate a visitor to Amsterdam. It's an emergency.' Eddie leaned toward a hexagon of small perforations in the glass. 'Her name is Sharon Powell.' He spelled Powell. 'She arrived this morning from Washington.'

The official turned and had a short chat with his computer. A wondering look stole across his face. 'A Sharon Powell arrived at eight o'clock this morning via KLM from Dulles International.'

'That's her. Where can I find her?'

'You'll have to ask the police. She's under arrest for drug smuggling. She was carrying twenty-five grams of cocaine.'

May 3 – 10:10 a.m.

T he room was sealed and draft free, and the blonde-haired Dutch
police chemist wore a white lab coat over her blouse. Concentrating
closely under the glare of tensor lights, she shook the first of the twenty-
fifth glassine envelopes empty.

Behind her, the slow movement of Mozart's twenty-third piano
concerto flowed serenely from a pair of CD speakers.

Approximately one gram of white crystals fell to the stainless steel
scale plate of a beam balance.

With a small pair of scissors, her surgical-gloved hands slit the
envelope neatly up two sides and gave it another shake. Five recalcitrant
grains fluttered down.

Now she took a tiny battery-driven vacuum cleaner, scarcely larger
than an electric toothbrush, and brushed the two interior glassine sur-
faces with the nozzle. She held the envelope up to the light, making
sure no particles still clung to it. Satisfied, she turned off the vacuum,
opened the collection chamber, and added its contents to the pile:
another ten grains.

She shifted the poise to the correct notch on the coarse-adjustment
beam, then moved the poise on the fine-adjustment beam. The scale
plate came into balance. The pointer indicated 964 thousandths of a
gram.

She entered the amount in her records.

Tapping gently with an unperforated steel spatula, she flattened the
tiny pile into a two-inch circle.

She dipped the tip of an eyedropper into a flask of clear reagent and
drew up half a dropper full of liquid. She placed one drop in the center
of the circle and four more at equidistant points a quarter-inch inside
the circumference. Almost instantly, five bright blue spots appeared like
points on a mandala.

She noted the reaction in her records.

Using the edge of a sterile scalpel, she separated the blue powder
from the white, nudging it off the scale plate into a paper cup. She
dropped the cup and the blue powder into the bag of burn trash.

Taking a pair of sterile tweezers, she selected four grains of the white powder at random and placed them on the stage of a laser spectroscope. She closed the chamber, pressed a button, and annihilated them.

As the chemical analysis appeared on her computer screen, she carefully noted it in her records.

Now she began on the second envelope.

The tapping at the door came a little before noon.

Vrouw Juliana Mengelberg had just taken a cup of boiling water from the microwave. With an annoyed glance into the next room, she lowered a tea bag into the cup and covered it with a saucer, letting it steep.

The tapping sound again.

'I'm coming,' she called, 'as fast as I can.'

Taking her cane, she crossed the living room and peered through the peephole. The face of a nun wearing an old-fashioned veil and round eyeglasses smiled at her.

Vrouw Mengelberg's annoyance melted. She opened the apartment door.

The nun wore a white habit, like one of Mother Teresa's Sisters of Charity, and she held a collection canister with the red-lettered words Save Our Children. 'Am I disturbing you, Vrouw Mengelberg?'

'Not at all, Sister. Come in. I was just fixing myself a cup of tea. Could I offer you any?'

The nun seemed embarrassed, hesitant to step across the threshold. 'I have no right to trouble you. As you can see, I've come to solicit a contribution for . . .'

Vrouw Mengelberg waved a hand, brushing aside any refusal. She could spot a thirsty nun. 'I've put aside five guilders – it either goes to you or the Salvation Army. Or would you prefer something stronger than tea?'

'Tea would be delightful.'

'Come in, come in. Have a seat. Would you like a little shortbread with your tea?'

'I hate to trouble you.'

Vrouw Mengelberg could see the good sister was tempted. 'No trouble.' She hurried into the kitchen as fast as her fused knee would allow. She took down a second cup from the cupboard and filled it from the tap.

Over the sound of splashing water, she failed to hear the footsteps behind her. The nun's hands were so light, so rapid, that they had

259

slipped round her neck before she was even aware of them.

As they choked, Vrouw Mengelberg had a feeling of something tearing inside her, a tremendous burning in her air-starved lungs. Blackness stabbed across her field of vision, followed by one last flash of the sink and the open tap, and then she crumpled into a small-boned, motionless heap on the kitchen floor.

'I'm sorry, Vrouw Mengelberg, but we need your window.'

The nun removed her veil and habit, loosened the two harnesses round her waist and chest, and undid the rifle stock and the barrel and breech that she'd worn strapped to her back. It was a relief to be able to relax her spine.

She cleared Vrouw Mengelberg's kitchen table and snapped the pieces of the weapon together. She fitted a silencer to the barrel and a high-power sight to the scope mount bases. She got a sofa cushion from the living room and placed it on the tabletop. It made a fine gun rest. She set four gleaming percussion-cap rounds beside the cushion.

She opened the window, drew up a chair, and peered through the telescopic sight.

On the far side of Herrengracht, the stone steps of the police station jumped into sharp focus.

The chemist stepped into the antechamber.

A Dutch narcotics cop looked up from his magazine. 'Took you long enough.'

'It's best to be thorough.' She handed him a small shopping bag with the logo of Amsterdam's most popular department store. It contained twenty-five freshly sealed packets of cocaine and crack. 'It's not bad stuff. Fifty per cent pure.'

The cop whistled. 'And the other fifty per cent? Lactose?'

She shook her head. 'You'd never guess in a million years.' She handed him the print-out of her report.

In a small windowless interrogation room in Central Headquarters, a Dutch narcotics inspector reviewed the chemist's report. He stared at Sharon with gray, troubled eyes. 'You realize it's a serious crime to import this amount of cocaine into Holland.'

'I realize that.'

'Was it for your personal use?'

She drank her coffee in short sips. She needed the boost, but she could feel a sour churning in her stomach. She shook her head. 'No.'

The inspector drew in a weary breath and frowned. 'For resale then?'

Dizziness caught her. It came swiftly and violently. Black spots swam before her eyes. Her cup clattered in the saucer and she quickly set it down on the table. It was a moment before she could bring the room and the inspector back into focus. She realized she had eaten nothing and had slept barely three hours in the last two days.

He was watching her curiously. 'Are you all right?'

'Fine.'

'Was the cocaine intended for resale?' he asked again.

'No. Not for resale.'

'For a friend, then?'

'I have no friends in Holland.'

He shrugged his shoulders, closed his notebook and rose. He was dressed in an American checked shirt and khaki trousers. 'You have the right to speak to someone from your Embassy.'

'I'd rather speak to someone from the World Health Organization.'

Shortly before 6 p.m., the nun waiting in Vrouw Mengelberg's kitchen picked up a burst of static. She lowered the volume on the micro-miniaturized radio receiver with de-scrambler chip that she wore like a hearing aid in her left ear. The static was followed by a male voice.

'Do you hear me, Sister Fredrieka?' The tone was furtive, almost whispered.

The nun spoke into the lion's head medallion of the carnelian signet ring on her left hand. 'I hear you perfectly.'

'She'll be coming out the front entrance in ten minutes. She'll have two guards with her and an officer of the World Health Organization.'

'World Health Organization?' The nun frowned. 'Why?'

'I couldn't overhear everything. But they're taking custody. Ten minutes.'

There was another crackle of static and then silence.

The nun snapped back the bolt of the rifle and loaded two rounds into the chamber.

She steadied the recoil pad against her shoulder, lifted the barrel, and centered the police headquarters steps in the telescopic sight.

At 6:10 on the dot a woman with light brown hair stepped out of the building and almost lost her life.

Luckily for her, the nun asked herself, where are her guards?

Her finger hesitated on the trigger. She swung the rifle with the woman, keeping her in the crosshairs as she came down the steps.

Alone. Hair curly, not waved. Eyes dark, not green. No freckles. No gray forelock.

Not Sharon Powell.

The nun swung the rifle back to the door.

In the next five minutes nineteen men and four women passed through that doorway, none of them Powell.

And then, a little after 6:15, two plain-clothes policemen in dungarees and an officious-looking type in a dark business suit ushered a blonde-haired woman out the door. She slid into the nun's telescopic sight, giving her a generous three-quarter profile.

This was the right hair and forelock, the right freckles, the right eyes, the right woman.

The nun's left hand brushed a thin film of sweat from her forehead.

She tracked Sharon Powell down the steps. Swinging slowly to keep her centered, she very gently increased the pressure of her finger on the trigger.

The bullet made hardly any sound hissing through the silencer; there was a semi-audible 'pfft!' like lips smacking, more than covered by the sound of a taxi screeching to a stop.

May 3 – 6:16 p.m.

As the cab turned into Herrengracht, Eddie saw Sharon Powell and three men coming down the precinct steps.

'Driver,' he cried. 'Stop.'

It was Eddie's bad luck to be riding with the one cab driver in all of Amsterdam who didn't understand a word of English. At least not the word 'stop'.

He thrust a 100-guilder note into the driver's face. 'Stop here!'

The driver slammed down the brake and shot him a burst of gutturals that he suspected had to do with not having change.

Eddie was out the cab door and into the street in one uninterrupted leap. 'Sharon!' he shouted. 'Sharon Powell!'

Sharon heard someone call her name.

Her head turned, eyes searching. A cab tore away from the far curb, tires squealing, a crazed contrast to all the cars and cyclists and pedestrians flowing down the street in orderly lanes.

At the same instant, she felt a tiny sting at the back of her neck, like an insect bite. Her hand instinctively reached back to rub the spot.

Her fingertip came away bloody. A wave of unreality broadsided her. 'Someone just shot at me.'

The man from WHO ripped off his jacket and threw it over her head. 'Keep down!'

Bending her in a kind of running crouch, her three escorts hurried her into a waiting black Audi. They piled in after her.

She peeked out from under the jacket.

A hand pushed her. 'Keep down!'

The door slammed and the sedan nosed into traffic.

Eddie squinted down Herrengracht into the late afternoon sun. He could see that the black Audi sedan weaving through traffic had a Swiss license.

The traffic light changed. He crossed the street, climbed the steps to the police station, and showed his DEA credentials at the desk. 'Do you speak English?'

The officer at the desk gave his credentials a skeptical look, then gave him an even more skeptical look and swallowed a mouthful of ham sandwich. Without the slightest trace of an accent, he said, 'I speak a little.'

He was not Eddie's idea of a cop. With his sunburnt face and beefy forearms he looked more like a bricklayer who'd put on a necktie and jacket for a wedding.

'That American woman who just left with three men in a Swiss Audi sedan – you've been holding her as a drug smuggler.'

'Possibly.'

'Her name is Sharon Powell.' Eddie began spelling the name.

'I can spell.'

'I need to see her. Urgent. Can you tell me where they're taking her?'

'Possibly.' The man turned and shouted something in Dutch. His voice boomed across the squad room. A woman shouted something back.

'You've caught us on an unusual day. We don't have any American drug smugglers.'

There was laughter behind him.

'I didn't make myself clear,' Eddie said. 'She just left with three men. You've either transferred her or released her.'

'The computer usually knows these things.' The officer entered a command on his keyboard. He watched the monitor screen closely, waiting for something. Apparently it came and he uttered a phrase that sounded like a Dutch curse. He snatched up the phone and punched three digits. A flood of Dutch followed. The only word Eddie recognized was the name Powell, repeated several times with growing impatience.

The officer slammed down the phone and sat looking at it.

Eddie had the cold flat feeling in his stomach that he'd lost the trail.

'Miss Powell has been released to the World Health Organization.'

The officer was speaking English so suddenly that it caught Eddie unprepared.

'I'm sorry? What did you say?'

'You'll find her at the AIDS convention at the RAI Gebouw.'

Miguel and Helen strolled through the International AIDS Conference like wealthy vacationing tourists. Helen had chosen to wear a Lagerfeld black silk dress with matching elbow-length gloves. The emerald cross hung from her throat like a beacon.

Bosch smiled, delighted at the way she looked, a queen among peasants. He held her elbow and maneuvered her through the exhibits and the milling, directionless crowd. She made him pause at every exhibit.

'This is a circus,' she said. 'We don't want to miss a single sideshow.'

He smiled. 'You're a skeptic.'

'I used to be. But I'm fast becoming an idealist.'

'Idealists are dangerous people.'

'Very.'

The hall of Amsterdam's RAI Gebouw, Amsterdam's largest exposition space, was crowded with restaurants, bookshops, galleries and boutiques run by various AIDS groups. Posters advertised art by Persons with AIDS, dance recitals by Persons with AIDS, seminars for relatives and friends of Persons with AIDS, a candle-light vigil for Persons with AIDS.

Helen stared at a pearl-and-ebony rosary designed by a Person with AIDS in Rwanda.

'Do you want it?' Bosch offered.

The price was marked in guilders and dollars. 'Over four thousand dollars,' she observed.

'Why not? You're the star here tonight.'

'No,' she decided. She pulled him toward a large booth that promised 'Help for Children with AIDS'. A three-paneled box featured grossly enlarged photographs of emaciated babies. 'Give the money to these people.'

'You can't be serious.'

'Of course I am.'

The curtness of the command irritated him. It testified to a major shift in their relationship. She was no longer the frightened woman he had locked in the conference room. She had turned the Sperilac factories into her own private fiefdom. The Indians worshipped her; the technicians and scientists relied upon her sharpness of instinct and clarity of vision; cartel quotas were already being exceeded. She had made herself indispensable.

And she was telling him not to forget it.

He took out his checkbook, sighed, and wrote a check for four thousand dollars. He handed it to the woman in charge of the booth.

The woman smiled and thanked him and suddenly he realized that she was a member of the royal family.

'Look, darling.' Tugging at his sleeve, Helen drew him into a book-stall. 'This should have been dedicated to us.' Her gloved hand held out a paperback book: *Cocaine and HIV: A Breakthrough?* 'Do you suppose somebody's been tattling?'

He examined the book. 'Author's a Swede. Outside our territory.'

She replaced the book on its rack. 'I wonder for how long.'

As they passed through a cluster of men in dinner jackets and women in floor-length gowns, a jeweled hand shot out. 'I want to talk to you about *that*,' a woman shouted. 'It's *gorgeous*!'

Bosch realized it was Elizabeth Taylor, and her finger was pointing at the emerald cross on Helen's neck.

'I'll catch you later,' Helen shouted back, obviously delighted with her own impudence.

Bosch smiled. 'Didn't I tell you that you were a star?'

'Your cross is the star, darling.' Helen took a compact from her sequined bag and smoothed powder on her cheeks. 'And I cherish it.'

Inside the breast pocket of Bosch's jacket, his cellular telephone rang. 'Damn. Excuse me, darling.'

But she had already wandered away to study a wall of hospice photographs.

He pulled the cellphone out. 'Bosch.'

'It's Kees Niewendam. Sorry to keep calling.'

Bosch watched Helen drop five hundred-dollar bills into a plastic cylinder labeled 'Publicize AIDS'. He lowered his voice. 'What the hell's gone wrong now?'

His chief of West European operations told him exactly what had gone wrong. 'And they've released her to the World Health Organization.'

Bosch watched Helen perusing pamphlets at a 'Save Zaire' kiosk. He cupped his hand over the mouthpiece, taking a chance that she was too far away to hear him, that too many voices were shouting. 'What the hell is WHO going to do with her?'

'They've scheduled her to address the conference. She goes on right after you.'

Mike felt a violent tightening in his heart. 'Sharon Powell is not to step on to that platform.'

'How on earth do you expect us to stop her once she's inside the conference hall?'

'I don't care how you do it, so long as you stop her. That's an unrescindable order.' He slammed the telephone closed.

'Trouble?' Helen stood at his elbow, a questioning eyebrow arched.

'The trouble's over.' He smiled and slipped the phone into his pocket. 'They found the data.'

266

May 3 – 6:30 p.m.

In the doorway of a rundown building in the heart of Amsterdam's red light district, a nun wearing round glasses and an old-fashioned white habit pushed the one button that had no name.

'Who is it?' a voice growled over the intercom.

'Sister Fred.'

The door buzzed open and she climbed two narrow flights of stairs laid dizzyingly end to end. The door on the second landing was ajar. A figure was sprawled on a sofa in front of the TV watching a news interview. A shot glass of Genever and an almost empty bottle of Heineken sat on the table. Sadistic pornographic magazines were scattered on the floor.

Sister Fred stepped into the apartment and closed the door. 'Job for you, Jan-Pieter.'

He drained the shot glass in a single, head-back gulp. His moist pink tongue-tip flicked insolently along his lower lip. 'I don't work after five.'

'This is an order from Mike.'

Eyes the blue of Delft tile flicked up. They were the glazed eyes of a five-times-a-day speed-baller – an addict who injected cocaine with his heroin.

Sister Fred did not trust those eyes. Nor did she trust the freshly scabbed track marks inside the left forearm.

Still, Jan-Pieter had a proven record of being able to break through security, at terminating politicians that other hitmen couldn't even get near.

'Who's the target?'

Sister Fred showed him a photo. 'She's in the exposition hall in the RAI Gebouw. The Green Room behind the stage. She has a guard.'

Jan-Pieter studied the photo. His expression was slack and apathetic. 'Nice tits.'

'Her name is Sharon Powell. You're going to take her these flowers.' Sister Fred set a basket of red and yellow tulips on the table. 'Plus a little surprise.'

She loaded six fragmentation bullets into the magazine of a Glock 9-

267

millimeter. The magazine was specially lined with foil. The gun itself was plastic. Neither the bullets nor the gun would set off security alarms. 'You'll only get one shot at her but you may need the others for the guards.' She snapped the magazine into the automatic.

Jan-Pieter belched noisily. 'I'll only need one.'

Sister Fred recoiled from a stench of onions and halitosis. 'I wonder. Can you even see straight?'

Jan-Pieter hefted the Glock in his right hand, spun it cowboy-style and, without even taking aim, shot a bullet into the open mouth of the Prime Minister. The screen on the 21-inch TV shattered with a pop.

'You're an asshole. Give me that.' Sister Fred fitted a silencer to the barrel and handed the gun back. 'Now get going. She's scheduled to speak in half an hour, and Mike doesn't want her stepping on to that stage.'

'Give me your comb. I have to look cute.'

Sister Fred's stomach contracted at the idea of sharing a comb with that blond mop. 'Haven't you got a comb of your own?'

'Someone picked my pocket at the day care center.'

'Then to hell with looking cute.'

'Trust me. I know my job.' Jan-Pieter held out a plump, grime-caked paw that betrayed the telltale puffiness of the long-term addict.

Sister Fred reluctantly handed over her comb. She'd have to boil it tonight. 'And while you're at it, brush your teeth and gargle. You smell like a fermented juniper bush. And wash your hands. They're filthy. No one will believe you're from a respectable florist's shop.'

In the Green Room behind the auditorium, Sharon paced to the window for the twentieth time. She stared out at the lights of Amsterdam reflecting off low night clouds.

She turned. 'How long?'

One of the WHO officials consulted his wristwatch. 'It shouldn't be long now. You've been wedged into the schedule right after Miguel Bosch.'

Sharon felt a jolt of disbelief. Eddie Arbogast had said it was Bosch, with his scheme of controlling Sperilac, who was behind all the killings. 'Miguel Bosch is speaking *here*? At the conference?'

'He won't take long.'

'But he's a criminal.'

'That's what the Americans say, but who knows?' The official shrugged. 'He's a philanthropist, that's what counts here.'

There was a knock at the door. Sharon belted back the last of her mineral water and squared her shoulders.

Another knock. Impatient.

'It's locked.' The Dutch policeman crossed the room and opened the door.

'Sharon.'

She turned at the sound of her name, saw Joe Mahler standing in the doorway, and ran to him.

'Damn it.' His arms closed round her. 'You had me scared stiff.'

Relief flowed through her. She allowed herself a moment of closeness to him.

'Would you mind telling me what's going on?' he said. 'I went to meet three planes – no sign of you. I was losing my mind.'

'There wasn't time to get in touch.'

'Finally a customs officer told me you'd been—'

She nodded. 'Arrested.'

'All six of you?'

'Just me.'

'Where are the others?'

'I'm the only one who made it, Joe. The others were killed.'

His face turned white but it was a slow process. '*Killed?*'

'Yesterday morning.'

'Christ.' He grabbed her by the shoulders and studied her. 'Are you hurt?'

'I'm OK. Just a little tired. And very nervous.'

'Can I do anything?'

'Thanks. I'll be fine after the speech.'

He was even handsomer when he scowled. 'Speech?'

'I'm addressing the convention.'

'Addressing the . . . ?' His eyes held amazement.

'It's our last chance. There's no other way.'

Jan-Pieter made his way past rows of cars in the parking lot, past loading bays at the rear of the convention hall. A stream of people was pouring through the stage entrance. They flashed passes at the gray-haired custodian, who waved them through.

'Excuse me, sir.' Jan-Pieter had to shout above voices babbling Dutch, French, German, Italian, English. 'I have an urgent delivery.' He held up the basket of tulips. 'Flowers for Miss Sharon Powell.'

The custodian frowned. 'Who?'

269

'She's going to address the delegates.'

'Then she's in the Green Room.' The custodian consulted a clipboard of printed schedules. 'Green Room, Green Room . . .' His finger came to a handwritten line that had been added to one of the schedules. He shook his head. 'Miss Powell is under strict security guard.'

'These were telegraphed from Switzerland.' Jan-Pieter showed the custodian the card: 'For Sharon Powell, from all her friends at WHO headquarters.'

'I don't know.' The custodian pondered. 'Switzerland, hey?'

'I could just knock and leave them outside the door.' Jan-Pieter smiled his most disarming smile.

'Pretty flowers like that wouldn't last two seconds in a place like this.'

'Or I could give them to the guard.'

'That's a good idea. Give them to the guard.' The custodian patted Jan-Pieter on the head. 'Go down that corridor and take a right.'

'We are honored to welcome Señor Miguel Bosch, industrialist and representative of the government of Colombia. Señor Bosch has a surprise announcement for us.' The young Belgian count who was acting as master of ceremonies signaled Bosch to come out of the wings.

The applause that greeted his entrance was a disappointment. Miguel Bosch was accustomed to cheers, tumult, fanfares, the audible, tangible signs of worldly respect. This audience, filled with half-baked doctors, shamans, and very angry sick people, had no respect and no hesitation in showing the fact.

He stood alone in a place that was uncomfortable for him, in a spotlight, greeted only by a patter of clapping.

'Your excellencies, ladies and gentlemen.' He placed his large-print text on the podium in front of him. He adjusted his reading glasses to bring the letters into focus. 'I am a man who is perhaps unknown to many of you. First, as Count Wilkaiser indicated, I am an industrialist and an entrepreneur. Second, I am, despite my credentials, someone who can be of considerable service to this cause, because, third, I am a multi-millionaire.'

He waited for the laughter to subside.

'In Deutschmarks.'

Now there was applause. He held up his hands to still it.

'Fourth, I sit on the boards of three pharmaceutical companies and two hospitals, and I run my own research laboratories. But last, and most significantly, eight years ago my own beloved daughter, Rosa, died of AIDS. This is the greatest pain I have ever experienced in my life.'

Bosch paused, as if bringing himself under control.

'You may make inquiries about me. You will receive mixed information. But there's one thing on which my friends and enemies will agree, I am a man of determination. And I am here tonight to create the mechanisms by which this plague will come to an end. To see that no more fathers and mothers suffer what I have suffered.'

Applause broke out again, even more enthusiastic this time.

'I do not speak wishfully or loosely or hyperbolically. My laboratories and clinics have produced results unrivaled by any of the major drug firms in the world. There is *now in existence* a drug that has proved in limited but thorough trials to be one hundred per cent effective against AIDS.'

An astonished silence overtook the auditorium.

'One hundred per cent? you're saying to yourselves. This man must be insane. Or a liar. If a drug one hundred per cent effective against this plague exists, why haven't we heard of it? Why aren't doctors prescribing it? Why aren't hospitals using it? Why aren't governments buying it and handing it out free to the sick? Why hasn't the dying stopped?

'Ladies and gentlemen, I can assure you I am not a liar, nor am I insane. Furious, yes, but not insane. The reason you have not heard of this drug can be summed up in one ugly word: money.

'Last year, twenty-eight billion dollars was spent worldwide on AIDS research and treatment. You heard me – twenty-eight *billion*. And who is pocketing this wealth? The purveyors of therapies that do not work – powerful medical and drug conglomerates who profit not from the cure but from the disease, who will be put out of business overnight by a *genuine* cure.

'These are the same people who brought us the war on cancer, and as you know, in the last thirty years, while cancer spending has increased by a factor of one hundred, cancer *deaths* have risen from one in twenty to one in three. What a way to run a war, hey? These people are selling us worthless, ineffective therapies whose only virtue is their price. At the same time they are suppressing far less costly therapies that have proved effective but for one drawback – the medico-pharmaceutical establishment cannot profit from them. Money, ladies and gentlemen. Money.'

He took a moment to polish his glasses.

271

'The medico-pharmaceutical establishment will try to suppress the cure for AIDS, just as many believe they have suppressed the cure for cancer. They will fight it with all the financial and governmental power they possess. They will fight until they can find the means to monopolize it, even if in the meantime hundreds of millions must die.

'And so I need your help. I am asking for assistance in funding. I wish nations, not individuals, to match my pledge to the Rosa Margarita Bosch Foundation For The Cure Of AIDS. Tonight, I am giving the foundation a check for fifty million dollars to be held in trust by the government of Colombia for completion of trials and tests. Within six months, I promise you, a cure for AIDS will be in general distribution and available on the markets of any nation that requests it.'

Applause exploded. Elizabeth Taylor was on her feet, tearing apart a bouquet and hurling roses at the podium. Miguel Bosch's heartbeat quickened. A glow spread through him. This was more like it.

'After I am through speaking, my colleagues will provide you with statistics and papers to show you how far we have come, how close we are to eradicating this scourge.'

'I pledge a million,' Ms Taylor hollered. 'And tell that girlfriend of yours to hock her rocks.'

It took almost sixty seconds for the laughter to die down.

'Please,' Bosch said. 'As grateful as I am to Miss Taylor, I need the help of countries, continents. Uganda, Thailand, Romania, Brazil.' He paused and his voice deepened. 'First come, first served.' He held out his arms and cried: 'First come, first *cured*!'

The audience came apart. Industrialists, finance ministers, sick men and women on crutches all pushed to their feet cheering. The message was clear: the toxic, overpriced, useless remedies were out with the garbage; a cure had finally been found – and Bosch was cutting out the pharmaceutical establishment.

The sound of applauding and shouting and stamping washed into the Green Room. Sharon stared at Joe Mahler. 'What has he done?'

'He's just pledged himself fifty million dollars and he's asked every AIDS-afflicted nation for more.' Joe shook his head. 'The Chinese will be worth a billion if he can produce.' He looked sadly at Sharon. 'My guess is, he *can* produce, can't he?'

'He can produce Sperilac,' she said. 'He's pirated the formula.'

Joe nodded grimly. 'Sperilac. I should have guessed.'

An usher appeared at the door. 'Dr Powell, you will be next. Would you care to follow me?'

As Sharon approached the wings, she could see Bosch on stage doing a Richard Nixon imitation, arms overhead, fingers spread in V for Victory signs.

An adorable little boy of ten or eleven, all blond bangs and bright blue eyes, stepped in front of her clutching a basket of tulips. 'Dr Powell?' he asked.

Sharon smiled. 'Yes?'

He raised the basket. 'This is for you.'

'Why thank you, and what's your name?'

'Jan-Pieter.'

'Thank you, Jan-Pieter.' She bent to plant a kiss on the little blond head.

Joe Mahler saw the gun before Sharon did. The barrel and silencer emerged like a snake from a garden, pushing their way through the tulip stems.

'Watch it!' Joe shouted, and back-handed the kid with all his strength.

The little boy toppled backward just as the gun went off.

May 3 – 9:05 p.m.

On stage, Mike Bosch bowed to the applause for the ninth time. As he raised his head he was aware of a whistling sound. A blow rocked through the podium. He looked down and saw that a bullet had splintered the wood two inches from his hand.

He turned toward the wings. Three grown men were pummeling a small boy who was trying to beat them off with handfuls of flowers.

A young woman stepped round them and came on to the stage. With a shock, he recognized her from her photograph: Sharon Powell, shaken but apparently unhurt.

Very well. Plan B.

Mike Bosch took off his reading glasses, transferred them to his left hand, and placed them carefully in his jacket pocket. He had only one recourse now, and his fingers found it: the syringe. He drew it out and curled it into his palm.

Smiling broadly, he strode toward Sharon Powell before she could reach the microphone.

'Sharon Powell,' Eddie gasped, out of breath from running. 'Where is she?'

The guard at the Green Room door pointed.

Eddie ran toward the stage. He could see Mike Bosch marching toward Sharon, twisting something in his left hand. Even at twenty feet, Eddie's eyes caught the glint of a needle guard as it fell to the floor and rolled toward the footlights.

Bosch's grin was wide and charming, his voice thundering. 'Dr Powell, my name is Miguel Bosch.' He stretched out his right hand in greeting.

'Sharon!' Eddie cried. 'His left hand!'

Sharon's head whipped round.

'My good friend Helen Weller has spoken highly of you.' Mike Bosch's right hand seized Sharon's. 'I'd like to congratulate you on your admirable work.'

Just as the uncapped syringe flashed forward, Eddie leapt, hurling his weight into Bosch's arm. The syringe flew spinning into the air and hit the stage with the sound of a tossed coin.

Bosch grunted as Eddie brought him slamming down to the floor. 'Damn you! Who the hell are you?'

'Call me an old admirer, Mike. I've been following you from way back.'

Guards seized Eddie's arms and pulled him off Bosch.

'My leg.' Mike Bosch tried to push himself to his feet and couldn't. 'I think he broke my leg.'

A woman in a long black silk dress swept past them. She took three steps on to the stage and stopped at the spot where the syringe had fallen. Eddie saw her foot nudge it under the hem of her gown. For an instant she dropped to a curtseying crouch. One gloved hand slipped to the floor, reaching under the pool of silk. When she rose, the syringe was gone.

She went to Mike Bosch and sank to her knees beside him. 'Darling, are you all right? Did that madman hurt you?'

'Watch out for that woman!' Eddie shouted. He tried to point, but one policeman had him in a hammerlock and another clapped a hand over his mouth.

'It hurts,' Bosch grunted, 'but I'll be all right.' He struggled to sit up.

'Don't strain yourself, darling. I worry about your heart.' The woman's voice was unnaturally loud, as if she wanted her words to be heard over the confusion by people in the fifth row.

Mike Bosch's face took on a perplexed look.

Masking the syringe in her glove, the woman jabbed it through Miguel Bosch's sleeve, emptied it and withdrew it. If Eddie hadn't seen it with his own eyes, he'd never have believed any human being could have the speed or the audacity. Her hand vanished into her evening bag.

For an instant Mike Bosch's mouth was open, his eyes wild, and then his head dropped back.

'Señor Bosch is having a heart attack!' the woman called. 'We must get him to a hospital!'

Her eyes met Eddie's. In that instant, even without her glasses, he recognized the woman standing at the rail of Mike Bosch's yacht: Helen Weller.

'Put him on a couch until we can get an ambulance! Gently, gently!'

Ushers and stagehands and members of the audience, proclaiming themselves physicians, rushed to assist.

The police released Eddie and ran to help. But he could see that Miguel Bosch no longer inhabited the flesh they carried from the stage. The body was dead weight.

As Helen Weller passed Sharon, huddled in Joe Mahler's arms, Eddie heard her say something remarkable: 'Now get out there and break a leg.'

'Ladies and gentlemen.' Count Wilkaiser tapped on the microphone with his fingernails to bring order to the hall. 'Please excuse the interruption. Everything is under control.'

The audience, unsettled and in motion, turned their heads toward him.

'Your attention!' he shouted. 'Please! I have an announcement. We have an unscheduled speaker from the United States whose presence has been sponsored this evening by the World Health Organization.' He consulted a sheet of paper. 'I am honored to introduce Dr Sharon Powell, the daughter of Nobelist Dr Lucas Powell.' He turned and inclined his head toward the wings. 'Ms Powell.'

The confusion in the auditorium gradually died down. Joe Mahler led Sharon to the rostrum, kissed her on the cheek, and whispered, 'Give it to them with both barrels!'

Feeling shaky and ill, Sharon forced herself to take three deep breaths. Her hands gripped the podium for support. She was scarcely aware that Joe had gone backstage to stand in the wings.

'Your excellencies, ladies and gentlemen,' she began.

'Louder!' someone called from the audience. A murmur began to swell in the vastness on the other side of the footlights.

Tears of exhaustion welled in her eyes. The stresses of the past three days were taking their toll. Don't give in now, she told herself. Not now!

She raised her voice. 'The previous speaker did not lie to you. A cure for AIDS exists, here and now. But I must inform you that Señor Bosch has misled you. The drug of which he spoke is not his to offer. It is the discovery of my father and has been the property of Forbes Biochemtech for over seven years.'

In the stillness that suddenly gripped the auditorium, she could hear her own voice echo.

'I shall spare you the history of deception, negligence and criminal interference that has prevented this drug from reaching the market before now. But I am here to tell you that the cure exists, and its name is Sperilac.'

She held up one hand to still the commotion in the audience.

'Please listen! Today I have given the World Health Organization records of trials and certain other data that verify the drug's efficacy. These are being reproduced and will be available for you at tomorrow's session. I am authorized to tell you that supplies of Sperilac will be offered to any laboratory or any government facility that wishes to conduct its own trials.'

A man in a wheelchair in the center aisle called out, 'What about those of us who need it now?'

'You shall have it,' Sharon replied. 'Forbes Biochemtech will make Sperilac available immediately for those in the most urgent need. If for any reason we are forbidden export from the United States, stockpiles are available in other parts of the world. And I am quite sure that access can be arranged within a matter of days. Furthermore,' Sharon's voice rose, 'we shall franchise production of the drug to any, I repeat, *any* government or reputable pharmaceutical firm on an immediate basis, forgoing red tape and bargaining.'

Let Lucinda Forbes wriggle out of that, she thought. Lynch mobs will pursue her down the streets if she tries to hold out now.

'We are here to bring you a cure, not to exploit you. There's been enough of that.' As her gaze met that of the man in the wheelchair, she felt tears break loose and flow down her cheeks. Her voice rose to a cry. 'Take heart, the exploitation is ended!'

The audience rose in a shouting, foot-stamping, program-tearing ovation.

'We're home free,' Sharon cried. 'Home at last!'

Then she fainted.

Afterward

Helen Weller lay by the pool of the hacienda and let her skin soak up the heat of the sun. She had become even thinner since Amsterdam, partly through a failure of appetite, partly because she loathed any sign of fat or self-indulgence on her body.

Gazing through prescription Ray-Bans, she reviewed the week's print-outs. 'Production's up five point five per cent.'

Larry Lorenzo lay on his stomach three feet away, covered only by a towel round his midsection, his head resting on his forearms. 'Your part of the business or mine?'

In the chaos following Mike Bosch's fatal heart attack, it had been necessary to organize a transitional management team. It was now Helen's job to supervise the manufacture of Sperilac and to co-ordinate production with Forbes Biochemtech under a special licensing agreement. It was now Larry Lorenzo's job to oversee the processing of cocaine and manage world distribution of the cocaine/Sperilac mixture. If present business trends continued, the posts would almost certainly become permanent.

'Your part of the business *and* mine,' Helen said. 'At these rates, we should be able to meet our market demand in . . .'

Larry raised himself on one elbow and punched keys on a calculator. 'Eight point six weeks.' His eyes fixed upon her. 'I'm not surprised. The Indians love you, your lab colleagues love you, your confederates in the cartel love you.' He moved closer. 'And I love you. Love is the perfect motivator.'

Helen studied the suntanned torso, middle-aged but still strong, the face with its slightly wolfish features, the hair drawn into a dark ponytail. She had no illusion that Larry possessed any more moral center than a common viper; hadn't he double-crossed the DEA, and didn't he keep a wife and child stashed in Bogota? But for the moment he was *her* viper.

'What about addict mortality stats?' he said.

'I don't have those.' Helen pressed two buttons on her radio phone. 'Key. can you find the latest NIH addict mortality figures? They should be on my desk somewhere.'

A minute later Key, looking deeply tanned in his yellow tank top, brought Helen a thick pile of print-outs. At first she'd felt qualms employing a professional assassin as a houseboy, but as Larry pointed out, Key knew the ropes, and in this business his skills were bound to come in handy.

She leafed through accordion folds of paper. 'NIH says the evidence is anecdotal and they won't have reliable figures for three months. But they estimate a seventy per cent drop.'

Since Helen had taken over day-to-day directorship of the cartel, virtually no unmixed cocaine was allowed on to the market. Sperilac had become the pasteurization process of the industry. Because it was also available worldwide in legal form through Forbes Biochemtech and their licensees, AIDS mortality had plummeted.

'I'd say that calls for a celebration.' Larry snapped a finger and pointed. Key reached into the shade of a palm, where the ice chest sat.

Helen heard a pop of a champagne cork, the fizz of escaping froth, and then she felt the stream of tiny ice-cold bubbles on her spine, prickling down from her shoulder blades to her bikini.

And then she felt the touch of Larry Lorenzo's lips and nibbling tongue.

'Moet eighty-seven,' he murmured. 'I love it.'

Helen knew she had no right, and yet – she was happy. 'Me too.' To think I once dreamt of being a nun, and wept for weeks when the Carmelites turned me down . . .

She took off the Ray-Bans and laid her head down and closed her eyes. She couldn't help sighing when she remembered the old days, and the woman she had been.

I wonder how Sharon is. I wonder if she ever thinks of me.

The Dutch Ambassador took three steps into Lucinda Forbes' living room, saw what was hanging over the fireplace, and stopped in his tracks. 'Van Gogh's "Lilacs".' His astonished eyes turned toward Lucinda. 'The last time I saw this painting it was hanging in Fiona Pullman's study.'

'She got tired of it; and I've come into some unexpected income.' Today Lucinda's jewelry was radiantly understated: an emerald at each ear to bring out the green of her eyes. 'Tell me, do you think it goes with the room?'

'Magnificently.'

'Liar. Van Gogh's pink clashes with mine.' She tweaked the

Ambassador's cheek. 'I'm going to have to get rid of it.'

'Get rid of it!' The Ambassador was shocked and pained.

'Do you suppose the Van Gogh museum in Amsterdam would be interested?' She knew he had been trying to buy the painting for the museum for ten years.

Now the Ambassador was cautious. 'How much are you asking?'

'Asking?' Lucinda had bought the painting for two reasons: to get a whopping tax deduction when she gave it away; and to snag the Ambassador. Recently widowed, he was one of the largest stockholders in Royal Dutch Shell; he was also a Count of Orange. Lucinda liked the idea of being related to the Queen of the Netherlands. 'I thought I'd *give* it to them.'

'My darling,' the Ambassador smiled, 'that's a splendid idea.'

'Naturally, you'll have to advise me.'

'But of course.'

She took the Ambassador's arm and pulled him toward the sofa. 'I'm so glad you stopped by.'

A voice said, 'Two clubs.'

Eddie Arbogast's mind was in Amsterdam, but unfortunately his foot was in Coconut Grove. A shoe kicked him under the patio table. His wife's.

'Didn't you hear Irma, honey?'

He snapped back to here and now. 'Right. Sorry.' He scanned his hand. 'Two diamonds.'

The bid went to Dottie with her new pink-rinsed hair. 'Three spades.'

Amy wasn't going to let Dottie get away with that. 'Three no trumps.' Which turned out to be the top bid.

Irma led the two of spades.

Eddie laid down his hand. 'Anyone want anything?'

Irma and Dottie were too horrified by Amy's slash-and-burn riff to answer. Eddie strolled into the kitchen and poured himself an iced tea.

So this is retirement. The toughest assignment yet. He added a sprig of fresh mint. But hell, I can lick it. After all, didn't I lick Mike Bosch? Sort of?

He began thinking of Amsterdam again. Nostalgically.

Sometimes, sort of is all it takes.

Once again his mind's eye saw that black-gloved hand giving Mike Bosch a dose of his own poison. Try his damnedest, Eddie had not been able to trace Helen Weller. He suspected she was in Colombia, almost certainly linked with the cartel. But there was no way of getting information out of the DEA. Not since Larry Lorenzo had burned them.

'Eddie,' his wife called, 'we'd all like some of that iced tea.'

Eddie sauntered back to the patio with a jingling tray load.

'We dealt you.' Amy nodded toward his cards, lying face down at his place. 'I bid two spades, Irma bid three hearts.'

'May I propose a toast?' Eddie raised his glass. 'How many guys can honestly say they've achieved their life's dream? I can. Helen Weller, here's to you.'

'Honestly. He never stops talking about her.' Amy raised her glass. 'Helen Weller.'

Irma and Dottie raised their glasses. Four iced teas clinked.

'Are you ever going to tell us who this Helen Weller is?' Dottie asked.

'Never.' Beaming, Eddie picked up his cards. 'Four clubs.'

On the afternoon of September 12th, in Washington, DC, at a handsomely converted movie theater at 15th and S Streets, the broadcast and print media covered the inaugural ceremony of the Andy Horner Institute, a foundation chartered with a quarter-billion-dollar grant from Vestcate International.

'Our purpose,' Dr Sharon Powell stated, 'is to commemorate the achievement of Dr Andy Horner by continuing the work to which he dedicated his life. We shall encourage young doctors to enter clinical practice and to explore promising alternative treatments to diseases. All too often outmoded therapies are prolonged while deserving therapies fail to find government or institutional funding. We hope, in helping to redress the imbalance, that medical knowledge and public health will both be advanced.'

Dr Powell announced first-year grants of half a million dollars each to eight young doctors in fields as varied as cancer, infant mortality, depression, multiple sclerosis, and heart disease.

Dr Powell and her husband Joseph Mahler then cut the pink ribbon on the door. They held the scissors together, like newlyweds cutting the first slice of wedding cake.

The Baltic sun had set and the city of Stockholm was bathed in early sub-Arctic night. It was December 10th, and in the *Stadshus*, the Town Hall, in the white chamber known as the Blue Hall, candles glowed on the banquet tables. Three hundred illustrious members of the international scientific, political and cultural communities had gathered to witness the annual presentation of the Nobel Prizes.

After an unusually brilliant flourish of trumpets, the King of Sweden told his listeners that Alfred Nobel had been a man far ahead of the technology of his time, and it was therefore completely appropriate that this year's prize in medicine should be awarded via satellite hook-up over the Internet.

For the first time in the history of the awards, the young King, himself computer-literate, then presented the medal and the red leather folder to a computer terminal.

Thanks to satellite-linked TV, Dr Lucas Powell, wheelchair-bound in Silver Spring, Maryland, was visible to the audience, a handsome figure in his white tie and tailcoat. Through the miracle of microcircuitry embedded in his computer, he was able to express audibly, though not in his own voice, his delight at receiving this, his second award.

'I am even prouder of this award than I was of my first, because it represents, potentially, a far greater reduction in human suffering. I say potentially, because all causes begin as lost causes, and most remain so. If I may be permitted to paraphrase another laureate, we fight for lost causes not only in the slender hope of victory, but also to keep the will to fight alive. We fight because we know that, should we meet defeat, that defeat may be the preface to our successor's victory.

'In the rare event that victory should greet our efforts, we must remember two things: any victory is temporary at best; and there are many who have paid the price for it. In my case, it was the hundreds of thousands, now totalling millions, who died in one of the most tragic plagues the modern era has yet known, a plague not only medical but bureaucratic and political as well. I thank the Swedish Academy for honoring their sacrifice and my efforts.

'And because she risked her life to bring hope out of darkness, I thank my daughter, Sharon Powell Mahler.'

On Christmas Eve, on the corner of V and 10th Streets, NW, in Washington, DC, a nervous and emaciated white man, newly arrived from Chicago, made his first local crack buy. Scuttling into an alley, he dropped the rock into his stem, poised the flame of his lighter under it, and inhaled until his lungs were filled.

In less than three seconds the familiar, reality-blotting sensations began to move in waves through his body.

His cure had begun.